PROMISE ME *this*

HANNAH BIRD

Also by Hannah Bird

Loveless Series

The End and Then (Book 1)

What's Left of Me (Book 2)

Author's Note

Dear Reader,

As always, it is a tremendous honor that you have picked up a book of mine. I'm so grateful to be able to create these stories, and Leo and Callum have especially captured my heart from the very beginning.

This book is about their love story, yes, but it also dives into Leo's grief journey over the stillbirth of their daughter twelve years prior. There are remembered moments of both her pregnancy and her loss, told through letters written to their daughter, Poppy. This subject is understandably a hard one for a lot of people, and I wanted to make sure you take care of yourself and your mental peace. Please read with caution, and if mentions of miscarriage, stillbirth, and infant loss are painful for you, perhaps pick up a different book of mine in place of this one.

And to any woman who can relate to the subjects in this book, I am so very sorry for the loss you have endured. You contain within you an immeasurable strength. Never forget that.

With love,

HB

In loving memory of my sister, Brandy.
And in honor of our beautiful mother, who has carried Brandy for
her whole life.
I love you, Momma.

Prologue- 12 Years Ago

Leona

If I didn't know any better, I'd think the city was on fire.

From this vantage point, the streetlamps and illuminated windows blur together into a sea of shimmering embers, like the remnants of a dying flame. I glance over at Callum, at the hard set of his jaw and the tenderness in his eyes.

So not a dying flame then, rather one that's just getting started.

"Worth breaking the rules for?" The corner of his mouth twitches as he speaks. His gaze hasn't left the valley; I can see the twinkling lights of Dublin dancing in the wetness that pools at the precipice of his lashes. Sadness has been hovering at the edges of the evening since we left the manor, threatening to spill over the dam of joy we've built up. We both know what's coming. We just want to put it off as long as we can.

I retrieve his hand from the gearshift, twining our fingers together and squeezing three rapid pulses. He's referring to the gate at the base of the mountain that he made me jump out of the car to push open, something enough other cars have done to join us at the viewpoint that my fears of breaking the law have eased. "Always is with you."

He chokes on a half laugh, half sob before wiping his nose with his spare hand and clearing his throat. "What am I going to do without you, Leo?"

My eyebrows lift of their own volition, but I choose to be nice and not chastise him for the despised nickname. It's our last night together, for a while anyway. The least I can do is let him get his way for once.

"Hmm, I don't know." A gust of wind jostles the car, bending trees and each blade of grass on its journey into the city below. "Perhaps you'll actually get enough sleep for once and your uncle can stop hating me for keeping you out all hours of the night."

In sync we glance at the clock on the dashboard. Seeing that it's just past eleven, I add, "Starting tomorrow night."

A muscle in his jaw ticks. He doesn't like it when I talk about life after I leave. He can't seem to fathom that I mean it when I say I'll come back.

Freeing my hand from his, I grab ahold of his chin, pressing my thumb into the familiar indent of the scar there. It's a permanent memento from his time playing GAA, some violent Irish sport I still don't understand despite the hours he spent trying to explain it to me.

"Hey," I whisper. His long lashes flutter as he finally lets himself look over at me. Why does God always give the best lashes to men? They bring his beauty to a whole other level, when he's already too pretty for his own good. "We're happy tonight, remember? You promised me. No sadness till the morning."

His gaze sobers, those bright green eyes studying my face intently as if he's committing it to memory. "Easy for you; you've had enough sangria to tranquilize a horse."

We both giggle. His is the steady rumble of thunder under my tinkling wind chime of a laugh.

"You took me to a Spanish restaurant; what did you expect?"

"I'll tell you what I didn't expect was for those prawns to still have eyes when they got to our table."

The mental image of him splashing his white shirt with shrimp guts as he attempted to behead them flashes in my mind, making it harder to maintain any semblance of composure.

He glares at me, trying not to show he's just as amused. "It wasn't funny! No food should be able to look at you!"

Laughter pools in my belly, mixing with the alcohol to drown out the sourness of knowing this is the last time we will be here, like this. For a while anyway. I unclip the seat belt and turn, hoisting myself clumsily over the center console and into the back seat. My black dress rides up, probably flashing him, but he isn't complaining.

He's staring at me now, in that heavy way he does. It settles like a weighted blanket over me, cocooning me in its warmth. I pat the seat beside me, holding his gaze all the while. "Come on back. There's plenty of room for both of us."

He glances over my head, through the rear window. "There are other cars here."

"And they're all too busy in their own back seats to care what we do in ours."

"You've got a point." He doesn't hesitate a second longer, clumsily forcing his significantly larger body through the narrow gap between the seats. When he lands with a solid thud next to me, he's flushed from the effort.

I reach down, sliding one high heel off and then the other. They weren't the most practical choice in footwear, I'll admit, though I had no way of knowing our walk from the street where we parked to the restaurant would be entirely comprised of centuries-old cobblestones. Walking back was all the more diffi-cult after the alcohol had flooded my system. A summer spent living here hasn't cured me of my surprise at how ancient even the most mundane of things—such as roads—can be. At least by American standards.

Pivoting in my seat, I hoist one leg over him and settle onto his lap. He dutifully grabs onto my hips, holding me in place. If I look up, I'll probably see another car behind us with a couple just as enamored. But I don't look up; I'm too busy memorizing Callum's face.

His blond curls are growing out, framing his ears and falling across his forehead. I tangle my fingers in them, earning the groan that passes through his parted lips. His angular jawline is covered with a dusting of scruff. In the final days, who has time for things like shaving and haircuts? That only takes away from the small bank of time we have left to spend together.

"How will I say goodbye to you?" His voice is a strangled whisper, desperate and pleading. I try to swallow around the knot forming in my throat, to no avail. He reaches for the long brunette wave that's fallen over my shoulder, and tucks it back behind my ear. The tenderness is enough to shatter me.

"You won't." I fight for a gasp of air. When did breathing become difficult? Where did all this moisture come from? He swipes a calloused thumb across my cheek, wiping away the evidence. "You won't say goodbye, Callum. Just 'see you later.' You'll see, it'll be May before you know it. Then we'll be together again for another summer. Then one more year and I'll graduate, and I'll be here permanently. It'll all happen so fast you'll wish you'd had more time alone, because once I'm yours, I'm yours forever."

"I like the sound of that. *Forever.*" His smile is an apparition. A trick of the light. "Can it start right now instead?"

"It started the moment you walked into that kitchen. I was a goner."

The tears spring forth once more, filling his eyes to the brim. He closes them, causing a tiny rivulet to spill over the swell of his cheek. It stalls in the hollow beneath, and I brush it away with my lips, tasting salt on my tongue.

His head falls forward, landing against my chest. The heat of his breath easily slips through the thin silk of my dress, warming my skin and sending zings of electricity right down to my core. His hands move away from my hips, brushing the tops of my thighs where my dress has ridden up. Slowly, painfully so, his fingertips travel upward. Beneath the hem of my dress and then the waistband of my thong. He's tugging at it and pulling soft cries of want from my lungs with the movement.

"Promise you'll come back to me." He mouths the words against my collarbone. He can't have spoken them aloud. How could he when I felt them in my soul?

"I promise."

One hand joins the other on my right side, confusing me for a moment until I hear a distinct snap of fabric. The elastic waistband of my underwear falls against my thigh, now torn in two. He quickly does the same on the other side, freeing me from them in the only way that would keep us from having to part for even a moment.

He glances up at me, and I seize the opportunity, covering his mouth with mine. The familiar taste of him, mixed with the bitterness of the red wine he drank with his dinner, is enough to sober me up completely. Every detail comes into focus. Our tongues brush against one another, sending a thrill of delicious heat all the way down to the apex of my thighs.

A whimper forms on my lips, vibrating against his. He reaches between us and fumbles with the button and zipper on his pants. I lean forward onto my knees to give him space to free himself, and he takes advantage of the position by biting my nipple through the thin fabric of my dress. "Bull's-eye," he mumbles, grinning.

I scoff. "You are a child."

"Am I?" His hand moves between us, two fingers curling into

me while he uses his palm to put pressure on my clit. "Because I feel like a grown man."

"Quit ruining the moment," I breathe, riding his hand in search of more of that exquisite pressure.

"Your body is telling me I haven't ruined anything." One wicked eyebrow quirks, and he grazes my nipple once more. Without the added layer of a bra, the rough scrape of his teeth cuts right through my dress, and the resulting jolt of pleasure settles somewhere in my abdomen.

"My body is an idiot," I say. At least I try to say it. It comes out a little more strangled than I'd like, proving his point rather than mine. His fingers slip out of me, leaving me hollow, and I have no control over the disappointed sound I make.

Then I feel him pressing against my entrance, and I forget about the argument I definitely wasn't winning. He's teasing me, just out of reach. The heat of the moment mixes with the remnants of alcohol in my bloodstream, making me languid and overconfident. "Get a condom."

He shifts his weight, retrieving the wallet from his back pocket and flipping it open. In the space where he usually keeps them, there is nothing. An expression of abject disappointment flashes over his face before his hand scrubs it away. "I forgot to replace it after last time."

Even the memory of last time—a week ago, in the little cottage in Cahersiveen, with the scent of hydrangeas floating through the window on the summer breeze—is enough to make me shiver. I shake my head. "It's fine; just pull out."

I don't miss the shock that passes over his face. "Are you sure?"

"Yeah." I lean forward, reach beneath me, and guide him back to my aching core. "I can't wait, Callum. I need you now."

"I'll pull out." He nods along with the words, confirming it with himself.

"You'll pull out," I echo. I lower myself one torturous inch, feeling my body stretch to allow him in. It's the first time I've ever felt him like this, without barriers. "It'll be fine."

His eyes are heavy-lidded, and he nods in that hazy way that feels like a dream. "You're right."

Grabbing firmly to my hips, he holds me still as he thrusts upward, filling me and drawing a moan from deep within my lungs. Tears prick at the backs of my eyes and I think I cry out his name, but he captures it with his mouth as it covers mine. We move in sync, giving as much as we are taking. I try to hold on to this feeling, to impress it upon my heart, because without it I don't know how I'll survive tomorrow.

I don't know whose tears fall first, but soon there is a mixture of both on our cheeks. His hands travel up my spine and weave into the hair at the base of my skull, clinging to me as we build higher and higher toward the precipice.

I roll my hips against him, that glorious pleasure building in my chest until it hurts so badly that I'm afraid I might burst. Forget the other people on this mountain, in this city, in this world. I cry out loud enough for every one of them to hear me, and I can't be bothered to care.

Before I've completely returned to myself, I feel Callum lift me off him as he shudders through his own release. His arms encircle me and pull me tight against him. My lips are level with his forehead, and I press them there, inhaling the familiar scent of freshly fallen rain mixed with the sweat that slicks his skin.

"Promise you'll come back to me," he says once more.

I cling to him, squeezing with all the strength I have left. "I promise."

Chapter One

Leona

The memory of our last night together plays on repeat in my mind, the light of it somewhat dimmed by the knowledge of what came after. It feels impossible that it's been twelve years since I stood on this street, surrounded by a green so lush it has to be fake. But it isn't, and neither is the quaint cottage situated on the end of a quiet road with fog-shrouded mountains looming in the distance beyond.

There was a time when I thought I'd never see it again. I never imagined the sensation of coming home could feel so like breaking in two.

White, gauzy curtains hang in the windows, blocking my view of the inside. Unlike the manor near the city where we lived that summer, this house has no imposing stone wall keeping people out. If I wanted, I could tiptoe around to the hip-high garden gate and see the hydrangeas his mother planted when she was a child. I could lose myself in their heady scent, their vibrant hues.

Not a good first impression if he thinks you're stalking him, Leona.

Aren't I, though? I remembered the name of the town where their family vacation home was back then. But the exact location of the cottage—the one he always swore he'd move to when he was older—escaped me. After taking a train to Killarney, and then a bus to Cahersiveen where I off-loaded my bags at the local bed-and-breakfast, I paid a visit to the post office. Or rather, the post *counter* in the local petrol station. One chatty mail carrier later and I had a general location, which the taxi driver understood well enough to get me here.

If that's not stalking, I'm not sure what is. But I push the thought away. I'm nervous enough as it is without worrying over which laws I've broken.

Fall is slowly creeping in, with tendrils of cold weaving themselves into the gaps of my knit cardigan. Gravel crunches under my steps as I approach the house. I try to hone in on the sound over the loud thrumming of my anxious heart. Over the internal monologue telling me this is the biggest mistake I've made in a decade. It doesn't take long before every cataloged failure of mine runs like a trailer for the world's worst movie across the screen of my mind.

So *one* of the biggest, then.

I don't recognize my own trembling hand rapping softly against the wooden door. I'm above my body, watching the horror movie play out. Maybe I've died from fear, and this is what the afterlife will be for me. The closest thing to a smile I can manage stretches my lips at the thought. Ireland would be the perfect heaven if it weren't for the inevitable come-to-Jesus waiting for me on the other side of the door.

Footsteps reach my ears, growing louder with every *thump*. The blood drains from my face in one swift rush. Suddenly the possibility that a stranger is about to open the door flits through my mind, and I'm tempted to turn tail and run. I have to force my feet to remain planted against the ground. The delicate amulet hanging from my neck is clenched in my fist, and I do my best to draw strength from it.

"You can do this," I whisper to myself.

The words stall on my lips when the door swings open, revealing a memory so real I feel the need to pinch myself. It's not like he looks the same, per se, but *enhanced*. Time has done him nothing but favors, as though it is fonder of him than anyone else. Callum is wearing wire-rimmed glasses instead of his contacts, something I always loved but he refused to do because glasses weren't cool enough for him back then. His once-unruly curls are tamed into a close cut on top of his head, held in place by a gel that makes them look slightly damp. Or maybe he's just gotten out of the shower.

The thoughts that follow, and the mental image that comes with them, are entirely involuntary. I shake my head, reminding myself those aren't mine to imagine anymore.

His eyes go wide when they land on me. The fire of betrayal, of hurt catches in their evergreen depths. Even after he schools the rest of his features into cool indifference, it remains there. Simmering.

"Leo." His voice is intentionally mechanical, and his jaw ticks as though saying my name is a crime committed against his better judgment.

But it's still *his* voice, and it strikes me right in the center of my chest.

A sigh of relief, equally as involuntary as the shower thoughts, escapes me. Somewhere deep inside, I was sure he'd forgotten me. But no, if the scalding anger in his eyes tells me anything, it's that he knows *exactly* who I am.

The realization puts a little steel back into my spine.

"Cal."

He leans into the doorframe, crossing his arms and looking down at me. Every possible bodily cue that shows someone's not wanted, he's giving me. "You know I hate being called Cal."

I stand up straighter. "You know I hate being called Leo." Leo is the name of hundred-year-old painters and celebrities who only date models half their age. Leona is beautiful, elegant, a gift passed down from my grandmother, who immigrated from France.

As if he can hear the spiel going through my head, he narrows his eyes. "Don't show up on my doorstep after a decade and insult me with a lie."

His tone freezes me in place, chilling me to the bone. I tug at the edges of my cardigan, wrapping them tightly around my middle. My stomach is rolling, and I have to draw a deep breath to take the edge off the nausea that threatens to overwhelm me.

It wasn't entirely a lie, after all. Leo *is* a boy's name, and I *do* hate it when people call me that. But the memory of the first time we had this conversation—back before he hated me—stands in stark contrast to the hostility rolling off him in this moment.

I can almost feel his hand, broad and gentle, lacing itself into my brunette waves. Cradling me close. In my memory, he nips the bridge of my nose where it's crinkled in disgust. The bite forces me to relax my expression because now I'm giggling, and his face flickers from broad smile to serious stare in the blink of an eye.

"Why do you insist on calling me that ugly name?"

"Because," he whispers, studying my face as if I really were painted by some old guy a hundred years ago. A work of art. Something worth revering. *"The shorter your name is, the more times I can say it in one breath."*

And then he'd said it, over and over, the hallowed syllables that make up a prayer.

He's watching me remember; I can see it in his eyes that are nearly as green as the grass in the rolling hills beyond the cottage. For a moment he softens, before the reality of the years that lie between that moment and today fall swiftly into place, dividing who we are now from the two twenty-somethings who loved each other more than life itself.

"Why are you here?" Despite his stern expression, the words are purposely flat and lifeless. None of the heat flooding his defined cheekbones finds its way into his question. He seems tired all of a sudden, like this sorry excuse for a conversation has aged him in a matter of seconds.

My gaze falls to my hand, locked in a choke hold around my necklace. I've never let myself imagine this day, really, and now that it's here, I feel completely unmoored. After everything happened, I pushed away any thoughts of this place, and Callum even more so. It was all too painful, too visceral, and it compounded my shame. It was so much easier to bury those feelings if I remained at home in a country that didn't know how it felt to have Callum's footsteps on its soil, away from any reminders of everything I'd lost.

Then the carefully constructed life I created began to crumble to the ground. My safe, albeit predictable marriage ended. Moving back in with my parents for the first time since graduating high school was painful but manageable. There were enough logistics to work out while wading through a divorce that my mind had very little time to wander.

But when the mundane job that was supposed to be my most dependable distraction had budget cuts that left me unemployed, suddenly I found myself untethered. *Unhinged.* In the span of two days, I both decided to come here and bought my ticket. In another twenty-four hours, I was landing on the tarmac. Now that I'm standing on his doorstep, it seems too little too late to come up with a way to say, *"Life has been broken ever since we last spoke and I made a terrible mistake and by the way, you had a daughter,"* with grace.

He pushes off the doorframe, dropping his arms to his hips. "Ah come on, Leo, I haven't got all day. Whatever it is you've come here to say, just spit it out already."

Someone must have lit a match under my ears, they're so hot. "I—"

"Daddy! Who is it?"

The small voice belongs to a sprite of a girl, ringlets of her father's blond curls tumbling over her shoulders in disarray. She runs up beside him, her head just barely level with his hip as she wraps an arm around his leg and peers up at me.

"You *have* a daughter."

Someone who isn't looking for it wouldn't hear the inflection in my tone, but the words are gunshots rattling in my head. I stumble backward, suddenly wishing I'd taken the cab driver up on his offer to wait for me at the end of the street. He had a smirk on his lips that I didn't entirely understand, like he knew something I didn't about the surly man waiting for me in this cottage seemingly plucked straight out of a fairy tale.

"Would you like some tea?" the girl offers, smiling bashfully up at me. She has a gap between her upper front teeth, and it gives her the faintest lisp. "I'm just after pouring some for my bears. They're the nice kind; don't worry!"

I swallow the thick lump in my throat, forcing each of the forty-three muscles it takes to smile to do their damn job even though I'm dying inside. I just hope it looks less painful than it feels. "No, sweetie, I shouldn't actually have come. But thank you."

How did it not occur to me that he'd have a whole life now, one that had no space in it for me? He has a family. A daughter, a partner, possibly more children. Together they are living out the dream we once painted for ourselves under this very same roof, a million years ago when we could escape to the countryside for the weekend and I wasn't yet a mother with no child to show for it.

Callum clears his throat, patting the girl on the shoulder and urging her back into the house. His ring finger is empty, but I draw no solace from it. He once told me Irish couples could be together twenty years before they'd finally tie the knot. It wasn't the legal marriage that bound them, but their commitment to one another. Something I always found beautiful until right this moment, as unfounded jealousy curdles in my veins.

"Niamh"—he says it like *Neev*, but I know it's spelled differently. The Irish and their consonants—"go on inside. Leo was just leaving."

I nod, choking on the sob threatening to crawl up my esophagus, and turn away. I didn't even have time to turn on the international plan for my phone, so there's no calling a cab for me.

"Leo, wait."

I pause, glancing over my shoulder at him. Niamh has taken his instruction and returned to her tea party with her bears. I imagine her in the kitchen, my favorite room in the house with its wide-open windows and their views of the flowers and the mountains beyond them. Her mother, a blurry, faceless person, comes into the room with a plate full of warm cookies, placing them on the table for her daughter to enjoy.

A fantasy I originally dreamed up for myself. One I never actually got to experience.

Callum's eyes are clouded over, shrouded in a language I've been away too long to remember how to speak. Looking at him, surrounded by this beautiful place, I feel entirely at home for the first time in forever.

And somehow, simultaneously, I am so incredibly lost.

He hooks one hand against the nape of his neck, the way he used to when his uncle had been especially hard on him about work. The gesture fits perfectly into my memory of him, filling me with the yearning to close the distance between us like nothing has transpired.

But it has. She did. And I will never be who I was before.

Callum pulls his gaze from my face after a few heartbeats too long, filling me with an emotion I don't have a name for. "Let me at least call you a taxi."

I nod once, then tilt my head back, letting a rare, proud ray of sunlight fall onto my cheeks. A part of me hopes its warmth can penetrate the ice surrounding my heart. That I'll be thawed and the pain of this moment will melt away. My hair, which fell to my waist until a day ago, dusts my shoulders with the movement. I draw in a breath so thick and full that it sparks a burn in my chest. When I let it flow out at last, the words, "Don't worry; I'll walk," ride on its coattails.

"You sure?" he starts to ask, but I'm already retreating. I wrap my cardigan snugly around my middle and pray the Irish weather will be on my side just this once.

Chapter Two

Callum

If someone had asked me twenty minutes ago if I believe in ghosts, I would've said, *Hell no*. But Leona Granger standing on my doorstep was nothing short of an apparition. Even after rubbing my eyes with the heels of my hands so hard stars have exploded across my vision, she's still there when I place my glasses back in their rightful position. She walks to the end of the street, brunette waves whipping in the early autumn breeze. When I knew her, her thick hair tumbled all the way down her back, stopping just below her shoulder blades. The memory of her silken, olive-toned skin under my fingertips as I brushed her hair out of the way to undo her bra clasp has my hands thrumming with electricity, begging to feel it again.

I squeeze them tightly into fists, killing the sensation.

She turns down the main road back toward town, disappearing behind a tall, downy cluster of violet foxgloves blooming in defiance of the recent cold snap. I firmly ignore the urge to run after her, to grab ahold of her arm and spin her around. To demand the truth. Every fiber of my being wants to understand why she never came back, why we're now two enemies on either side of a front line rather than fighting whatever that darkness filling her eyes is together.

I shake my head, disappointed in myself for letting her affect me so deeply still. If I've learned anything in the last decade, it's that there isn't a reason. Some people are just selfish and incapable of handling a real relationship when the going gets tough, and I can't continue to let them take up space in my mind. Not Catherine, and not Leo either. Not anymore.

"Daddy! We need more tea!"

Niamh's voice snaps the cord of tension running through my body. With an exhale, I release it, letting the pulsing anger slow to a dull throb in my chest and then fade away completely. Just like Granda taught me. As the only father figure in my life, the first time he saw me holding Niamh in my arms with both our faces turning red as I complained about Catherine leaving and Niamh cried for her mother, he took it upon himself to teach me that I couldn't hold on to feelings like that anymore.

"Society will tell you a man is a fighter, a soldier, an angry thing," he'd said. *"But that little girl doesn't need any of those things. All she needs is a soft place to land."*

He was right then, and he's right now. As the sky grows steadily overcast—because the only dependable thing about sunshine here is that it's fleeting—I pivot on my heel and walk back inside, shutting the door behind me with my anger and resentment firmly on the other side of it.

My footsteps echo on the light oak flooring, creating a steady rhythm to align my breathing with. As I round the corner into the kitchen, the smell of flowers comes in with the crisp breeze. I stalk past Niamh, grabbing the back of the neck hole on her large sweater and tugging it up over her head, resulting in resounding giggles that fill the room with music.

"Oh, I'm sorry, is that not how you're supposed to wear it?" I slide the windows closed, locking out the cold wind that's picking up speed from the impending rain. An inkling of concern for Leo walking in the frigid mist trickles into the back of my mind, but I quickly push it away. I shrug my own sweater up over my head, turning myself into some weird semblance of a turtle. I tried it once while desperate to snap Niamh out of a tantrum when she was a fussy toddler, and it became the only surefire way to make her smile. A sight I desperately need to see right now.

When I turn around, she falls over laughing, and something loosens ever so slightly in my chest. "What? I thought it looked better this way!"

"No, you look silly!" She clutches her favorite bear to her chest, a matted, lumpy thing barely hanging on at the seams. It was the first gift I bought her. When Catherine showed me the positive pregnancy test, I ran to the closest store and picked the softest toy I could find. That was long before I knew the baby inside her was a little girl who would become my whole world. Who would stay that way even after Catherine was no longer a part of it.

I swallow back the lump rising in my throat, willing myself to forget. To show Niamh joy rather than pain.

"I look silly?" I exclaim in a theatrical voice, flattening my hand over my heart. "But I look like *you!*" I drop to all fours and crawl slowly toward her, earning another peal of laughter before she squeals in delight.

When I finally reach her where she sits at the table, feet dangling and toes sloppily painted purple—listen, I do my best— she yanks them up before I can grab onto one and tickle her. My plans thwarted, I change tactics, hooking an arm around her midsection and hoisting her into the air above me, where I blow raspberries on her stomach while she screams.

"I only wanted more tea!" she shouts, gasping between bouts of deep belly laughter.

I settle her back into her seat, then tug the sweater off her head and smooth the resulting frizz from her curls. I shrug back into the neck of my sweater and do the same to my own hair.

"If it is tea the lady wants"—I bow to her—"then it is tea the lady shall get."

"Thank you, Daddy." She grins at me, flashing the gap between her two front teeth.

Bending down to plant a kiss on the top of her head, I steal a quick inhale of her strawberry kid's shampoo. "Anything for you."

I make my way over to the sink and refill the electric kettle. Once it's set to boil, I relax into the counter to wait. Niamh resumes her storytelling with her stuffed animals, only now she's mimicking one knocking on a door, and the other coming to open it. The poor bear who has knocked is making whimpering sounds as the bear who opened it growls at her.

Kids certainly know how to humble you.

I have to remind myself that Niamh is only interpreting a five-second interaction, without knowing the many layers that lie underneath. The long years that led to that moment. I'm justified in giving Leo the cold shoulder. After all, she can't just show up twelve years later uninvited and expect me to simply forgive and forget. Surely that's what she was going to ask me to do.

A nagging thought echoes through my mind. *What if it wasn't?*

I remove the glasses from my face and return my hands to my eyes. The pressure distracts me from the pounding ache filling my head, starting in my temples and pulsing its way into a crown of pain.

Why else would she come here after all this time? What could she possibly have to say that could fix what she did? She abandoned me without so much as a parting word. I spent years agonizing over piles of letters, recorded voice mails, saved texts from before she went silent, trying to find the missing link where it all fell apart. I analyzed every touch we exchanged on our last night together, each whispered promise in the airline terminal the following morning.

Her face floods my mind, defying my efforts to scrub the memory of it out of my eyes with brute force. If I had let myself think of her for more than a fleeting moment prior to today, I would've hoped that her actions had dampened my connection to her in some way. But even now as she makes her way to God knows where in the steady rain that patters against my windows, I can feel the invisible tether stretching out between us, loosened but ever present.

Those arctic-blue eyes still pierce my soul, the unique golden rings in her irises drawing my gaze as quickly as they did the first time I saw her. I've only met one other person with eyes like that since—my very own daughter, with forest-green eyes that she inherited from me, and two golden rings that she was gifted by the universe, it seems, simply to remind me of the woman I'd lost.

It's too much, all of a sudden, and the wave of delayed emotions comes crashing down on me, no longer able to be kept at bay by simple anger. Disappointment echoes in the chambers of my heart, bouncing off a few ounces of relief. There's a fathomless pain taking up too much of the air I need to breathe, and I'm no longer hurting for what Leo did but the combined effort of her and Catherine in ruining me for any woman who could ever come after.

"Daddy, are you crying?"

Niamh's delicate voice draws me out of my wallowing, bringing the hot wetness on my cheeks into focus. I tug my sweater sleeve over my hand and scrub the tears away, replacing my glasses to shield my daughter from some of my pain.

"I'm all right." I clear my throat. "I thought you were playing."

She peers up at me with curious eyes, cocking her head to the side and giving her teddy a squeeze. "We needed more tea."

Spinning around, I notice the kettle has shut off, meaning the water is done boiling. I shake my head, disappointed in myself for letting a ghost from the past rattle me to the point I'm likely scaring my daughter. I can count on one hand the number of times she's seen me cry, and none were when she was old enough to remember.

Dads are supposed to be brave for their daughters. Dads are supposed to know what to do. *A soft place to land.* I have to be strong so she can know she's safe to be weak with me, not the other way around.

Once the tea sachet has steeped for long enough, I remove it and add some milk before lowering it to Niamh's outstretched hands. At just shy of five years old, I can finally trust her to carry the full-to-the-brim cup across the room without leaving dribbles of pale brown liquid for me to clean up later.

Watching her return to the table, all I can think about is watching Leo walk away. The nagging feeling at the edge of my brain wants to know why she came. The more mentally stable half says good riddance. Niamh and I don't need any more disappointment in our lives. Things are stable now, in this plateau of peace we've found after so long spent trudging through a valley.

When neither voice wants to surrender in the war over my emotions, I do the only thing I can think to do. What any grown man would surely do. I retrieve my cell phone from my back pocket and swipe a finger across to unlock it before dialing the one person who will know what to say.

My mam.

Chapter Three

Leona

The shock-induced determination that got me here is slowly ebbing, and panic creeps in to take its place. I try to focus on putting one foot in front of the other. On the thud of my footsteps against the damp earth. Walking, navigating, *getting soaked to the damn bone*—all of it is easier than thinking of what just happened.

I've been trudging through the Irish countryside in a haze of forced distraction for a solid thirty minutes when the unrelenting drizzle starts to threaten my sanity. My cotton V-neck clings to my skin in that suffocating way that damp clothing does. The woven texture of my cardigan does nothing to keep the rain out. Just when I'm about to give in to the overwhelming desire to rip all my clothes off and walk the rest of the way in the nude, a silver taxicab pulls up alongside me.

"You need a lift?" the driver says. It's the same gentleman from earlier, midforties with a web of fine lines fanning out around mischievous hazel eyes. He's wearing a black adidas tracksuit that's two sizes too big for his thin frame and has a cowlick that makes a tuft of hair stand at attention on the crown of his head.

I've never been more grateful to see anyone in my entire life.

"Yes, please!" I jog around to the passenger door and climb in, deflating into the seat. The car lurches forward as he shifts gears, turning my stomach in a way I forgot manual cars did. Before today I haven't ridden in one in…well, since Callum dropped me off at the airport twelve years ago.

"Didn't go so well with Cal, I take it?"

The rolling in my stomach intensifies, and it has nothing to do with his driving.

The driver seems to read my expression, because he answers my unspoken question. "He and I go way back. If he was sharp with you, don't mind him. He's always like that."

All I can think is, *He wasn't when I knew him*. Did my leaving hurt him so badly that it honed all his soft edges into razor blades? I can't bear to think that I damaged Callum in that way. That I stole his kindness with my own cruelty. But I can't say any of that, so instead I say, "He doesn't like to be called Cal."

The driver studies my face for a moment longer before letting out a soft snort of laughter and glancing away. "No, I suppose he doesn't. But I've never let it stop me, and you shouldn't either." We roll to a stop in front of a gathering of sheep making their way across the road. Their backs are spray-painted bright blue to identify them as part of the same flock, though I notice one sheep with a neon-pink marker. She's out of her element, away from her family. "I'm Padraig, but my friends call me Podge."

He's holding out a hand for me to shake; I can see it in my peripheral. I tear my eyes away from the misplaced sheep to face him, taking his hand in mine. "Leona. Nice to meet you."

"And what do your friends call you?"

I consider the question for a moment, taking a sad inventory of the lonely life I've created for myself. Melissa was probably the closest I've gotten to a person in quite some time, but she hasn't spoken to me since her brother and I divorced. The few work friends I thought I had didn't so much as glance my way as I gathered my things and left, for fear that being laid off was catching. A sigh leaks out of my lungs. "I don't have many friends."

He presses his lips together and nods his head once. "Right. Well, Cal is a grump, but he's one of the best friends I have. So maybe give that one another chance on a day when he's not being a prick."

The last of the sheep make their way to the other side of the road, bleating loudly at us for rushing their travels. Padraig pulls forward and I'm nauseous again. I'm beginning to think this is how I'll be spending my entire trip. Though after how today has gone… "I don't think that'll be much of an issue. I'm not here for long."

He casts a sidelong glance my way. "Don't let him run you off that easily."

Something about Padraig's chattiness eases my desire to shut this tender topic down. I extend my arms to let my hands hover in front of the vent, heat filling them once more. "I think I might've been the one to run *him* off."

"Ah, explains why he made you walk back to town."

"I actually insisted."

His eyes go wide as he turns onto the main street running through town, arriving an hour sooner than I would've on foot. "Now why'd you do that?"

I shrug. "Five miles is a lot farther than I thought it was." A blank stare meets my gaze. I'm confused for a moment before I realize my mistake. "Um, I don't know how far that is in kilometers, sorry."

He shakes his head, chuckling. "Far enough to be washed up for dinner, apparently. Now there's only one inn in town, so I assume that's where you're headed. Unless you're staying with one of those friends you don't have."

I glare at him, earning a full-on cackle.

"Bridge Street Bed-and-Breakfast it is, then."

My gaze drifts out the window, lazily tracing the shapes of the two-story buildings lining the street in various shades of pastels. When I arrived earlier, I moved with blinders on, focused solely on my destination. I forgot to pay attention to the local market where we'd stop in to grab the ingredients to make crepes sprinkled with sugar and layered with slivers of strawberries. The pub near the riverfront where we'd eat lunch when we first got to town for the weekend passed by without me noticing. The imposing stone church used to drop my jaw with its incredible architecture. Now its proximity causes my lungs to squeeze so tightly I'm afraid I'll never breathe again.

"We're here."

Padraig's voice snaps me out of my trip down memory lane, and thank God for that. I go to pull a few euros from my wallet when his hand lands gently on my forearm, halting any of my movement. He's shaking his head, having anticipated my protest before I can form the words.

"I have to pay you, Padraig!"

"I told you, call me Podge. And you already paid me this morning." He removes his hand, using it to scratch at his dark hair that's taking on more gray streaks than I'd imagine he likes. "Any friend of Cal's is a friend of mine."

"*I told you*, we're not friends."

"I think that, too, sometimes." A mischievous smile plays on his lips, softening his angular features. "But he always proves me wrong. Now go on! There's paying customers out there waiting."

I hesitate for a second longer before he makes a shooing motion and I resign myself to owing him. With one foot already out the door, I call over my shoulder, "Thanks, Podge."

"Anytime!"

The car accelerates away behind me as I step up to the turquoise door of Bridge Street B&B. Luscious green vines climb the white facade, nearly covering the gold lettering that marks this place as the only hotel in town. It's only been a few hours since I stopped by to store my luggage, but it feels like it's been years. My bones are heavy in my body, dragging me down. I trudge forward, opening the solid wooden door with a grunt and a prayer that my room is ready now.

The makeshift check-in counter at the front of the foyer is unmanned. It's nothing more than a console table with a fat notebook on its surface and a key box mounted to the wall behind it. My luggage still sits in the corner where I watched the owner tuck it away this morning. Not a good sign.

A lilting voice reaches my ears from farther down the hallway, so I follow its trail. My gaze travels over the cream-colored walls, which are decorated with pictures of the local fishermen's boats docked along the river. The gallery is broken up by a set of double doors on my right that open into an intimate living room lined with bookshelves. The owner is nowhere to be seen, so I close the doors behind me and continue on. The corridor's tall, wooden-paneled ceilings leave lots of wall space for the boat portraits, some of which are so old and tattered the edges are fading into a vignette.

I pause to study a particularly weathered image of an elderly man standing proudly on the bow of his boat. The riverfront surrounding him is still wild in many places, yet to be developed into its modern state, but I can just see the spire of that ancient church in the distance. Surrounded by so much history, I'm reminded that all this existed long before my own personal tragedy, and will go on long after me. It makes the pain slightly easier to bear when I remember it is finite.

I find myself at the foot of a broad, wooden staircase with the hallway continuing off to the right and an ajar door to my left. That familiar voice trills on the other side of it, so I push it open, revealing a cozy kitchen complete with ornately carved wooden cabinets and doilies on every surface. The frazzled woman who accepted my luggage earlier turns to me from where she's leaning against the counter across the room, and I see a phone pressed to her ear. A glimmer of what appears to be amusement flashes in her eyes when she catches sight of me. "I've got to be going now. Talk to you soon."

With that, she ends the call, sets the phone down on the counter, and turns to face me while settling her hip against it. The movement strikes me as somewhat familiar, tugging at a memory, though I don't know which one. She smooths her wild silver curls back from her face and smiles at me. "Got caught out in the rain, did ya?"

A blush warms my cheeks, which is honestly a welcome relief from the chill that has taken over my body. "Unfortunately, yes."

"Happens to the best of us." The corners of her mouth twitch into a smirk. "I'm Siobhan, by the way. You were in such a hurry earlier I hardly had time to catch *your* name, let alone tell you mine."

The heat spreads to my ears. "Sorry about that. I'm Le— well, as you said, you already know my name." I tug at the hem of my shirt, pulling the soggy fabric away from my body.

"That I do." She studies me for a moment, her cool green gaze traveling from my rain-flattened hair to my damp Keds. "So, Leona, are you traveling with anyone? Friends? A husband, perhaps? We get a lot of honeymooners along the Wild Atlantic Way."

I glance down at my left hand, half expecting to see the solitaire diamond I wore there for the past five years still resting on my finger. Even the tan line it left on my skin has faded and evened out, all records of our marriage washed away. I can still see Nick's face the moment I placed it in his outstretched palm, an expression of relief that echoed my own softening his features.

Siobhan clears her throat, reminding me there's a question still hanging in the air between us.

"No," I reply softly. "Just me. I came to visit someone I used to know."

My own words reach my ears, breaking me in their honesty. My throat constricts, and all I can think is I better not start crying in front of this woman. I beg my own heart to just let me get into my room so I can fall apart in peace.

Siobhan hums something like understanding before stepping forward, away from the counter. She's wearing a flowy tunic-style top that sways with each step. "Well, unfortunately it is just me running this place and I've not gotten to your room yet. We had a full house last night, unusual for this time of year. I've been scrambling this morning, but I'll get right to it. It'll take me thirty minutes or so." Her gaze travels over my damp clothing once more. "I can make you some tea or coffee to warm you up while you wait?"

Panic quivers just below my breastbone, threatening to become a full-on earthquake. If I'm left alone with my thoughts for more than a couple minutes, I'm going to break down. I can't do that in this kitchen where people might see me. Before I can think better of it, my survival instincts take over. "I can help; I don't mind."

One of her barely-there eyebrows quirks up. "You sure?"

I nod, probably more vigorously than necessary, but I'm desperate. "I used to clean houses with my mom in high school." Not to mention the late-night cleaning sessions when I couldn't sleep, haunted by my own grief. Nick would wake up to a sparkling house, grinning like he'd won the lottery by getting a wife who'd rather scrub an oven than rest. "I find it relaxing."

That same glimmer from earlier returns to her eyes, but she simply nods. "Right then, follow me."

I do as I'm told, joining her outside the kitchen. She gestures down the hall to the right of the stairs. "That's my personal space; my room, office, and a closet. Guests don't usually need to go there, as you can almost always find me in the kitchen, but should you be looking, that's my wing." She takes to the stairs, one wrinkled hand gripping the banister to steady herself. "You'll be in the converted attic room." She tosses a smile over her shoulder that instantly takes ten years off her face. "It's my favorite spot in the house. You can even see the river on a clear day."

"Then why isn't it yours?" I ask as we reach the second level.

"With these knees?" She gestures toward her legs, that tunic brushing her thighs. "Not a chance. Now I just save it for those guests who I feel will appreciate it most."

I smile. It feels odd on my face, like stretching a muscle after too long spent stiff. "What made you think I'll appreciate it?"

She opens the second door off the landing, a narrow one that reveals a closet stocked with everything one might need to clean a room. She gathers a caddy of supplies from the floor and a pile of sheets off the shelf, which she hands to me. Her gaze meets mine as she does it, something familiar and comforting glinting in her emerald irises.

"Just a feeling," she says. Her chin juts toward the stairs, which continue upward. "Come on, let's get you a clean room."

Between the two of us, it takes just under fifteen minutes before the room that was once an attic is sparkling, the lemon cleaner mixing with the fresh scent of rain coming in through the open dormer window in a pleasant way. I lug my suitcase up the two flights of stairs and settle it next to the white antique writing desk in the corner of the room by the door. Collapsing onto the bed, I train my gaze on the wallpaper, a floral print with winding wisteria vines that stretches all the way to the vaulted ceiling, and let my vision go blurry at last from the unshed tears.

My phone, now connected to Wi-Fi, vibrates in my pocket. I retrieve it, unlock the screen, and click on my mother's message.

MOM

Let me know when you're settled. Dad and I are leaving for the cruise this evening. Left your key under the doormat in case you need it. Love you, Mom.

Her signature sign-off on the text splinters my heart, making me miss her. But even more heartbreaking is what I can read between the lines of her message.

In case you need it. Meaning in case I come crawling back home with my tail between my legs, something I distinctly wanted to avoid doing. Which is why I left my key with them in the first place. I didn't need a way back to their home, the empty nest I invaded, though they'd never admit as much to me. I was finally taking control of my life and facing my demons. Finally attempting to repair the damage that I've caused.

In case you need it, meaning in case I fail. Something I'm apt to do.

I used to be successful. Full of promise. I was a straight-A student all the way through sophomore year of college, destined to become the journalist I always dreamed of being. Then I came home from Ireland, and everything I was became lost in the wake of tragedy.

The first person I ever failed was my unborn daughter. I've been doing the same to everyone else in my life since that day— so much so that it has become a personality trait that my mother feels the need to account for.

Thoughts of my daughter, which have been hovering at the

edge of my mind all day, suddenly force their way onto center stage. The fist that has been clenching my throat releases, allowing a sob to claw its way out. With tears blurring my vision, I scramble across the room, grab the notebook from my front suitcase pocket, and bring it with me to bed.

Tucked under the covers, I turn to the first blank page, not letting my gaze settle on any of the anguish scribbled before it. I click open the pen I've been using as a bookmark, and I talk to her the only way I can anymore.

My Darling Poppy,
I've made it to Ireland after a long flight—and a lot of years. Dublin is lovely, but the countryside is otherworldly. I like to imagine you here, running through the fields and laughing at the sheep. The breeze coming off the bay travels up the river to Cahersiveen, filling the air with salt and movement. I imagine you would've had your father's hair, and that breeze would have driven your curls crazy. In the most beautiful way, of course.

The flight was mostly uneventful. There were two babies on the plane, seated a row in front of me. I heard grumbles from other passengers as their cries disturbed their sleep, but I didn't mind it. Those poor little ones didn't know why their ears hurt from the pressure, only that they did. You can't blame them for that. Instead of complaining, I simply stared out the window. Frost crept like fogged breath over the glass, cutting me off from the dark ocean below. I felt a bit like a fish in a bowl, with the whole world on the other side of the glass. Only no one was looking in at me. Though I can't decide if that's a good or bad thing.

I wish you were here with me on that plane, sweet girl. I think a lot about what you haven't seen, what you'll never get to see. In the first few months after I lost you, Mom sent me a song written by a woman in a similar situation. In it, she said when a child dies that God takes them back to the beginning of time and shows them how it all unfolded. I like to believe that's true. That maybe you've seen far more than I ever have. You'll have to tell me all about it when we're together again.

I saw your daddy today. And your sister. Can you believe you have a sister? She looks just like Callum, the way I always knew you would. They make quite a pair. Quite a family.

I don't know what I thought I'd find when I got here. I guess I didn't let myself think about it, out of fear. Fear that he'd forgotten. Fear that I never could. In all that fear, I forgot that he'd have a whole life that doesn't include us. That by finally telling him about you, I could be damaging something he's built in our absence.

Now I don't know if it's logic or that fear

that's making me hesitate. I'm so tired of being afraid. I let myself give up everything, bury my head in the sand, and hope that it would keep me safe, all because I was afraid to suffer again. To lose anything that could hurt me the way losing you did.

What if it's too late to right my wrongs? What if I've kept silent too long?

I'll do my best, Poppy. My best is all I can do.

I love you, honey. I'll be seeing you.
Momma

Chapter Four

Callum

"The one day a week I don't see you, and you're calling me."

I pinch the bridge of my nose, reminding myself her effort at a joke should not get such a rise out of me. "Love you, too, Mam."

"Of course you do. I'm the best!" She chuckles to herself. "So how's my favorite child?"

Luckily she can't see my eye roll through the phone, or I'd be smacked upside the head. I let my gaze settle once more on Niamh. "Love, Granny wants to know how you're getting on."

"I just saw her yesterday!" she calls over her shoulder, not breaking the role-play she has going with her teddy.

"The two of you are one and the same, aren't you?" I grumble. My fist finds the center of my chest, rubbing at the knot that is my heart. No luck massaging the pain away. When my hand begins to tremble, I decide it's best to take this call away from listening ears and amble down the hall toward my room.

"She's my pride and joy." I can practically hear Mam beaming on the other end. She's probably knee-deep in cleaning supplies, trying to keep her little inn afloat. In a town with less than two thousand people, most of them fishermen, it's hard to find help. And she's terrible at asking for it. "Now what did you need, son?"

My breath stalls, unwilling to form the words now that the time has come. Part of me still feels like it was all a dream. For as long as I don't speak the words aloud, it can remain theoretical. Leo showing up on my doorstep will stay a fever dream I've since woken up from, rather than a real-life problem I have to find a way to deal with. I've had my fair share of nightmares involving her; why should this be any different?

The sound of Mam clearing her throat expectantly drags me back to reality rather abruptly.

In a voice quieter than I thought myself capable of, I finally mumble the truth into the speaker. "She's here."

"Who's here?"

"Leona." A pause follows my words, opening like a chasm that I desperately wish I could throw myself into. I train my gaze on the gauzy white curtains I haven't gotten around to swapping out, hoping focusing on something will help the emotions settle. Finally, when I no longer feel as though I'll burst into an unbecoming fit of tears, I add, "The American girl."

Another pause, this one so long I'm nearly convinced she's not even holding the phone up to her ear when she finally says, "Right, yeah, the one you hogged the cottage with over that whole summer. I swear every weekend you were off to Cahersiveen; no clue why you bothered paying rent in the city. And now you live there so none of us get to use it!"

Not the point, Mam. "You have the inn. Why would you need to stay in a holiday home in the same town?"

"Doesn't matter. Just wanted to point out your granda never offered it to *me*." The sound of a faucet turning on adds static to the background of her nonhelpful commentary. She's being especially sharp today, and not nearly as nosy.

A thought occurs to me. "Have you seen her? Is she staying

there?" It's the only inn in town. Unless she was just driving through, she'd have no other choice. But if she were driving, why'd she walk away from my house? A bus, then?

The water shuts off, the following silence quickly filled with the sound of Mam huffing her way to presumably the front entry, where she keeps her guestbook in a makeshift check-in desk. "Erm no, I don't think so."

Something in her voice sets the hair on the back of my neck to standing. "Would you tell me if you—"

"What is she here for anyway?" she asks, cutting me off.

Her question completely derails my train of thought, redirecting it back to the sight of Leo on my front porch. Her big blue eyes gazing up at me, more guarded than I've ever seen them. There was a time when they were a deep pool that I could dive into, no bottom in sight. Now there are stone walls on the other side of that shimmering blue, keeping everyone out. Or perhaps just me.

I collapse onto my bed with a strangled sigh, letting the phone fall beside me, still close enough that my mother's voice will carry to my ear. Not that it's helping much. "I don't know. She wouldn't say."

"Interesting," she croons. "Don't you find that interesting, Callum?"

"Not particularly. I find it grating. Annoying. *Infuriating.*" I practically growl the final word. "But certainly not interesting."

More huffing as she deserts the desk, satisfied with her fruitless investigation. "Come on, love. You can fool anyone else, but you can't fool me. I know deep down you're dying to know what's brought her here after all this time." She takes a loud sip of something, lubricating her vocal cords for more lecturing. "Perhaps you'll finally find some closure. Maybe even rekindle what you once had. You were so happy then."

It feels like a lifetime ago, that summer. But in some ways it's like it just happened yesterday. For four months I lived and breathed Leo. Every minute that I wasn't working as an intern at my uncle's shipping company was spent with her. I'm convinced I got more sleep in Niamh's newborn stage than I did back then. When I came home from work, she'd just be getting back from class, ready for another adventure. We drove through the mountains more times than I can count. Ate more sausage rolls from the petrol station for breakfast than my doctor would appreciate before setting off on a weekend trip to the country. I fell asleep beside her each night. Woke up to the scent of her citrus shampoo on my pillows every morning.

That knot has returned to my chest, threatening to take my breath away. "Too much has happened, Mam." I close my eyes, pretending the first thing I see isn't Leo straddling my hips, leaning over me with a grin as wide and bright as the moon, hair falling around us in a secret curtain that closes us off from the world. "Niamh deserves better than someone who can leave without so much as a goodbye. We've had too much of that in our lives already. Besides, last I heard, she was getting married."

A low hum sounds in the back of Mam's throat. "All I'm saying is, people change, and you have to be willing to let them."

"You don't unders—"

"I've got to be going now. Talk to you soon." The line goes dead, leaving me to wallow in a bed of my own making.

The worst part about having an almost five-year-old for a best friend is that no one is around to distract me after nine o'clock. Theoretically earlier, but after she's asked for at least three glasses of water that she doesn't drink over the course of an hour, she finally drifts off to sleep, leaving me alone with my thoughts.

I have those thoughts to thank for the two bruise-like bags bulging underneath my eyes this morning. Once Niamh drifted off at last and my duties as her father ceased for a while, I found myself falling through memories in rapid succession. Memories I haven't let myself revisit in years.

There was the time I spent a whole day trying to convince Leo that black sheep were in fact real and not just metaphors, driving through endless farmland until dusk shrouded our view of the flocks. All the fuzzy black bastards made a fool of me that day, hiding in plain sight, as if they were on Leo's team instead of mine.

I found myself reclining on the roof of a crumbling bit of ruins in a cemetery at the top of a hill. *"The only place in Ireland where you can see three counties from one spot,"* I'd proudly told Leo. Her eyes swam with wonder as she gazed out over the fields, tracing the patchwork of their borders with a fingertip gliding through the air. It was the first time she kissed me, her lips sweet and wind-chilled when they covered mine.

Then I was inside her, enveloped in the warmth of her embrace once more, listening to the soft moans she tried to suppress as I made love to her in my bed. The walls in that manor were so thin, I'm sure everyone could hear us. But I didn't mind then. It still fills me with a spark of pride now, thinking back, knowing that everyone else knew she was mine and I was hers.

That spark becomes a flame that fills my lungs with smoke, choking me on the memory of goodbye. I still had hope then, as I watched her walk toward airport security. She threw a reassuring smile over her shoulder, and I let myself believe she meant it when she said she'd come back to me.

But she didn't come back. And I can't forgive her for that.

Mam texted to cancel Sunday dinner yesterday after our chat, citing a long list of check-ins to prepare for, which left me alone with my thoughts and a four-year-old for far longer than is healthy. Staring at the door all afternoon waiting for Leo to return, not sure if I was hoping or dreading, followed by my unplanned trip down memory lane last night still has my nerves feeling raw and unsteady as I drive to the inn. I slam too hard into a pothole, eliciting a cry from Niamh. I miss my turn and have to circle back. I nearly flatten one of Eoin's sheep in the process.

By the time I'm parking in front of Mam's place, Niamh is practically racing to get out of the car. "Are you trying to kill me? Or just that sheep?" She stomps up the steps, pushing open the large wooden door with a grunt and a glare thrown over her shoulder.

"Just myself," I grumble under my breath, locking the car before following her inside.

"Granny! Daddy almost hit a sheep!"

"Did he now?" Mam calls from the kitchen. We make our way down the hall, finding her there dropping a dollop of fresh cream into a ramekin. She wasn't kidding about having a full house, given the breakfast spread she's prepared. The scent of bacon floods my nose, and before she can stop me, I've swiped a rasher from the nearest platter and downed it. She levels a hard stare my way. "He actually did hit one when he was just learning to drive. The poor thing had to be—"

"Mam!" I slap a hand over each of Niamh's ears.

"What?" She's the picture of innocence, shrugging at me and then making wide eyes at Niamh. "I'm just telling the truth. You shouldn't lie to children, you know."

"You lied to me all the time!" I groan, releasing Niamh at her insistence. She skips over to the cupboard where her stepping stool is kept, retrieves it, and sets it up next to Mam.

"Name one time." She points at me with the knife she's using to scoop jam from the jar, stopping my hand midreach for another rasher.

I swipe it quickly, dodging her advance. "Remember when you told me our dog went to live on a farm?"

She scoffs, caught red-handed, then swiftly changes the subject. She glances down at Niamh, who's busy at work preparing a scone for herself with generous dollops of cream and jam. "Didn't you ever teach him to chew with his mouth closed?"

Niamh sighs too heavily for a child her age, shaking her head. "I do my best."

"On that note I'll be running to the bathroom and then leaving you two to it. Unless you have any other insults or embarrassing stories for me?" I ruffle Niamh's hair, further loosening the already crap plait I attempted this morning.

She glances up at me. "Well, your hair is getting a bit shaggy…like a sheep's."

"You two deserve each other," I say, placing a kiss on Mam's wrinkled cheek. "See you tonight!"

"See you tonight!" they call in unison, already ignoring me with their heads tucked close together as I leave the room.

Chapter Five

Leona

Exhaustion is one hell of a drug, helping me sleep longer and more soundly than I have in months. I cling desperately to the void of endless slumber, but eventually reality drags me out of it kicking and screaming.

Literally.

My memory of the nightmare fades faster than I'm able to grasp it, leaving me panting and confused. I blink my way into awareness, taking in my surroundings. Floral wallpaper. Racing heart. Exposed beams. Sweaty palms. Open window.

Oh God, the window. Half the town probably heard my cries. I scramble to my feet, pad across the threadbare rug, and tug the window shut. A cursory scan of the street reassures me it's early enough in the morning that most people are not yet out and about. The few early risers ambling past look none the wiser, lost in whatever audiobooks or playlists fill the headphones tucked into their ears.

I flatten my hand against my chest. Poppy's amulet presses into my palm, reassuring me of her presence. After five rounds of measured breathing, I finally feel stable enough to make my way to the door. As the only room on this level, I have to travel down to the second-floor landing to use the bathroom. Two knocks assure me it's empty, so I push my way in and lock the door.

I brace myself on the porcelain pedestal sink, catching sight of my wild gaze in the mirror. Sweat slicks locks of my dark hair to my temples where they've fallen from my haphazard bun. I untangle the elastic band and drop it on the floor, followed by my damp pajama shirt and shorts. They pool on the chilled tile around my feet, and I keep my gaze trained on them so I don't have to see my naked body in the mirror. The sickly olive-toned skin, the too-frail arms, the silver stretch marks that still form parentheses around my navel as a reminder that it was once Poppy's home. The only one she ever knew earthside.

I turn to the glass-enclosed electric shower in the corner and crank the dial all the way up before powering it on. Steam glazes over the mirror steadily until I'm safe from my own reflection and all the reminders it contains of the dream I can't seem to shake.

Precious heat melts the tension in my shoulders when I step into the shower at last. Luckily there are travel-size soaps lining the shelf, since I've left mine buried in my still-packed suitcase upstairs. I take one and unwrap it, lathering it in my fist before wiping away the dried tearstains on my cheeks and the slick sweat from my weary body. With my eyes closed, I can nearly pretend I haven't made the grave mistake of coming here, thinking I could...

Thinking I could what? What was I hoping to achieve? For the first time since coming up with this harebrained plan, the reality of what I've done crashes down on me. I am the captain of a sinking ship, and I just untethered myself from the only dock keeping me afloat, thinking I could sail across the ocean to patch my holes.

I shut the water off but leave my eyes closed, sucking in breath after measured breath, hoping more oxygen is what my brain needs to finally kick into gear and figure out how to fix this.

The doorknob jiggles, startling me out of my trance. It's quickly followed by a knock.

I glance around, suddenly hit with the realization that I've forgotten to bring two crucial supplies with me: clean clothes and a towel.

The impatient person knocks again before trying the knob once more, as if my silence has made them question their own assuredness of it being locked. It still is; thank God for that.

"Someone's in here." My pathetic voice sounds foreign to me. In my thirty-two years on this earth, I've never figured out the right thing to say when letting someone know I'm occupying a public bathroom. Everything I've come up with sounds equally awkward.

Quiet falls on the other side of the door, and though the person is no longer knocking, I don't hear their footsteps retreat either. After a long pause spent holding my breath, I hear a low voice that freezes every shivering muscle in place.

"Leo?"

Oh. My. God. "Callum?"

I'm sopping wet and getting colder by the minute, but high-voltage shocks of embarrassment run down my spine, doing their best to warm me.

"What are you doing here?" His voice is forcibly empty of any emotion. Against my better judgment, I'm filled with the longing to see his face, to know what feelings he's suppressing. He may be good at speaking with a level head after years spent training under his uncle, but I've always been able to read the truth in his eyes, and right now I'm desperate for it. Even if the truth is that he hates me.

"I'm, erm, showering." I glance at the pile of sweat-soaked pajamas on the floor, realizing they're my only option. A thin white T-shirt and cotton shorts. I slip one damp foot into the bottoms.

"The shower isn't running," he states matter-of-factly.

"I know. I'm done now." My shorts are on, grossly laminating my skin.

He rattles the doorknob again impatiently. "Can you come out then?"

"One moment." I grimace, slipping the shirt over my dripping hair. I can feel the fabric clinging to my wet body, just like on my walk home yesterday, and the déjà vu is astounding. Not to mention incredibly unpleasant. "Okay."

I pull the door open to see a red-faced Callum with one fist raised, ready to knock again. Our eyes meet momentarily before his gaze travels down my body, halting on my chest. If it's possible, his face grows even redder.

I follow his gaze, realizing the fabric has been made see-through by my damp state. Fantastic.

Crossing my arms over my breasts, I train my gaze on our feet, unable to face him. "I forgot a towel."

"I see that," he chokes out before catching himself and clearing his throat. "Now what in the *hell* are you doing here?"

It's the third time he's asked me since the moment I stood at his doorstep, and I'm no closer to having an answer than I was in that moment. I'm floundering, my mouth opening and closing like a fish out of water, when Siobhan ascends the stairs with a stack of towels in hand.

"Leona! I forgot to bring you a towel." She steps around the tall, broad wall that is Callum, her mouth and eyes forming identical O's when she takes in my drowned-rat appearance. "Oh my."

I take the towel she's offering to me, avoiding eye contact with Callum all the while. He turns to Siobhan, mouth set in a grim line. "Mam, why is she here?"

Mam. Fantastic. If this trip went any further south, I'd be standing in Antarctica.

Siobhan glances back and forth between the two of us as I do my best to dry my water-logged tendrils and still use my elbows to cover my chest. An expression of realization that seems a little overdone dawns on her face. "Oh, is *this* the American girl?"

I chance a peek at Callum's face, finding barely suppressed rage lacing the twitching muscles in his jaw. Nerves form a knot in my throat that I nearly choke on.

"I tell you Leo has shown up out of nowhere and then a random American woman comes to check in and you're telling me you're just now connecting those *glaringly obvious* dots?" His voice pitches higher, threatening to become a full-blown yell. My gaze travels to the other doors down the hall, worrying he'll draw more guests to this unfortunate gathering.

Siobhan waves a hand through the air dismissively. "Son, I see so many people a day, it all blurs together after a while."

Something in her tone tells me she's full of shit, but I'm not one to insert myself into other people's family drama, so I don't mention it. Instead I gather the now-damp towel strategically in my arms and clear my throat. "While you two work this out, can I please put some different clothes on?"

Siobhan says, "Sure, love, I'll go put on the kettle," at the same time her son grumbles a strained, "Yes, *please.*"

I nearly fly up the steps to my room, faintly hearing Callum bite out, "Keep being so forgetful and I'll put you in a home," as I close my door.

Dressed in an oversize sweater and a pair of baggy jeans—the most conservative outfit I could find after my unintended peep show—I brace myself as I head downstairs to rejoin Callum and Siobhan. I seriously considered staying in my room until I could be certain he'd left, but that's what a coward would do. And a coward is exactly what I'm trying to *stop* being, even if yesterday didn't exactly constitute my best effort.

My steps falter when I cross the threshold of the kitchen. Callum and his mother are locked in a whispered argument, both leaning a hip against the counter in an identical pose. But at the table in the far corner, stuffing her face with a bite of scone—the source of the delicious aroma filling the room, if I had to guess— sits his daughter.

Her wild curls are barely being tamed by what looks like a sloppy French braid. Two thick strands spool around her face in an angelic frame. There's a smudge of cream on one of her round cheeks, and a dimple embedded there when she smiles at me.

The ache that fills my heart is almost enough to bring me to my knees. She's everything I've ever imagined our daughter would look like, down to the long fingers currently clutching her breakfast. The ones that match her father's hands perfectly.

I blink to clear the mist from my eyes, but it doesn't stop the barrage of memories. When the doctors first told me something wasn't right with our baby, I couldn't comprehend it. I had only just realized I was pregnant; how could anything be wrong with her? I was scared, of course, because what twenty-year-old mom isn't. But I was also deeply in love with her already. She was as real to me as Niamh is here in this room.

Then that *something* had a name. Trisomy 18. A birth defect and a death sentence in one. They tried to prepare me for what was to come. There were mentions of miscarriage and stillbirth, of comfort measures if neither of those came to pass. The doctor stared at the floor as he rambled medical jargon in an attempt to manage my expectations for the baby I carried.

"We'll know more when you're further along, but most babies with Trisomy 18 develop fatal heart defects," he told me. *"If she*

survives to birth, she'll likely be incredibly small, and may have several deformities."

I couldn't fathom it. From the moment I found out I was pregnant, I pictured the little girl sitting at this table. Her father's hair. Her father's long, lean limbs. I wanted her to have every part of him that she could, because I couldn't imagine a more lovely person to take after. No words of warning could steal that image from my mind.

There's a heavy silence filling the room, drawing me in like a black hole to fill its emptiness. Niamh has gone back to sucking jam off her fingers, completely unbothered by the palpable tension. Callum and his mother, however, are staring at me.

I wrap my arms around my middle, holding on to what is already gone, as if there is still a chance she can be saved.

"Niamh, can you go play in the living room for a bit," Callum says. His mouth cradles the words gently, no hint of his obvious anger leaking through.

She scans the room with observant eyes, finally landing on my face before giving a soft nod and getting down from the table. When she passes me on her way to the door, she stage-whispers, "If you make yourself a turtle, he can't be angry anymore."

My brow furrows, fear temporarily pushed aside. "If I do what?"

"You know," she says, and then she shrugs into the neckhole of her olive-green sweater until only her face is showing and she grins, that dimple popping once more. "A turtle."

A gruff combination of what seems to be a snort and a groan escapes Callum's tight-lipped frown, while Siobhan takes a sip from her mug to hide her smile.

I swallow past the lump of nerves in my throat and offer a watery smile. "I'll keep that in mind."

She nods, satisfied, and skips from the room with her sweater still framing her face. I shut the door softly behind her and turn to my audience of two, bracing myself against the solid wood for strength.

"Callum—" Siobhan begins as a warning.

"You need to leave," he says, cutting her off.

Siobhan smacks him on the back of one arm. "That is no way to speak to my guest!"

He winces but trudges on with eyes that nearly scorch me with their fire. "She's no guest. She's a ghost from the past who had no business turning up." He takes two steps toward me and then stops, as though approaching a wild animal whose actions are unpredictable. "Whatever you want, since you can't seem to tell me, I have no use for. The time for explanations is long gone."

I drag my voice out of the depths of my fear. "Callum, I didn't come here to hurt you. I just—" My words hang in the air between us. *Didn't I though?* my thoughts whisper. Everything I have to tell him could only bring him pain. There's no way to heal the wounds I left behind without adding new ones in their place.

I reach for my necklace, gripping it tightly for strength. His gaze tracks the movement, and for a moment the veil of anger falls away from his face, leaving him exposed. It's that glimpse of concern, the ripple of longing that reassures me I still know this man. I have not ruined him.

Not yet.

"Go home, Leo," he whispers as the shield falls back into place. "There's nothing for you here. Not anymore."

Tears well in my eyes, burning me with their need to fall. I glance at the ceiling, praying they'll stay put long enough for me to leave this room.

"She's not going anywhere," Siobhan says, drawing her son's attention like a cracked whip.

He balks at her. "The hell she's not."

"The hell she is." His mom crosses her arms, planting her feet firmly in defiance. Early morning sunbeams stream in through the window behind her, framing her in an aura of light. I've got to hand it to her; despite being half his size, she's not one bit intimidated by her son. "You're not running off my much-needed employee."

"Your *what?*" Callum and I say in unison. My eyes widen, confusion clouding my thoughts. As if they needed any more scrambling.

"That's right. I've hired her as a housekeeper to help me keep up with demand." She raises an eyebrow at Callum, daring him to disagree. "I can't be cleaning these rooms by myself any longer; I'm too damn old."

His glare moves from her to me. I'm not sure what game Siobhan is playing, but suddenly I'm desperate to be on her team. Besides, until two minutes ago I was thirty-two and unemployed. Not a good look.

"Come on, Callum. I'll stay out of your hair," I plead. My pride hates me for it, but I'm in no position to be anything but humble.

"Not likely," he bites out.

I try to mask my wince by shifting to face Siobhan, eyebrows furrowed in a desperate plea for further assistance.

"Niamh stays with me during the day while Callum works," Siobhan explains. She abandons her post at the kitchen counter, grabs a scone from the platter on the table, and takes a bite. For her, at least, the argument is over.

"Apparently *that* free labor wasn't enough," he mumbles.

"She's four!" Siobhan says around a mouthful of food.

"Almost five," he corrects.

"I won't bother you; I promise. I'll walk the other way when you enter a room. I won't speak to you. You'll barely notice I'm here." I don't have a clue how I'm going to accomplish what I came here to do while fulfilling that promise, but at least the space will give me time to come up with a plan.

The corners of his eyes turn down as a bone-deep weariness fills his expression. My hands ache to reach for him, to draw him close and let him sink into me in a move as familiar as my own existence.

But the time for that is past, as he said. I don't deserve those pieces of him any longer. He'll go home to Niamh's mother, and she'll be his comfort, as she should be.

With a curt nod, he pivots on his heel, heading toward the door I'm guarding. "I'll see you this evening, Mam," he says as he exits the room. His arm brushes mine in passing, filling my lungs with sand.

When it's just us left in the kitchen, Siobhan settles her amused gaze on me and sighs. "Sorry for him. Despite my best efforts, he's still got a bit of his father in that stubborn brain of his." She pats the seat beside her. "Come have some breakfast."

My gaze flickers from her to the door Callum just escaped through and back. "Um, Siobhan, now might be a bad time to tell you, but I can't legally work. I don't have a visa. I'm just here as a tourist."

"Not a problem," she says, shrugging. "You'll get free room and board and a bit of cash under the table."

I shift my weight. "Without a visa, I can only stay in the country a maximum of three months."

"I'll take three months of help over zero any day." She pats the chair beside her once more. "Come eat."

Forcing my legs to move, I stumble across the room. When I'm finally seated next to her, she passes me a plate from the stack in the center, winking at me as I take it.

"I, for one, have always wanted a ghost in my bed-and-breakfast. Attracts the tourists."

Chapter Six

Callum

I stare at the computer for the appropriate amount of hours, albeit with none of the necessary focus to do my job, as the clock ticks steadily toward the end of the workday. *It's not my fault*, I reason. *It's hers*.

True to her word, shocking as that may be, I didn't see Leo when I picked Niamh up last night or dropped her by this morning. And after Mam caught the few cursory glances I tossed toward the staircase, a glint in her eyes telling me she was reading too far into it, I've heavily considered parking at the curb this evening and waiting for Niamh to come outside.

I roll my shoulders, willing the tension to eke out of the muscles there. I'm not going to let Leo disrupt my life. Not again. I'm a grown-ass man, a father, for Christ's sake. I can march into that bed-and-breakfast and retrieve my daughter without trying to catch a glimpse of those familiar brunette waves or straining my ears for the musical lilt of her voice drifting down the hall.

Elbows braced on my desk, I let my forehead fall against my calloused palms. This shouldn't be so fucking difficult.

I walked through the pain of losing her once. I rebuilt my life, better than it ever was. I met Catherine; we had Niamh. I survived the pain of being left behind yet again. My walls are hard-won, forged from steel and unrelenting determination to not let lightning strike a third time. Whatever minute desire exists within me to see her, to touch her, is left over from a past life. I'm stronger than that.

Granda's old clock chimes five o'clock as if to say, *You're going to have to be.*

The heavy wooden door of the inn falls closed behind me and I strain my ears for any trace of my daughter. The weathered photographs hanging on the wall, donated to Mam by local fishermen proud to show off their boats when she opened the business, reflect my passage back to me in their glass frames as I walk down the hall. I peek my head into the living room, nodding at the couple gathered around a selection of fruits and cheeses by the fireplace. No sign of Niamh. The kitchen is surprisingly empty, too, and so is the garden beyond it.

As I pace toward my mother's room, a growing sense of dread fills my chest. The longer I linger, the more likely I am to run into Leo. The fact that there's a flicker of hope behind the wall of anxiety makes me quicken my step.

I knock twice before opening the door, only to find Niamh's pile of toys undisturbed and the sound of a shower running coming from Mam's adjoining bathroom. Which means my daughter is not with her. The alternative doesn't bode well for me.

Taking the steps two at a time, I reach the second-floor landing with the same speed as my pulse: rapid.

Niamh's voice spills out of an open door at the far end of the hall. I move toward her on instinct, even as every alarm bell in my brain starts screaming, *Something you don't want to see is up ahead. Turn back.* Like passing a car crash, though, I have to see it. Her.

Leaning against the jamb for strength, I fold my arms over my chest. Leo is mopping the hardwood floor while Niamh sits criss-cross in the desk chair and chatters away about how the next-door neighbor's cat is pregnant with kittens, and they've offered to let Niamh name them when they're born. She rattles off options, starting with characters from her favorite movies before moving on to candies I never let her eat enough of, in her opinion. I'd give her an industrial-sized Mars bar right this second if we could retreat without me being seen.

Leo keeps her gaze trained on the floor, but a half smile plays on her lips as she listens. Her shoulder-length hair is tied back from her face, which is flushed and coated with a light layer of sweat. She's dressed for a workout in a skintight long-sleeve shirt and black leggings whose knees have grown discolored, most likely from doing exactly what she's doing now, which is kneeling to take a sponge to some of the more set-in spots on the hardwood.

If I'm not careful, I'll lose myself in watching her. And around Leo, I can't afford to be anything but careful. Especially when it comes to protecting Niamh from what I know is an inevitable disappointment.

"Niamh, can I have a moment with Leo?"

My daughter falters mid stream of consciousness, and both of them startle at my voice. Leo glances up, eyes suddenly alert, that soft smile long gone from her lips. I will myself not to miss it.

"Daddy, her name is *Leona*," Niamh chastises. "Kinda like Fiona the ogre."

I press my lips together to choke off the chuckle trying to escape my throat. Leo, to her credit, looks quite pleased that my own daughter is standing up against the long fought-over nickname.

For some reason that sparks the anger anew in my chest. Soon it's roaring in my ears, prickling my palms. I clear my throat and force out the most level tone I can. "Niamh, downstairs, please. Go find your granny."

Hearing the shift in my voice, my daughter tosses a surreptitious glance Leo's way before scrambling out of the chair, across the still-damp floor, and down the hall. I train my gaze on the tiny trail of footprints left behind, reminding myself why I have to hold on to the anger.

Because without the anger, there's only hurt. And I've had enough of that to last a lifetime.

"So you're really doing this then." It's not a question, really.

Leo deposits the mop and sponge into the bucket of water with a splash. I glance up to find her knotting her hands together in front of her stomach, gaze guarded and watchful as it meets mine.

"Doing what?" she asks softly.

I gesture around the room. "Staying. Working." *Ruining my life,* I almost add.

She shrugs. "It's the least I can do for Siobhan for letting me stay here."

Something about my mother lending her a hand after watching me suffer all those years ago stokes the flame inside me.

"Won't your husband be missing you?" I snipe.

She doesn't even flinch. I'm almost convinced she's turned to stone. "We got a divorce."

I push off of the doorjamb with a scoff, striding across the now-dry floor until we're only a few steps apart. Easy enough to close the distance if one wanted to, but of course I don't. I plant my feet firmly where I'm at, close enough to intimidate, far enough not to find out if she still uses that citrus shampoo.

"So you got a divorce and thought you'd come running here? And what, we'd pick up where we left off like you never disappeared in the first place?"

My voice pitches higher than I'd like it to, and it's then that she flinches. White-hot shame licks at my spine, but I force myself to turn it to fuel for the fire rather than an extinguisher.

"It's not like that, Callum." Her voice quivers, but she pushes past the break. "It was a year ago. I'm not here because of Nick." She draws a deep breath while my own stalls in my chest. "I'm here because I left things unfinished."

The snort that rips out of me is so harsh it grates my throat. "That's putting it mildly."

Something like a warning flashes in her wide blue eyes. "That's not fair."

"You know what's not fair?" I growl, jamming a finger in her direction. "Thinking you've met your soulmate just for them to drop off the face of the earth without so much as a 'fuck you, see you never.' Next thing you know, that soulmate is getting married, and you realize they probably just moved on and didn't have the courtesy to let you down easily. *That's* not fair."

Her head shakes nearly imperceptibly. "That's not what happened."

"What did then?" I demand.

Every atom in my body quivers with anticipation, with hope. Hope that I'll finally get some semblance of closure. That I'll be able to walk away from this moment with that angry gash from my past at least stitched up, if not entirely healed. But she falters. Her mouth—with those perfect pale rose-colored lips of hers— parts just to shut again. And I'm once again reminded that I'll never get the truth.

Her hands come unclenched, instead moving to cradle her abdomen. Odd, that. She's folding in on herself, and this ache to hold her expands rapidly through my veins until I know I need to retreat lest I find my arms reaching for her of their own volition.

I scoff at her silence and turn to leave, to find my daughter and go home, when I find the words for the warning I have to give. I may not be able to protect myself from these feelings resurfacing, but I can protect Niamh. I have to.

"Just don't do this thing"—I wave a hand toward the desk chair where Niamh was sitting, and Leo's gaze flickers in that direction, something like grief flashing across her face—"with Niamh. Don't encourage her. She's had enough disappointment in her life."

Before she can respond, if she even wants to, I stalk out of the room and down the stairs to find Niamh sitting on the bottom step with my mother, the both of them suddenly busying themselves with studying a banister.

"See, it's loose!" Mam says while attempting to wiggle the immovable wooden rod.

"We're leaving," I say, ignoring her while scooping Niamh into my arms in a way I haven't since she was smaller. With every year that passes, she careens closer to wanting complete independence, while I struggle to find my footing in a world where she doesn't need me for every little thing. As if she senses that I need this, though, she doesn't object to being held. She simply lays her head against my chest and lets herself be carried to the car.

Once home, I go through the motions of dinner and the bedtime routine on autopilot, all the while floating somewhere outside my body. Leo's words—or lack thereof—have left me unmoored. When Niamh finally drifts off to sleep, I strip out of the slacks and button-down that my uncle insists are necessary even from my home office and don a T-shirt, gym shorts, and the worn pair of Adidas tucked into the bottom cubby of my wardrobe.

I flick the light on in the garage, the slightly damp scent of the space filling my nostrils. Two neon-green kayaks are mounted on the far wall, with waterproof coats and wet suits strung up on the racks to their right. A small lawn mower sits in the closest corner to my left alongside the limited assortment of gardening tools left over from long-ago summers when my mother would come here with her parents and plant flowers in the garden that I now maintain.

In the opposite corner, a barbell and several plates sit haphazardly arranged in my excuse for a home gym. On good weather days—or hours, for that matter—I can go for runs along the rolling hills to get my heart pumping blood through my desk-weary veins. But some days the rain doesn't let up or the night finds me unable to sleep, and I resort to lifting weights in the perpetually damp sanctuary of my garage.

After a few stretches and warm-up sets with just the barbell, I load a plate on either side and force my now-loose muscles to deadlift the weight. The burn that courses down my back and up the length of my thighs gives the unspent anger somewhere to go. It anchors me in my body. It empties me of thoughts of a brown-haired, blue-eyed woman that I can't figure out how not to want —or hate.

I add another plate on each side and repeat the motions. Beads of sweat pool along my brow and run down my spine. My breath grows ragged, but I force myself through the desire to stop, to lie down, to wallow in these feelings that are resurfacing with a vengeance.

The first mistake I make is not listening to my body as it screams for rest. The second is adding yet another plate to each side. On my best day, this kind of weight is a personal record for me. Today is not my best day.

Pain shoots down my leg, and I falter, dropping the weight with a clang that's nearly loud enough to wake Niamh clear across the house. I limp backward and collapse onto the stool in the corner while what feels like lightning strikes shoot from my right hip all the way to my toes. I glare at the barbell as though it's to blame for my stupidity, before hobbling back into the house and all the way to my shower, which I make as hot as possible.

When I finally collapse into my bed, too tired and wrecked to even clothe myself, I focus on the feel of the sheets against my skin. On the shadows dancing across the ceiling.

I don't allow myself to think of Leo. I certainly don't let myself wish she were here.

But in my dreams, she is.

Chapter Seven

Leona

It takes no time at all for Siobhan and me to fall into an easy rhythm. Despite my fear that her son's resentment will somehow leak into her feelings toward me, she remains steadfast and positive as I get my footing under me. Though I suppose I would, too, if someone suddenly took all the toilet cleaning off my to-do list.

Each morning she writes the day's arrivals in the guest book on the console table in the foyer. I watch from my window until Callum has driven off, and then I make my way downstairs to check which rooms need cleaning. By that time the beautiful breakfast spread Siobhan prepares each morning has been thoroughly picked over by guests heading out early to continue on their road trips along the Wild Atlantic Way.

My stomach growls its disapproval as I gather my cleaning supplies.

The work is not glamorous by any means, but it's simple and quiets my brain in a way that I start to crave in the hours after everything is finished. There are never enough rooms for all the thoughts I want to escape.

Which is why I find myself tiptoeing downstairs after all the guests have gone to bed, carrying a handful of rags and a bottle of furniture polish that I found buried in the back of the supply closet.

The midweek slump—as Siobhan calls it—is in full effect, meaning there were only two guests to prepare a room for today. Even after providing stay-over service to our other guests, I found myself with nothing to do come four o'clock. Which is unfortunate, because after last night's warning from Callum, I needed the distraction more than ever.

Add in a lonely dinner eaten in my room and a lot of fruitless sulking until the light faded from the sky, and it's no wonder I'm resorting to my late-night cleaning habits.

I start in the foyer, spraying a blue microfiber cloth with the furniture polish before setting the bottle aside and getting to work on the check-in table. The pine-scented cleaner triggers a memory from my childhood, when I'd watch my mother clean her parents' home every Saturday after my grandparents became too fragile to do the detail work themselves. I try to lose myself in the monotony of cleaning, in the memory of a time when everything was simpler and life hurt a lot less, but Callum's face as he warned me away from Niamh pulses in the back of my mind.

My eyes burn as I consider his words. The disgust that laced them when he accused me of running here for a rebound from Nick. How could I blame him, really, for jumping to that conclusion? From the outside, for anyone who wasn't a part of our marriage, it certainly wasn't a leap. But while Nick had loved me with kindness, while he had been an absolutely safe and secure choice, losing him never felt like much of a loss. It felt like a natural progression. An inevitable rite of passage, like high school graduation. The thing you've been working toward all along.

When Nick and I got together, several years after Poppy died, it wasn't that we fell in love, per se. It was that my soul recognized him for who he could be for me. What we could be for each other. Nick was a shade tree for my bruised and weary heart to rest beneath. His love was gentle and demanded nothing of me except that I exist. He did not ask difficult questions. He had no desire for children. He was the perfect place to hide.

In return, I fulfilled my role as the placeholder wife. I held the door open dutifully for the day when his true love would come along. When she did—with her blonde hair, mile-long legs, and pure admiration for the way Nick simply *existed*—I swear we both loosed a sigh of relief.

Because I remembered how it felt to love someone like that. Had done it once.

So Callum was wrong. I didn't come here because of Nick. I didn't even come here because of losing my job, really. When I logged into my computer last week to find an email saying I'd been made redundant, it didn't devastate me. It hit me like a splash of cold water to the face.

Suddenly I was awake. I was alive. And I was thirty-two years old and still grieving with the same intensity as the day my daughter died, because I'd isolated myself in that grief. I'd built a silo out of my heart and locked every grain of love I'd felt for Callum, for Poppy up inside. With the doors ripped open, I found it as fresh and raw as the day I'd put it away.

My life became a tunnel with the end in sight, and I realized I'd one day reach it without ever giving that love to the people who deserved it most.

And I was sorry, so sorry. Sorry for hurting him. Sorry for failing Poppy.

I stare at the wood grain, now polished so thoroughly that I can see my crumpled face reflected back at me. My frown lines deepen as I purse my lips and draw in a deep breath through my nose before releasing it slowly. I don't want to cry. I don't want to spend my life being just *sorry*.

Rising slowly to my feet, every muscle in my back screaming in protest, I set my sights on the living room. The fireplace is dark and cold, so I fumble along the wall until I find the lamp in the corner of the room and switch it on. It casts a dull, buttery light over the spines lining the bookshelves. There's a large window on the far wall that overlooks the street during the day but is clothed in heavy drapes for the night. Beneath it, a small love seat with tufted fabric beckons.

I pad over to the wall of books. There is no rhyme or reason to the way they are arranged, at least not one that I can decipher. Books on ornithology are nestled against classics; modern romance titles share a section with fantastical epics. It irks some part of my brain, but beyond that window the night has grown thick with darkness and sleep is trying desperately to tempt me in, so I leave that reorganization for another restless night.

A pale green spine captures my attention. In emerald filigree, *Anne of Green Gables* graces its binding. My mother's favorite. I hook a finger in the top of the book and pluck it out from its place between one of William Shakespeare's more melodramatic plays and the encyclopedia for the letter E.

There's a quilted blanket thrown over the back of the love seat beneath the window, and I toss it haphazardly across my legs. I resign myself to read a few chapters in the hopes that it'll lull me away from my anxiety and maybe, just maybe I'll finally be able to sleep.

A heartbeat later my eyelids flicker open at the urging of Siobhan. I blink her into focus. Her silver hair is combed into a loose chignon, and a cream-colored cable-knit sweater lends itself to her natural elegance. She's so bright I'm convinced she's glowing from within, until I realize it's the sun that illuminates her.

Blink. "What time is it?" *Blink blink.*

She chuckles. "Relax, it's early yet. I just like to get the fire started so the room can be warming for the guests." She reaches out to rub my bicep, which is mottled with goose bumps. "Guess I should've gotten here sooner."

I peer around her, finding the roaring hearth at the same time the sound of crackling wood breaks through the cotton clogging my ears. My throat is still thick with sleep, so I clear it as I sit up.

"I'm so sorry. I didn't mean to fall asleep here."

Her gaze drops to the bottle of furniture polish, which has tipped over by the leg of the love seat, before trailing up to the copy of *Anne of Green Gables* that remains open to the very first chapter in my lap. The corner of her lip quirks. "No worries, Leona. My home is your home."

My heart stills as I study her face and only find sincerity. Home. When was the last time I truly thought of any place as such?

Here. It was here, this town, the man in the cottage on the hill. It was twelve years ago.

I blink again, this time to clear the mist that has fogged over my vision.

"Thank you," I finally manage to squeak out.

"Not a worry." She pats my shoulder gently. "Though if you'd like to continue this ridiculous standoff with my son—which I don't approve of, just for the record—you might want to get a move on." She glances at the delicate gold watch dangling from her thin wrist. "He'll be here in the next five minutes or so, if I had to guess."

I jolt off the couch, nearly knocking Siobhan on her backside as she stumbles away to make space for me. "I'm so sorry!" I say, planting a hand on each of her shoulders to steady her. She's shorter than I am, and lean like her son and granddaughter, but I can feel her muscles beneath my touch. She's a strong woman; my attempts to brace her instead stabilize me.

Her breathy laugh assures me she's fine. "Go on, Leona. And grab a rasher on the way." She pinches my side affectionately. "Can't have you withering away on my watch."

"Thank you, Siobhan." Determined to clean up my mess, I bend over to collect the furniture polish and rags. When I turn back for the novel, though, she's already grabbed it.

"You take the polish; I'll put away the book." She flips it over to study the title. "Oh, *Anne of Green Gables.* One of my favorites." Her bright green gaze lifts from the cover and narrows playfully when meeting mine. "I knew I liked you."

The grin on my face feels good. It feels like waking up.

She shoos me toward the door, and I jolt into action, realizing I've eaten up precious moments of escape time with my clumsiness.

The door to the kitchen is propped open, the way I've learned she does on weekdays when guests are more likely to be up early. The gentleman whose luggage I helped carry upstairs when he arrived yesterday on business is already bent over the spread, selecting a fluffy croissant from the aromatic pile. He smiles at me as I pluck a rasher up with my bare hands, careful not to touch anything else around it, and deposit it in my mouth before heading for the stairs without so much as a word tossed in his direction.

He's checking out today. Not like I'll ever see him again, so no need to worry that he probably thinks I'm a little bit feral.

Just as my foot lands on the first step, I hear the solid thud of the front door shutting at the end of the hall. I don't allow myself to look back until I'm rounding the landing, where I hope I'm at least safely out of sight from whoever has just arrived.

The first thing I notice is that Callum's limping. The second is that *he's* noticing *me*.

I shove down my curiosity, my desire, anything living within me that feeds the urge to run back down the stairs. To run to him.

Instead I turn, letting the curtain of my mussed hair fall between us, and return to my attic.

Chapter Eight

Callum

"You walked in on her showering?" Padraig says, eyes wide. He takes a sip of his beer while the corners of his lips pull into a wicked smile, earning a scowl from me in return. "And still had the nerve to tell her off about talking to Niamh? When did your balls get so big there, lad?"

"She was done showering," I clarify, pinching the bridge of my nose. With the way this week has been going, I'm either going to succumb to a migraine or a heart attack.

Padraig raises his eyebrows at me, that shit-eating grin growing ever wider.

"She was dressed, Podge!"

I realize too late that I've raised my voice, drawing the attention of several patrons in the pub we're occupying. I glance over at Dermot—the bartender and owner who has one foot in the grave, he's so ancient—and nod my apology.

"Sure, yeah, whatever you say." Podge chews at the inside of his cheek, trying to contain his amusement at my suffering. "Did you see anything good?"

I immediately regret telling him this story. First, because now the image of Leo with dripping wet hair is flooding my brain. She stares up at me, shocked as a deer caught in headlights, with her full lips popped apart in a gasp. Her shirt clings to her breasts in a way that makes my dick betray my brain. Not exactly fond of logic, that one. I shift in my seat, suddenly not fitting into my pants as comfortably as before.

Second, and even more troubling, I regret it because there is a small part of me that feels like I'm betraying Leo by sharing something so personal. The rolling in my gut is directly tied to the corner of my brain that still thinks she's mine to protect, despite the years and evidence to the contrary.

Forcing myself not to read into which reason causes me to say it, I reply, "Let's just drop it, yeah?"

Padraig leans back in his chair, raking a hand through his hair that then settles at the nape of his neck. He studies me for a long moment before shaking his head in what can only be described as bewilderment. "What happened with the two of you's anyway? I'd consider myself your best friend, since you don't seem to have any others, and you've never mentioned her."

Now it's my turn to lean back with a groan. My beer sits untouched on the table between us, and suddenly the idea of drinking it makes me sick to my stomach. Every Friday at five in the afternoon, like clockwork, I log out of my computer and Padraig turns off his taxi light and we meet here for a beer or ten to decompress. We've been doing so for three years, ever since I moved here permanently after deciding Niamh deserved to grow up in a slower and safer environment than Dublin. My uncle didn't like the idea of remote work at first, but I've kept up with the demand and am on a fast track to take over the shipping company when he retires next year.

Not that he'll ever admit to eating his words.

Even before the move, Padraig and I were close enough. We met on one of the few trips Catherine and I took to the summer cottage before Niamh was born, when she needed a taxi to get from one place to the next even if it was right down the street because her belly was so round and ankles so swollen. She hated being pregnant, resented how it changed her body. Padraig would crack joke after joke, trying to lighten her mood. While unsuccessful, he did manage to endear himself to me in the process.

When Niamh was born, my circle of friends shrank to become unrecognizably small. With everyone in their late twenties, no one was inclined to come hang out with an infant on a Friday night. They were out living their lives, and I can't say I blame them. Padraig, however, is ten years older than me and content with the pace of my life. He's just as happy to join me for a beer as he is to come over and help build a tree house for Niamh in the backyard. If that doesn't make someone a best friend, I don't know what does.

I chew at the edge of my lip, filling my mouth with the taste of iron. How do you admit to a fellow grown man that, as a thirty-four-year-old father, you still cling to the pain of a love lost when you were twenty-two?

Padraig is watching me expectantly, letting silence grow between us into something vast enough for me to fill. With a sigh, I resign myself to at least try.

"She was an English student at the college in Maynooth when I lived there during my internship with Darren." My uncle was truly just doing a favor for Mam, as he admitted to me later, but he saw something in me during that summer working at his company that made him keep me on. I've been moving up the ranks ever since. "Studying abroad for the summer. We lived in the same manor and spent every waking moment together that we weren't working or in school."

I pause, gathering my thoughts, and Padraig spins his hand in a gesture that says, *Go on.*

I glare at him, not one to be rushed, but continue. "When she had to go back to the States at the end of the summer, we'd already decided we wanted to be together. To make it work." An old, familiar insecurity has me shaking my head. "At least, I thought we had. She was supposed to come back the next summer, and then move here permanently after she graduated.

"For a few months after she moved back to the States, things were perfect. We spoke all the time, wrote letters." An involuntary smile tries to take over my face as I remember the late nights spent talking after she finally got out of class. So much for getting more sleep after she left. *Sorry, Uncle Darren.* "Then she'd go days without responding, and when she did, it was like talking to a completely different person. There was no life in it anymore. That went on for another few months or so until one day she just stopped answering altogether. I never heard from her after that."

For years I shamelessly stalked her social media, desperate to understand what happened. I watched from a distance as she graduated, studying the photo of her in her cap and gown for hours and wondering why her smile never touched her eyes like it used to with me. I waited for her to announce a job in journalism like she'd always dreamed of. Part of me still imagined she'd call me out of the blue and finally explain things. I told myself if she just gave me a reason, I could accept it. Even if it shattered me.

"She announced she was seeing someone a few years after that. Last I saw, they were engaged." I blocked her on everything that day, unwilling to bear witness to the rest of her life without me. "That's when I met Catherine. Because apparently life wasn't done fucking me over just yet."

Padraig shifts in his seat, draining the remainder of his glass. He tries to make eye contact with Dermot to request a refill, but the bar owner is locked in conversation with one of the local fishermen seated at the counter. Rows upon rows of liquor bottles line the wall behind Dermot. Some of that whiskey has been aged longer on his shelf than it was in a barrel. Experience tells me there's no end in sight to the old man's rambling, so I slide my untouched beer across the table, and Padraig takes the now-luke-warm beverage with a resigned sigh.

"Let me get this straight," he says, then swallows a swig of amber liquid. He wipes his lips with the back of his hand before continuing. "You're mad at her for flaking on a promise she made at what, *nineteen years old?*"

I wince, realizing how ridiculous it sounds when spoken aloud, without any of the nuance accompanying it. "Twenty," I mumble under my breath.

A guffaw escapes his lips, returning our neighboring patrons' attention to us once more. I wave a hand in apology, urging them to go on about their business. When they finally look away, I level a glare on my friend.

"You wouldn't understand. We were young, but our feelings were real." At least for me, they were. The possibility that she never truly reciprocated them has haunted me for years.

"I'm not saying they weren't, man. But can you imagine someone hating you for the stupid shit you did at twenty?"

Dermot finally notices the state of our drinks, bringing over two sloshing pints. "*I* still hate you for the shit you did at twenty," he grumbles, his voice sounding like he's been gargling gravel for the last fifty years. A lifetime of smoking will do that to you. He slaps Padraig on the shoulder affectionately before turning to me, an arthritis-riddled finger pointed at my friend. "Bastard stole a fifth from behind my bar."

"And you made me clean the jacks for the next six months straight," Padraig replies, rolling his eyes. "I think I've well made up for it, don't you?"

Dermot makes a sound like he's coughing something up before waving his hand to dismiss us and returning to the counter.

Padraig chuckles, and I find myself joining in. Surprise flashes in his eyes. "There's a laugh! Jesus, never thought I'd hear it again."

I steal one of the fresh glasses Dermot delivered, and finally take a swig, but it can't hide the amused smile playing on my lips.

A nagging thought tugs at my attention. What if I *am* wrong to still be angry at her? She showed up after all this time and was met with nothing but hostility. No wonder she hasn't explained her reasons for coming. I haven't exactly given her the impression that they'll be met with anything other than anger.

Just as I feel myself softening to the idea ever so slightly, the front door opens, and my hackles raise instinctively.

So much for that.

Leo scans the room before her gaze lands on Padraig. For a moment the corners of her eyes crinkle and I see her truly smile for the first time since she returned. But the expression, which hits me like a blow to the chest, fades instantly when she realizes I'm the one sitting next to him.

Her smile falters and her hand finds that oval-shaped amulet hanging from a delicate gold chain around her neck. It's a nervous tick she's developed in the time since I knew her, and I can't explain the pang of sadness it fills me with every time she does it. Perhaps it's because the woman I knew was so fearless, so carefree that the sight of her faltering betrays every memory I have of her.

Or perhaps it's the fact that I'm the one she's afraid of.

She starts walking toward us, and I force myself to study the grain of the wooden table rather than watch her approach. Hurt and anger and sorrow are swirling in my gut, filling me with the worst kind of nausea. It's a sensation I've been hit with more times since she arrived than ever before in my life, and I can't help but resent her for it.

"Um, hello." Her voice wavers, and I can't help it. My gaze travels up to meet hers, and suddenly I'm certain I'm going to be sick or punch something. Possibly both. Anything to suppress the urge to hold her and take away her anxiety.

The anxiety I'm causing.

"Hello there, Leona," Podge says cheerily. "Nice to see you stuck around for the week!"

A grin tries to form on her face but falters. "I'm actually helping Siobhan out with cleaning for a bit, just until she can find more permanent help."

"Well why can't you be the permanent help?" He props one ankle on his other knee, settling in for the conversation. Meanwhile my spine has turned to steel.

Her gaze flickers from him to me and then back, before she murmurs a noncommittal, "Oh, you know."

Padraig follows her gaze, scowling at me in disapproval. *Oh, he knows.*

A scalding surge of resentment causes my good sense to exit the premises. How can she show up after all this time and have everyone instantly on her side? Doesn't she understand how deeply she hurt me? Don't they understand, after being abandoned by both her and Catherine, why I'm not keen to open up old wounds once more?

"This isn't exactly keeping your distance," I snap, wincing at the sound of my own harsh words. Too late. I can see the lashing hit her, but the regret her expression fills me with does nothing to rewind time and stop me from saying the words in the first place.

"I—well, your mother—I mean, Siobhan," she stutters. She presses her lips together and inhales deeply, her breasts rising with the motion. Not that I'm staring at her breasts. *Damn it, Callum. Focus.* "I needed to get groceries, and Siobhan said you'd be here, Podge."

Of course my meddling mother sent her. She knows Padraig and I meet every Friday afternoon. She and Niamh usually have a movie night to celebrate the occasion.

I've done everything in my power this week to avoid running into Leo when dropping off and picking up my daughter. And I've been doing a damn good job, I'd say. Aside from seeing her short, dark hair swinging to shield her face as she rushed up the stairs on Wednesday morning, I've mostly managed to pretend she's not even here.

My mother won't stand for that, apparently.

"Listen, I'm sorry. I didn't mean to interrupt." Leo extends her hands palm out like she's trying to prevent a snarling animal from leaping at her. Shame threatens to take over when I realize that snarling animal is me. I shrink in on myself, utterly crestfallen, when her rose-pink lips turn down at the edges. "I just need a ride."

Padraig snickers at the same time color fills her cheeks. Realization dawns on her, and she quickly corrects herself. "A *lift*. I need a lift."

But it's too late. Our gazes lock as we both travel back in time, to the first memory we share.

Chapter Nine

Leona

I'm wearing a channel into the rug with my pacing, but I can't help it. I've called the taxi company five times now trying to get a ride to the PPS office in Newbridge. No one's answering, and at this point a train won't get me there in time for my appointment. Learning to rely on public transportation is proving to be a real pain in the ass.

My teeth sink into my lower lip as I dial the number once more, hoping the sixth time's the charm. I have to find a way to get there. These appointments book out months in advance, and I can't start working to pay the rent until I have an Irish social security number assigned to me.

The door to the communal kitchen swings open, revealing a petite man named Jude who immigrated here from India last spring and always makes enough curry to share. He's the friendliest of my housemates, and the only one I've shared more than a couple words with in the week I've been here. There is a set of sisters who pass by without so much as a look offered in my direction and an older gentleman who mostly keeps to himself, but with classes getting underway, they're all I've been able to meet. The *entire second floor is lined with doors like a hotel, so I imagine there's more where they came from.*

"Hey, Jude." I smile at him and hang up the phone call, which has once again landed in hold-music purgatory. Or hell. Definitely hell.

"Nice to see you, Leona." He passes through the doorway, and another man, younger and unfamiliar, follows in his footsteps. "Callum and I were just talking about ordering lunch. Do you have any plans?"

Wavy locks of golden-blond hair sit like a halo atop the stranger's head. I do my best to acknowledge Jude's question, but I can't force my gaze to meet his. It's locked on this man, Callum, and I'm not sure I'll ever be able to look away.

You know those moments in your life when you become distinctly aware that everything's changing? Not gradually or in pieces, but all at once, with a clarity and awareness that comes out of nowhere. I felt it for the first time at my favorite uncle's funeral when I was thirteen, and again at my high school graduation. I even felt it when lying in Grant Foster's bed freshman year of college after losing my virginity to him. The lens I was seeing the world through suddenly zoomed out to include the entirety of my existence, from beginning to end, and then zoomed back in on the moment, leaving me too aware and vulnerable.

This moment, when I'm met with a green-eyed gaze that turns my heart into a hot-air balloon threatening to lift me out of this place, is one of those. I can't tell you why, but the second Callum enters my line of sight, I'm certain nothing will ever be the same again—least of all me.

"Nice to meet you," Callum says, his voice dripping from his tongue like molten honey, languid and lyrical. He offers his hand to me. "Leona, is it?"

I'm so busy staring at him that I forget how to be a normal person for a split second. His hand hangs in the balance between us, a question quirking his golden-blond eyebrow.

"Oh, um, yes. I'm Leona." I wipe my palm on my jeans before clasping his hand. "Leona Granger. Nice to meet you. I just moved in."

"From America, yeah?"

"Yes! From Tennessee." I raise my eyebrows at him. "How'd you know?"

He ends the handshake, and I cradle my wrist in front of my stomach, trembling with an anxious energy. His now-free hand draws a circle in the air around his lips as he says, "Your accent."

Duh, Leona. *My God, he must think I'm an idiot.*

Jude, meanwhile, is watching the interaction with entirely too much amusement. He's searching his phone—presumably for takeaway options—but leaves his gaze trained on us all the while.

"Of course. Makes sense." Heat creeps up my neck steadily until it's tickling the apples of my cheeks. I clear my throat, sounding like a drowning person getting their first taste of air, before tearing my gaze away from Tall Blond and Handsome. For the greater good, also known as my pride. "Sorry, Jude, I'd love to, but I've got to get to the PPS office in"—I check my phone—"fuck, thirty minutes."

Callum blinks at me, amusement tugging at the corners of his lips. His full, framed-by-stubble lips.

"Shouldn't you already be going? That's in Newbridge, no?" Jude says, interrupting my staring contest with Callum's mouth.

I groan, throwing my hands up in the air. "Yes, but I can't get ahold of a taxi and it's too late to get a train or bus. You wouldn't be able to give me a ride, would you?"

Jude starts to shake his head, but Callum shocks us both by bursting into laughter. Not even minimally contained laughter, either. He's full-blown dying in the kitchen entrance. Jude and I exchange several confused glances before Callum finally inhales enough oxygen in between guffaws to let us know what's so funny.

"So sorry, it's just that, in Ireland, asking someone for a ride has a bit of a different connotation, if you know what I mean." He scrubs a hand over his jaw, attempting to wipe away his cheeky grin. He's unsuccessful. "Sorry, I know you meant a lift. I do. It just surprised me, is all."

His implication finally reaches the last part of my brain firing on any cylinders, and my blush catches flame. If they couldn't see it before, the heat in my cheeks tells me they certainly can now. I glance from him to Jude, shaking my head in horror.

Jude is older than us, likely in his midforties if I had to guess, and he just takes the joke in stride. "Relax, Leona, I knew what you meant. Unfortunately I don't have a car here, or I would be happy to. But you're right, it's too late for the train. When I went, it took me nearly an hour to get there with the different routes you have to switch between."

I feel like I might vomit, a result of the combination of embarrassment and nerves swirling in my gut. The landlord, Ainne, is giving me two more weeks to get settled and pay rent. I can't do that without a job, and I can't work without that number.

"Ahem."

The sound of Callum clearing his throat draws my gaze reluctantly back to him. How is it that ten minutes ago I couldn't look away, and now the thought of facing him fills me with self-consciousness?

The edges of his eyes are still crinkled in amusement, but he's managed to get the cocky smile under control. He crosses his arms over his chest, impressive biceps fully on display. "I have a car."

Desperation overrides any self-preservation telling me riding in a car with a strange, albeit gorgeous, man I just met is not the wisest decision. Besides, I'm not exactly in a place to turn down the favor. "Would you mind? I'd be happy to pay for the gas."

He shakes his head at my offer while he retrieves a set of keys from his jacket pocket, swinging them around his index finger. The universe continues to shift under my feet, making me wonder if I'll ever stand on solid ground again.

"Don't worry about it. I'd be honored to give you a ride."

Padraig's amusement quickly sobers when he sees the look in my eyes. Callum, meanwhile, seems to have seen a ghost.

Does he remember that first moment as I do? With fondness, despite all that has happened. Or does he regret ever making that tongue-in-cheek offer, knowing what became of us as a result?

I tear my gaze away from him, letting it flit about the bar without settling too long on anything in particular. The lighting is dim and seemingly powered only by gas lanterns hung haphazardly throughout the room. The walls are exposed stone in various shades of brown and gray. The old bar is made from weathered barnwood, if I had to guess. It's a cozy place that feels a bit like stepping back in time.

The elderly gentleman behind the counter tips his flat cap at me, smiling beneath his scraggly white beard. I offer him a grin in return that doesn't reach my eyes. Like everything else about me, it's become an echo of the joy I was capable of the first time I stepped foot in Ireland.

"Ah, Leona, I'd be happy to give you a lift," Padraig says, drawing my gaze back to him. I scan the pint glasses on the table, counting two empty and two just getting started. He catches me looking. "It's taken me an hour and a half to drink those two; I'm good to go."

I nod, and Padraig rises from his seat. Callum starts, reaching out, and grabs his friend's arm so tightly his knuckles turn white.

"Are you sure you're good, man?" Callum asks, a fierceness in his eyes replacing the disgust I've been getting since I arrived.

Padraig's eyebrows furrow at his friend, and he yanks his arm out of Callum's grasp. "Yeah, why would you even ask that? You know I'd never drive if I weren't right as rain."

Realization dawns on Callum's features as he glances at me before training his gaze on the tabletop. "Right. Sorry."

Padraig is still studying him, and I can practically see the moment the lightbulb goes off over his head. "You wouldn't be wanting to drive her, would ya? Since all you've had is a sip."

"No," we say in unison, twin vines of panic lacing our vocal cords.

Padraig glances between the two of us before nodding once. "All right then. Just checking." He claps a hand down firmly on Callum's shoulder, who is still focusing hard on a drink ring staining the table. "Sorry to bail on you, but duty calls."

"Thanks, Podge," I murmur. He grins at me and rests a hand gently against the small of my back to turn me toward the exit. The last I see of Callum is his gaze, hollow and unreadable, finally lifting to meet mine. Just determined to see me out of his safe haven, I suppose.

The brisk, early evening air does wonders for my blood pressure, cooling my feverish face and bringing me back down to earth. Padraig escorts me over to his cab and opens the passenger door for me to climb in before jogging around to the other side. He's wearing an identical tracksuit to the one I saw him in that first day. I'm convinced it's the only type of clothing he owns. Or a self-imposed uniform.

"Sorry about him. I didn't realize quite how badly you got under his skin," he says, shifting roughly into gear before pulling onto the street.

I scan the passersby on the sidewalk, all bundled up against the incoming chill of night. I've never been here in the winter, but

I remember Callum telling me that the temperature isn't what gets you. It's the wind that cuts right through your clothes.

"I told you we weren't friends," I mumble.

We roll to a stop at a red light. As some pedestrians cross in front of us, Padraig taps on my leg, dragging my attention away from the window. My hot breath leaves a foggy circle behind on the glass.

"D'you know he wasn't always this way?" His face has grown as serious as I've seen it, and he watches me intently for a reaction to his words. He must find what he's looking for, because his eyes soften at the edges and his eyebrows lift, opening his expression up. "Who do I think I'm talking to; of course you know."

Something sinks inside me when I realize Callum must've explained our history to Podge. I couldn't have expected him not to, but the shame is there all the same. Still, curiosity gets the better of me. "I'm not sure what you mean by that."

The light changes and we start rolling forward again. I can already see the sign for Aldi up ahead, and I start to feel a bit stupid for even asking for a ride—*lift*—in the first place. Then I realize Siobhan knew how close it was when I asked, and still sent me to crash her son's guys' night.

She's a determined old bird; I'll give her that.

The fine lines surrounding Padraig's mouth deepen as he offers a grim smile. "All right, since you're so good at keeping a lid on things, you can pretend I didn't tell you what I'm about to. 'Cause he's my friend and I shouldn't be ratting him out, but you both seem to need a little nudging along."

He navigates the car into the lot in silence before he parks and shifts in his seat to face me. "You can't be blaming yourself for the way Cal is acting. He holds on to a lot of anger, and it comes from a plethora of sources. He doesn't seem keen to let go of any of them, least of all you."

My eyebrows furrow. "What else could he possibly be upset

over?" Callum has the perfect family, a child and a partner somewhere and his mother nearby. I know he used to have a lot of hurt over his father leaving them to go off gallivanting in the UK somewhere, but other than that he has a pretty full life.

One I'm hell-bent on ruining, it seems.

Padraig shakes his head with a sardonic snort. "Oh, Leona, how little you know."

"Enlighten me then," I say, drawing my feet up onto the seat and hugging my knees closely to my chest. It makes me feel secure, like whatever blow is coming won't find a place to land and will thus be forced to pass me by.

A heavy sigh escapes his barely parted lips. He runs his fingers through his hair, the silver strands glinting in the light of the setting sun. "Niamh's mother, Catherine, left them when she was just after turning two years old. She resented having the baby, being tied down. She had an affair, and then she ran off with the lad to Barcelona when Callum caught wind.

"He begged her to reconsider, told her how Niamh needed her mam, but there was no changing her mind. She signed over her rights and never looked back."

I sit dumbfounded in a puddle of my own shame, feeling ridiculous for assuming everything was perfect. Don't I hate it when people make assumptions about *my* life? They'd take one look at Nick and me and then scan the floor for toddlers, always following up with a nonchalant, *"When will you two be having children?"* as if there was never any other possibility than things going perfectly. Get married, buy a house, have babies, live happily ever after. In that order.

I did to Callum what they always did to me, only I assumed he was already at the finish line.

Grief for him comes in waves, a tide tugging at the sand around my heart. First his father, then me, then Niamh's mother. Callum's been abandoned by nearly everyone he's ever loved.

How can I blame him for not wanting me here? How can I blame him for trying to protect Niamh from the same fate?

When I think of all he's been through, all Niamh's been through, there's rage, too, sparking in my veins. "My God, how could someone leave their daughter like that?" You get the most beautiful gift in the world, a stunning, *living* child, and you walk away like she's nothing?

Tears are threatening to fill my eyes, and I force myself to draw in a big enough breath to contain the ocean of pain inside me. Or at least to try.

Padraig is shaking his head again, now staring out the window as a smattering of rain begins to make music on the windshield. "Hell if I know. But it tore Callum apart. Now he practically kills himself trying to be enough for Niamh, trying to bear all that pain himself, so she never has to feel it."

As heartbreaking as it is, the words thaw my heart ever so slightly. Because that's the Callum I remember. The one who would walk through fire to bring help to someone in need. The man who would do anything for anyone if it meant sparing them pain.

The memory of him standing in the airport terminal in Dublin fills my mind. I can still see him, stone-faced as could be, trying to remain strong so I'd be able to walk away. He knew if he showed any chinks in his armor, I'd never let him go. I'd miss my flight, abandon my degree and the dreams it would help me achieve, all to remain with him.

When we parted, it was with a tendril of a promise dangling between us, holding us together even across an ocean. One that I, and so many before and after me, have broken when it comes to Callum.

I press my lips firmly together, holding back a sob that threatens to break loose. After a long, pregnant pause has passed us by, I finally find the ability to form words again.

"I'm going to run inside. No need to wait for me. I didn't realize how close it is, and I can easily walk home. I only need a few things."

"Are you sure?" Padraig asks, gaze scanning the weeping sky through the window. "You'll be walking in the rain. Again."

"I don't mind," I whisper. Before he can respond, I exit the vehicle and close the door. I trudge forward, through the biting cold, willing the rain to wash my spirit clean.

Chapter Ten

Callum

id he have to put his fucking hand on her back?

The sight has left me with red-tinged tunnel vision. All I can see is my friend's hand settling into the curve at the base of Leo's spine, guiding her the way I used to. I can practically feel the heat of her body beneath my fingertips, or perhaps it's just my rage setting me alight. I try every method Granda taught me to relax. Breathe in through the nose, out through the mouth. Count backward from one hundred. Imagine each of my appendages filling with warm, golden light that spreads through my body until I'm filled to the brim.

Okay, that last one was for falling asleep, but it does the trick anyway.

It's just Podge, I remind myself. *He's not trying to fuck your ex-girlfriend.*

Oh God, is that how I'm thinking of her now? Like a tree I've pissed on to mark my territory. It's been twelve years, for Christ's sake. I've got to get a grip.

I drop a handful of euros on the table and stand, leaving behind a lot of wasted beer and along with it, I'm hoping, this bout of insanity that's overtaken me. Dermot studies me with a hint of suspicion folded into the million wrinkles between his eyebrows. Frazzled and utterly spent, I nod in his direction and take my leave.

The steady static of voices that fills the bar falls away when I step out onto the sidewalk, leaving me feeling like I've stuffed my ears with cotton. The world is at once muffled and incredibly clear, and it takes a moment for me to find an equilibrium. There's a tension headache building in my temples, and I cup my jaw, tugging it left and right like I've just been punched, attempting to relieve the pain.

No dice. The sky opens up right on schedule, spilling a steady smattering of rain on the pavement. And, consequently, me. I tilt my head back the way Leo did the day she showed up on my doorstep, only instead of soaking in rays of sunlight, I'm attempting osmosis.

Why am I doing this to myself? She's just a woman who, if I'm honest with myself, I don't know in the slightest anymore. We've both lived entire lives in the time we've been apart. Letting her presence drive me to this level of stress is ridiculous.

The moment Catherine stepped out the door, I swore I was done wasting my time on flighty women. Niamh is my world, and she deserves my undivided attention. And she certainly doesn't need to watch her father repeat the same mistake ad nauseam, leaving her thinking this is how relationships should be.

There's a bit of resolve still left in me, though I have to dig deep to find it. I shrug into it like a stranger's coat, foreign in fit but functional nonetheless. I can do this. I can ignore Leona Granger, for as long as she remains on my side of the Atlantic Ocean.

"Daddy, what does it mean to have 'cowlike reflexes'?"

I pause midstroke, leaving the comb lodged in Niamh's damp curls. She scoops another bite of porridge into her mouth, patiently watching her favorite television show while I attempt to form a plait with her rebellious locks. Now she's added understanding her question to the list of things I'm not succeeding at this morning.

"Could you give me an example?"

"Yesterday I knocked cleaning stuff off the table, and Leona caught it before it fell all the way down. She said she had 'cowlike reflexes' and that's why she caught it so fast."

I press my lips tightly together, suppressing a grin, even as my headache from last night threatens to return. "I think what she probably said was 'catlike reflexes.' Like the neighbor's cats that wander into Granny's garden. Even when you scare them and they fall off the wall, they still land on their feet. It means they have really good balance."

"I've never scared the cats." She turns to look up at me, eyebrows furrowed. "Have you been scaring the cats?"

I'd be lying if I said I hadn't rushed them a time or two, making growling noises just to startle them off. I'm not exactly a fan of always being the one to find the cat-poop land mines in the garden, usually with my nicest shoes, no less. Despite my best efforts, the food scraps Mam feeds them keep the felines coming back for more jump scares.

Rather than lie to Niamh, I do what any parent does best with questions better left unanswered. I dodge it. "What do you think cowlike reflexes would be?"

She considers it for a moment, facing forward once more. Her feet kick back and forth in the chasm of space between her chair and the floor, a metronome to keep pace with her thoughts.

I'm about to secure what I can confidently say is my best plait to date when she turns unexpectedly to face me once more, yanking the tiny lock from my fist before letting out an impressively baritone, "*Moooooo.*"

As I watch in abject disappointment, the plait unravels within seconds of being released. I lock my hands on my hips and give Niamh my best pout. "Now why'd you go and do that? I was just after finishing!"

Niamh shrugs and offers me a cheeky grin. "Cowlike reflexes."

I burst out laughing, any twinge of anger forgotten. This is the part of parenthood no one warns you about. There's all the talk of sleepless nights and endless sicknesses and relentless questions once they're old enough to talk. What everyone forgets to mention, however, is just how damn funny kids can be.

At least, mine is. Can't speak for the other sorry bastards that didn't create their own personal comedian. Pride swells in my chest, and I envelop my daughter in a quick hug, squeezing her to me as hard as I can without suffocating her. "Love you big."

She forces out a reply with each tiny gasp of air she's able to suck in between the gap in my arm. "I love. You. Big. Too."

When the emotion releases its grip on my heart enough that I can function, I step away from Niamh and assess the situation. "Bad news bears, we're going to have to start all over."

Rather than deflating like I expect, she perks up. "Leona had her hair in two plaits yesterday. Can you do two plaits, Daddy? So I can match her?"

I bite down a little too hard on the inside of my cheek, and the metallic taste of blood coats my tastebuds. Two shout-outs for Leo in one morning. I guess Neruda was right about love being short, and forgetting being the bastard that takes his sweet time.

"Erm, I don't really know how to do two plaits, hon."

"You could watch a video like before!" She scoops another spoonful of porridge, unbothered by the idea of being stuck here for another thirty minutes while I watch some woman on the Internet plait a mannequin head's hair at half speed.

All for my daughter to look like Leo. Pure agony.

When she realizes I've not set to work on pulling up a tutorial, she looks over her shoulder at me, bottom lip in a pucker. "Please, Daddy."

Fuck. Can't say no to that.

"Right, okay." I grab my phone from the counter nearby, loading up the best video I can and slowing it down to a speed I can at least somewhat comprehend. Niamh gives a satisfied *harrumph* when she sees she's been victorious. As if she's ever known anything but.

"Leona says lots of other funny things as well." The kicking resumes, making it even more difficult to hang on to her now-dry curls that are slick and soft as silk. "She calls the bin a garbage can." A fit of giggles follows her attempt at an American accent.

I smile despite myself. Curiosity creeps up on me, and before I know it, I'm asking, "Do you see her often?"

I don't know what I expect the answer to be, since I warned her away from my daughter in no uncertain terms.

Niamh's head tilts to the side. So the braids will be uneven, then.

"Not really. She comes downstairs to clean after breakfast is all finished. Granny says she sleeps real late. Sometimes we all have lunch together, though. She's nice, Daddy." She hums softly to herself for a second, considering her words. I've never met a more thoughtful almost-five-year-old. "It stinks that you hate her so bad."

Out of the mouths of babes. Shame colors my cheeks, and it has nothing to do with how catastrophically crooked these plaits are looking. "I don't hate her," I murmur softly, more to myself than to Niamh.

"Then how come your voice gets all mean and scary when you talk to her?"

"Because, love—" I pause, unable to form the right words. How do you explain something like this to a child? And even more upsetting, if my grudge can't be justified to a child, what business do I have holding on to it?

A million tiny pinpricks fill my throat like I've swallowed my mam's sewing kit. Not for the first time, the burden of being alone in figuring out how to explain all the ins and outs of the world to my daughter overwhelms me. I find myself wishing for a mother —not Catherine specifically, but a kind, faceless presence filling the role—to help me explain that life is full of hurts, and sometimes they're inflicted by other people. On purpose or by accident.

"Leo—*Leona*—and I knew each other a really long time ago, and there are just some things about that time that make Daddy sad to remember." I tie off her plaits with two tiny rubber bands and silently thank God that she can't see and critique my work. I place a kiss on the crown of her head, always the finishing touch. "But you're right, I shouldn't be mean. I'll try to do better."

She holds up her pinky for me, the way she saw in one of the kid movies she makes me leave on repeat for days, and waits for me to accept it before saying, "You twinkie promise?"

Okay, so she misheard the character in the movie. But this one is too cute to correct. "I twinkie promise." I give her pinky a little shake to seal the deal. "Now let's go enjoy some of that sunshine before it's too late. I heard there might be a storm coming in tonight."

Chapter Eleven

Leona

My body aches in places I never thought possible, and I'm wondering if this is the beginning of the end for me.

Turning thirty didn't scare me the way it did for so many of my acquaintances. Like every birthday before it, I ushered in the day with a peace settled around my heart, knowing I was one day closer to seeing my baby again. What I hadn't been prepared for was the way my body would start taking to hurt like a fish to water. One night spent sleeping in a less-than-ideal position and I'd wake up with a crick in my neck that would hang around for a week.

A few summers back, Nick and I joined some coworkers of his for a tubing trip on the lake one weekend, and I landed on my hip wrong after being thrown into the water. That hip still gets stiff when I sit for too long.

Turns out cleaning rooms day in and day out, bending over to tuck and untuck sheets, scrubbing showers to keep them fresh for guests, and the many other tasks that make up my new job require being a level of in-shape that I apparently am not. I hobble into the kitchen after turning over the last room for today's arrivals, and I'm met with an amused snort from Siobhan.

"Now you know how I felt all the time before you came along." She giggles, the youthful sound existing in direct contrast to the lines on her face that are filled with a lifetime of stories.

Occasionally, when she's not knee-deep in the garden harvesting veggies with Niamh and I'm not elbow-deep in a toilet, she shares some of them with me. My favorites, the ones that involve Callum, she seems to save for especially busy days when I most need the pick-me-up. From the way her eyes light up when she reminisces about his wild teen years or his mischievous toddler phase, I can imagine it boosts her mood just as much.

"Coffee?" She holds out the mug she's just filled.

I take it with a thankful nod. "Yes, please."

The sound of my slurp slaps my ears at the same time the bitter liquid graces the back of my throat, warming me from the inside out. I hum my thanks, rest a hip against the counter opposite Siobhan, and join her in staring out the window.

"You'll let me know if I get to running you too ragged, won't you, love?" She takes a sip of her coffee while her gaze, green as the grass in the garden, shifts from the window to me. I don't know how I didn't notice right away that she was Callum's mother, with eyes like that. "Though I must admit, it has been nice having the help."

I smile softly, shaking my head. "I don't mind. It's good to be kept busy."

Something flickers in her expression. "What were you doing before you came here? I thought I remembered Callum saying you wanted to be a travel journalist back then. Is that what brought you back?"

"Sharp memory you've got there." I wince even as I force the words out in a lighthearted tone. "No, I was working as a legal editor. The firm I was working with downsized, making me redundant."

She grimaces. "Sorry about that."

I wave a hand dismissively. "It was just a job. There will be others."

Her head tilts as she studies me, and my skin feels suddenly transparent, letting her see everything I like to keep hidden beneath the surface. I have to fight the urge to squirm under the spotlight of her stare.

"If you're not passionate about your job, what are you passionate about?"

The question hits me square between the eyes. What *am* I passionate about? I used to have a laundry list of answers for that question. Travel being at the very top. It's what brought me here in the first place, way back when. It's why I wanted to spend my career visiting far-off places and peoples and writing about them so others would be inspired to do the same.

After I lost Poppy, trudging forward with my degree felt like wandering through a dark tunnel in an attempt to end up in a brighter place. Then my father's friend offered me a job after graduation at his law firm as a legal editor, and at the time the grief was still so fresh that I had no energy to seek out internships or fight for a spot at an agency. A job being handed to me was the first bit of grace I'd received from the universe in two years, and I decided to hang on to it for dear life.

Then there was Nick, who had roots the size of a redwood. After meeting him at a conference and falling into a safe kind of love, his dedication to remaining in his hometown forever meant I moved there, too. He had no desire to travel, and I had no desire to make him, so I let my passport expire. Along with it went any chance of returning to my original dream. Getting a new one when changing my name back after our divorce was done more out of routine than actual plans to use it.

Sadness burns the backs of my eyes, and I hope Siobhan can't see it in my expression. With the way hers softens, though, I imagine she can.

I may not have loved Nick in the all-consuming, earth-shattering way that I did Callum, but I did love him. It was gentle and safe, steady as a heartbeat. The loss of it left its own kind of scars.

"You know," I finally say after clearing my throat. "I'm trying to figure that out."

She nods with her lips pressed into a grim line. Her hand that isn't holding a mug reaches out and settles over mine where it rests on the counter. "When Callum's father left, I had a lot of figuring out to do. It takes time, but time is all it takes."

"I like that. Time is all it takes."

"Thanks. I stole it from someone, I'm sure." She winks at me, a grin softening her somber expression from before. "Feel free to steal it from me."

I chuckle, feeling the tension in my shoulders release with the act. "Don't mind if I do."

"Now listen, the rooms are all done and this is likely one of the last nice days we'll be seeing for the next few months, so why don't you go on down to the market at the community centre. Just bring a raincoat this time; you know how quickly the weather can change." She reaches out and pinches my shoulder softly before adding, "See if a little exploring won't bring that travel bug back to life."

Siobhan was right. Strolling down the sidewalk after a much-needed shower and change of clothes, I can't help but squint my eyes against the blistering sunlight. Everything appears more vivid, from the pastel shades on the shops lining the street to the green of the mountains in the distance. A wild wind sweeps through the town, tossing my hair this way and that. Summer is making its last stand on a random day in the fall, and I'm admittedly grateful for it.

The farmer's market is bustling, with lilting music weaving in and out of the many conversations taking place between merchants and patrons. The frenetic energy adds a bounce to my step. As I move into the fray, a fleeting thought dances through my brain.

I wish Callum were here with me.

I shake my head, dismissing it. How can I still wish for someone's company from twelve years ago? After all, there's no way it's this modern-day, prickly and solemn Callum that my heart is longing for. It's the version of him that I knew back then. The one who oozed charm and positivity. Who could turn a trip to the social security office into an adventure.

A booth featuring various hand-carved wooden magnets captures my attention. I pluck one from the display board, turning it over in my hand. Someone has carved the outline of Ireland into the face of it, then marked the spot where Cahersiveen lies along the southwestern tip with a tiny heart. It reminds me of one of those mall directories with a *YOU ARE HERE* sticker plastered over the entrance.

"How much for this?" I ask the gentleman behind the table. He glances over at me from where he's bargaining with an elderly woman over the price for one of his more elaborate creations, a custom cutting board from the looks of it.

He squints his eyes at the piece in my hand before glancing up at me. "Five euro."

I remember how Callum taught me to play this game, especially as a tourist. Removing two coins from my pocket, I hold them out for him to see. "I've got four."

His gaze flickers between my palm and my face before he finally glances back at the woman still waiting for him to match her price and decides I'm the easiest negotiation he'll get today. "Fine, yeah. It's yours."

"Thank you!" I toss the coins into a waiting jar and take my leave, listening as he tries to explain to the woman why she can't have that cutting board for a fiver.

I shove the magnet into my purse, and I imagine it joining the collection in a box on the top shelf of my parent's spare bedroom closet. The collection that started when Callum drove me to Newbridge that day. After finishing up at the PPS office, I met him back at the street corner where he'd dropped me off. He was leaning against the hood of his car, his golden hair being tousled by the breeze. When I approached, he held his hand out with a satisfied grin on his face, dropping a green, shamrock-shaped magnet into my outstretched palm.

"To commemorate the day you became an Irish citizen," he said. *"If only in the eyes of our tax law."*

The memory brings a smile to my face even as my heart squeezes tightly in my chest.

I pass by food stations and stands featuring handmade jewelry. One woman tries to draw me in with the promise of a tarot reading. I shrug her off with a polite, "No, thank you," wishing I could explain that when the worst thing has already happened, the future no longer carries any wonder. It is just something that will happen, with or without you, and the only thing you can do is survive it. Until you don't.

The last stall I come to is filled with woven baskets overflowing with children's toys. There are trains carved from wood and painted in every primary color. A display of blocks is stacked on the table in the shape of a pyramid with hand-painted letters reading *MAEVE'S TOY CHEST* on the front of them. My gaze is drawn to a hanging mobile, meant to dangle over a crib and mesmerize the infant inside. Each little woodland creature is strung up with silky ribbon in various shades of pink.

"Those are made out of wool, if you can believe it." A woman —Maeve, I presume—approaches me from her seat in the back of the tent. "Handcrafted each one of them myself. Took ages."

I marvel at a tiny bird perching on the ring of the mobile, amazed at the amount of detail in its markings. "That's incredible."

"My dad taught me as a child, and I've been doing it ever since. He doesn't like to admit it, but I'm much better at it than he was."

The corners of my mouth twitch at her comment. "I'm sure he's proud of you."

"Oh yeah, he loves that I carried on the tradition."

I can see her watching me out of the corner of my eye, but I remain focused on the miniature elephant resting in my palm. Suddenly a lump forming in my throat makes it difficult to breathe.

"Do you have any little ones?" she asks, cocking her head to the side. Her dangling silver earrings brush the hollow of her neck. "I can give you a discount since it's the last market of the season."

My mouth opens and then falls to a close without any words traveling out. I draw in a deep breath, forcing it past that lump, and hold it for what feels like an eternity. When I finally release it, I clear my throat once before glancing over at the woman.

"I do, yeah. But she's eleven now. Too old for a toy like this." I let it fall from my palm, instantly missing the feel of the scratchy wool against my skin.

"Oh wow, you don't look old enough to have an eleven-year-old. Good on ya!" She pinches her stomach in the place where we all carry a bit of extra skin and fat, especially after stretching to accommodate a growing infant. "I hope to be looking as good as you when mine's eleven. Just had her last June—my first—and I don't have to tell you this I'm sure, but it's a life changer."

"That it is," I whisper. I try to imagine what I'd tell her if my daughter really was still here. If she'd made it to eleven, and I'd lived through all the terrible twos and first days of school and the encroaching teen hormones making their way onto our horizon. Part of me nearly believes the story I'm weaving in my head. That I'll go back to the inn, and my daughter will be kneeling next to her grandmother in the garden, proud of the turnip she's just uprooted.

I realize the words I want to tell her as a mother of a baby who died are no different than the ones I'd tell her if my daughter had lived. The strong breeze shifts, hitting my eyes as I turn to face her. I'm hoping it's enough of an excuse for her not to question the stray tear that leaks onto my cheek before I swipe it away. I pull a few bills out of my wallet, the equivalent of what the mobile would cost, and hand them to her, earning a confused expression.

"Use it to get your daughter something she needs. Or something you've been wanting for her. And give her a big squeeze when you get home and hold her extra before she goes to bed tonight. And try to remember how lucky you are to have her, even when you're tired beyond belief. Sometimes I still feel the weight of mine on my chest, and I miss it more than I can bear."

The last part is barely above a whisper, and I don't know what she interprets from the syrupy thickness of my somber voice, but she nods with round, teary eyes before saying, "I will. Thank you."

"You're welcome," I reply, and I walk away from the mobile and all the other toys I'll never get to need. I've barely made it ten feet when I stumble to a stop as my eyes meet with a pair of questioning green ones.

Callum stands in line for an ice cream stand, with Niamh too focused on the treat coming her way to notice me. But he does. I don't know how long he's been watching, but the ravine between his brows tells me he's seen too much.

For a half second I debate going over to him and explaining myself. Trying to patch up the confusion with another tall tale. Adding another layer of things I have to unravel when I finally come clean.

Then Niamh tugs at his shirt to let him know it's their turn to order, and the wind shifts, blowing my hair across my field of vision, and I remember the look on his face when I walked away from his table last night.

I keep walking, and he makes no effort to stop me.

Chapter Twelve

Callum

Go to her.

Over and over, despite every excuse I threw internally this afternoon as I watched Leo, my brain rebutted with the same command. *Go to her. Comfort her.* It didn't matter that I had no clue what was wrong, no clue why she was touching that infant mobile with a sort of reverence that wedged itself in the small space between my heart and my rib cage. Even if I couldn't offer more than fumbling words and a gentle touch, I had to try.

But I didn't. Instead I hesitated, and Niamh distracted me and before I knew it, Leo was walking away. I should've been happy about it; after all, the more space the better when it comes to her. But as she disappeared from the market in the early afternoon sunshine, it felt like a part of me trailed after her.

Niamh lands a solid kick against my spine at the same time a whistling gust of wind threatens to bust my eardrums, and the combination jolts me from my ruminating. I glance at the clock on my bedside table. Glowing red numbers let me know that it's just past eleven. Another gust buffets the side of the house, causing the old cottage to groan under the assault. After one of the loveliest days of weather we've had in weeks, it almost feels like the universe is trying to punish us for enjoying it too much.

I'd love to roll onto my back, but Niamh has now curled up in a ball against me, pinning me in place. No matter how old she gets, the minute there's a bit of bad weather, she comes padding down the hall, pushes open my door, and whispers, "Daddy, I'm scared."

No matter how old *I* get, those words melt me in place. Which is why I'm currently occupying ten percent of the overall surface of my own mattress.

As if the other woman in my life is getting a bat signal from her granddaughter to interrupt my sleep schedule, my phone lights up with a call from Mam. I groan, reaching for my cell while trying not to jostle Niamh. When I pick up, Mam huffs, "There you are."

"Hello to you, too."

"Took you long enough!"

"It's the middle of the night," I growl. Niamh stirs beside me, and I resign myself to the fact that I'm going to have to leave my warm bed and take this conversation into the hall. I slide ever so carefully out from beneath the covers, tucking Niamh in to keep her cozy in my absence. She looks like a cat curled up with how tightly wound she is, and my lips stretch into a smile as I tiptoe out of my bedroom. Into the receiver I whisper, "What is it, Mam?"

An exasperated sigh drifts over the line at the same time I hear something metallic clattering in the background. "Ah shit," she grumbles. The static of a phone being shuffled around joins the whistling wind in grating against my ears before she finally pulls herself together and breathes into the microphone once more. "The power is out, and I'm trying to get a fire going before the guests start freezing in their rooms and come looking for warmth."

I can practically see her clambering around the living room, knocking over fire pokers and giving herself splinters as she tries to stock the hearth. I pinch the bridge of my nose and press my back into the wall, letting it support me for a moment. "What can I do?"

"Have you got firewood?"

The image of my empty rack in the garage, still waiting to be refilled after the last cold snap, fills my mind. It's the one task I always forget about, and Mam knows it. "No, I haven't gotten around to it yet."

"Might want to head this way before it gets too bad and your power goes, too."

With a groan of frustration, I walk to the kitchen and peer out the window, quickly noting the power line dancing in the wind. "Right, yeah. Let me get Niamh ready and then we'll be heading that way."

"See you soon." *Click.*

I pivot on my heel and march back down the hall, accepting that I've gotten just about all the sleep I'll be getting tonight, which is exactly zero. Upon returning to my bedroom, I flip on the bedside lamp and gently shake Niamh's delicate shoulder. I've barely managed to rouse her and slip her shoes onto her feet when the room goes dark.

Shrugging out of my coat, I hang it up on the rack by the door before doing the same with Niamh's comparably tiny one. The matching gray peacoats look comical next to one another. I glance down at my little girl, and she gazes back at me with sleep-laden eyes. "Come on, love." I scoop her up.

Her head falls against my chest, and soon she's soundly asleep once more. I make my way down the hall, the sound of the wind muffled by the many rooms of the large inn. A handful of guests have already congregated in the living room, where they sit scattered about on different furniture, all soaking up the warmth that the fire offers. A quick scan of their faces comes up empty. I've just resigned myself to embark on a search for my mother when she steps into the room with two bleary-eyed gentlemen behind her, their arms linked together under the plaid blanket they've wrapped around themselves to keep warm.

"Have a seat over here, on the chaise. You'll be toasty in no time," Mam offers, gesturing to the lounge chair adjacent to the hearth. The couple nods and follows her directions, snuggling closely together on the old floral chaise.

"Everyone all right?" I whisper, trying not to wake Niamh again. I smooth a hand over her hair, which has nearly completely fallen out of the plaits from this morning, but she insists on keeping them in so she can match Leo.

"Everyone's grand; just a bit of frostbite here and there. Who needs toes anyway?" She chuckles at her own exaggeration.

"I'm sure everyone's toes are intact, Mam." The winters here are mild enough, although I wouldn't be choosing to hang out in five-degree weather without heat if given the choice. Clearly, since I'm here.

Something registers in my mother's thoughts, rippling across her expression. She crosses her arms and surveys the room. "Now, I haven't seen Leona."

Electricity sparks down my spine at the mention of her name, reaching all the way to my fingertips, which clench onto Niamh a little tighter. I do my best to maintain a neutral expression, but I see the moment Mam notices my reaction because her lips stretch into a Cheshire grin.

"Why don't you go up and check on her?" She drifts over to the one open sofa, collapsing onto it as though all energy has suddenly left her. "I'd do it, but I'm just absolutely knackered from all this running around." Her arms stretch out, and she makes grab-hands at me. "Give Niamh to me; us two gals will warm up by the fire."

"Convenient," I grumble. I shift my weight from one foot to another, weighing my options. I don't know how to face Leo after ignoring her in the market, but that's not exactly something I can share with my mother. "I'm sure if she were cold, she'd come down here."

"I wouldn't have known there was a fire going if Siobhan hadn't come to tell us," one of the gentlemen—an American, according to his accent—offers from his spot on the chaise. "We were resigned to cuddle naked for warmth."

His partner gives a cheeky grin that's a bit too suggestive for me to feel comfortable witnessing. Or perhaps it's the mental image of Leo and I doing the very same that causes me to flush.

Either way, leaving the room and the plethora of watchful gazes behind before my skin crawls right off my body suddenly seems like the least awful option.

"Fine, I'll go get her." I settle Niamh beside her granny and head for the hall, my steps echoing back to me. I don't let myself think about what I'm doing—*can't*, really. If I do, I'll never make it past the second-floor landing.

When I've finally reached the top of the stairs, the backs of my knuckles bounce softly off Leo's door, barely penetrating my eardrums, let alone the solid wood. I shake the tension out of my shoulders and try again, this time firmly rapping my fist in a staccato of knocks.

There's no sound on the other side of the door. No bed

creaking or footsteps tiptoeing my way. I close my eyes tightly and let out a resigned sigh before clearing my throat. I knock once more and call out, "Leo?"

Nothing. Surely she's not grown to be this hard of a sleeper. Is she ignoring me on purpose?

Right, she can freeze then. No need for me to stand on this landing shivering while she makes a point with her grudge by giving me the silent treatment. I've made up my mind to leave her when suddenly my hand moves of its own volition, reaching for the doorknob and turning it. Before I can come to my senses, I'm over the threshold, standing in the chilled moonlight of her room and staring at a sleeping Leo for the first time in a dozen years.

I can't explain the feeling that takes over my entire body in that moment. I stagger forward, drawn to her inexplicably, even as my brain roars that this is a mistake. *Leave her be*, it urges, the exact opposite message from this afternoon. *Let her suffer.*

But she *is* suffering, and that's why I can't stay away.

She's dreaming, I can tell that much. With a moan of pain the likes of which I've never heard, she tosses and turns in her sleep. Her legs thrash beneath the sheets, and despite the cold, she's broken out in a thin sheen of sweat that sets her forehead to shimmering in the moonlight drifting through her window. The wind rattles it in the frame, but the noise isn't reaching her wherever she's gone. Neither is my voice, calling to her.

"Leo? Leo, love, it's Callum."

My forward motion only stops because I'm now at the edge of her bed, drawn to her as I always have been. Except she used to be a sun I wanted to orbit, and now she's a whisper I have to lean close to understand.

I reach for her shoulder, suddenly desperate to break her free from whatever dream has her face wrenched in such suffering. I hesitate when a slow tear spills over the apple of her cheek and down, down, down into the hollow of her throat. My mouth goes dry all of a sudden, and I forget my own name. There is only Leo and Leo's pain and my desire to protect her from it despite everything.

I shake off the foreign feelings, coming back to myself with a snap. I'm being a creep, staring at her like this while she sleeps. I need to wake her, get her downstairs to warmth, and then go stand out in the wind and rain for a bit so I can calm the fuck down.

"Leona," I say, much as it pains me, and give her shoulder a gentle shake. With a jolt, she comes alive, fear flashing in the blue abyss of her eyes before recognition and confusion swirl together in her expression.

"Callum?" She tugs the covers up over her chest, groggy yet aware enough to be bashful. "What are you doing here?"

In fairness, my gaze had traveled down to the outline of her breasts in her thin pajama shirt. She definitely is freezing, if the impression of her hardened nipples against the soft fabric was any indication. I force my gaze back to her face, even more mesmerized by that sight than I was by her breasts. Jesus, I need to pull myself together.

"Power's out," I finally manage to choke out. It sounds like I'm going through a second round of puberty. "Mam's got a fire going downstairs, and all the other guests are warming up there."

Her eyebrows furrow, unsatisfied. The sound of the wind is the only answer to my words, and finally I realize she's not asking why I'm here, in this house. She's asking why I'm here, in her room, *touching* her. Christ.

"Erm, I knocked." I jab a thumb over my shoulder in the direction of the door while taking a step away from the bed. "Called your name a few times. Started to think the frostbite had gotten ya."

She considers this for a moment before sitting up and shifting her legs to dangle over the edge. "It's not *that* cold," she says, but she grabs a sweater from the floor and shrugs into it.

Probably for the best, or I'd likely start drooling, much to our mutual embarrassment. I turn and head for the door, leading the way to warmth. And sanity. "Yeah, try telling that to my mam."

She falls into step behind me with an agitated groan, mumbling, "I've got a few things I'd like to say to her."

"You and me both," I reply, practically falling down the stairs in an attempt to put enough distance between us.

Chapter Thirteen

Leona

For a man who just barged into my room in the middle of the night without permission, Callum is certainly in a hurry to get away from me. As soon as we step into the living room, he mutters something about going to check all the windows and then disappears without further comment.

Scattered throughout the room are our various guests, some halfway to sleep and others fully there.

Not ours, I correct myself. *Siobhan's.* Getting too attached will only deepen the pain when this situation inevitably implodes. When I'm left running away once more with my tail between my legs and skin marred with the shrapnel of my poor decisions.

I brace my shoulders and draw in a deep breath, trying to let all those feelings flow out on the exhale.

The fire is roaring, its luxurious heat reaching me all the way at the threshold. The light of it dances off the spines of books lining the shelves along the wall. A young couple from London are currently drifting off in the love seat beneath the window with their child nestled between them. The memory of Siobhan shaking me awake in that same spot vies for my attention. I shake my head softly to dislodge it. She hasn't asked any questions about my sleeplessness, and I haven't offered answers. It's a silent deal we've struck between us.

I can't help but wonder if she'd still want to share a secret with me if she knew all the others I carry. The ones that sent me running from that market today, leaving Callum in my dust.

"Come over here, Leona. We've got room," Siobhan shout-whispers, gesturing to the space at the other end of the couch closest to the fire. Niamh is curled up underneath a weathered afghan, her head resting in her grandmother's lap.

I make my way to them, doing my best to avoid the floor-boards that I've discovered are rather creaky, before settling into the lumpy cushions. The warmth of the fire, now just a few feet away, floods my body. For the first time since Callum woke me, I realize just how cold I was. Sometimes it takes things returning for you to understand just how much you missed them while they were gone.

"Sorry about all this," Siobhan offers. She smooths an absent-minded hand over Niamh's mess of curls, which are slowly unraveling from a set of braids. "Most of the country has under-ground power lines now, but they keep forgetting about us out here in the rural areas. Not usually a problem till we get one of these windstorms."

I wave a hand dismissively. "It's no problem. I'd take this over a tornado any day."

"Would you be getting those often?" she asks, eyes wide in horror.

I shake my head. "Not too frequently where I'm from. The Midwest gets the worst of it."

"Still, I'd say one is one too many."

"And you'd be absolutely right." I draw my feet up onto the sofa, tucking my knees into my oversize sweater and resting my chin on them. The honeymooning couple from Chicago are fast asleep on the chaise across from us. I check back in on the small family occupying the love seat and discover they, too, have drifted off. The only people still hanging on—two girls in their early twenties—are laid out on their stomachs on a makeshift cot in the corner of the room, scrolling through one of their phones and giggling softly.

Despite the less-than-ideal circumstances, it reminds me of sleepovers with my cousins as a child. My older brother and I would pile up on pallets our aunt had constructed on the floor, her two sons joining us for a movie night that would last into the wee hours of the morning. It was the best part of growing up so close together, having a built-in set of best friends. As we grew up and went off to college, then married—and divorced, in my case—everyone spread throughout the country and our bonds stretched thin at the seams. I make a mental note to text Brian in the morning and remind him he has a sister who loves him, even if she's shitty at showing it.

The door creaks open, revealing a slightly out-of-breath Callum sporting two damp shoulders and blond hair turned bronze with wetness. If his expression weren't so terse, I'd be tempted to ask why he felt the need to check the windows from the *outside*, but the hard set of his jaw keeps me quiet.

"Windows are all secured," he huffs. He removes his rain-splattered glasses and lifts a corner of his maroon Henley to wipe the lenses clean, flashing a strip of golden skin and hardened muscle along his waistline. A pair of low-slung sweatpants completes the just-rolled-out-of-bed look, and I can tell by the way they hug certain *attributes* of his body that he neglected to wear any boxers underneath.

I look away, the heat of the fire suddenly growing so intense that my cheeks catch flame.

Siobhan studies my face for a moment before the corner of her mouth twitches. She sits up abruptly, bracing Niamh's head with one hand as she shifts. "You know what, I've actually just remembered I need to check that all the cats are all right—"

"I thought those cats belonged to the neighbors," I ask, but my voice is breathier than I'd like and she continues speaking over me.

"Leona, could you hold Niamh for me?" She finishes, meeting my gaze expectantly.

Everything about me stills, including my heartbeat for a concerning moment. I gaze down at the little girl between us. Her lip quivers in her sleep. My pulse echoes the tremor.

I haven't held a child since Poppy. Since they laid her little body on my chest, light as a feather but heavy on my heart. If I concentrate hard enough, I can still feel it. The cool metal of her amulet turns to the warmth of her skin against mine. One pound and nine ounces of absolute perfection.

Something shifts in the air between us as Siobhan takes in my hesitation. The quirked edge of her mouth falls, and she turns to look at Callum, who's staring at me like his glasses aren't working quite right.

"Erm, I've got her, Mam." He steps forward hesitantly, like he's waiting for me to object. "But I'm sure the cats are—"

"Thank you, son!" She shifts out from underneath Niamh's head while supporting it with her arm. Callum slips into the vacated space and tugs the edge of the blanket up around Niamh's cheek once she's settled against him.

Before either of us can get a word in edgewise, Siobhan has skittered out of the room.

My gaze finds Callum's, and we shake our heads in unison. A nervous laugh escapes my lungs, and my attempt to swallow it sounds more like I'm choking.

After clearing my throat for the third time, I finally manage to speak. "What do you think she's actually doing?"

Callum considers the question for a moment before letting out a heavy sigh. "Probably listening with a cup pressed to the door."

The mental image elicits a sharp laugh, and I press my lips firmly together to trap the noise before it wakes Niamh and the other guests. If I didn't know any better, I'd swear the corners of Callum's lips pitch into the echo of a smile. One blink and it disappears.

Niamh stretches in her sleep, drawing our attention down-ward. Her tiny foot slips out from underneath the blanket, coming to rest against my hip. I stare at it, counting her toes once and then five more times, before looking away and drawing in a ragged breath.

"What were you dreaming about?"

"Hmm?" I jerk my head back to face Callum. He's watching me carefully, studying my reaction. I'm too tired, too raw with emotion to hide whatever he's seeing.

"Upstairs, you didn't hear me knocking because you were having a dream. A bad one, from the looks of it." He winds one of Niamh's curls around his finger before letting it fall back against her cherub cheek. "Do you remember what you were dreaming about?"

I shake my head too quickly, training my gaze on my knees still tucked inside my sweater. The image of a faceless doctor burns the backs of my eyes. He walks into the hospital room where I've just delivered my daughter, alive and healthy, and rips her from my arms. I swallow the hard lump rising in my throat as I picture him walking away while Poppy tries her best to cry for me, only no sound comes out of her lungs. When the door closes behind them, it never opens again.

"If you'd rather, we can talk about the market."

A quick study of my peripheral tells me Callum wants that as little as I do, if his subtle wince is any indication. I stare at

Niamh's toes. It's easier than facing her dad, though the margin is slim. "I'd rather not. And I can't remember my dream."

I don't know if he's trying to be more amicable because Niamh is between us, albeit asleep, or what, but he hums his understanding before replying, "I'm the same. Can never remember my dreams, even the good ones. And I'm sorry for not speaking to you."

"Hm?"

"At the market."

"I thought we weren't going to talk about it."

He holds his hands up. "That's all I wanted to say."

I was certain there'd be a whole line of questioning about the stall I was standing at and the tears on my face when he appeared, but maybe he didn't see any of that. Maybe that moment was mine and mine alone.

I turn to face him, laying my head on my knees. It's the first time I've really let myself drink him in unabashedly since returning, and for a moment I become completely unmoored. He is as familiar to me as my own reflection, and equally as haunting. There's a lifeline stretching between us, impossibly taut and fragile, and I'm desperate to make it last. A thought pops into my head, and I can't help myself. "You remember that time you fell asleep on the boat ride to Skellig Michael and shouted Marge Simpson's name out in your sleep?"

He balks at first, and then his shoulders begin to shake with barely suppressed laughter. It's the happiest I've seen him in my presence since I arrived, and it fills my chest with light.

"What I remember is that you didn't tell me I did it," he sucks in air, struggling not to burst into full-blown cackling, "and so I was incredibly confused when the captain kept making wet-dream jokes at me while talking like Homer the whole trip back."

I bite the inside of my cheek, but a snort escapes my nose. I clap a hand over my face to trap the noise, trembling with the effort.

He shakes his head at me, amusement sparkling in his eyes. "You were certainly something back then."

The shift in his tone hits me like a dart to the lung, letting all the air out. I realize I want him to still see me as that fun, enigmatic girl he once knew. Hell, *I* still want to see me like that. Even though it's impossible, I find myself wishing for it all the same.

"What about now?" I ask, my voice hushed.

"You're different." He narrows his eyes at me. "Meeker than before."

My skin prickles at the comment. "Who says I wasn't always like this?" I reply, jutting my chin out.

He scoffs, tilting his head as if to say, *Come on.* "You once convinced an entire pub to take shots with you to celebrate you passing a round of exams."

"Hardly an impressive feat in a country known for its drinking habits."

He spreads a hand across his heart in mock offense. "Haven't you heard how hurtful stereotypes can be?"

I roll my eyes at him, earning a grin that highlights the angle of his cheekbones sloping into the hard cut of his jaw. His gaze flickers over my face in a way that makes me both self-conscious and bold, though I'm not sure how.

"Am I really all that different?" I ask, trying to lean into the boldness.

The fog of amusement clears, leaving his true emotions bare. He's hurt, and the sharpness of it cuts me to the core.

"You're still you," he mutters. I don't know if it's the steady hum of howling wind or the crackling of the fire or the darkness settling close around us, but he looks straight at me and I realize that he's about to be completely honest, whether I'm ready for it or not. "You're still beautiful; that could never change. Still a hard worker and more endearing than you have a right to be, since my best friend has clearly betrayed my loyalty to take your side." He chuckles to himself, though the sound takes on a harsh edge. "But you've changed. You had to, because the person I knew wouldn't have done what you did. Wouldn't have dropped out of thin air without so much as a goodbye, and then shown up over a decade later like none of it happened."

I deserve it; I know that I do. But the words slice through me all the same.

"It *did* happen." I draw in a shaky breath. "And for what it's worth, I'm so very sorry."

He deflates like an untied balloon, and when he speaks, his voice comes out raw. "Why did you come back, Leo? After all this time."

I gnaw at my bottom lip, gaze skirting around the room. The girls in the corner have fallen asleep at last, leaving us cocooned in this moment together. Alone in the world with only each other. I realize this isn't the time or place for everything that has to be said, but I can't go one more second without giving him something. Anything.

And besides, if he doesn't hate me now, he will when he knows the truth. I'd selfishly like a few more moments like this before I have to suffer the consequences of my own actions.

"I wish I could believe that my reasons would make any sense to you, Callum." My vision fills with unshed tears, blurring the image of sleeping guests and crackling fire and my very first love. I blink twice, bringing his face into focus once more. "But Ireland"—and what I can't say, *him*—"is the place where I've felt most at home in my life. So when everything started falling apart, it was instinct."

"You mean the divorce?"

I snort harshly.

He meets my gaze with confusion, and I grimace.

"Not exactly. It wasn't any one thing, really. But when the divorce finalized, I moved home with my parents. It was meant to be temporary." I shake my head, mostly at myself. "Then I lost my job, and all of it at once just brought up a lot of things I'd managed to bury. In all that pain, the only thing I could think to do was buy a plane ticket to yo—"

I stop myself, glancing away so I don't have to see the shock register in his expression.

"A plane ticket to *Ireland*," I say, correcting my almost-mistake. "The last place that felt truly right."

After a long pause, he finally speaks in a voice softer than I thought him capable of. "If it didn't feel right with the guy, why'd you marry him?"

There's the million-dollar question. And before I can answer it, Niamh stirs between us, wiping one of her eyes as she peers up at her dad with a pitiful pout.

"Daddy, can I have some water?"

He holds my gaze for so long without replying to her that she opens her mouth to ask again. The words are poised to fall from her lips when he breaks our stare at last. "Sure, love. One second." He rises from the couch, and Niamh stretches into the empty space he leaves behind, yawning for what feels like millennia.

Callum crosses the room and settles his hand on the doorknob, but just as he steps into the dark hallway to make his way to the kitchen, he turns to glance over his shoulder and whispers, "We're not finished here."

It's everything I hope to be true, and yet, in this context, everything I dread. I nod wordlessly, a gesture that he returns, and then glance away so I don't have to watch him leave.

"Cats are all good!"

Siobhan's voice startles me with its sudden appearance. She lets the door fall shut behind her, traipsing over to the couch.

"Granny, the cats belong to the neighbors," Niamh groans.

Siobhan glances up at me with the most theatrical expression of shock I've ever seen before planting her hands on her hips and smirking down at her granddaughter. "Now that you mention it, you're absolutely right, my girl. I must be losing it in my old age." Niamh sits up to make space for her, and she settles on the couch, pulling Niamh to her side. She tucks a strand of silver hair behind her ear and smiles. "Now, what did I miss?"

Chapter Fourteen

Callum

Eoin, who has managed to forgive me for nearly flattening one of his sheep last week, calls just after dawn to let me know the power's turned back on. I lean forward and rest my elbows on my knees, prompting my back to scream at me for falling asleep propped up in a wooden dining chair. My ass has gone numb and I'm fairly certain my hair smells like the old, decrepit wall of books I used as a headrest. I need a shower, a warm liter of tea, and a lot more distance between myself and Leo than this room currently offers.

Standing brings with it another round of bodily anguish. Bracing one hand against the back of the sofa, I reach down with the other and brush a matted curl away from Niamh's forehead. She stirs, glancing up at me groggily. Her eyes are framed with a fan of damp black lashes. Just the sight of them squeezes my heart.

"I'm tired, Daddy," she whimpers. A fat tear pools on the precipice of her eyelid. Niamh is many things, but a morning person after being kept up on and off all night is not one of them. Even as an infant, she coveted her sleep.

"I know, love. Let's go home."

I come around the sofa as she sits up, removing her feet from where she's propped them on Leo's lap. Unwilling to glance in the woman's direction lest the tap of intrusive thoughts come back on, I simply toss the blanket Niamh unwittingly disturbed back into Leo's general vicinity. Even my mother, who is usually the earliest of birds, remains sound asleep.

Probably exhausted from all that meddling she did last night. I huff a quick laugh at my own joke, even as I lean forward to place a kiss against the crown of Mam's head before heading for the exit with Niamh on my hip.

"Racing home so soon, son?"

Shit. I glance over my shoulder at Mam, who is getting to her feet with a grunt and a prayer. She waddles over to Niamh and me, working out the same kinks in her back that I had. For a moment I catch a glimpse of myself thirty-five years in the future, and I shudder.

"Yeah, Eoin's after calling. Power's back on at the cottage, so I thought we'd hurry on so there's more room on the couch without this one." I give Niamh's side a squeeze for emphasis, which she swats away with a scowl on her face.

Mam glances over her shoulder, and I can just see the corner of her mouth twitch when she looks at Leo. I fight the urge to follow her line of sight, knowing that seeing her will hurt more than help. The need to hold her last night had been visceral, and I can't be letting feelings like that simmer. They'll boil over eventually, and we'll all get burned.

When Mam's gaze returns to me, her lips have formed a full-blown grin. Not done meddling quite yet then.

"The two of you's have a good conversation last night while I was out herding cats?"

I roll my eyes at her. "You and I both know those cats were fat and warm in the neighbor's house." A quick glance around her assures me Leo is still fast asleep before I add, "What's your game, old lady?"

Mam chuckles and tosses her silver hair over her shoulder. "No game, son. I just think, underneath all that anger, you care for her still. Would it be the worst thing in the world if that were to blossom into something more?"

I clamp a firm hand over Niamh's ear a little too late, though from the soft snores falling out of her parted lips, I think we're in the clear. "Things between Leo and I are over. They've been over. Don't go dredging up things better left buried. Soon she'll leave again. I don't want to go through that a second time, and I certainly don't want Niamh going through it. Surely you can understand that." With a last stern look tossed in my mother's direction, I begin stalking toward the door again, ready to return to my house where the only two residents are at least sane.

She follows me into the hall, but pauses at the threshold while I continue walking away. I've managed to get my coat on and have Niamh's in my fist when Mam's soft voice calls after me with a haunting, "Just think about it."

I spend the entire drive home trying to do anything *but* think about it.

It doesn't take long after we cross over the threshold for Niamh to groggily make her way into the living room and curl up on the couch, drifting back to dreamworld. I settle in beside her and turn on a guilty pleasure home improvement show, trying to lose myself in the predictability of it. The steam from my tea envelops my senses in its malty aroma, bringing me back to life with every sip. But with that comes the sudden and sharp aware-ness of my conversation with Leo last night, and then I'm doing exactly what my mother told me to do.

I'm thinking about it.

Thinking about her face drenched in anguish as she slept.

About the flash of recognition, of *relief*, when she saw me before confusion took over. I'm envisioning her breasts beneath her thin tank and the curve of her neck hollowed out by the firelight and her eyes twinkling with laughter as we fell back into old roles we once knew so well. And more than anything, I'm thinking about the word she never finished saying. It's that singular word, more so than the coffee, that's got me jittery.

You. She was going to say *you.* As in *me.* As in she bought a flight here in the midst of all her tragedy because the only thing that she was sure of in that moment was her need for me.

After all this time. After a marriage and a dozen years and even more that I probably can't imagine, I'm still that person for her in a moment of crisis. Her home. Her soft place to land.

What does it say about me that the very thought fucking *thrills* me?

I jump to my feet, checking to make sure I've not woken Niamh, before striding down the hall to my home office. The computer whirs to life reluctantly, as if angry that I've disturbed it on a Sunday. While it drags its feet on the loading screen, I yank open the doors of the wardrobe in the corner, scanning the top shelf until my gaze falls on the target of my search.

The nondescript box is buried under layers of shoeboxes and file folders from over the years. I tactfully remove it without disturbing the other precarious items on the shelf, bring it with me over to my desk, and settle it on my lap as I sit.

It's a plain, unmarked box that should definitely be labeled, *Why the fuck do you still have me?* But it isn't, and I'm too exhausted to ponder that question anyway. I remove the lid as my desperation grows hot at the base of my neck, scanning the contents for the object of my desire.

I comb through various magnets and postcards and ticket stubs, not letting my gaze settle on them for too long lest the emotion brewing in my stomach become full-fledged nostalgic heartbreak. I find what I'm looking for beneath a dried sprig of foxglove, drawing the USB drive out carefully so as not to disturb the brittle stem.

My heart is now firmly lodged in my throat. I watch the files painstakingly load onto my desktop. I drum my fingers against the wooden surface of the desk, but the sound can't seem to penetrate the roaring in my ears. Slowly the images become tiny little thumbnails of a past I tried to forget. Tried to bury so deeply that I'd never again find myself sitting here, tears burning the backs of my eyes and breath coming in short gasps as what I thought would be the rest of my life is once more laid out before me; a highlight reel of the singular summer it turned out to be instead.

The images make up a road map of our time together. There's Leo with a shamrock magnet held up proudly beside a younger, softer version of her face. A hazy, ethereal image of her kayaking through a cavern at the edge of the sea fills the screen. I click to a photo of Leo leaned backward over a too-steep castle wall, kissing the Blarney stone while some old man who works there holds on to her sides. I snort at the memory, how I complained every time she dragged me to more touristy shit, all the while loving every minute spent watching her eyes light up at each iconic ruin or natural landmark or filming location for *PS I Love You*.

I click past another image, this time of her tiptoeing across the hexagonal rocks at Giant's Causeway, to find the final photo, the one I stared at more nights than I care to admit after it all came to an end. She's standing at the edge of the Cliffs of Moher, and her long hair whips around her face in a brown flurry. Even in the midst of all that movement, there is a stillness in her striking blue eyes as they gaze at me on the other side of the camera. A smile spreads across her face like a meteor shower, miraculous and astonishing, forcing onlookers to stop and bear witness.

A true Leo smile. The kind I worked so hard to draw out of

her every chance I got that summer. The likes of which I haven't seen on her face since she walked out of my life all those years ago.

I know this woman like the back of my hand. It kills me that I do. But it's like learning where Christmas presents really come from or that your parents are fallible creatures, just as prone to mistakes as you are. Once you know it, there's no un-knowing it.

The image of her face last night fills my mind once more in all its haunted glory. I don't want to care, but I can't help it. I want to do exactly what I told Mam to do and leave it buried. But the need to unearth all those tattered pieces of her and hold them close fills me as fervently as the need to breathe. At the same time I want to push her to the other end of the earth so I can free myself from this torture at last.

With a heavy sigh, I lean back in my chair, drawing a hand through my greasy curls. I need a shower. Or a stiff drink. Possibly both, simultaneously.

I didn't want to believe after all these years that she could still affect me like this. I thought I was stronger, more mature. That my priorities were in order at last. But it's becoming apparent that there will be no end to this until I can finally understand why she did what she did all those years ago. I know Padraig is convinced she was a dumb twenty-year-old who didn't know any better, but he's wrong. I wasn't nothing to her. I wasn't some out-of-sight, out-of-mind summer fling.

You don't buy a plane ticket in the midst of your life falling apart for a summer fling.

I close out of the program, but it's no use. The image of her is burned on my brain. I down the rest of my now-cold tea and force myself to stand, weary as my legs feel beneath me. The box goes back where it belongs, fitting into the jumbled mess of the wardrobe about as well as this new version of Leo fits into the picture I had in my mind.

Sloppily and incredibly out of place.

I force it in regardless, grumbling to myself all the while. "You just have to figure out why she's here, and then you can let her go. Wipe the slate clean. Move on."

Yeah, right, says the voice in the back of my head. Bastard.

Chapter Fifteen

Leona

The sound of voices drifts up the stairwell and underneath the gap in my door, letting me know that the other guests are beginning to stir. I roll away from the fading floral wallpaper and the echoes of socialization, clamping a pillow down over my head to block it all out.

It's been nearly a week since the windstorm, and though I'm fairly certain our vow of avoidance has been made null, I have a new reason to skip breakfast.

Waking up on Sunday morning brought with it all the worst symptoms of a hangover, despite having none of the fun the night before. Sitting across from Callum in the darkness, I could sense the veil of resentment and pain growing thin between us. I could almost see him clearly for the first time since I came back. But then the sun came up and filled the room with light, leaving me feeling raw and exposed, like I'd ripped a bandage off before the wound was fully healed.

It doesn't help that every time Callum's seen me since, he's tried none-too-discreetly to get me alone and finish our conversation. Something that, in the light of day, I have no clue how to do.

My phone buzzes somewhere on the bed, vibrating the

mattress against my cheek. I fumble through the sheets blindly until I feel its cool metallic surface beneath my touch. When I see my mother's face filling the screen, I exhale a sigh of relief.

I accept the call and immediately place it on speakerphone, not bothering to unbury my head from beneath the pillow. "Hi, Mom."

"Hi, baby! You sound far away; is something blocking the speaker?"

I dig my way out of the cocoon, sitting up in bed and bringing the phone to my ear. "Better?"

"Much better! How *are* you?" Mom asks, her voice full of zest after their two-week vacation. I hear a deeper voice rumbling in the background, and then she adds, "Dad says hello and he misses you."

"Tell him I miss him, too," I reply with a smile. There's a muffled echoing of my sentiment and then the distinct squeak of their back door swinging open as I imagine she steps outside to enjoy the cool Tennessee fall morning. With my eyes closed, I can picture the ancient oaks along the property line with their leaves giving a last, vibrant stand before succumbing to the cold weather in a few weeks. It's early there, so the sun will still be resting below the treetops, casting an orange glow across the sky that blends with the foliage.

The fact that even an image as beautiful as that one doesn't fill me with homesickness is telling.

"We just got home last night, and he's already knee-deep in planning the next trip," she says, chuckling softly. "I thought retirement was supposed to be for resting."

"You and I both know you'd hate staying home all the time and only getting out for Bingo on Thursday nights."

"You're absolutely right." She takes a sip of something, her slurping echoing through the receiver and making me cringe. "But would a couple weeks at home kill the man?"

"He did spend an entire career sitting at a desk. Can you blame him?"

Dad retired early as one of the highest paid accountants at Stabler Electric, a multimillion-dollar automation and energy management company. Whatever that means. I gave up trying to understand the jobs of his coworkers after joining them for my fifth annual Christmas party as a teenager. They were mostly attended by old men with unruly white nose hair who talked nonstop of combining technologies to achieve real-time automation with the bright-eyed interns who soaked up every word out of their mentors' mouths. I'd hover at the edge of the room, waiting for the night to be over.

After I was old enough to drive, I skipped them altogether.

Once my brother and I were done with college and married off to our respective spouses—that is to say, officially off our parents' purse strings—my father made the decision to go ahead and retire. He and my mother had saved up more than a measly nest egg. They squirreled away an entire hard-earned coop, which only made moving home and crashing their party that much more devastating.

I settle against the wrought-iron headboard, stretching one arm out while the other clutches the phone to my ear. "I miss you, Mom." The words are a whispered admission, but she hears them loud and clear.

"I miss you, too, Leona. When are you coming home?"

My heart lurches at her words, mostly because I don't feel like the place that she's referring to *is* my home. I don't know if I really have one anymore, if I'm honest.

"I don't know, Mom. I've still got a couple things to take care of here first." My gaze drifts to the window and the slate-colored sky beyond it. A stillness fills my mind at the sight of it, despite all that I'm juggling internally.

"Are you doing all right on money?"

"Yeah, I'm working under the table for the owner of the inn where I'm staying." I giggle before adding, "Don't report me to the Irish authorities please or you'll get me deported."

"My lips are sealed," she says, and I imagine her drawing pinched fingers across her lips before tossing the secret over her shoulder. She's been doing it since I was a child, back when my biggest secrets were that the boy I liked in kindergarten had tried to hold my hand on the playground.

Inconsequential, but she kept it like an oath.

"The owner is actually Callum's mom, if you can believe it." The line goes dead for longer than it ever takes my mom to form a sentence. I grow nervous in the silence, adding, "Small world, huh?"

"Extremely," she murmurs.

This time I let the silence stretch out between us till it turns a shade of awkward that's not typical of our conversations.

"Leona, what exactly are you doing there? You haven't mentioned Callum in years, and all the sudden you're flying halfway around the world to see him." She pauses, letting the dust settle around her words. "I just don't understand what the goal is here."

"There's not a goal, really." I bring my finger to my mouth, nibbling at a stray cuticle. My sweet mother, after years spent managing a household for two busy kids and a workaholic husband, still breaks everything down into a goal and steps to execute. In her world, there is a plan and a set of milestones to hit for every task. If you're not checking off your to-do list, then why even waste the time? Traveling constantly in their retirement is just as much for her as it is for my dad. Plan a trip, check the trip off the list, rinse, and repeat. It gives her purpose in life.

Something she's terrified I don't have. And I'm beginning to understand her worry.

"Well, what did he say when he saw you? Surely he has a wife now, some kids." She adds the last part flippantly, but I hear the moment she regrets it. Her thoughts nearly audibly snap into place, clamping her mouth shut around the end of her sentence.

"He, um, hasn't really said much." I close my eyes, picturing his face the day I showed up on his doorstep, stone-cold and sharp. It morphs into the man that sat across from me in the firelight, open and yearning for answers, with a sleeping Niamh stretched out between us. "He has a daughter."

Mom hums sadly on the other end of the line. "How old?"

"She'll be five in January." I know because she reminds me all the time.

"Can I ask you something? Without it upsetting you?"

I feel the tension coiling in my neck, and I tuck a pillow behind me as if it can relieve this type of ache. "Sure, Mom."

"Is he the father?"

A sob lodges itself in my throat, cutting off my access to oxygen. My trembling hand finds its way to my cheek, and suddenly I realize it is wet with tears I never felt falling. *When did they begin?* When I heard my mother's voice? When I said Callum's name?

"Yes," I whisper, using what little air is left in my lungs. "I have to go, Momma."

"Oh, baby," she sighs. "I'm so sorry."

"I'll talk to you soon." I hang up before she can reply.

The emptiness of the room presses in on me as soon as I sever the connection, feeling like a sinus headache building in intensity, only it's my whole body being compressed. Half-blind with tears, I reach for the notebook and pen on the bedside table. Drops fall from my eyes onto the page, blooming into swirls of salt and ink as I pour my heart out to our girl.

My Darling Poppy,

I don't know what it is about talking to my mother that always makes me want to talk to you. Wouldn't it be incredible if I could just pick up the phone and call? Ask you how your day has been? I wonder what your voice would've sounded like.

When I first found out I was pregnant, those were the kinds of things I wondered about. Would your voice be high and lilted or low and thick like molasses? Would you talk a lot like your grandmother or not so much like your father? How would your handwriting look? How would you smell?

These are the things I will never get to know, and it's the not knowing that kills me.

Dreaming of you was such a short-lived joy. Three days is all I got. From the time those two lines appeared on the test to the moment I sat in the doctor's office with a stone-faced university physician telling me I needed to seek another opinion. She hadn't seen this kind of ultrasound outside of her textbooks, but something didn't look quite right and she wanted to be sure.

Two weeks later, a man in a white coat sat across from me and said blasphemous words like incompatible with life and miscarriage. He never said when the baby is born, he said if. He said words I'd never heard before, and didn't even offer me a tissue as I sobbed in my chair, clutching a stomach that hadn't yet grown to accommodate your presence. I was just shy of four months along, and I was already falling so deeply in love with someone that I might never get to meet.

How do you live with a tragedy like that? How do you function?

The truth is, I didn't. That numbness held me so tightly in its fist that there was no room for anyone else, not even Callum. It took me days to return a simple text from him, and I just flat out ignored the phone calls. I disappeared from social media. I'd just gotten back from seeing my parents for Thanksgiving, so there were no attempts made to visit me. I did just good enough on my finals to pass, and not a bit more.

After a few weeks spent walking through a haze, I returned to the doctor for another ultrasound. They were wrong. I could feel it. You were alive and you were going to be just fine. I'd call Callum up the next day and tell him the whole crazy story, and we'd cry and laugh together and then everything would be okay.

But they weren't wrong. That day when I walked into the blinding sunlight after an hour in the dim ultrasound room, I shattered into a million pieces. And I didn't call Callum. I called my mom.

I didn't speak. I just dry heaved into the phone, and she heard and understood what I was trying to say but couldn't. *I need you, Momma.* And so she came to me, her child, as all good mothers do. She told Dad that I needed help with some last-minute Christmas shopping, and then she made it to me in record time.

There are sacred secrets kept between a mother and a daughter. Like when I started my period on a brisk December morning in the eighth grade, and she quietly brought me one of her pads and then took me to the grocery store. We bought pads and tampons and a jumbo cupcake that we shared in the parking lot while she told me all about her first period. When we came home, my dad asked why I hadn't gone to school, and Momma just said, "She had the stomach bug, but she's feeling better now."

She kept this secret just as she kept all the others. Just as I kept yours.

When she asked me who the father was, I did what I felt I had to. I told her he knew, and he didn't want anything to do with us. What a lie, of course, my love. Your daddy would've come for you, just as my mother came for me, if only I'd let him. But my grief was an ugly, selfish thing. I felt like I had drawn the shortest possible straw, and I wanted to wallow in it. I didn't want to share you with him because he couldn't possibly know how I hurt. His pain couldn't possibly compare.

Misery might love company, but grief is a loner convinced that no one could understand.

And the truth is, my love, that now I have all these thoughts and explanations for how and why and what I felt back then, but at the time I couldn't fathom any of it. I was numb aside from the pain. I only ate because it fed you. I only slept because it's when you kicked the most. I'd fall asleep giggling, that manic laughter that comes as a prologue to tears. I missed you with a bone-deep ache, and you weren't even gone yet.

I begged Momma not to tell Dad, and so she didn't. I locked myself in my apartment. I stayed alive for you. Kept up with classes for the future I still wanted you to have, against all odds. I read a story about a girl with Trisomy 18 who lived to be forty years old and decided that you were going to be just like her. There was no other outcome that felt fathomable.

Grief, of course, is unfathomable. Even when you're in the trenches of it. Maybe especially then.

Everyone keeps asking me why I'm here, what I'm hoping will happen. I ask myself that, too. Am I selfish for wanting to tell Callum after all this time, when it will only bring him pain? It's my selfishness that kept you a secret. My selfishness that put me on that plane. It would certainly be on brand.

But I don't want to be a selfish mother. And I don't want your memory to die with me. Your life was painfully brief. I can't bear for your memory to be also.

I just want you to know that I'm sorry it took me so long to do the right thing. There are some secrets that don't need to be kept.

You will always be my daughter. But you're Callum's daughter, too.

I love you, honey. I'll be seeing you.
Momma

When my tears finally dry to a crust at the corners of my eyes, I slip out of bed and don a simple white linen button-down and a pair of loose-fitting jeans. They were snug on me when I packed them in my suitcase two weeks ago, but today they hang from my hips in a strange way. One glance at myself in the floor-length mirror in the corner of the room tells me what I should've already known: I'm not eating enough. I can't keep skipping breakfast.

When I hit the second-floor landing, I see that there are three rooms with their doors propped open. No doubt the same three rooms will be written in the notebook on the entryway table. A workload that will take me no time at all now that I've gotten into the swing of things.

A quick knock on the bathroom door tells me it's unoccupied, and so I rinse the evidence of my sadness away and quickly braid each side of my hair back from my blanched face.

I don't look *good*, per se, but I look a little less like death, which will have to do.

Siobhan doesn't let me get two steps into the kitchen before muttering, "My how the tables have turned."

I grab the last scone, runt of the litter if I've ever seen one, and a couple cold rashers of bacon, both the only meager bits left of the hours-old breakfast spread.

"What are you talking about?" I ask around a mouthful of bread and jam. She scrunches her nose up at me in disgust, so I cover my mouth after the fact, although it's too little too late.

Her silver curls sway when she shakes her head at me. "First he was avoiding you, and now you're the one avoiding him." She clucks her tongue in disappointment before adding, "You two are going to put me in an early grave."

"I'm not avoiding him…" I start to say, but I don't even sound convincing to myself.

"Sure, you're not."

The only way to win this debate is not to engage, so I decide to change the subject. "Where's Niamh?"

She glares at me pointedly, letting me know she's onto me, but she still takes the bait. "She's next door at the Sullivan's. One of their cats is after having kittens, and they said she'd be welcome to come see them."

"Did she ever decide what to name them?"

"Not yet!" a familiar voice calls, drawing our attention to the doorway. Niamh kicks out of her boots and drops her raincoat where she's standing, letting it splat on the floor as she skips over to us. "They were so cute, Leona! You've got to come see them."

Just as I open my mouth to answer, my stomach lets out a startling growl so loud I'm certain the whole town has heard it.

"Now, hon, you can't be living off a few old rashers and a prayer. I'm off to the shops with this one soon as I fix her hair, but in the meantime there's a pub just up the street that has nice food.

Get you a bite to eat and put some meat on those bones." Siobhan pokes my ribs, making Niamh giggle. "They have a sticky toffee pudding that's to die for."

"Oh, bring me some, please!" Niamh pleads. Siobhan hoists her onto the countertop with a grunt and begins unraveling Callum's attempt at double French braids. And I thought his singles were sloppy.

"I've got three rooms to clean upstairs," I say, trying to catch Siobhan's eye. She's already doing so much for me by letting me work in exchange for boarding and a bit of spending money. I don't want to take advantage by leaving the rooms till late.

"Nonsense," she scoffs, waving a hand at me. "We aren't full up tonight, and this one's spending the night while her dad goes off hunting with Podge. It'll be grand. Bring us back a toffee pudding to share and all will be forgiven."

"And then we can go see the kittens!" Niamh says.

I smile at her as warmly as I can, though my heart is still feeling a bit fragile. I'm about to turn around and leave when Niamh gives me the world's most earth-shattering grin as she adds, "Granny's gotta fix my plaits cause Daddy's no good at doubles. But he keeps practicing 'cause I told him I wanna look just like you!"

The tops of my ears grow hot, and my nose burns like I'm going to cry. All I can manage is a nod and a pinch of Niamh's arm. When I finally squeak out, "Just like me," it sounds like someone else's voice.

Niamh is blinded with pride, but Siobhan notices something is off. Before she can enter a new line of questioning, I pivot on my heel and head for the door and the much-needed walk in fresh air that awaits me.

The Bridge Street Bed-and-Breakfast is not far off the main strip. I've barely been walking five minutes before a black awning with gold lettering appears through the mist. I duck inside

McDonough's, and I'm welcomed by a dimly lit pub occupied by exactly one person: the bartender. He's my age, possibly a little younger. With close-cropped dark hair and bright blue eyes, he's more than pleasant to look at.

Not that it matters.

He glances up from the glass he's polishing and does a quick once-over of my body. "Take a seat wherever you'd like," he says warmly, gesturing only to the barstools directly in front of him rather than the many tables and booths spread throughout the restaurant.

I'm halfway tempted to choose the farthest corner booth anyway, simply to have the alone time, but then he'd have to cross the entire restaurant to serve me, which feels a bit rude. I select the leather-topped barstool directly across from him instead, climbing on as he settles a laminated menu on the glossy wooden counter in front of me.

"Can I get you anything to drink?" he asks, his voice surprisingly raspy considering his clean-cut look. He's wearing a black vest over a white button-down, and he's rolled the sleeves up to his elbows, exposing the pale skin of his forearms.

I glance back down at the menu, though I can still feel his eyes on me. "Just a Coke to start, please. And could I have a Caesar salad?"

He nods, retrieving a glass bottle of Coke from the mini fridge behind him and popping its top off before placing it in front of me. It's quickly joined by a small glass containing two ice cubes and a slice of lemon adorning the rim.

"Could I get some more ice?"

"Right, yeah, forgot you Americans love your ice." He uses the metal scoop to collect a few extra cubes and plops them into the glass.

I pour the soda while he types my order into the touch screen at the other end of the bar.

"So what brings you all the way to Cahersiveen by yourself?" he asks, retrieving the rag from his back pocket and twirling it absentmindedly in circles. The sinew of muscle on his exposed forearm flexes with the movement.

"Just trying to get away for a little while." It's the closest to blasé that I'm capable of sounding, and I hope it doesn't sound as flimsy to his ears as it does to mine.

He stops swinging the towel and leans forward, bracing his hands on the counter in front of me. "Without a tour guide?" he asks, and I know immediately that he's flirting with me.

It should feel good. It's been a long time since any man blatantly flirted with me. But it makes me think of Callum, and that makes me want to cry.

A bell dings, drawing his attention away from me. I'm certain I've dodged the bullet when he returns from the back with my salad and then resumes his stance.

I squirm in my seat, trying to get comfortable. "I'm pretty good at finding my way around."

"Well, that's too bad." He steps away and stretches his arms up over his head, locking his fingers together and letting them settle against the base of his neck. His blue gaze is startling and vivid, full of confidence, so I focus instead on the yellow stains in his armpits. "I happen to be great at showing the tourists around."

The armpit stains make him feel less perfect, and it releases some of the tension building in my spine. I snicker softly, taking a bite of my salad and chewing slowly. When I finally swallow, I reply, "Oh yeah? You give tours to all the single women that come through town?"

"Not all of them." He winks, letting his arms fall to his sides. "Just enough to be good at it."

"Right." The slight smile falls from my face. "Well, Godspeed on that side hustle."

He cocks his head curiously and bites at his lower lip as he considers me. I wonder how I must look to him. Then I decide I don't care to know.

"Could I get a couple pieces of sticky toffee pudding to go, please? And how much do I owe you?"

He adds the order in and tells me my total, taking the bills when I hold them out to him while managing to look genuinely disappointed.

When he hands over the packaged-up cakes a few minutes later, my salad remains half-eaten, but I can't bring myself to finish it.

"Thanks for"—I gesture awkwardly at the picked-over meal —"this."

"Anytime," he replies, a crooked smile returning to his face. "I'm Colin, by the way. You'll come see me if you decide you want that tour, yeah?"

All I can do is nod, tight and succinct, before backing all the way to the door and making my escape.

"That was fast," Siobhan says as I deposit her and Niamh's cakes onto the kitchen counter a few minutes later. The two of them are all bundled up, ready to head to the grocery store, and I find myself hoping they don't bother to invite me along.

"I'm nothing if not efficient."

She glances at the dainty gold watch on her wrist and then back at me. "You've barely been gone twenty minutes. You can't have eaten that quickly."

Niamh glances over at me from where she's sitting at the table, lacing up her shoes, and smiles, exposing that gap between her front teeth. The gesture takes up her whole face and more than a reasonable amount of my heart. "Did ya come back 'cause ya missed us?"

"Right, that's exactly why." I nod, giggling, before my gaze cuts to Siobhan. "That and the pesky bartender."

"Oh, Colin? Pay that charmer no mind." Siobhan shakes her

head at no one in particular. "He's just about as bad as a stray dog with the way he'll hump anything in heat."

"What's that mean?" Niamh asks, ever curious.

Siobhan balks for a moment before regaining her composure. "Erm, it means he wanted to take Miss Leona out on a date, but she said no." Something occurs to Siobhan, and her gaze reverts to me. "You said no, right?"

"Right."

"Oh good." She shudders with relief before shrugging out of her jacket.

I wave a hand at her. "No, please don't let me interrupt your plans. I'll be fine while you two go to the store."

"Nonsense. One doesn't simply abandon a friend who's just been—"

"Humped?" Niamh offers.

Siobhan bites her knuckle to hold back a laugh. I'm not so composed.

While I work to contain myself, Siobhan gathers a few spoons that clink metallically in her fist as she carries them to the table along with the two cakes. "No, love, not humped. *Harassed.*" Glancing over her shoulder, she gestures for me to join them. Niamh pops open the first container the moment it's placed in front of her. "Especially when said friend bears warm sticky toffee pudding."

"Yum!" Niamh groans, scooping a bite into her mouth.

"No one tells Callum," Siobhan warns, spoon aimed at each of our heads in turn. I'm unsure whether she's referring to the situation with Colin or that we're eating dessert before dinner, but either way, Niamh and I nod in agreement.

Then we dig in.

Chapter Sixteen

Callum

"So we've gone hunting," Padraig says.

"Yep."

He shifts next to me as I scan the rolling hills. "Hunting for?"

"Pheasant, some woodcock."

He starts to snicker, ever the sense of humor of a child, but manages to swallow it. "And we haven't brought guns?"

My gaze cuts to him. The wrinkles around his eyes deepen as he offers me the world's most sardonic smile. Our breaths come out in twin puffs of smoke, evaporating into the cold air between us. I roll my eyes at him and then look away. "What's your point?"

"My point," he says, full-on laughing now, "is that without the guns, this is really just two lads gone bird watching."

I frown at no one in particular. The man is not wrong.

Granda used to bring me out here on his hunting trips. I never much cared for the guns or killing things, but I enjoyed the time spent with him and his two hunting dogs. Even now, several years since his passing, it's here that I feel the closest to him. It's here that I can think the clearest.

"My gun permit expired just after Granda passed. I haven't gotten around to renewing." I shrug, and Padraig's laughter subsides. "Just needed some fresh air, I suppose."

"There's quite a lot of fresh air closer to home, and these clothes aren't required to enjoy it." He gestures to his head-to-toe army-green sweater and slacks. The look is completed by a flat cap, like a true Irish gentleman. A stark contrast to his usual tracksuits.

"In fairness, no one asked you to dress like that."

"*You're* dressed like that!"

I glance down at my ensemble, which closely resembles his. Minus the cap. "Yeah, but I can pull it off," I say, offering my best attempt at a cocky grin.

"Oh, fuck off, man." He punches my shoulder firmly.

A shot rings out somewhere in the distance, and we both follow the sound with our gazes. The tall grass ebbs and flows under the constant wind gusts, looking more like the ocean surface than a hillside. A babbling creek nearby adds to the cacophony of nature sounds filling my ears, but I don't mind the dull roar. Beats the nonsense circling my mind.

Padraig takes a seat on the slick surface of a boulder, retrieves a protein bar from his pack, and rips it open. I join him, immediately regretting it when the dampness starts to soak through my pants. Hazard of being out in nature in a country known for its rain, but still.

"What's going on, man? You've been out of sorts all week." Padraig takes a bite of the bar and starts to chew with his mouth open. My least favorite thing about him. I glance away.

Padraig has been nothing but a solid friend to me over the years. He had my back when Catherine ran off, and he treats Niamh as if she were his niece rather than a nuisance. But he's not the one I really wish I could talk to about this.

Granda always knew what to say, but more importantly, he

knew what to do. He embodied everything a man should be, everything I want to be, even until the very end. That ever-present tide of grief rises to the surface, and I swallow thickly over the lump that forms in my throat. Padraig catches the bobbing of my Adam's apple but doesn't comment.

He may not be as wise as my grandfather, but he will listen. He will try to help. And at this point I'll go crazy if these thoughts don't stop pinballing around in my head.

I open the levers and let the balls drop out. "I talked to Leo last weekend, during the storm."

"Oh yeah?" Padraig replies a little too enthusiastically. He clears his throat before continuing. "How'd that go?"

I press my lips firmly together and shake my head. "For a moment it felt like nothing had changed. Like the past twelve years hadn't happened at all, or happened differently at least. The way they were supposed to." My hands begin to ache with how harshly I'm wringing them. "But there's something guarded about her, in a way that she wasn't before. And I just know that's what's going to be the death of me if I let her get too close again."

His eyebrows nearly hit his receding hairline. "So what I'm hearing is, you want her to get close again?"

"What? No!" I shake my head, glaring at the horizon. How dare it exist? How dare it be so beautiful when all of this is so damn ugly and complicated? "I want answers, and that requires getting close. But I don't want more than that, if that's what you're asking."

"Yeah, sure. And I'm going to shoot that pheasant with my imaginary gun." He aims at the bird in the grass twenty feet from us, which I'm amazed he's spotted considering its brown feathers blend into the landscape, and fires a make-believe shot. The sound he makes with his mouth startles the bird, and it flies off. "See? We're both good at lying."

"I'm not lying," I say, growling in frustration. "I'm being serious, Podge."

"Right. Let's pretend for a moment that you do get the answers you want. What then?" He shifts to face me full on, crumpling the wrapper in his fist. "What are you hoping to gain? Do you plan to forgive her? To forgive yourself? And then what, you send her packing?"

I bite down too hard on the inside of my cheek while considering the question and wince at the throb of pain. I tell myself I'll respond to him once it subsides, but the truth is, I'm just biding my time, waiting for the answer I don't have to materialize in my brain.

What exactly am I expecting to do with the answers once I have them?

What I desperately want, I realize, is to be free. Free of the pain I didn't even realize I still carried. Free of the anger. Free of the rejection. I don't want to want Leo anymore. Because I do, underneath it all. It's there in the aching of my hands to reach out and touch her. There in the longing to draw her close and comfort her, despite the way she has wrecked me in the past.

That's the thing about Leo. When she's yours, she enhances everything. The world is brighter, tourist traps are unprecedented adventures, every roadside stop is a magnificent view.

But when she's not, the world is ruined. The rose-colored glasses fall away. I want to see in color again, and I don't want to need her to do it.

"I want to finally understand so I can close that chapter." I shake my head, and my cheeks heat at the way my voice cracks. Hopefully Padraig brushes it off as a side effect of the weather. "And then I want to let her go."

He nods but doesn't comment. The bird watching resumes.

"Where's the prettiest girl in the entire world?" I call, my voice echoing down the hallway of the inn. I'm standing in the foyer, trying not to track leftover mud from my shoes across Mam's shiny floors. I cock my head to the side and allow myself to actually notice how clean everything is for once. There's no dust gathered on the old photographs, no scuffs along the walls. The inn has never looked this spotless before.

Guess the new housekeeper is panning out to be a real help after all.

A twinge of guilt passes through me. Once things with Leo are done and dusted, she'll go back to America and Mam will be missing the help. I add finding a permanent housekeeper to my mental list of to-dos so my mother doesn't disown me for running off her employee.

"Out here, Daddy!" Niamh shouts, drawing me back to the moment.

I follow the sound of her voice all the way through the kitchen, pausing briefly to greet Mam where she's loading clothes into the washer, and out into the garden. The early evening air has settled in cool and dry since the rain has subsided, and Niamh's taking advantage of the briefly clear sky to run around in the grass, chasing after a rather bedraggled-looking mama cat.

"Daddy!" she screams when she sees me. She abandons the cat, who I swear sighs in relief, and bounds over to me. With a running leap, she flies into my arms, and I squeeze her tightly as I spin around in circles. Her shrieks of joy pierce my eardrums in the best possible way.

"I missed you," I say, leaning back to gaze at her face. "Did you get bigger? What have I told you about getting bigger overnight?"

"I didn't get any bigger," she says, giggling. "I did have sticky toffee pudding though."

"That was supposed to be our secret!" Mam scolds, propping the doorframe up with her hip as she watches the two of us with a scowl.

"Oops!" Niamh says, her lips popping on the *p*. Her pale skin has taken on a tinge of red from exertion, making her look more like a baby doll than a real-life girl. I wonder, not for the first time, how someone so precious came from me.

"Oh, so you and Granny are keeping secrets from me now?" I pinch her side, earning another fit of giggles. "What else did you get up to while I was away?"

"We played puzzles, and Granny let me try on dresses from her closet that smelled like dirt—"

"Come on, now!" Mam interrupts. She tries to look indignant, but the amusement on her face is apparent.

"—oh, and Leona got humped by Colin at the pub!"

Both Mam and I audibly choke. Even the cat, who has slinked over to the stone wall while Niamh is distracted, pauses to make sure she's heard correctly.

I recover first. I set Niamh on the ground and crouch to her level. "She did *what* with Colin?"

Niamh glances at Mam for reassurance. "Granny says it means they're going on a date!" Her lips form a confused pout.

The sense of betrayal is a shock to say the least. There's no reason for it. Leo's not mine, I know that. She hasn't been for a very long time. But my heart seems to have forgotten that bit of information, given the way it's throbbing in my chest.

"Now, Callum, that's not what I said," Mam says. "It was a joke I made that she's taken out of context—"

"It's fine," I bite out, cutting my mother off. The edges of my vision are beginning to blur, whether from tears or anger, I can't be certain. All I know is I have to get out of here before everyone present reads too much into whatever it is I'm feeling. Including myself.

Mam frowns, fisting the towel in her hand at her hip. "Niamh, why don't you go get cleaned up?"

Niamh raises an eyebrow at me. After my responding nod, she takes off for the door.

Once she's safely out of earshot, Mam launches the inquisition. "You know, for someone who swears he's not interested, you seem awfully"—she scans my face, chuffs—"*interested.*"

I study my hands. Pretend I don't notice them trembling. The numbness in my mind is fading fast, replaced by an all-too-intense awareness that my mam is getting uncomfortably close to being right. "I said it's fine. She can date who she wants. It's no business of mine."

"She's not dating Colin," Mam scoffs.

"Doesn't matter." I turn to her and shrug, trying my best to look unbothered. "Hey, I forgot I needed to stop by the shop before picking Niamh up. We're out of some… things. Do you mind watching her a bit longer while I go get those?"

Her arms cross over her chest. "Sure, love. Go take a drive. Sort out whatever that mess is you've got going in your head. 'Cause it *is* a mess."

I sigh heavily. Of course she knows. Haven't I learned anything being a parent? They *always* know.

"Thanks, Mam," I mumble.

Just as I pass her in the threshold, Niamh comes running across the tile floor. "All clean, Daddy!"

"Yes you are!" I try to keep my voice light, but it comes out strangled. Her eyebrows scrunch. Even at this age, she doesn't miss much.

I'm her soft place to land. One deep breath in, followed by a slow exhale. I just have to make it to the car. Then I can lose control.

"Love, I just realized I've forgotten to pick something up from the shop. Would you mind staying with Granny a bit longer?"

"Can I have more sticky toffee pudding?" she asks, grinning mischievously.

A snort from behind me answers before I can, but I still add, "Sure you can."

She squeals, "Did ya hear that, Granny?" and races around me, my strange tone—and presence—already forgotten.

I exit the kitchen and practically bound down the corridor, desperate for a wall of crisp, fresh air to slap me in the face and quell these feelings. Whatever happened, it's none of my business. Leona Granger, and whoever the fuck is humping or not humping her, is *none of my business.*

The sooner I get that through my thick skull, the better.

I don't even see the living room door opening through the haze clouding my vision. Not till the person exiting it collides with my chest.

"Oof," Leo huffs, rocking back on her heels to steady herself. One delicate hand reaches up to cup her nose, causing her next words to come out nasally. "I'm sorry, I should've looked where I was going—"

She glances up, eyes watering, and drops the hand. "Oh, it's you."

Her proximity does two things to my brain: First, alarm bells go off. The volume could be equated to a thousand birds cawing simultaneously. Or one really loud nuclear bomb.

Second, whatever leash I'd been maintaining on my emotions snaps. Implodes. Another, more dangerous nuclear bomb.

"Callum?" Her eyebrows furrow as she tries to peer around me. "Is everything all right?"

"Grand. *So* grand. Couldn't be better, honestly." The tightness in my chest is threatening to suffocate me. I rub my sternum, but it's no use. "Heard you had a run-in with Colin at McDonough's."

Redness immediately floods her neck and cheeks. If she tucked her hair back, I'd bet it reaches all the way to the tips of her ears. It's something I desperately wish I didn't know. A piece of her I want to give back, along with all the rest that still take up residence in my heart.

"Siobhan told you?"

"Actually"—I step around her—"Niamh did."

She calls after me for reasons I don't want to read into. I keep walking, for the sake of us both.

"Callum, it was nothing. He made a pass at me; I rejected it." She grabs my elbow just as I reach for the doorknob. "It was nothing."

"You don't owe me an explanation," I say, glancing down at her over my shoulder. "Not for that, anyway."

Her hand falls away. I almost regret the dig. *Almost.*

I open the door, letting that first gust of cold air rush in. My head is pounding, heart aching, chest tight. All signs point to a heart attack. Or Leo's presence. Lately they've felt the same.

"Look, Leo." I turn, facing her but looking through her. It's the only way I'll maintain even a shred of my resolve. "It doesn't matter. None of this"—I gesture between us—"matters. Whatever happened back then, it was nothing. We were two stupid kids."

She folds her arms around her middle. "I just thought after last weekend—"

"I was wrong," I interject. "Last weekend, I was wrong when I said we weren't finished here." I take another step away from her, from the hold I can't afford for her to still have on me. "Clearly we are."

Tears fill her eyes. "Callum."

It nearly breaks me, my name on her lips, but I hold firm. This morning, talking to Padraig... I was a fool to think that I could ever understand, that I could ever have closure. There's no such thing as closure for this. It'll be a wound I have for my whole life. I just have to learn to live with it.

"I think it's time for you to go home, Leo."

She inhales sharply. I want to comfort her even now, but I stop myself.

"Have a good life."

The only sound that follows is the thud of my footsteps against the sidewalk as I walk over to my car and climb in, shutting the door on this chapter once and for all.

Chapter Seventeen

Leona

I'm frozen in shock.

I try to focus on the grain of the wooden door, tracing the loops and lines with my gaze. I try to find the seam in the yellowing floral wallpaper. I try, I try, I try.

For far too long, that's all I've been doing. Trying to move on, trying to build a life, trying to do the right thing. I'm exhausted down to my core.

Since returning, I've felt resentment from Callum. Confusion. Even anger. But the apathy flowing off him today, an emotion I never thought him capable of, is what hurts the most. It feels like I've just been hit with a deadly dose of radiation. I stretch my arms out in front of me, half expecting to find them covered in bubbling burns.

I don't know how long I've been lying in bed, stuck in a state of suspended animation, when my door creaks open. Siobhan peeks her head through the crack she's created and frowns apologetically.

"I knocked but you didn't answer."

I blink twice. Swallow. Try to remember how to talk to people. "Sorry, I didn't hear."

Another frown. "Are you all right, love?"

"Mm." It's the best I can muster.

She steps inside completely, shutting the door behind herself. "I heard you two talking in the hall." She knocks on the wall above the writing desk. A hollow *thunk* answers her. "Too thin for secrets, I'm afraid." She closes the distance between us and sits on the edge of the bed. "I'm sorry, Leona. I tried to explain to him. Niamh simply misspoke; you know how kids can be. They pick one thing you say and repeat it without including context." She tilts her head, studying me. Her face is wrought with concern. "He's gone off to clear his head. Didn't want to be around Niamh in this state."

My heartbeat stutters. "He's a good father."

"That he is." She gnaws at her bottom lip like she's fighting off saying more. Unsurprisingly, she loses the fight. "But he's a terrible"—she waves her hand toward me—"*whatever* he is to you."

"Nothing," I say, even though it causes a bone-deep ache. "We're nothing to each other."

Her mouth flattens into a grim line, but she lets that one slide.

"Can I get you anything?" She shifts her weight. Fidgets with her watch. I can practically see her brain working to find a way to smooth this over. To make it right. Ever the hostess, she's trying to take care of things. Only this is something a scone and a scheme aren't going to fix.

Suddenly I'm so hot. My face, neck, ears burn. My heart fucking *burns* with all this love that has nowhere to go. Love meant for Callum, for Poppy, turned malignant from lack of use. "I just need some air," I croak, forcing myself out of bed.

"Right." She rises alongside me. "I'll just give Podge a call; he can take you anywhere you need to go."

"He takes the weekends off." I scan the room, looking for my jacket. It's slung over the chair of the writing desk, where my journal for Poppy lies open. I grab the jacket and shut the journal, letting the pretty floral cover shield the anguished words that lie within. "Besides, I'd like to walk."

"The sun will be setting soon," she says, worrying at her bottom lip. She pulls her phone from her back pocket. "He'll do anything I ask. I'm practically the lad's second mam."

I shake my head at her, lips flattened into a grim line. "It's really okay. Thanks anyway."

I step around her, not bothering to wait for her response. Out of the corner of my eye as I round the top of the stairs, I see the phone lift to her ear, but I don't wait. I just go.

"Where are you off to?" Padraig asks, hanging his arm out the window. He's driving alongside me as I make my way down the sidewalk. Passersby are beginning to stare at the girl being stalked by the taxi driver, but I do my best to pay them no mind. It's not lost on me that this is a mirror image of him finding me trudging home from Callum's in the driving rain. Only this time, the last thing I want is a ride.

A lift, I correct myself.

"I'm just getting some air, Podge. It's fine." I'm looking anywhere but at him. The chimneys adorning every rooftop. The empty flowerpots hanging from wrought-iron posts. The sky with its streaks of pink and gold. "Go back to enjoying your night off."

"Sure look, I could go on and leave you here, but Siobhan's after calling. And if I don't do what Siobhan asks, she'll stop inviting me for Sunday dinner. I quite like being invited, even if I can't always make it. So respectfully, I'm more scared of her than I am of you. Get in the car."

"No."

"All right then."

He pulls ahead of me, and I let out a sigh of relief. But the victory is incredibly short-lived. The reverse lights come on, and then he's backing into a vacant spot along the curb. I do my best to pick up the pace, but I've only made it a few yards ahead when he comes jogging up beside me.

"Is that why you wear the tracksuits?" I cast an irritated glance in his direction. "To chase after unwilling customers."

He laughs, jolly as ever, like I'm joking. I'm not.

"I happen to think I look good in them." He smooths his hands over the pudge of a beer belly on his otherwise lanky frame. "Makes me look slender."

"Mhm, sure they do."

"Please try to remember," he says, casting a hand over his heart, "that I am not the enemy. There's no need to go insulting my figure. I'm sensitive, you know."

I stop on the sidewalk, turning to face him. "I'm sorry, Podge," I say, doing my best to sound earnest. "You're right. Thank you for being a friend to me. I'm clearly not very good at being one in return."

"Apology accepted." He hooks an arm around my shoulders, tugging me into what I think will be a quick embrace. But soon he's walking forward, still holding me hostage. "Now, let's go handle your sorrows the true Irish way. With a stiff drink."

"That doesn't sound particularly healthy."

He smirks, casting a sidelong glance my way as we step into the pub that he and Callum frequent. I pause for a moment, expecting to see him here, but a quick scan of the room yields no dejected blond Irishmen.

"Well, I promise not to tell your therapist if you won't," he says. He tugs a stool out from the bar, offering it to me.

I take the seat, and he joins me, calling over to the elderly bartender for a round of beers. I mouth, *"Cider,"* over his shoulder, and the gentleman offers me a conspiratorial wink. "I don't have a therapist."

"Neither do I." The drinks are settled in front of us, a dark red ale for Padraig and a pale cider for me. We clink them together in a sad excuse for a toast. "Here's to a poor man's version of mental health care. Slainte."

"Slainte." I take a sip, the syrupy fizz temporarily providing a balm to my wounds. "I think that's just called alcoholism."

"It's only alcoholism if you think you need it." He slaps his palm against the counter, startling nearby patrons. And me. His eyebrows pull close as he studies my face intently. "Do you need that alcohol to feel better?"

"No," I answer honestly. Of all the possible vices I could've developed after losing the baby, self-isolation seems to be my drug of choice. Alcohol I can take or leave.

"Then we're grand." He sips his beer, offering me a sad smile, as if he understands all that I've left unsaid in my simple answer. I like that about Padraig. He was born with the very rare gift of being able to read a room.

"Should I be worried about *your* drinking habits?" I do my best to make it sound like a joke. I remember how to make jokes, right?

He snorts, and I crack a relieved smile.

"Don't you be worrying about me, now. Dermot here keeps me in check. He'd deliver me right to rehab's door if I ever got out of hand." He and the bartender exchange a respectful nod. "So, Siobhan gave me the outsider's rundown, but do you want to tell me what happened with your man?"

"Not my man."

He rolls his eyes. "It's just a phrase."

"I know," I say flatly. "I just wanted to be clear."

He puts his palms out in a display of innocence. "Sorry. What happened with not your man?"

I glare, and he snickers. I've surprised myself by drinking half the pint glass already, and the warmth of the alcohol has reached my veins. My shock has melted, and along with it the desire to keep everything tightly wound inside. It would be so nice to finally unravel, even just for a moment.

"I went to McDonough's yesterday for lunch, and the guy working there made what could be interpreted as a pass at me."

Padraig swallows the last sip of his beer before signaling Dermot for another. "Colin?"

"Yeah."

"It was definitely a pass at you, then." He thanks Dermot for our refills, and the older man tips his cap at us. He has kind eyes, and it makes me feel safe here, in his bar. Like I can set a bit of my armor down.

Oh God, the alcohol's already making me sappy.

"Anyway," I groan. "Siobhan made a comment about it in front of Niamh that she repeated—"

"As she does."

"—and Callum took that *some* type of way. I don't know how to explain it really. He told me I could date whomever I wanted. Then he told me to go home." The words come out in a rush, and I realize as soon as I finish saying them that I feel like a weight has been lifted off me. I giggle, and it feels so good to laugh. "It's ridiculous, honestly."

Padraig studies me with a quirked eyebrow. "It is."

"I've never seen him act that way before. It was so unlike him." My voice sounds whiny even to my own ears. I down another glug of alcohol, trying to drown out the noise.

"He's sensitive when it comes to you, and it makes him act like an idiot."

My stomach drops and I level him with a hard stare.

"I'm not making excuses for him, if that's what you think. It was just an observation."

"That's not why I'm staring at you."

"Then why are you staring at me?" he asks, running a hand through his hair. The silver strands woven into the dark ones catch the low light of the bar lanterns, shimmering softly.

"You said he's sensitive about me." I swallow thickly. What did Dermot do, mix syrup into my drink? "What do you mean?"

Padraig gives me a look that says, *Don't play dumb.* "It's clear that he cares about you. No one reacts that way to someone they don't have strong feelings for."

The *harrumph* that escapes my lips is a bit harsher than I intend. "Well, considering he told me that what happened between us back then was nothing, that we were just stupid kids, I'd say you're probably mistaken."

"Sometimes the lies we tell others are really just the ones we're trying to believe ourselves."

I raise my eyebrows at him. "That was surprisingly insightful."

He tips his half-empty glass at me. "I'm smarter when I'm buzzed."

I swallow the rest of mine. "Ironically I only get more stupid."

He laughs, and my stomach gurgles, and I feel tears forming in the corners of my eyes, but I blink them away.

The room is filled with groups of people chattering and drinking away the worries of their weeks. I let the hum of noise fill my ears for a moment, not trying to decipher any of it but rather letting it all form a steady roar that makes me feel less empty. My gaze flits from face to face, not settling on a particular one for more than a heartbeat. Looking at all these people, I wonder who they miss and if those people miss them back. I wonder what they're sorry for, and if any of us deserves to be redeemed in the end. I certainly hope so, for all our sakes.

"Leona," Padraig asks, his voice cutting through my reverie. "I'm going to ask you a question, and I don't want you to shut it down right away. I want you to humor me, if only for a moment."

I nod. There's another drink in my hand. I don't remember it arriving, but I'm grateful it's here.

Padraig's eyes dance around my face, searching for something. "Do you still love Callum? Did you ever?"

There's no judgment in his tone, no hint of a challenge or test. He's not measuring my worth by my response. He won't think less of me, I can already tell, no matter what the truth is.

It's for this reason that I decide to share it with him, this tiny piece of my truth.

My eyes fill with tears, and this time blinking doesn't work. They fall just as the words do, tumbling over my lips. "I never stopped."

He nods once, as if this is what he suspected, and then offers me his bar napkin. I blot away the tears, embarrassed to be crying in public, and then I wave Dermot down at the other end of the bar.

"Can we get a round of shots, please?"

Chapter Eighteen

Callum

I drive for what feels like ages, though there aren't enough roads in Cahersiveen for that to be true.

For a while I let the full range of ugliness unravel from within me. Every color of jealousy, the entire spectrum of anger. My knuckles turn white from clenching the steering wheel. Just when I think I've felt it all, grief like an extended epilogue brings up the rear.

My glasses fog over. I tell myself it's from the heat flowing out of my car vents, but then a bastard tear rolls down my cheek. I try to blink the moisture away, determined not to crash on this single-lane road that winds between vast fields of farmland. The sun has set, and twilight arrives on its heels, turning the world to a delirious shade of purple. It feels wrong, the way the sky swirls and flows into darkness. All that beauty grates against me like a pad of sandpaper. Or maybe I'm just projecting my own discontent onto it.

Bingo, my inner monologue snipes. I stop the car.

The disappointment—in myself, in this entire situation—hits me like an avalanche. Buries me beneath snow and debris till I can no longer breathe.

For what feels like an eternity, I sit in my car and stare directly ahead, unseeing and suffering. This morning I was certain all I wanted was answers so that I could finally be rid of her. Now just the *suggestion* that she might be seeing someone else has turned me into a complete neanderthal. I can tell her to go back to America all I want, but the aching in my chest—a sickness that nearly turns my stomach—is rooted in the desire for her to stay.

I was kidding myself. I will never be free of her, nor do I want to be.

My phone rings, slicing the silence of the night in half. I scramble for it, hoping beyond hope that it's Leo. Even if she's just calling to tell me to go to hell for being a jealous prick, I'll take it. I'll take it in a heartbeat over never hearing her voice again.

Everything inside me sinks when I see that it's Padraig.

"Hello?"

"First of all," Padraig slurs. "Do you know that you're an idiot? Like, the king of all idiots?"

I remove my glasses and run a hand over my face. "Glad the word is getting around quickly about how much of a fuckup I am."

He hiccups and then giggles. He's well and truly drunk. "Just had to make sure you knew."

"Was there a 'second of all' coming, or did you just call to make me feel worse than I already do?"

"Well, I definitely wanted to do that, so I'm happy that came across." There's a dull roar of chatter in the background. I hear Dermot's voice asking if the two of them would like another round.

Two of them?

"Podge, who are you drinking with?"

"*Second of all,*" he shouts, ignoring me entirely, "we need you to come pick us up. We're very, very drunk."

"We?" I ask, but I already know.

"Me and your lady, lad!" He guffaws, and I have to pull away from the phone so that the sound doesn't burst my eardrum. "That's funny. Lady lad. You're a lady lad for getting mad. Hey, that rhymed!"

I shift the car into gear and start driving, not waiting for him to confirm the obvious. My heart takes up residence in my throat. I wouldn't be able to speak even if he stopped babbling long enough to give me the chance.

This may be the only chance I have to tell her how I feel. To find out if there's a chance in hell to bridge this gap between who we used to be and who we are now. It could already be too late, but I'll be damned if I'm not going to try.

In between his ramblings and laughter, I hear a familiar voice call to him.

"Who are you talking to?" Leo says, sounding far away at first and then suddenly closer when the phone shuffles and she groans, "Oh, *God.*"

The call disconnects, and I press my foot down a little harder on the gas.

Leo's always been a playful drunk. When I walk into the pub to find her foxtrotting across the floor with Dermot, I'm relieved that this part of her has remained unchanged.

I've never seen the old man move so fast. The song—a traditional tune with an up-tempo—comes to an end just as he dips her as far as his hunched spine will allow.

She comes up grinning, breathless. Until she sees me.

Even though she schools her face into something resembling

impassivity, her eyes betray her. They're a violent storm, but not the type to run away from. The kind I want to chase.

How I ever convinced myself I wanted nothing more than answers from her is beyond me.

"I'm here to take you home," I say, ignoring Padraig's raised eyebrows and shit-eating grin. He's sitting on a barstool watching us like a cutthroat tennis match that he's got front seats for.

She grits her teeth, staring me down intently. "I'm sober enough. I can walk home."

I study her for a moment, realizing she's telling the truth, and suddenly amusement sparks deep in my throat. It's foreign and glorious against the emptiness my shame left behind. I have to cough to cover up the smile my facial muscles desperately want to form.

"So why didn't you?"

She blanches. "What?"

I don't know why I do it, as precarious a position as we're in, but I take a step closer. "You knew I was coming. You could've left immediately. But you didn't; why is that?"

Her mouth opens and then closes again. She realizes her hand has been shown. I still feel guilty enough about what I've done not to bask in the victory.

"Let's get him home"—I jab my thumb in Padraig's direction, where he's gradually slumping farther by the second—"and then you and I need to talk."

She grabs her small brown purse from underneath Padraig's head, the closest thing he could find to a pillow, resulting in a resounding *thump* of his skull against the hardwood. She looks sorry before she wipes the emotion off her face. "No thank you," she says, shoving past me to head for the door. "I don't think we have anything left to say to one another."

I'm momentarily stunned by the electricity of her touch, even something so minor as a brush of her shoulder. By the time I start to speak, she's already halfway to the exit. I jog to catch up with her and grab her elbow loosely to hold her in place.

"Leona—"

She stops dead in her tracks and stares down at the place where our bodies connect. It's unreadable and cold, two things I've never known her to be.

I drop my arm to my side.

"I'm so sorry for what I said. I didn't mean a word of it." I let the words hang in the air between us. I wonder if it's just wishful thinking that warms the atmosphere a few degrees over the next couple heartbeats. "Just get in the car please. I need to talk to you."

She studies me, taking my measure. Deciding if I'm worth her time. I stand up straighter under her scrutiny, hoping to be found forgivable whether I deserve it or not.

Her gentle nod unravels me. It takes everything in me to lock my knees and keep standing.

Quickly, before she can change her mind, I gather my friend and usher the two of them out the door to my waiting car.

We ride in silence for longer than I've ever been quiet around Leo, the only sound to break it up being the muffled snores coming from Padraig in the back seat. When we're finally to his apartment—a studio on the second floor of a jewelry store a few streets from the river—I turn to look at him over my shoulder and then glance at Leo.

"I can't believe you went drinking with Podge, and he's the one who came out of it unconscious."

My attempt at humor barely reaches her. It's the minor twitch of her cheek that acts as my glimmer of hope, even though it could've simply been a coincidence.

"You've made it clear you don't want me here," she says, and her voice sounds unspeakably sad. Hollow and cavernous. "Just get him inside and then we'll get this over with."

I press my lips together. She looks toward the window, pressing her forehead to the glass. I've been dismissed. The magnitude of the damage I've done hits me square in the face, and I'm not sure that I'll ever be able to undo it.

I study the curve of her delicate jaw, the swoop of the brown wave dusting her shoulder. I ache to reach out and touch her. In the same breath I wish I could wring my own neck. Here I am, staring at the only future I've ever been able to see for myself, and I've been doing everything in my power to burn it to the ground.

How will I ever teach Niamh about forgiveness when I'm this bad at giving it? At deserving it?

I exit the car and collect Padraig from the back seat. Leo doesn't give us a second glance.

Once Padraig is safely tucked into bed—fully clothed because I don't love him that much—I slip back into the night and lock his door behind me. I store his spare key under the doormat and walk to the car with my head hung low.

There's no reaction as I collapse into the driver's seat. For a moment I wonder if Leo's fallen asleep, but then I hear a soft whimper escape her lips. It's so, so much worse than I thought.

She's crying.

"I'm sorry, Leo. I had no right to be upset about Colin. You are free to date whomever you want, of course—"

"I told you," she interjects, still talking to the window, "that it was a misunderstanding. He hit on me. I left the pub. End of story."

I let my head fall against the headrest. "I know that. I know that you wouldn't, that you aren't—weren't—like that. I just…"

Her gaze cuts from the window to me, the blue turned black by the moonlight. "You just what? Got jealous?"

I nod. "I don't know why I'm so sensitive when it comes to you."

To my surprise, she laughs.

"Do I want to know?"

She shakes her head. "It's just that Podge said the same thing. That you're sensitive about me."

I shift in my seat, feeling exposed. "And what did you say to that?"

"That he was full of shit."

I don't know what comes over me, what makes me think I can be so bold, but I reach for her hand where it rests on her knee, and I grab onto it for dear life. Her gaze falls to our joined hands and stays there for a long time.

"I've never been great at getting out of my own head." I rub my thumb over her knuckles. There's a new scar on the swell of the first. A story I don't yet know but want to desperately. "Something about you, though, has always made me feel so distinctly alive. So fully present in my body. Every sensation is more intense. The good…and the bad."

I squeeze her hand three times and then release it. "I'm sorry the only thing you've seen since you came back is a whole lot of bad."

"I haven't exactly given you a reason to show me the good."

"All you've ever deserved," I say, holding her gaze with my own, "is the very best."

Her eyelids flutter closed, and she winces like she can't believe the words coming out of my mouth. Like the very suggestion that she deserves goodness is painful for her.

"You do, Leo. I wouldn't lie to you."

She bites the inside of her cheek and draws in a deep breath. When her eyes open, the sadness from before has been tucked away. "Shouldn't you be driving?"

I glance ahead at the quiet street, illuminated by a fat moon overhead. "I suppose I should."

Houses become scarcer with every kilometer we travel. The moon is big and bright, illuminating our path with a silvery light that makes this all feel like an impossible dream. I've had so many like it. Dreams where Leo came home to me and we'd drive for hours like we used to, content just to be in each other's presence once more. Something I never thought I'd take for granted. Strange to realize that's what I've been doing for the past two weeks.

"Why did you come to get me?" she whispers. Her tone isn't accusatory. It's baffled.

The edges of my vision go blurry with moisture. I blink it away. "There was a time when I told you I'd always show up for you. I promised it." I shake my head at the darkness, at the impossibility of all that has happened. "I've been doing a really bad job keeping my word, haven't I?"

She snorts, and it makes me smile. "Haven't we all?" she muses. A shuffling sound catches my attention, and I turn to see her shifting in her seat to face me.

The grin on my face grows infinitesimally bigger. Once she was an open book for me to read at my leisure. Now, this small grace of her turning to face me feels like I've struck gold. My gaze cuts to her every chance I get, trying to capture as much of this new version of her as possible.

"You're different now."

She rolls her eyes. "So are you."

It seems so obvious, but it's just now occurring to me that she doesn't know this version of me. A father. Responsible. Accomplished in my career. She only knows the parts I've shown her, which are admittedly some of the worst.

"Hi, I'm Callum." I stick out my hand for her to shake. It hangs there for an awkward second before she hesitantly grabs hold. "I have a four-year-old named Niamh who is the light of my life. I work as a manager at my uncle's shipping company, though before you think it, I assure you it isn't nepotism. Someone very important taught me that." I give her a wink.

"I like cycling in the summer and hunting at my granda's old lodge in the winter. I'm pretty sure I'm developing an allergy to dairy." My voice grows somber, and she giggles at the dramatics. I stop the car at a crossroads and turn to meet her gaze head-on. "And I'm kind of an asshole to the woman who broke my heart."

The amused look leaves her eyes, and they open up into infinite pools of water. I'm tempted to dive right in.

She grips my hand firmly and shakes it once. "I'm Leona. Divorced. Jobless. Dust in the wind. And I'm so sorry for breaking your heart."

Chapter Nineteen

Leona

The torture of my inner turmoil is enough to sober me up.

He'd never lie to me, and it kills me that I can't say the same. That lying is all I've been doing since the day I found out I was pregnant. Lying to Callum, to my parents, even lying to myself.

I want to believe him, that I deserve goodness. But I'm afraid, once he knows the truth, that he won't even believe himself.

His eyes are red-rimmed the way they get when he's emotionally on edge, and his freckled skin is flushed. That gorgeous blond hair is in a tangled disarray, marred by frustrated hands raking through it. I want to touch him, to smooth his rough edges over. I want to run far, far away from this man who makes me feel more than is safe for my fragile heart.

I realize I've been too lost in my thoughts to pay attention to where we are going when he turns onto a familiar driveway. Rather than the inn, like I would've expected, his headlights fall on the fairy-tale facade of his quaint cottage. He pulls around the side of his home and parks. In the glow of the moonlight, I can just make out the tops of the hydrangea bushes peeking over his garden gate.

Air whooshes out of me at the sight. Tears prick the corners of my eyes.

Callum follows my line of sight and smiles when he sees the bushes swaying in the breeze. "You always did love those flowers. Did I tell you Granda helped Mam plant them as a Mother's Day gift for my gran one year when she was little?" His voice falters, and it draws my gaze to him. "She loved them just as much as you."

I remember the story, but I love to hear him tell it so much that I just nod. When he talks about his granda, his voice goes soft in a way I adore. The man has always been the most important person in Callum's life besides his mother. "How is your grandfather?"

He shakes his head, still facing the bushes. "He passed a couple years ago."

Instinct has me grabbing his hand before good sense can convince me not to. His gaze cuts to me, wide with surprise and yet raw with gratitude.

I let the moment linger. I won't be the one to let go.

As if he can hear my thoughts, the corner of his mouth quirks. He squeezes my hand once and then releases it. "Would you like to come inside?"

"I'd like that," I whisper. I'm afraid if I raise my voice any higher, it'll shatter the magic we seem to be suspended in.

The house is just as I remember it. Pale cream walls and blonde wood floors fill it with light, even in the darkness. Those gauzy white curtains have an ethereal glow, adding to the fairy-tale feel. He's made a few updates to the kitchen, painted the cabinets white and replaced the countertops, but the bones are still there. It's just enough to remind me that time has passed, but it doesn't feel like it's so far ahead that I can't catch up.

Callum paces across the room and opens the cabinet above his fridge, the movement exposing the skin of his lower back. I want to reach out and slip my hands under his shirt, tracing the warm expanse of his body until I've learned all that is new and noted what remains unchanged. The desire is thick in my throat, heavy in my hands.

I'm so distracted by the warmth flooding my cheeks and the space between my thighs that it takes me a second to recognize what he's holding in his hand when he turns. The bottle of amber liquid is wrapped in a simple white label. He sets it on the countertop and pinches the neck to rotate it until the words *Writers' Tears* come into view.

I gasp. "I cannot believe you still have that!" I walk over to him, taking the bottle in my grasp. He settles his hip against the countertop beside me, so close that if I moved even slightly, I'd brush against him. I have to force myself to remain completely still.

"Of course I still have it." He crosses his arms over his chest, his bicep caressing mine. I force myself to draw in a normal breath so he doesn't know how deeply this all affects me.

I turn the bottle over, marveling at its mere existence. We bought it on a whim while perusing a touristy shop in County Cork. Knee-deep in essays for my literature classes, it seemed the perfect lament to my chosen career. But in the car as we drove away, he made me a promise that he wouldn't open it till I returned after graduating. We'd drink it to celebrate my career and our reunion.

Now here it is, twelve years later. Unopened. Its intact seal is a testament to two of my greatest failures.

"Why didn't you drink it?" I breathe. "Or throw it out?"

He shakes his head. "Hope. Or stupidity. Probably both."

"I'm sure your ex-wife loved that." I don't know why I say it, but I do. And then it's out in the open and I can't take it back, no matter how jealous it makes me sound.

He shifts awkwardly, which only serves to bring us closer together. His heat is now a constant at my side.

"We were never married," he says gruffly.

I hum my understanding. "Well, shall we drink it?" I ask, glancing up at him to find him studying me intently. We're so close that we're sharing the same postal code. We're sharing the same breath.

He nods, pivoting to reach for a glass in the cabinet behind us. His hand finds the back of my head and cradles it gently, shielding me from the door's sharp corner as he swings it open. I don't miss the way his pupils dilate, the way his breath halts. It gives me a glimmer of satisfaction to know that I affect him this much.

Just as much as he affects me.

Once a glass is poured for each of us, we clink them together, the whiskey sloshing dangerously close to the rim. Callum's gaze never leaves my face as I take my first sip and wince when it burns my throat.

"Why didn't you become a writer?" he asks, cocking his head.

I take another gulp, trying to taste the vanilla and caramel notes that the bottle promises are inside, but all I'm getting is the fire. "What happened with Niamh's mom?"

He snickers and takes another sip from his glass. "I asked first."

"I'll show you mine if you'll show me yours?"

Heat flares in his eyes, and he swallows even though he hasn't taken another drink. I fight to keep the blush from creeping up my cheeks, but I know it's no use.

"Relax," I say, touching his arm. "It's just an expression."

He narrows his eyes at me. "Quit avoiding the question."

"I'm not!" I flatten my hand over my heart. When he doesn't stop glaring, I add, "Fine, Jesus."

"Atta girl."

I set the now-empty glass down and then hop up onto the counter, resting my back against the upper cabinets with a weary sigh. "I guess I just realized how hard it would be to break into that career field, to make any money doing it. And besides, my dad's friend offered me a good-paying job fresh out of college. I would've been really dumb not to take it."

It's the same reason I've given everyone for the past ten years. I've said the words so much they no longer ring hollow. They just sound a little rehearsed. I study my fingernails, picking at a loose cuticle. My real motivations for giving up on my dream got buried along with every other true thing about me, for the exact same reason: it hurt too much.

If I were honest, I'd tell him that I didn't go after my dream job because I'd already lost something I loved more than life itself. The idea of pursuing travel journalism, of risking the pain of losing that too, was just too much to face. It was easier if the choice was mine. Easier if I was the one to walk away before the universe could rip it from my hands.

If I were honest, I'd take the opportunity to tell Callum about our daughter. But I'm tired and this moment is too fragile and I'm still a coward. So I don't say any of it.

"Catherine never really took to motherhood. Thought of Niamh as a burden. She missed her life before, and she really missed being able to sleep with whomever she wanted." He pauses for emphasis, letting that gavel smack down hard on the truth. "She ran off to Spain with some man she met online. Never looked back."

It's a horrible enough truth that I look just as shocked as the first time I heard it. Padraig's secret gossip will remain safe with me.

"You wanna know the worst thing about all of it?" Callum asks, shaking his head in disbelief.

I can't imagine anything worse than a woman abandoning her toddler. "What's that?"

"In Ireland, the only way for a mother to sign over rights to the father when they're unmarried is by putting the child up for adoption, and then the father has to adopt the child. I had to adopt my own daughter." He sucks air in through clenched teeth. Every muscle in his face is strained and tight with the effort it takes to say the words. "The parent who wanted her had to fight for her. How ridiculous is that? Thank God her mother was agreeable."

The desire to comfort him, to take away all that has caused him pain, is all-consuming. I can't fight it anymore, no matter how badly I know I should. I reach for him, and he glances up at me. He doesn't resist as I pull him to me. He steps into the space between my knees and lets himself be held.

He still smells of rain and soap and something else distinctly him, something so fresh and breathtaking that I've never smelled anything like it since. I bury my nose into his neck, trying desperately to imprint it on my brain. I didn't know the last time I saw him would be the last time. As far as I knew, the year would pass and I'd be back here with him, and we'd have a whole lifetime together for me to inhale his scent. But now I have the privilege of knowing any moment could be the last, and so I cling to the details with all I have in me.

"I was wrong earlier," he says, his breath rustling my hair.

Reluctantly I pull back. Just far enough to see his face, not enough to let him go. He cradles my jaw with one strong hand and traces his thumb over the swell of my cheek.

"The way we felt about each other back then… It was intense. That kind of feeling can't last. It'd burn you alive." He says it like he's trying to convince one of us it's true, though I can't guess which. His gaze, which had fallen to my lips, returns to mine.

"But it was real, wasn't it? We were young and it was fleeting, but it was real."

I want to pull his glasses away, to leave no barriers between us. But more than anything, I want him to see me clearly. I lay my hand over the top of his, feeling the ridges of his knuckles and the warmth of his skin. My next words come out in a rush.

"Still is."

Suddenly our mouths are a breath apart and I have to release his hand because it moves to lace in the hair at the base of my neck. I arch my back, pressing my body flush against him. My nipples harden against the plane of his chest. Warmth pools in my belly when I feel the length of him straining against my inner thigh.

He tugs at the fistful of hair, tilting my head back and exposing my throat. His lips trace the line of my jaw, down the sensitive skin of my neck. It is there that he places his first kiss, in the curve where neck becomes shoulder, before he trails back up to my ear. I'm panting, clinging to his biceps, and still he takes painstaking care to move slower than I ever thought time could pass.

His teeth scrape against my earlobe, his hot breath falling in tendrils across my skin. Just when I think I will have to beg, he relents, pulling back so we're face-to-face.

"I want nothing more than to kiss you right now." I nod, desperate, but he presses on. "I want to pick you up off this counter and carry you to my room. I want to make love to you as the man I am now, not the boy I was before.

"But if we're going to do this, Leo, we've got to take it slow. You've got to be absolutely certain that this is what you want." He swallows hard, and I do, too. "Loving you isn't something I can survive a second time."

I nod because I can't speak, and he folds me into his embrace completely. It's the only thing in that moment that keeps me from coming undone.

The first thing I smell when I step into the bed-and-breakfast is the sweet aroma of fresh crepes. It's nearly eleven at night, so I wonder for a moment if my senses are deceiving me. When I round the corner into the kitchen, though, I find Siobhan plating up one of the thin pancakes next to a spread of toppings she's laid out for the two guests standing by the door to the garden, embracing haphazardly.

"That's not who I sent to give you a lift," Siobhan says.

I glance over my shoulder at Callum, who is trying desperately to contain his grin as he ignores her and asks, "Why are you cooking at this hour?"

Siobhan aims her spatula at the couple in the corner. "Meet Chase and Eden. They're taking a belated honeymoon around our beautiful country and stopped in for the night. Glad you came back, Leona, as I was just about to give up your room!"

I roll my eyes at her as I reach out to shake their hands.

"Nice to meet you both," I say, sounding surprisingly chipper even to myself.

"Nice to meet you," the woman, Eden, says. She has dark auburn hair that falls in a straight curtain down to her collarbone and eyes even greener than Callum's, which I didn't realize was possible. Her skin is littered with freckles from a lot of time spent in the sun. She leans into Chase's side, a man with dark hair and a half-sleeve tattoo, and affectionately pinches his waist. "This is my husband, Chase." She preens as she says the word so sweetly it comes out honey-coated.

Chase's chest puffs out with pride. He offers us a lazy grin. "Are you guests here, too?"

I smile. Wow, I'm doing that a lot tonight. "No, I actually work here, for Siobhan. I sleep up in the attic."

"And the starstruck one back there is my son," Siobhan adds gruffly.

Callum steps up to shake their hands. His cheeks are flushed red when he turns to his mother. "Do you cook in the middle of the night for all your guests?"

Siobhan's gaze cuts to Eden, who exchanges a glance with her husband before he nods softly. Immediately, in a gesture I'd recognize in a heartbeat, her hands fall to her stomach.

She smiles at him as she speaks. "We're actually pregnant," she says, her voice taking on a dreamlike quality. "Not too far along, but the morning sickness has set in. Though why they call it morning sickness is beyond me." A heavy sigh escapes her lips as she turns to face me. "I'm sick all. The. Time."

Callum snorts. "I remember that with my ex." He waves a hand to excuse himself. "Sorry, I know it must be miserable. But congratulations on the baby."

His voice becomes warm velvet as he offers his congratulations. I can see in the way his features soften, in the far-off look in his eyes, that just the mention of a baby brings him back to a wonderful place.

I'm so jealous in that moment I can barely breathe.

"Thank you," the couple responds in unison before Eden adds, "Anyway, I'm still figuring out how to navigate the nausea."

"And I told her anything bready like crepes always helped me," Siobhan says.

"Hard candy, too," I mumble. Callum's gaze flickers to me, and I avoid it.

"What was that?" Eden asks, eyebrows raised.

I find a loose thread hanging from my sweater and grab on,

twirling it around my finger until the circulation is cut off and the tip starts turning red. "Hard candy. Like Jolly Ranchers, or here they don't have those but any flavored candy like that will work. Crackers, too. Basically, just don't ever let yourself get hungry."

Eden smiles, and it takes up her entire face. She's beautiful in the way a rainy day is beautiful. Refreshing. Life-giving. "Thank you; I'll try that."

Siobhan is watching me closely, and Callum's hand cups my elbow to get my attention. I pull my gaze away from where Eden's hands still cradle her nonexistent bump to meet Callum's.

His eyebrows furrow. "How'd you know all that?"

I shrug and force my voice out while holding back every lick of emotion behind a dam. "Lots of my friends have kids."

He considers me for another moment, and I panic when I realize he might press for more answers. But then the sound of Siobhan scraping the bowl for the last bit of batter breaks whatever tether was anchoring him to me, and I loose the breath I was holding.

"Well, I hope something works and you can get a bit of relief," he offers the woman before turning to his mom. "Where's Niamh?"

His mother points with the spatula down the hall. "She's asleep in my room. Do you want something to eat before you go?"

"No, I'd better get her home." Callum glances between Siobhan and I, clearly trying to decide how to go about this exit. After how close we were just a little while ago, it feels odd to have this distance between us. For a moment I think he's going to hug me goodbye, but he places a hand briefly on my bicep instead. "Good night, Leo."

"Good night, Callum." I smile at him, a little bit relieved, and hope I'm turned enough away from his mother that she cannot see. That flicker of desire burns to life once more in his eyes, and then he's turning and marching out the door before anyone else catches it.

"Good night, son!" Siobhan calls pointedly, but the door falls to a shut on her words. An awkward silence settles around us, with only the sizzling of the pan to break it up.

"So are you two…?" Chase asks, gesturing toward the door. Eden swats him before I have a chance to infer what he's asking.

The front door closes somewhere down the hall, and a tightness fills my chest to know Callum is leaving. It feels ridiculous. I know I'll see him again. But getting close to him tonight, hearing him say that he wants something with me, no matter how slow we take it… It makes being apart now impossibly painful.

"He wants to know if you two are a couple," Siobhan finishes for him, staring intently at me. "In fact, all of us would like to know."

She plates the last crepe and carries it over to the table. I gather a couple of bowls filled with strawberry slices and sugar and follow her lead. Chase and Eden take a seat at the table, loading up their plates with silent efficiency.

"It's, um, complicated." I grab a crepe and start filling it, hoping a stuffed mouth will spare me from this conversation.

No such luck.

"Might want to uncomplicate it, because he's delicious," Eden comments, snorting at her own observation. Chase covers his mouth to drown out the noise of his own resounding laugh. "I meant the crepes are delicious. Truly an honest mistake."

"I'm working on it," I say, keeping my head down.

"Well, don't work on it for too long," Eden says. She glances at her husband, and the love on her face is plain for anyone to see. It's almost painful to behold. "Don't wanna let a good one slip away."

"Eden would know," Chase adds. He scrunches his nose at her, and she sticks out her tongue in response. "She was the queen of playing hard to get. Almost cost her this dime piece." He gestures to himself.

"You weren't going anywhere," Eden says, rolling her eyes.

"Damn straight." Chase swallows the last of his crepe. "But I can't let you get too cocky."

The two of them go on laughing. Meanwhile Siobhan is watching me silently. I meet her gaze, and she offers the tiniest smile. The closest thing I'll get to approval tonight, in front of guests.

I nod, accepting it, and say a silent prayer that I won't let us all down.

Chapter Twenty

Callum

"Be careful, Niamh!" I call, but she's already sprinting up the stairs to the door of the bed-and-breakfast and letting herself in.

"Be faster, Daddy!" she replies before ducking through the entrance. The last thing I see is a flash of her unraveling plait, and then the door snicks closed.

"Yeah, Daddy, be faster," Padraig teases. He's walking up the sidewalk with his hands stuffed into his tracksuit pockets, looking a tad worse for the wear. Two bold purple bags hang under his eyes. His hair is disheveled in some places, matted in others.

"First of all, I told you only to call me that in private." We both arrive at the door at the same time, and I clamp down on his shoulder. "Second, you look like hell. I can't believe you let an American girl drink you under the table."

"Would you be quiet with that? I have a hard enough time finding a date without adding a rumor that I'm a lightweight to the mix." He grabs my face and plants a kiss loudly on my cheek, drawing the attention of two grannies walking down the street opposite us who quickly glance away. "There, your punishment. Now we're a couple, *Daddy*."

I wipe my cheek with a disgusted groan. "You're a terrible kisser."

"You're a terrible friend!" He crosses his arms and gives me a once-over. "It's been nearly twenty-four hours since you dropped me at my gaff and ran off with Leona, and I've yet to receive an update on what happened in my absence."

Now I'm really checking our surroundings for prying eyes. I remove my glasses, cleaning them with the corner of my shirt, while I contemplate how much I'm willing to share.

"Holy shit, did you shift her?" Padraig asks, mouth agape.

"What the fuck are we, twelve? No, I didn't shift her." I replace my glasses so I can glare at him properly.

"Well, something happened." He points at my face. "You always do the glasses thing when you're nervous."

"I do not," I say, adjusting them on my face. *Guess I do.* I sigh heavily, glancing around a final time before lowering my voice. "We didn't kiss, I swear. We almost did, but I stopped it before it got that far."

"Ah, go on, lad!" His face is lit up with glee, every wrinkle around his eyes showing with how broad his cocky grin is. It falls a fraction when my words catch up to his excitement. "Wait, what? Got that far? That's literally first base, Cal."

"You know I hate when you call me that."

He shrugs. "And I'm not scared of you, so deal with it." He leans against the stone facade of the inn, crossing his arms over his chest. "So tell me about this almost kiss? Had to be good; you're practically glowing."

"I brought her back to my place after dropping you off. Just to clear the air." He gives me a look. "Okay, to apologize for being a huge asshole; is that what you wanted to hear?" He nods, and I fight the urge to smack the smirk off his face. I might, if he weren't right on top of being smug. "But we got to talking about

Catherine and Leo's career, and then we wound up discussing the past. *Our* past."

I shake my head, at a loss for words to describe what came next.

My fingertips still buzz with the feel of her hair between my fingers. If I focus hard enough, the scent of oranges and lemons still surrounds me. The same shampoo after all this time. I wonder for a selfish moment if she kept using it because I once told her how enticing the scent is. It makes my chest swell with pride.

But it's the memory of her skin against my lips, her breath coming out in short rasps, that burns deep in my gut. The way she pulled me to her, clinging to me like she couldn't get close enough, her breasts swelling against my chest...

I need to stop this thought in its tracks, or I'll end up with a boner at Sunday dinner.

When I come back down from cloud nine, Padraig's eyeing me with a look I can't place.

"What?" I ask, embarrassed at how hoarse my voice sounds.

He shakes his head. "I'm just happy for you, man. You've been licking the wounds Catherine gave you for too long now. It's about time you let yourself be happy again."

With a groan, I smooth a hand over my hair and then let my thumb and forefinger find my temples, pinching them lightly.

"What?" Padraig snaps, shifting his weight. "You haven't already ruined it, have ya?"

"No, it's just..." How do I convey the turmoil going on in my brain? The worries are so numerous I counted them instead of sheep in order to finally get some rest after tucking Niamh in last night. Or early this morning. Time has lost all meaning for me.

He waits, and I decide an incomplete thought is better than none.

"It's just that I have a kid now. I have to think about how this will affect her. If Leo up and leaves again, how will Niamh handle that?" My voice breaks, and I clear my throat in an attempt to cover it up. The flash of pity in my friend's eyes tells me he heard it anyway. "It's been hard enough on me to deal with both of them leaving me. How much worse would it be for Niamh if she lost two mothers?"

I clamp my mouth shut as soon as the words leave my tongue. Who said anything about Leo being Niamh's mother? I'm racing so far ahead of myself that I've crossed the finish line before the gun's gone off.

Padraig snickers, as if he too knows this, but clears his throat to cover the sound.

I glare at him, but only because I'm incapable of glaring at myself. It's an unsatisfactory substitute for self-loathing.

"What I'm trying to say"—I splay my arms wide in exasperation—"is that if I'm going to do this, I'm going to do it right. I've got to take things slow. I've got to make sure we're on the same page so no one ends up getting hurt."

Because I meant what I said to Leo. I couldn't survive loving her—*losing* her—a second time.

Padraig's gaze darkens, his spine straightening as he pushes off the wall of the inn. I'm taller than him by a few inches, and he has to look up at me to meet me in the eye, but when he does, I feel suddenly small and fragile.

"Look, I know it's hard to put yourself out there." He winces like the comment could apply to both of us. "But I really think you're doing the right thing, for what it's worth to you. Leona, she… she really cares about you."

He stares intently, as though he can force me to believe him with sheer determination. I try my best to let the words warm me from the inside out, like a hot breakfast after a morning spent hunting in the cold. Granda would make quite the feast, and it always helped thaw out my bones.

I shake my head and offer Padraig a grin that doesn't quite reach my eyes.

"Grand. Now I'm going to get my ass inside before your daughter eats all the Yorkshire pudding." With that, he pinches my shoulder once more and then releases me. He grabs the brass handle and steps inside, holding it open with his foot for me. I suck in a deep breath and follow, letting the weight of the solid wood carry the door to a close.

I stand with my back pressed against it, watching as Padraig makes his way to the kitchen without looking back to ensure I'm following. There's a weight still sitting like stone in the base of my stomach, taking up so much space I'm not sure that I'll be able to eat.

I can't explain the depth of my reservations to Padraig because I don't fully understand them myself. I know that the feelings are there between Leo and me. There's no denying that after last night. Even the anger at her since she arrived has only been heightened by the love that still remains underneath. Deny it all I want, it's still the truth.

But there's something haunting Leo beyond our unfinished relationship. Something more than a broken dream. There's a sadness so vast and deep that its darkness pulls me in like a black hole. The Leo I knew was a bright and unruly thing. The one I held last night was tamed, tampered down. Subdued. She's drowning, and it kills me that I can't tell what is holding her under.

Every time she hands me a piece of herself, it feels like a half-truth. She forgets that when someone knows you as well as you know yourself, they can sense the lies you tell. Even if they're ones you honestly believe.

I want so badly for her to open up to me completely. To let me see all the dark and hidden parts of her so I can love them anyway. I want her to understand that her heart is safe with me, that I will not hurt her, no matter what the truth is.

It's too soon to expect so much, but I hope for it all the same.

Deep down, though, worry still nags at my brain. It's the part of myself I loathe, the voice of melancholy reason that suspects the worst in people. I don't want to listen to him, but his concerns drift through my consciousness anyway.

What if it really is that bad?

I shake my head because it can't be. I have loved her across time and an ocean and what felt like an insurmountable mountain of resentment. That love has survived every attempt I've made to squander it, to kill it. Despite all my reservations, the moment I held her in my arms, there was no denying it. And now that the floodgates are open, nothing could stop the rushing torrent.

Niamh walks out of the kitchen and bounds up the stairs without sparing a glance in my direction. "Leona! The roast is ready!" she calls, excitement pitching her voice up.

Nothing, I assure myself, *except when it comes to my daughter.*

"Afraid the door will cave in if you don't keep holding it up?"

Mam's voice startles me, making me realize how deeply I'd slipped into my thoughts. I shake my head and then my limbs, loosening them up as I step away from the door. Mam wipes her hands on the tattered gingham apron tied around her waist. Her eyes narrow, and I know she's soaking up every bit of body language she can, trying to put together the clues into a bigger picture of what's going on.

She's too good at it, after making a career out of people watching. It makes my skin crawl.

I force my walk to remain steady, schooling my face into careful indifference as I close the distance between us. She cocks her head and presses her lips into an impish grin.

"You two were out awful late last night."

I lean a shoulder against the wall, eyeing the stairs to check for my daughter and Leo. Mam tracks my gaze, and that grin deepens.

Busted.

I long ago learned not to lie to my mother. She can scent a fib on you like a bloodhound. Instead I survived my teenage years with partial truths that rang just true enough to go undetected, but not so complete that I didn't get to keep the best parts to myself.

"We had things to talk about," I say, keeping my voice level. Unaffected.

She hums softly, nodding to acknowledge my statement. Sometimes I wonder if she was a garda in a past life with the way she can interrogate you with silence, letting it drag out so long you feel the urge to fill it.

Not today. I look down at her with equal intensity, reminding myself that I'm an adult and I don't owe my mam an explanation for staying out late.

Footsteps rumble above us, and a door slams closed.

"That'll be Niamh with Leona," she says, drawing out Leo's name longer than necessary.

"That it will be."

Her pale-blonde eyebrow arches, unimpressed, when Niamh turns the corner on the landing and comes thundering down. Right on her heels is Leo, looking brighter than I've seen her since the day she showed up on my doorstep. Her hair flows freely, dusting her shoulders with every step. She glances up at me, and though that heaviness still fills her gaze, there's a bit of light there, too, vying for control.

The air I was inhaling stalls in my throat. My heartbeat trips over itself. Leo pauses on the top step, hand dangling on the railing, bottom lip caught in the vise grip of her pearlescent teeth.

Mam clears her throat, and we're forced to break our eye

contact to look at her. Niamh has disappeared past her into the kitchen, unbothered by the electricity sparking through the air.

"I'm happy for you two," Mam says, causing Leo to blush and me to start grasping at straws. She holds up a hand to cut me off. "I don't need to know the details. Just wanted you to know you're not sly." She gives me a pointed look. "Never have been."

She pivots on her heel and marches back into the kitchen, leaving Leo and me alone in the hall.

Leo starts down the steps again, slower this time without a kid to chase after, and maintains my stare the whole way. When she enters my orbit, I catch that citrus scent first, followed by the soft gust of minty air that flows out of her lungs and tickles my face. Goose bumps prick my flesh. All the woman did was sigh, and every part of my body is leaping to attention.

Every. Damn. Part.

"How'd you sleep?" she asks, gaze flitting over my face, my chest, and farther down. I hope beyond hope that she can't see what's so obviously there.

"Don't know," I say, shaking my head. "Felt like something was missing."

She tucks her hair back as she flushes deeper, the pink reaching her ears the way it always did when I let her know how badly I wanted her. It's a part of her that remains the same, and I savor it in the midst of so much newness. Like the silver loop now piercing the rounded curve of her ear, twinkling in the dim hall light, that I reach out to touch.

Her spine straightens, and she looks me dead in the eye, that red tint to her cheeks making her blue eyes sparkle. She's wearing a little makeup, I realize, and it only serves to make her more perfect than anyone has the right to be.

"Ask me how *I* slept."

Her tone, the demure fire burning in her irises, makes me perk up. My hand falls back to my side in a closed fist. "How did you sleep?" I rasp.

A half smile. A delicate hand, grasping my bicep first and then trailing up to my shoulder, which she uses as a perch to pull herself onto her tiptoes. She leans into me, bringing her lips to my ear the same way I did to her last night.

"Soundly," she whispers, and it carries both the heat of her expression and a layer of relief. "I dreamed of you."

Before I can respond or catch my breath or grab her waist and drag her into the living room and make love to her against the dusty old books, she turns and lets herself into the kitchen, leaving me gasping in the hall.

Chapter Twenty-One

Leona

My Darling Poppy,

I'm in love with your daddy.

I always have been—always will be, I'm sure—
in love with him. It never went away, even after all
this time. Even after I met Nick and fell into a
simple kind of love and tried to build a life that
didn't revolve around the center of my universe. Nick
was a different planet, someone else's sun, but he
did what he could for the time that he was mine.
You can love more than one person at once, baby.
You can be a good person and a bad person at the
same time, too.

When I was pregnant with you, I had to go to
the hospital a lot more often than women with
healthy pregnancies. They took measurements, let
student nurses into my ultrasound room, studied
every inch of me from the inside out. For a lot of

them, I was a learning opportunity. A cautionary tale. Never a person, never a mother in mourning.

There was one ultrasound tech, though, who saw me as more. She was young, with soft brown skin that smelled of cherry-blossom lotion and an even softer voice. She believed the best in me, and the best in you, too. Every time she located your heart-beat, she'd announce it with the same amount of relief, masked with a blanket of joy. She'd often smile-frown at me and say, "You're so selfless, love, carrying that baby even when you know how it'll go."

I wasn't what she said, though. I was selfish even then. Selfishly hoping you'd prove them all wrong, sweet girl. That you'd defy the odds. Sometimes when you were especially active at night, I'd imagine you'd be born healthy. Imagine calling up Callum and saying, "You'll never believe it, but we have a baby!" And he'd bring us home to the rolling green hills and the foxgloves and we'd be happy there, the three of us.

But you didn't, honey. You did exactly what you told us you would do. You were honest like that, right from the start. You must get that from your daddy.

I haven't be—

"Leona?" Niamh calls. She's peeking a single green eye through the cracked door, studying me where I sit at the writing desk.

I drop the pen and use it as a bookmark, close the journal around it, and shift in my chair. I take a deep breath and let it flow out before saying, "You can come in, Niamh."

She shoulders the door open and steps into the room, casting her gaze along the flowered wallpaper and high beams, then on my clothes hanging in the open wardrobe across the room and a particularly messy bed that I'm suddenly embarrassed for her to see.

"Daddy doesn't make me fix the bed either," she muses, padding over to it and hopping up. She perches at the edge with her feet dangling and smiles at me.

"Oh, he doesn't?" I can't help it; I smile, too. Despite the particularly dark bit of memory lane I was just traveling down, Niamh's presence diverts my path, and now I'm seeing another, more pleasant recollection. "That's probably because he doesn't like making his bed, either."

Her eyes go big, and her mouth forms a small O, which shows off the gap in her front teeth. "How did you know?"

I shrug, dismissing the mental image of Callum's messy room in the manor where we both lived. "Lucky guess."

She shakes her head, completely amazed. Kids are so easily impressed. Peering past me to the desk, she asks, "Whatcha writing?"

I glance at the journal and my smile falters. "I was writing a letter to someone."

"Your daddy?"

The edges of the spring flowers on its cover begin to blur. "No, not my daddy."

"Your…mam?" Her voice is soft, hesitant. It draws my gaze back to her even as it turns my heart on its head.

"No, Niamh, not my mom either."

Her eyebrows, which had been perched high on her forehead, scrunch together in response. "I don't have a mam."

I cross my arms over the arched back of the wooden dining-chair-turned-desk-chair and rest my chin on the apex. "I'm sorry." I may not know children, at least anymore, but I do know grief. Perhaps in this way I have something to offer her. "I know it's not the same, but you do have Siobh—your granny. I never had grandparents growing up, and I would've loved to hang out with a cool grandma every day."

She giggles, but her gaze falls to the floor. "I don't really miss her. I don't know her."

She doesn't have a lot of words, at almost five years old, to explain how she feels, but those simple ones crack something open inside me. Turn the air in my lungs to needles that prick me with every breath.

"Hey," I say, drawing her gaze back to me. It's misty and wide-open, those golden rings shining in a sea of green. It's like looking into a warped mirror, where I'm younger and things are different colors, but the feeling is the same. "She really missed out, because I know you, and I think you're pretty great."

She grins and wipes at her eyes with the backs of her hands. "You're pretty great, too." Her head tilts the way her father's does sometimes when he's curious. "Are you somebody's mam?"

I press my lips together, swallowing the thick sorrow that rises into my throat. There's pride, too, underneath. Pride that I am, in fact, someone's mom. But I can't explain it to Niamh, and I certainly can't explain it to Callum. Not yet.

It's what I was trying to tell Poppy. That I had the moment to be honest, to come clean, and I didn't take it. Because I'm selfish.

Because I'm afraid.

I shake my head, loosening the bolts of worry and tension and sadness. Niamh takes it for an answer and hoists herself off the bed. "The roast is ready. Granny sent me to get you."

"Oh good," I reply, rising from the chair. "I'm starving."

She swings open my door and launches down the stairwell, frightening me with her speed. I bound after her, barely remembering to yank the door shut behind me. She's already to the bottom floor when I round the landing above it, but I stop in my tracks when I see two sets of eyes trained on me as I take to the last flight.

Niamh disappears into the kitchen, past Siobhan, who stands guarding the doorway with her hands perched on her hips, but all I can see is Callum. He's leaning against the wall, arms crossed over his chest, which is heaving with the effort to breathe. A deep, velvety pleasure licks at my spine when I realize my mere presence is making it hard for him to take in air.

His lips part softly, and I draw my own in between my teeth. His hair has this permanent windswept look, showing off the various shades of gold and buttery yellow and even undertones of rich brown. Beneath his glasses, I watch his gaze trace the length of me and come up sparkling with satisfaction. He's wearing a tight-fitting quarter-zip sweater in a shade of cream that hides no contour, conceals no muscle.

"I'm happy for you two," Siobhan says, cutting into the tunnel vision I've developed for her son. I blush, glancing at her just as she turns to Callum and adds, "I don't need to know the details, just wanted you to know you're not sly." She murmurs something else to him that I can't quite make out and then turns to the kitchen door, casting a wink in my direction before disappearing inside.

I force my body to move once more, one foot in front of the other bringing me closer to where Callum waits for me by the kitchen door. He's watching every movement my body makes, and I feel myself preen at his attention, desperate to let that glow warm every part of me. The dream I had last night, which resulted in my messy bedding, returns to the forefront of my mind, replacing the sadness I'd been wallowing in before Niamh marched into my room.

It was the first time I'd dreamed of anything other than the baby and actually remembered it after waking up. In the cool, silvery winter sunlight I woke, the taste of Callum's tongue lingering on my own. The scent of rain and soap and sweat filled my nostrils, and my breath came in shallow gasps.

Before I know it, I'm in front of him, peering up into the endless fields of evergreen grass that reside in his eyes. A lazy half smile tugs at his lips, and it emphasizes the scar in his chin. I want to lick it so badly I have to bite my tongue or I'm afraid that I might.

"How'd you sleep?" I ask. It's the first thing that comes to mind. I can feel the heat rising to the tips of my ears, can see his gaze cut straight to the telltale marker of my embarrassment, so I take a moment to focus on anything else. Unfortunately for me, that focus falls straight to his body, which is now so close.

Bad decision. Very, very bad decision.

"Don't know," he replies, his voice rough like he's been gargling gravel. There's an unmistakable ridge pressing into his dark chinos. I force my gaze upward, but I'm salivating. "Felt like something was missing."

His gaze tracks my hand tucking my hair behind my ear, and then he reaches for me and my heartbeat stutters. I feel the warmth of his fingertips on the shell of my ear, where my cartilage piercing loops through. When we lock eyes, there are wildfires in that forest of green.

His words, and his obvious desire, fill me with a sense of bravery I don't normally feel. I straighten my spine. I let him see me, without folding in on myself, and wear the depth of my longing for him on my sleeve. It's the least I can do. The most honest I can be.

"Ask me how I slept."

The man actually gulps, swaying away from the wall like I've knocked him unsteady. "How did you sleep?"

This bold version of me reaches for him, touches the scalding skin of his arm and travels upward, taking note of the way his breath hitches when I dig my nails into his shoulder and pull myself onto my tiptoes.

My lips find his ear, the way his did mine last night, and I decide it's time to return the favor. To torture him the way he tortured me.

"Soundly," I whisper, letting my breath drift down his neck. "I dreamed of you."

Then I slip away and through the door, mostly because I'm truly a coward, but also because that responding flare of heat in his eyes makes me feel a little bit like prey.

And as the predator, he gives chase.

Just as I've let the door fall closed behind me and Padraig's gaze has cut to me from across the room where he's loading his plate, Callum clambers into the kitchen. I force myself not to look over my shoulder at him, but from the way Padraig and Siobhan's eyes go wide, I know he must look absolutely feral.

There are two seats left at the table. I sit with my back to the door, and yet I could tell you every movement Callum makes to take his place opposite me; I'm that attuned to his body. I'm that on edge.

It's my first time joining them for a Sunday dinner, what with the storm last week and my arrival canceling it the week before. The latter I was informed of later, by a very tipsy Padraig at Dermot's pub.

"Quiet night at the inn?" Padraig asks, choking a bit on the forced pleasantry.

"Only a handful of guests, and most are out to dinner," Siobhan replies, stabbing at a potato with her fork.

Callum hasn't moved a muscle since he sat down. His plate is still empty, and his gaze tracks every move I make to fill mine. There's a promise in his eyes. A promise that while he does intend to take things slow, as he said, when the time comes, he'll be ready to devour me.

"Ahem," Siobhan says, not clearing her throat so much as snapping the taut line anchoring Callum to me. "I already prepared the food. Any more steam between you two and it'll be overcooked."

Padraig bursts into laughter, and Niamh follows suit, not wanting to be left out even as she's glancing around in confusion. A giggle bubbles up my throat next, and then it blooms into full-blown belly laughs. Siobhan snickers at her own joke, and dawn breaks over Callum's face as a smile lights up his features.

Just like that, the trembling energy between us dissolves. Not gone but tucked away. For now.

We eat our dinner in between bouts of laughter, whether it's a clever innuendo from Padraig or Siobhan or a hilarious joke from Niamh. When we finish, my belly and heart are equally full, and it's a sensation so intensely lovely that it nearly brings me to tears. Padraig challenges Niamh to a round of checkers in front of the fireplace, which she accepts with a gleaming grin.

"Take it easy on him," Callum cautions, smoothing a hand over her hair. Her braid has nearly come completely undone, so much so that I only know it was originally a braid because it's her go-to style. She and Padraig race down the hall, and Siobhan encourages us to go be spectators while she cleans up the meal.

"You cooked; I can clean!" I argue, but she's already shaking her head.

"You clean everything else in this house," she says. "Let me do this. It does my heart good."

I press my lips together, determined to disagree, but she makes a shooing motion at me. Callum grips my elbow and tugs me toward the door with a wink. "Come on; they need an audience."

I let myself be dragged away, too distracted by the feeling of his firm hand to put up much of a fight.

I'm trying to remember how to have a normal conversation. How to do anything but drool over his strong, capable hands. Scrambling until we're halfway down the hall, and I spew the first thing that comes to mind. "Why do you continue to braid Niamh's hair if you're so bad at it?"

Oh perfect, an insult. *What's wrong with me?*

To his credit, Callum just laughs, taking it in stride. "I know they aren't the prettiest plaits in the world, but they make her happy. Believe it or not, they used to be a lot worse. But she saw them on a lady in a store one day and couldn't stop talking about them. I started watching video tutorials online to figure them out."

I hum amusement, ducking under his arm as he holds the door open for me. I catch a whiff of his deodorant, and it feels oddly intimate, like I've caught him fresh out of a shower.

The mental image sends a thrill down my spine.

Padraig and Niamh are sitting crisscross on the floor in front of the fire, contemplating whether her double skip was in fact legal, when we enter the room. They don't even notice our presence. They don't even notice the oxygen has left this space.

Callum presses his hand to my lower back, guiding me toward the couch where we sat during the storm. How has it been only a week?

His words on that night drift back to me on the tendrils of heat wafting out of the hearth. *We're not finished here.* Glancing over at him, across the polite amount of space he left between us when we sat, I can't help but hope he was right.

Chapter Twenty-Two

Callum

It takes every bit of willpower imaginable for me to leave Leo the hell alone. For days, every time I see her, I'm nearly drowned in the desire to touch her in any way possible. I feel like I'm in secondary school again, where just the brush of Aisling Murphy's hand against mine could get me hard. When Leo glances at me from across the kitchen or greets me while bent over to tuck sheets onto a bed when I pass the open doorway, it's nearly impossible not to march into that room and ruin the pretty bed she's made ourselves.

But I'm taking things slow, I remind myself. Even if it's excruciating.

When I've just about hit my limit on self-restraint, the universe intervenes. A shipment gets misplaced somewhere between China and Ireland, and Uncle Darren tasks me with solving the problem. I'm up to my eyeballs in middle-of-the-night phone calls to make up for the time difference and hours-long computer work that makes my head feel like it's about to explode. After a few days I finally locate the misplaced shipment in Turkey and get it rerouted to its rightful destination in Dublin. Darren sends me a curt "Well done, lad" email, which is the highest praise I'll get from my mother's stern older brother.

I stand from my desk, every bone in my body crying out in relief, and slam my laptop shut. With the amount of overtime I've already worked this week, I've more than earned the right to knock off a bit early today. I'm just about to grab my keys and drive over to get Niamh when, for reasons I won't even admit to myself, I reroute to the shower. After a quick refresh, I retrieve styling gel from where it's rotting in the back of my medicine cabinet. A few globs make my hair look slightly more tamed. My hand hovers over the contact lenses I rarely if ever use anymore, but I think better of it, instead swiping an unopened bottle of cologne that Mam bought me for Christmas last year off the counter and misting the air to walk through.

It's probably the most ridiculous twenty minutes I've ever spent in my adult life, but when I load into the car and pull away, I feel a giddiness of anticipation that wipes away any embarrassment.

Bridge Street Bed-and-Breakfast is bustling with activity when I arrive. Guests loiter in the halls, chatting with one another and nursing drinks. The door to the living room is flung open, and more couples and families are scattered about, some reading various titles sourced from the bookshelves and others taking a note from Niamh's book and dominating their friends in checkers. I scan the room but come up empty, so I continue down the hall.

In the kitchen Mam and Leo are playing bartender for two women with easy smiles and friendly brown gazes so similar they have to be related somehow. They all glance over at me and then quickly go back to the task at hand, except for Leo. Her gaze remains with me, crackling with the same tension I've been suppressing all week. Hot licks of pride stroke my spine, making me stand taller under the spotlight of her gaze.

"Not going to greet your mam, huh, son?" Mam rolls her

eyes in commiseration with the woman she's handing a margarita to, complete with the sloppiest salt rim I've ever laid eyes on. "I swear, we raise them, and then they wipe their hands of us, content to forget we changed their nappies all those years."

The woman grabs the drink from Mam's outstretched hand and clucks her tongue. "Don't I know it. My children will sooner put me in a home than change mine when the time comes." She turns to me, shakes her head, and waggles an outstretched finger at me. Her wrist is laden with silver bangles that make her chastisement sound more like music. "You be nice to your mam," she says with a thick Northern accent. "You put her through hell that you can't even remember."

Her sister? Cousin? takes a simple Jameson and ginger ale from Leo, who has ducked her head, though I can see the round swells of her cheeks from the grin she's trying to hide. The friend links arms with my admonisher and raises her glass to me. "Don't let Naomi beat you down. She's only bitter that her son forgot her birthday."

Naomi softens, leaning on the other woman for support, and then pretends to wail. "I'm all but dead to him. I'll just wither away to nothing!"

"See," the woman says. "Dramatic."

They continue tittering at one another as they exit the kitchen, joining the other guests in the living room.

"What's all this anyway?" I ask before hooking an arm around Mam's neck and planting a kiss on her head. Leo peeks up at me, her gaze roving over my gelled hair before meeting mine and raising her eyebrows. I shrug and then release my mother. "And where's my kid? Don't tell me she's after forgetting me or I'll *wither away to nothing!*"

"Leona had the lovely idea to host a cocktail hour for our guests to start the weekend a bit early." Mam pinches Leo's side affectionately. "And she's off somewhere playing with one of the guests' children." She waves her hand dismissively at the ether.

"You came up with all this?" I right the frames of my glasses as if it will bring Leo into focus. But she already is, sharper than anything else in this room. It's disorienting, and yet I can't look away.

She presses her lips together in a polite smile. "Just thought it'd be nice for our guests."

"*Your* guests?" I ask, my heart skipping a beat. "Spoken like someone who plans on sticking around awhile."

Her gaze flickers from me to Mam like she's going to get in trouble for what she said, but Mam looks as thrilled as I feel. She loops an arm around Leo's waist and hugs her close, smiling as she tips her head against Leo's. "You stay as long as you like, Leona."

She melts into my mother for just a moment before stepping away abruptly and sweeping margarita salt off the counter with a broad stroke. "I'm just glad they seem to like it."

I'm tempted to grab her by the shoulders and shake her, to tell her it's okay to let go of whatever it is that's holding her back. I have to remind myself that it takes time to let yourself be vulnerable. Something I know better than most. So instead I just offer her a genuine smile when she meets my eyes once more, and hope it's another drop to refill her well.

Shrieking that I've become numb to over the years pierces the silence as Niamh comes storming into the kitchen, followed by a little boy around her age with vibrant red hair and skin that burns at the thought of the sun. He tags her just before she can cut outside to the garden, and then bolts away now that it's Niamh's turn to give chase.

"No, you don't," I say, hooking an arm around her waist and scooping her into the air. "Time to go."

She continues running—which looks more like swimming

with the way she's flapping—for a few seconds before collapsing dramatically into a rag doll. "I was winning!"

"No, you weren't!" the boy retorts.

"Say thank you for playing."

She does as I instructed, and the boy stalks off to find his parents. I settle her onto her own two feet, and she crosses her arms over her chest with a pout. "I *was* winning."

"And I believe you," I say, smoothing a hand over her hair. "But I've got a surprise that I thought you'd like more than kicking some poor lad's arse."

"Callum," Mam scolds.

"Bum," I correct.

Mam shakes her head while Niamh and Leo giggle. Leo's wiping off the whiskey bottle and recapping it but smiling at my daughter all the while. It does worse things to me than watching her bend over to make a bed.

Niamh practically dances from foot to foot. "What's the surprise?"

"Wouldn't be much of a surprise if I told you, would it now?"

"Would too!"

"Would not!" I counter. She relents with a heavy sigh more worthy of a teenager than a small child. Man, I'll be in for it when those years come. I offer her my hand and she takes it, and then I steel myself for part two of my plan.

When I glance up at Leo, she's watching Niamh with a gaze that's unreadable. Maybe in another life, where we spent the last twelve years together, I'd be able to read it as easily as plain English. But in this one, I'm at a severe disadvantage. One only time will make up for, I'm realizing. And time is what I intend to get.

"Would you want to join us, then, Leo?" I ask like the thought has just occurred to me.

Mam smirks, but she tears off a piece of soda bread and shoves it into her mouth to hide it.

Leo returns from wherever her mind had drifted off to, glancing again between Mam and me. "Oh, I couldn't. I've got to help Siobhan."

"Nonsense, go on," Mam says, waving a hand. "Everyone'll be going off to dinner soon anyway. You can help me clean up tonight." She looks pointedly at me but continues directing her voice to Leo. "If you come home, that is."

"I will."

"She will," I say, speaking over Leo.

We glance at each other, laughing nervously. Niamh calls jinx.

"Then it's settled." Mam wipes her hands off on her pants, smiling at both of us and then gesturing toward the door when no one moves. "Go on, then."

We all jolt forward at once, heading for the exit. Niamh chatters excitedly about what the surprise could be, and Leo listens politely. When we make it to the car, I load Niamh into the back seat and then hold the passenger door open for Leo. She stops between me and the car, her body so close I can see her chest rise and fall with her breathing. The pendant she always wears dips under her neckline, and when my gaze traces its journey, I see the lace of her white bra strap peeking through the wide knit of her coffee-colored sweater, and all the blood drains from my head.

"Where are we going?" she breathes, training her gaze on my throat rather than my face.

"You'll see," I say, and then I allow myself one spectacular mercy. I rest my hand against the base of her spine and guide her forward.

"We're skipping rocks!" Niamh squeals, bolting from the car the moment it slides into park.

She bounds across the dirt lot in no time, coming to a stop where it turns to pebbled shoreline. I glance at Leo, and she's smiling. It's slight, but it's there, and it splinters my heart into fractions.

"Ready?"

She nods excitedly, and we exit the vehicle together.

As we make our way over to where Niamh is already tossing rocks across the surface like a seasoned pro, I can't stop myself from stealing glances of Leo out of the corner of my eye. I'm waiting for some flicker of recognition, a widening of the eyes or for her mouth to pop open with a soft, *Oh.*

It looks the same, this place, as it did all those years ago when I brought her here to teach her how to drive a manual transmission. The lot is large and mostly empty, save for the occasional fisherman that posts up by the lake. It seemed the perfect place to teach her without witnesses, as was her request.

I never considered how at risk it put my car of being sunk in the lake until afterward, when we were breathless from laughing so hard and my transmission was halfway to being shot. Even after an hour of guiding her through the motions, she could barely get the car going without stalling. A passenger princess she was destined to be.

If I focus hard enough, I can still feel the soft warmth of her hand underneath mine as I guided her to first gear, then second. Out of the corner of my eye, I see her hand flex, and I know that she's there in the memory with me.

When she glances up at me, I'm already staring, and she looks away quickly, but a suppressed smile forms all the same.

"Leona, come watch! See how far I can throw them?"

"I see!" she calls; then she lowers her voice for only me to hear. "It's a miracle she still calls me by my name, despite your terrible influence."

My hand covers my heart. "I call you by your name!"

Her eyes roll so hard in my direction, I'm concerned that it might hurt. I balk in mock innocence, but then I lean in close, invading her space, as we come to a stop at the shoreline. I can smell her shampoo. I can see the rings of gold in her irises. It's all too much but not enough.

"Selfishly, I'd like to keep your nickname to myself."

"Wouldn't want it to catch on," she murmurs, glancing at my lips. "I hate it anyway."

"No"—I take her hand in mine, featherlight yet anchoring —"you don't."

She shakes her head. "You cocky bast—"

"Your turn!" Niamh interjects, shoving a flattened pebble into Leo's other hand. If she sees the ones we've joined together, she doesn't comment. "You know how, right, Leona?"

Leona crouches down to her level, removing her hand from mine, and I miss it instantly. It's dangerous, this need for her. I know it, and yet I can't find it in me to hit the brakes.

"You know what? It's been a really long time. Why don't you teach me how?"

Niamh practically glistens with joy as she takes Leo's outstretched palm and folds it around the rock just so, angling her pointer finger along the smooth ridge and anchoring her thumb on the flat top. Then she hurls an example throw, which skips an impressive five times before sinking into the center of the lake.

"Now you go," Niamh says, smiling at her protégée.

"Here goes nothing." With that, Leo lets the little rock loose, and it plops dramatically into the water and never resurfaces.

I bite my lower lip to suppress my laughter, and Leo plants her hands on her hips, glaring at the water.

Niamh stares at the spot where the rock disappeared, and then gives a world-weary sigh too big for her tiny body. "This is going to take more work than I thought."

Between her drama and Leo's disappointment, I can't hold back the laughter anymore. It rolls out of me in waves, and both ladies glare at me for different reasons.

"Hey, no one's born an expert," Leo groans, shoving my shoulder. It surprises me and promptly knocks me off-balance. Before I can catch myself, I go tipping into the frigid water, landing on my knees.

"Oh, now you've done it," I growl. Niamh screams, and Leo joins in. Both of them run toward the car, but I'm faster than my sedentary job gives me credit for. I hook an arm around Leo's waist in a matter of seconds and then I'm dragging her back toward the water kicking and screaming while Niamh doubles over in a fit of giggles.

"Please! No! It's too cold!" she pleads.

"Shoulda thought about that before you pushed me." I splash into the water, already wet up to my hips from the fall, and then she really starts to squirm. "Better plug your nose."

"Don't you dar—"

But I dare.

I let go of her, determined to drop her into the water, but she's cunning when she wants to be. She clings to my arm, dragging me down with her. The cold zings up my spine, electrifying me, and I shoot to my feet, sputtering water just as Leo does the same.

"Bastard," she says, finally finishing her insult from earlier. She wipes the water from her eyes before fixing me with a glare, but a light has come on in their depths. A flame that I'm determined to feed kindling.

Her clothes, that knitted sweater and slim-fitting jeans, are slick to her body, and I'm suddenly not cold anymore.

Giving her my best shit-eating grin, I say, "This look suits you."

With a warning splash, she replies, "Don't push it."

We trudge over to where Niamh stands at the edge of the water, arms crossed with a disapproving frown turning her into an admonishing mother rather than my child. She hates to get dirty, and she hates to be splashed. This behavior, as far as she's concerned, is unacceptable.

When I get close, she holds out a finger to keep me back. "I don't wanna get wet."

"Neither did I," Leo huffs, but it turns into a laugh. And then we're all laughing, two of us shivering, as we make our way back to the car.

The stars are just starting to wink at us in the darkening sky, and the evening breeze chills me to the bone, but the image of Leo doubled over with laughter—truly consumed by joy—for the first time since her return is enough to make my inevitable pneumonia-induced death worth it.

"Can we get takeaway?" Niamh asks, hopping into her booster seat.

"Sure, there's a shop on the corner up the road," I say.

Leo's eyes go wide as she joins us in the car after ringing out her hair as best she can. Her teeth are chattering to the same tune as mine, but at the sound of deep-fried food, she perks up. "Can we get a spice bag?"

"How could we not?"

"With garlic mayo and curry sauce?"

"Mixed together?" Niamh's lip curls around the question.

I roll my eyes. "That's just as disgusting as it was twelve years ago, but sure. We'll get all the sauces."

Niamh giggles, and Leo settles into her seat, satisfied. I rest my hand atop the gearshift, ready to get on the road. Just as I start to move toward first gear, Leo places her hand over mine, guiding me through the motions, and I know that she remembers. I'm realizing neither of us could've truly forgotten.

Chapter Twenty-Three

Leona

"What on earth are you cleaning now?"

I glance over at the doorway, where Siobhan is peeking in with her eyebrows scrunched together. Dusting my hands off on my cotton pajama bottoms, I check my work. The bookshelves have all been emptied and wiped down, and are now ready to be refilled. I'm surrounded by stacks of books that run the gambit from historical romance to bird watching, each sorted into their respective genre.

"The shelves were a bit dusty, and I thought it'd be easier for guests to find books to read if they were organized into categories."

She swipes at the sleep pooled in the corners of her eyes as she makes her way across the room. Her nightgown dusts the floor, its yellowing lace edges frayed from years of wear. A thick wool shawl is draped over her shoulders, and suddenly I realize how chilled I am.

Siobhan selects a tattered copy of *Pride and Prejudice* off the top of the romance stack, turning it over in her hands. "Do you not sleep well, Leona?"

The grandfather clock in the foyer chimes then, low and

resounding, punctuating her sentence. It's two in the morning. I've been at this for an hour.

I study my nails. Painting them was my first distraction. When that didn't work, I came downstairs. "Occasionally I have a hard time, and it's easier if I clean instead of tossing and turning in my bed."

Her head tilts to the side. "Is it something with the room? I could get you a space heater if it's too cold up there, or I think they make little machines nowadays that make noise if the house creaks too much for your liking—"

"The room is perfect, Siobhan," I interject. "It's not a new thing."

Concern couples with understanding, filling her features. "The divorce then?"

I scoff, more harshly than I intend. It doesn't go unnoticed. "It long predates the divorce."

"What did your ex-husband think of it?" She makes her way over to the couch and settles in, props an elbow on the back, and rests her chin in her palm so she can still see me, as if I'll disappear otherwise.

"He didn't," I mutter. I try to comb through the memories of our marriage, fuzzy as they seem even now, just a year out. Nick was kind, albeit disinterested. Our marriage was not an unhappy one, just a blissfully neutral bandage that patched up the gaping wound of my twenties. "Nick didn't know what he wanted, I think, and so he convinced himself he wanted me. Until the person he did want finally came along."

Alarm flashes in her gaze, but I wave a hand, dismissing her concern.

"It's okay. I'm truly happy for him," I say, and I mean it. When he told me he wanted a divorce, that he'd found someone else, someone that felt truly right, it only broke my heart because

I felt I'd failed someone yet again. It didn't break my heart to lose him.

She nods, accepting my sincerity for what it is.

"What is it that keeps you up, then, if I may be so intrusive?" Her tone is gentle, open to being shut down. The dim light cast from the fireplace softens her wrinkled features while making her gray hair shimmer. She looks ethereal, like a wise enchantress from one of the fantasy novels I'm now restacking in alphabetical order.

I don't know if it's the cocoon of night or her willingness to go unanswered, but I find myself wanting to offer her some truth, even if it is sparse and mostly useless.

"The way I left things with Callum still haunts me in a lot of ways." I offer a grim smile to the bookshelf, unable to face her while I speak. "He deserved better than I gave him."

"But you're here now," she replies, her voice laced with forgiveness that I could never offer myself. "That's got to count for something, right?"

My shoulders fall, the effort to hold them up suddenly impossible. The nightmares have gotten worse as Callum and I have gotten closer, leaving me raw and ragged at the edges, with tendrils of my resolve trailing behind me. I turn to her, taking in the genuine interest and compassion filling her expression. It makes me brave for just a moment. "You don't think it's too little, too late?"

She shakes her head. "No such thing." Her arm extends from where it was resting on the back of the couch, and then her hand is dangling in the space between us, palm up. I take it, and she cradles my hand gently, as though it is breakable. "Besides, as happy as he's been now that he's gotten over himself, I'd say you've more than made up for the way you left. You were young then, Leona. You've got to give yourself a little grace."

Tears prick at the backs of my eyes. I glance at the floor while blinking them away. I want so badly to accept her words, to let them wash over me and make me clean, but there are sins she doesn't know about. Ones I doubt she'd find as forgivable as simply cutting off contact with her son.

It hits me then, the fear of not only Callum's reaction but Siobhan's. I realize how deeply I respect her, how much I want her to respect me. To trust me. How will she feel when she realizes I kept the knowledge of her first granddaughter from her? How will she ever look at me the same way?

She won't. And it's something I need to accept. I can build these bonds all I want, but they are walls made of sand. When the tide comes in, when I finally tell the whole truth, they'll all be washed away.

"You're good for him, Leona, whether you believe that about yourself or not." She offers me a close-lipped smile when I finally face her again. "And you're certainly good for me." Her tone shifts, lightening up. "This place has never looked so clean or done so well, if I'm being honest. Callum has helped where he can, and I do my best with it, but you're really something special. This inn"—she gestures to the ceiling, and the rooms beyond it —"is my baby. The only thing that's ever been truly mine. After Callum's dad left, I spent those years in the city raising him as best I could. And his granda helped, giving us the summer cottage to escape to on the weekends. And then my brother, bless him, took Callum under his wing at work.

"But with him grown and gone, I had nowhere to pour myself into. Buying this place with the money my father left me when he passed was the first thing I ever did just for me. Not for my ex-husband, not for Callum. For Siobhan." She smiles. Her gaze is faraway, and I don't dare to interrupt, to break the enchantment. "I love it. And it does my heart good to have someone else love it just as much. Especially as I'm getting older. It's hard to keep up with it all."

She rubs her hands together, marveling at the wrinkles there. I wonder if the age surprises her as it creeps up, the way it does for me. I don't know when I began measuring my age as a yardstick from the date Poppy died, but for the past few birthdays all I could think was, *It's been ten years. Eleven years. Where did these gray hairs come from? How have I aged when my own reason for living never will?*

"Well," my voice croaks on the word, but I press on, "I'm honored to get the chance to help."

Now the smile is for me, a precious gift, and I tuck it away into my heart for the day when she will no longer look at me with such graciousness.

The air grows heavy around us, not like a weight but like water, the way floating in a pool feels the same as being held. I want to stretch that feeling out. I don't want to go back to my cold bed and nightmares.

Tentatively I push my luck. "What happened with Callum's dad, if you don't mind me asking?"

Whether it is a gift of the years that have passed or her own work to overcome it, or both, she barely reacts to the question. A wince that is hardly more than a blink, and then she's recovered.

I remember Callum telling me his dad wasn't in the picture, that he hadn't been for much of Callum's life, but I never pressed for more information. Questioning him felt like being offered a look at someone's wound and then jamming a finger into it. Which I guess is what I'm doing now, but the wound seems a lot less raw for Siobhan than it did for her son.

With a sigh, she pats the cushion next to her, and I come around to join her on the sofa, abandoning the remaining stacks of books.

"Callum was—is—my life. And now Niamh is, too. But sometimes people stumble into being parents, rather than planning for it and desiring it with their whole hearts. And when that happens, half the people stumble into the purpose of their existence, and the other half fall into a role they didn't know they never wanted until it was theirs.

"I knew I wanted to be a mam, and Callum's father obliged, but when it came time to be a parent, he found the suit didn't quite fit." Her expression sours around a rueful frown. "In fairness, once that boy came along, I gave all of myself to him. I didn't leave anything else for my marriage. That wore on his father. Can't say I blame him."

A pang in my heart hits without warning, stealing my breath away. I recognize myself in her words, and it's a difficult mirror image to behold. "You were just doing what any good mom would do."

Her gaze is haunted as it holds mine intently. "I had my reasons. Some he understood, and some that only made sense to me." Those words hang in the air between us, heavy and full. I'm almost certain if I reached out, I could gather them in my hands. "I'm sure you had your reasons, too."

The way she's looking at me, like she can see all the way through to the ugliness, sends ice running through my veins. A shiver skitters down my spine, and she offers me her shawl, which I decline. "I think I'm actually going to head up to bed." I fake a yawn that turns into a real one. I'm hoping I can do the same thing with sleep. "Thank you for checking on me. I'm sorry for waking you."

She pats my knee, a claddagh ring that I've never noticed before glinting on her finger. "No need to be sorry. You're not the only one who has things that keep her up at night."

She rises from the couch and pads across the intricately designed rug, then the hardwood floor, the *swish swish* of her nightgown highlighting her steps. Halfway into the dark corridor, she glances over her shoulder, holding on to the doorjamb for support. "Try to get some rest, Leona. You deserve it."

With that, she disappears. I douse the fire, waiting for each shimmering ember to die off, remembering a city skyline that twinkled in the same way from my vantage point high on a mountain. When at last it goes dark, I make my way upstairs, still unable to believe her.

Chapter Twenty-Four

Callum

"Would I be seeing a lot more of my son because you love me so much," Mam says by way of greeting, "or because a certain brunette upstairs has captured your attention?"

I scowl at her, grateful that Niamh has already escaped to the neighbors to check on the kittens so she's not privy to this conversation. I cross my arms over my chest and give her a measured look. "Actually, I've been secretly cataloging every antique in this place so I have an idea how much money I'll be making when you pass on."

She slaps the towel she was using to cover fresh bread against the counter, hard enough that I'm certain she'd rather it was my head. "Callum Walsh, you take that back!"

"Ask stupid questions," I say, reaching to pinch a piece of bread off and barely escaping with my hand still attached. "Get stupid answers."

"Imagine if I'd said that to you when you were in your 'why' phase. Why is the sky blue? Why are the trees tall?" She counts them off on her fingers. "I've humored a lot of stupid questions, son."

"I'd hardly call questions about environmental science stupid."

She grumbles something, but not loud enough for me to hear. I take it as a victory.

"Anyway," I say, still keeping a healthy distance between myself and that weaponized towel. "Thank you for watching Niamh today. I owe you one. Maybe I'll sell off one of these antiques and buy you something nice."

She glares at me, unamused, so I shrug and head for the exit. "Tough crowd."

Before I can shut the kitchen door behind me, she calls, "Callum?"

I turn, half expecting a ball of raw dough to be flung at me. It wouldn't be the first time. But instead her expression has softened, the ravine of a wrinkle between her brows dissecting her eyes.

"What's the story, Mam?"

"Be careful with her," she says, pointing at the ceiling. We both know who *her* is; she doesn't have to explain. "I think she's been through a lot more than either of us realize."

"What makes you think that?" I ask, though from the look on her face, she knows I'm hedging. So I'm not the only one who's sensed it, that sadness in Leo.

"Sometimes you can just tell," she says with a sigh, and then she goes back to kneading the bread, her shoulders slumped beneath the weight of her suspicions.

With a quick jolt of my head that barely counts as a nod, I duck out of the room, not allowing myself to exhale until I'm halfway up the first flight of stairs. Mam's words stick in my head like an annoying jingle; I already know they'll be there all day.

In a way, it's a comfort to know I'm not the only one who sees it. I'm not crazy. But it also worries me, and in some dark corner of my heart there's a twinge of jealousy. That my mam gets to be around her 24-7. That she's privy to thoughts of Leo's that I've not yet earned access to.

When I reach the second floor, the door to the bathroom is propped open and, to my surprise, Leo is inside, giving the shower a wash. A memory of the first day I ran into her here, soaking wet from the shower with her breasts visible through the thin layer of her white T-shirt, lodges in the forefront of my mind. She senses my presence, turning toward me. It's all I can do to keep my gaze from dropping to her chest, searching for her dark nipples pebbled beneath damp fabric.

"Callum, you're here early. And on a Saturday." Her tone is polite, borderline customer service. It's not the way I want to hear my name on her lips. I'd rather it be punctuated by a moan or a sigh or…

God, what is wrong with me? I shift my weight, trying to get comfortable in my suddenly snug pants.

Her eyebrows rise, beckoning for me to speak. I swallow thickly, finally freeing up enough space in my throat for my voice to pass through. "Speak for yourself, cleaning this early on a Saturday morning. Do you ever sleep?"

I meant it as a joke, but she winces, and guilt immediately pools in my gut. I scramble for a way to fix it, my mouth opening and then closing, but she puts a hand up to stop me. "It's okay." The corners of her lips turn down, and she tilts her head to study me. Her chest rises and falls on a deep crest of breath before she looks back at the task at hand. She's resumed scrubbing when she adds, "You've seen what the dreams do anyway. Not like it's a secret."

The night of the storm flashes in my mind. I've been so focused on the dream of *me* that she mentioned having, that I forgot about the one I practically had to pull her out of by force. For a second I worry that I'm the star of the nightmares, too. Then I remind myself not to be a self-centered prick.

I lean a shoulder against the doorframe, watching quietly as she rinses the shower walls and then steps out, her bare feet landing on the towel she's left spread on the floor as a makeshift mat. Her toenails are painted with a bright pink polish that matches her fingers, I realize, and it's the kind of intimate detail that overwhelms my senses, like finding out her bra and panties match.

Now there's a mental image.

Shaking my head, I get myself back on track. We need fresh air and open roads and anything else to clear the fog that fills my brain. If we stay here any longer, I'll be tempted to do something I shouldn't, especially with my daughter liable to walk in at any moment.

"Erm, so." She looks up at me from where she's been drying the stray water splatters off her legs. She's wearing neon-orange gym shorts, and they make her olive-toned skin look especially dark in comparison. I gulp. "I was thinking. You've been here nearly a month now, and we haven't taken a single adventure together."

Her eyes go wide, the blue impossible and endless. "An adventure?"

I nod, puffing out my chest a bit. I knew this was what she needed, what *we* needed. The fact that, even after a dozen years, I can accurately guess what will make her happy is enough to fill my heart with warm pride. "There are two sausage rolls in the car with your name on them."

"An adventure *and* sausage rolls?" She gasps, slapping a hand against her heart. "Is it my birthday?"

I pretend to check a watch that doesn't exist. "I don't know, I didn't think it was March yet, but I could be wrong."

Her mouth parts ever so slightly, and she blinks once. Twice. "You remembered when my birthday is?"

An ache like a wildfire spreads through my chest, making the next inhale nearly impossible. How little did she think she mattered to me, that I would forget her birthday? Did I not make it clear how much I cared?

The devil on my shoulder wants to know if that's why she walked away. If she didn't think there was anyone she was leaving behind who cared about being left.

With a shiver, all those thoughts splinter and disintegrate. Those days are over and done. What we're doing now is building something new and precious. Something that cannot be so easily broken. I want to believe it. I have to.

"Of course I remember," I croak. I offer her my hand, and she takes it, allowing herself to be led out of the bathroom. I pull her toward the stairs, and all the way up to her bedroom, opening the door to let us in. Early morning sunlight has spilled into the room, casting its beams along that atrocious floral wallpaper I never could convince Mam to replace. The bed is rumpled but made, like she set the covers into place and then sat atop them. The wardrobe is open, and I feel the intense urge to cross the room and thumb through each blouse, each pair of pants. The fabrics that get to touch the parts of Leo that I burn for.

She steps past me into the room, crossing over to the wardrobe. As if she can read my thoughts, she runs a hand along the hangers, pausing on each piece before going on to the next. When her hand lands on a baby blue sweater that I know will set her eyes alight, she removes it from the hanger, tossing it onto the bed. Then she does the same with a pair of jeans.

Her gaze finds mine, and it's twinkling with amusement. Both thumbs hook into the waistband of her shorts, and she raises an eyebrow in question. "I have to change."

Without breaking eye contact, I reach behind me, push the door shut, and then collapse against it.

She's pulled the top half of her hair back into a clip, leaving her ears exposed. I watch as the telltale flush creeps up her neck, beneath the diamond studs she's wearing, all the way to that tiny silver hoop.

The shorts come down painstakingly slow, over the plains of hard muscle that made her thighs my favorite place to grab, a solid anchor to hold on to when I was driving myself deep into her body. They fall into a puddle of fabric around her ankles, and when I finally allow my gaze to rise to what has been revealed, the sight of black lace panties barely covering what they're meant to sends a rush of blood straight to my dick.

"Leo," I groan, unable to mask the desire in my tone, "I'm going to have to look away for the next part, or we'll never make it out of this room."

Her lower lip pokes out slightly, letting her disappointment show, before a heavy sigh follows the gesture. "You're probably right." She turns to face the wardrobe, thinking she's doing me a favor, and then begins to raise her shirt over her head. All I see is the perfectly round swell of each ass cheek covered by black lace before I force myself to look away.

There's a writing desk in the corner, and a floral journal resting on its surface. It so closely matches the wallpaper that I find myself chuckling. Between the rustles of fabric being dragged over skin that I'd much prefer she left uncovered, Leo asks, "What are you laughing at?"

"Not you, love." I shake my head at no one. "Never you. I was just thinking this journal you have matches the decor—"

"My what?" There's an edge to her voice. Before I can answer, she's across the room, now fully clothed save for those pink-painted toes. She places herself between me and the desk. "About those sausage rolls…"

I take her narrow hip into my grasp, pulling her flush against me so she can feel exactly what the show she put on does to me. She sucks in a breath of air, eyes going heavy-lidded as she gazes up at me. I want nothing more than to cover her mouth with mine, to taste the air she'll inevitably breathe out, but I only allow myself the gift of her body pressed against mine. I note every curve and swell and valley, wishing I could imprint the feeling of it on my mind and recall it at any time.

Leaning in close until our lips are nearly touching, I whisper, "No need to be embarrassed about your diary." Then, before she can reply, I back away. She moves with me at first, a pulse in my direction, but catches herself. I open the door, holding it wide for her to escape through, as heat and something else war in her expression. "Let's go; the rolls are getting cold."

She blinks, clearing the fog from her eyes, and then offers me an excited smile, the journal all but forgotten.

"Right," she says, retrieving her shoes from beneath the desk, "Now where are we off to on this adventure?"

Chapter Twenty-Five

Leona

The marks of civilization slowly fall away as the distance between each cottage fills with fields of rolling hills speckled with grazing sheep. Soon, mountains rise up around us like skyscrapers, their spires reaching into the wisps of cloud cover. Gurgling rivers rush under the stone bridges we drive over, flowing into lochs that might as well be oceans for how far and wide they stretch. I marvel at the sights as they pass, silenced by my unladylike shoveling of two sausage rolls, one after the other, into my growling stomach.

"Hungry, I take it?" Callum asks, chuckling.

I nod, wipe my mouth with the back of my hand, and crumple the paper wrappers together to dispose of at our destination. Speaking of which…

"Where are you taking me?"

He casts a sidelong glance my way, flicking at the indent of his chin. "You've got a little something—"

"Oh," I interject, swiping at my face. "Did I get it?"

He glances over at me again to check and immediately snorts. "May I?"

I nod, leaning toward him. His eyes dance between me and

the road as he reaches over and cups my chin tenderly in his hand, rubbing a thumb over the skin with a sort of reverence I'd forgotten was in his nature. I wonder if he touches every woman like that.

If he does, I don't want to know.

Even after I see the crumb fall into the crack between my seat and the center console, he doesn't let go. Instead his thumb finds my lower lip, trailing from the corner to the very center and pressing gently. My skin tingles where he's touched. I don't dare breathe, afraid that if I do, it'll break whatever trance we're in.

Boldness is not usually my forte, or it hasn't been for many years, but when Callum is near me, I feel it spark to life in my veins. My spine straightens, my shoulders brace. I do things like strip my shorts off right in front of him, without ever looking away.

I do things like biting the tip of his thumb.

Heat flares in his gaze when it cuts to me. A moan forms in the back of his throat, and his glistening teeth peek out to dig into his lower lip. One deep breath is drawn in, then two. He's a more responsible driver than I could be in the situation; he manages to keep us on the pavement. Every time he has to look at the road, away from me, I swear he winces like it pains him.

"We're going," he says at last, clearing his throat with the words, "to the Ring of Kerry. And *you're* going to be the death of me."

I sit back in my seat, letting my pulse return to its normal cadence. "Why?"

He shakes his head. "Because you're fucking beautiful, and you're wearing tiny black panties, which I shouldn't know, but I do, and I can't *un*know it, and—"

"I meant," I interject, giggling, "why the Ring of Kerry?"

A scoff cuts out of his throat, but it's punctuated by a wry grin. "I always told you I'd bring you when you came back."

It's not meant to be a barb, but it pierces me all the same. I tip my head toward the window, peering out at the sweeping landscape as it passes, trying to let go of the past while a piece of it rests in the little amulet nestled against my chest. I reach for it to anchor myself to her.

When I lived here, driving was what we did. It's how we spent every spare moment where I wasn't working or in school and he wasn't busting his ass for his uncle. We drove to every corner of the country. Well, he drove, and I napped between talks about our dreams for our lives. *One day,* I'd muse, *we'll be riding through the streets of Bali or Australia or Madagascar. We'll see the world together.*

I wanna see the ports all the ships are coming from, he'd add. *So I can picture them when I sign off on each arrival one day.*

One day seemed like such a mystical, far-off concept at the time. But it was ours for the making, or so we thought. When I glance over at him—at the way the sunlight makes the pale blond hair on his forearms shimmer where he's pushed up his sleeves, at the swoops and swirls of his hair, at the scar in his chin—I imagine this moment as some image that my younger self could've seen in a crystal ball, not realizing all the hell that came in between then and this *one day.*

Up ahead, the road winds through a narrow arch like a train tunnel carved right into the mountain. As we pass under it, tour buses travel in the opposite direction, their tops narrowly missing the roof of the tunnel. We climb higher, the road rising up the circumference of a grand valley spread out below, dotted with lakes and clusters of dense forest and small cottages with smoke rising from their chimneys. When we've nearly reached the rim, a café appears on our left advertising gelato and sandwiches. Callum slows, then pulls into a spot opposite the café. The nose of the car comes to rest against a barrier just before the sheer drop of a cliff.

"Ready?" he asks, staring straight ahead rather than at me.

I study his profile, the hard lines of his jaw and the bridge of his perfect nose. His eyelashes are blond and usually I cannot tell how long they are, but from the side I can see them fan out and nearly hit his glasses when his eyes are wide, watching, like they are now. He must sense my gaze, because he turns to face me, offering a twitch of his lips that I suppose is meant to pass for a smile.

"Come on, I've got something to show you."

I nod silently, because now that I'm this close to him in the cab of a car that's parked on top of a mountain, it feels like the years never passed at all. Like I've stepped through a wrinkle in time and found myself back in Tallaght that night, overlooking Dublin, with the worst of life still ahead.

"Right, then," he says, grabbing the door handle, and steps out into the brisk breeze.

I follow suit, grabbing the jacket I brought along from the back seat. Up here, the wind has a bite, and despite the fact that the sun has briefly decided to grace us with its presence, a shiver runs down my spine.

Rather than walking toward the trunk of the car, in the direction of the café behind us, Callum follows the barrier we parked against toward its end some twenty feet away from us. "You coming?" he calls over his shoulder. It jolts me out of the trance I've fallen into, and I force my feet to follow him.

When we reach the edge of the barrier, I realize there's a dirt path that stems from it, descending a few feet and then swooping off to the left. Callum offers his hand to steady me, and I take it. I don't have the heart to tell him that his touch is a lot more of a hazard than the sharp drop-off on our right.

Once we've rounded a sessile oak, lush and green despite the cold, our destination comes into sight. A large boulder that juts out over the valley below, veins of moss dissecting its chalky gray surface, stands in solitary guard. Callum guides me toward it, steadying me as I traverse the smaller chunks of rock that make a haphazard staircase up to their grander counterpart.

"Wow," I breathe, trying to take in everything beneath me. The tall, evergreen grasses sway and bow beneath gusts of wind sweeping through the valley. Smatterings of boulders, none as grand as this one, break up the endless green. All around us, mountains rise up like they are a crown, the valley a king's head, and we've just been lucky enough to witness his coronation. "This is incredible."

My hair is whipping against my face. I run a hand through it, holding on to what I've gathered at the back of my head so that when I turn to look at Callum, I can see him clearly. When I do, he's already watching me, a lopsided smile on his face and mist that must be from the wind filling his eyes.

"I'm glad you like it," he says, his voice almost a hum it's so pleased. "It's the best place in the world."

Normally when people say that, I'm tempted to ask them if they've *seen* the rest of the world. If they haven't, how can they be sure that Disney World or the Empire State Building is truly the pinnacle of what this earth has to offer? But now, with this expanse before me, I finally understand. There can be no better place than this.

"I can see that." I offer him a broad smile, letting it take over my face completely. When he returns it, my heart triples its step.

"In the summer I like to cycle here. Sometimes I can convince Padraig to come with me. There are trails that wind through the valley and you gain a hell of a lot of speed." His hands brace on his hips. We're so close that his elbow brushes against my arm. I make no effort to move away.

"I wish we'd come here before."

The words are out before I can stop them, though I desperately wish I could. Callum's gaze falls to the stone beneath our feet, his shoulders slumping.

"I'm sorry, forget I said that." My whisper is barely audible above the wind, but he hears it. I know he does, because he looks up at me, tilting his head to the side as he takes me in.

"I was going to bring you here when you came back." He scuffs his shoe against the boulder. His eyes are solemn and calculating, a mixture I never thought I'd see on his face. "I always thought I'd propose to you on this rock."

As much wind as there is swirling around us, all of it is knocked right out of me. My lungs empty themselves in protest, my veins constrict, my heart grows tight as a clenched fist. I can see it. I wish so badly I couldn't, but there it is, right in front of me.

The life we could've had.

If I'd called him the moment the test was positive. If I'd gotten on a plane, abandoned my degree, and come back to him. In this life, Poppy was healthy, because everything only went wrong when I started making bad decisions. In the version of our lives where I made the right ones, she was okay. She was alive.

We'd raise her in the little white cottage. I'd write for a local paper or get a different job entirely, and we'd take Poppy to stay with her granny every day while we worked. She'd have wild blonde curls and green eyes like saucers. She'd play with the neighbor's kittens and run around with half-done French braids at all times.

Niamh. I'm picturing Niamh, who wouldn't exist in this version of our lives. I can hear the wistfulness in Callum's voice, but he doesn't know what it is he's wishing for. A life where his daughter never existed. A life where his other daughter didn't die.

I almost tell him in that moment. When he looks at me with that intensity burning in his gaze, I almost spill my guts right on the boulder. It's selfish, the desire to lay it all out for him.

Because I want him to understand why I didn't return, to know that I never meant to break my promise. I want him to love me again, if that's even possible. I want to be forgiven.

But how could I add any more pain to a loss I already can never undo? Is the desire to tell him really about what's best for him, or is it me simply trying to unload this sadness on another person, on the *only* person who could come close to understanding the profundity of my loss?

Perhaps the right thing to do is to carry it, pain and all. To protect him from the regret I will live with forever.

I press my lips into a thin line, swallowing back all the words that want to pour out of me. When I'm certain that I've got them contained in the small, cancerous cell of my heart, I open my mouth to speak.

And Callum captures my words on his lips.

His arm sweeps around my back, pulling me to him, while his other hand moves to twine in my hair. I'm shielded from the wind, enveloped in the heat of his body, the scent of him coursing through me and bringing me to life. Our lips move in tandem, opening and exploring. When his tongue presses against my lips, I open for him, and then we are tasting one another and breathing the same sacred air.

I can feel the hard contours of his chest. My hands cling to the fabric of his sweater, drawing him closer but never close enough. I want to forget everything but this. Everything but him and me.

The one thing we ever got right.

Chapter Twenty-Six

Callum

The frigid wind whips frantically around us, but it cannot penetrate the sensual heat of Leo's tongue moving in tandem with mine. I'm warmed by her hands clinging to the small of my back. In return, I cradle her jaw, and the flush of her desire works as kindling for the fire beneath my fingertips.

She tastes familiar and brand-new, all at once. Something shatters inside of me. I'm not sure if it's my resolve or the bitterness I've held on to all these years, but I'm left trembling with need. We are flush against one another, the softness of her stomach pressing against my hard length. Her back arches, driving her breasts tightly into my ribs. I want all of her. Damn the cold and the cars driving past and God's own viewpoint of this fucking boulder. If she'd let me, I'd lay her down right here and show her just how badly I've missed her.

A groan forming deep in my chest dissolves into a whimper when she pulls away. Her cheeks are wet, and so are mine. With whose tears, I couldn't say.

I stroke a thumb over her supple skin, wiping away the pain we've both carried for far too long. I may not know everything that burdens her, but I know enough. I know that I'm capable of shouldering the weight.

"Let's go home, Leo."

Her mouth, red and swollen where I've bitten and sucked and licked, parts slightly, like she intends to speak. Something flashes in the depths of her eyes, and her lips clamp shut. She nods instead, weaving her hand through mine and allowing herself to be guided back to the car.

As we wind along the narrow road that leads back to the valley, and beyond that, Cahersiveen, Leo remains quiet. Her gaze is trained on the window, the glass fogging each time she exhales. If it wasn't for her hand balanced on my left knee, and her thumb gently sweeping back and forth in comforting strokes, I'd be terrified that I've driven her away.

"Penny for your thoughts?" My question is punctuated by the windshield wipers squeaking to life to combat the sudden drizzle.

Out of the corner of my eye, I watch her lips quirk upward, but the gesture does not carry with it any sense of amusement. It's hollow. It's pained.

I fight the urge to lurch the car to the side of the road, grab her by the waist, and haul her into my lap, where I can hold her closely and protect her from whatever memories cause her to suffer so. Our kiss made me feel triumphant, and yet it seems to have done the opposite for her.

"I'm thinking about fear," she says matter-of-factly. Her voice is quieter than the rain, and I have to strain to hear her clearly. "About how it changes you, and how, if at all, you can change it."

She's facing straight ahead now, but her eyes are unseeing, gone to a place I can't quite reach.

I clear my throat, nervous for the answer to the question I can't stop myself from asking. "What is it that you're afraid of?"

A harsh chuckle scratches its way out of her throat, followed by a silence that grows so long and thick I'm beginning to think it's all the answer I will be getting.

"I guess I'm afraid of failing the people I love. More so than I already have," she muses. I stop at an intersection and take the opportunity to look at her fully. She's rolling her amulet between her thumb and forefinger, smiling sadly at the windshield. "I'm afraid that I'm a selfish, awful person who will harm everyone I touch."

It's so much unadulterated truth—and pain—that it knocks the wind right out of me. I stare at her, entranced and confused. Every fiber of my being begs to reach for her, to comfort her, to assure her that she is not the horrible thing that she thinks she is.

But there's a whisper, a tendril, a thread in my heart that hesitates, and it is the thing I remain anchored to. It is the thing that keeps my arse in my seat.

Twelve years ago, if Leona had whispered that confession to me in a different car, on a different mountain, I would have vehemently disagreed with her. But then she left, and she never came back. In the absence of any facts to the contrary, I blamed it on her selfishness.

What if she's right? Doesn't she know better than anyone else what her faults are? Granda always said to listen when someone tells you who they are. My ears are perked, but my heart isn't ready to hear it.

A horn blares behind me, and Leo snaps out of whatever trance she'd fallen into, glancing at me and then over her shoulder in one quick motion. The smooth expanse of her neck is disrupted only by her thrumming pulse, the only indicator of the torrent that moves beneath her cool surface.

I pull forward as she settles back against her seat, and reassure myself that truly selfish people never realize how selfish they are. And they certainly aren't horrified at the possibility.

Back at sea level, the mountains rise up around us like a hand cradling us safely in its palm. The road winds toward home, flanked by fields of grass bowing beneath the same wind that fights with me for control of the car. We travel over stone bridges and gravel roads, past rivers and lochs with water so dark it reflects the overcast sky. Leo remains silent for so long I'm convinced she's fallen asleep, which would not be out of character for the version of her I knew.

When we've reached the outskirts of town, she shifts in her seat to face me, drawing her knee up and tucking one foot under her other leg. She studies me for a moment. I can feel her gaze sweeping over my skin, scalding everywhere it touches. I remember the taste of her, the feel of her swells and valleys against my body, and that heat travels farther south than I'd like it to while driving.

"What are you most afraid of, Callum?"

I cut a quick glance in her direction, and she raises her eyebrows in response.

"What? I showed you mine"—there's a weight to those words that I have to force myself not to read into further—"now you show me yours."

I'm no stranger to introspection, but rarely have I held up a mirror internally and liked what I saw. Granda, God rest his soul, made me do it when he was alive. He asked the hard questions, because he knew they were the ones that made you a better person in the end. Leo has always been that way, too. I've never been forced to look more closely at myself than that summer when she'd ask me about my hopes and regrets, when she'd have me list the things I'd change about the world and ways I wanted to be better than my parents. It occurs to me how much Granda would've liked her, and a pang of sadness lurches through my heart.

I clear my throat, turning on my indicator for the road that will take me past Eoin's fields and up to the cottage. Leo's eyebrows scrunch together as the vehicle veers right, but she doesn't question that I'm taking her to *my* home rather than hers.

"Probably being left behind," I manage at last, hating how fragile my voice sounds. I've worked endlessly to patch up that vulnerability, and yet the truth comes out as raw as ever.

Lips press against my shoulder, so warm I can feel them through the fabric of my sweater. Just a kiss. She doesn't speak, doesn't offer me a way out. She's letting me know she's here, but that the stage is all mine.

With a sigh, I will myself to elaborate. "I've been abandoned by a lot of people in my life. My dad, Catherine—"

"Me," she whispers.

I glance in her direction. "Yes, and you." I don't make excuses for her, and she doesn't ask for them. Yet another reason that I can't believe her when she says she is selfish. "You, and even my granda. When he died, it felt a lot like betrayal, even though I know he couldn't help it."

I've never said those words aloud, and it feels like a giant weight has crumbled off my shoulders. Granda was old. His body had started to fail him. He held on for a very long time, and part of me feels like he did it for me rather than a desire to stay alive. He gave me something that my own father could not be bothered to, but still I wanted more. More time. More memories. More guidance.

The car falls silent around us when I cut the ignition. The sun is hiding behind a tuft of clouds, leaving a gray haze hovering over the world. Splatters of rain still hit the windshield here and there, but for the most part the storm has subsided. For now, at least.

"So many people have left me, but you are the one who has haunted me all these years. Not Catherine, the mother of my child." She winces, but I press on. "Not my own father. You. And I've never been able to figure out why that is."

I shift in my seat to face her. Tears burn the backs of my eyes. After not crying for years, this time spent with her has refilled the well that long ago dried up. I remind myself to be embarrassed about it later. "I loved you more than anything, Leo. And that didn't go away just because you stopped talking to me. Just because you never returned. It grew like a virus in your absence. It festered. It made me bitter." I shake my head, and my next inhale rattles my lungs. "I'm not blaming you. It's my fault for how I handled it. I just want to know why. Why didn't you come back?"

She swallows thickly, her throat constricting. I'm afraid she'll clam up and leave the question unanswered once more, but she sighs and folds in on herself. "I didn't know how to, Callum." Her hands are clasped together in her lap, wringing so harshly I'm sure her skin will turn red. "I wasn't the same person anymore, and I didn't think I could have the same life I was meant to before…"

Her voice trails off, and I lean in, following it to the edge of my seat. I want to know what happened that made her feel that way. What could she possibly think would change the way I felt about her? We were younger then, but I knew. And once I've made up my mind about something, or someone, it's nearly impossible to change. That's why deciding I hated her in her absence is making it so excruciating to find that I don't.

Hate, after all, is born from love. And it's the love that still courses through my veins, now that all the fire has burned up and run its course.

"Isn't it enough," she says, glancing up at me beneath tear-dampened lashes, "to know that I wanted to? To know that I agonized over it, that I suffered for it, that I loved you even as I tried to move on and forget that I did." Her trembling hand finds mine. "Isn't it enough to know I never stopped?"

I remove my hand from hers and step out of the car. Her jaw

goes slack, and I swear her skin turns a sickly shade of green. But I don't walk away from her. I walk toward her, circle the car and open her door before offering my hand. She takes it, rising hesitantly from her seat, gazing up at me with barely guarded hope.

"It's enough," I say, hushed so my voice doesn't shake. "For now, it's enough."

Her reply is lost on the wind and on the whisper of my lips against hers.

Chapter Twenty-Seven

Leona

I'd shatter if he wasn't holding me together.

His arms sweep around my waist and then lower, over the swell of my ass and into the dip below, scooping me off the ground and into his embrace. I wrap my legs around him, clenching my thighs to hold myself up and eliciting a guttural groan from him in response.

I take advantage of his mouth opening to let the sound escape, dip my tongue into the warmth, and brush against the silk of his own. A decade may have passed, but our bodies know this dance. We move in perfect harmony, ebbing and flowing, as if made for this and only this.

In some far-off corner of my consciousness, I hear him kick the door of the car shut behind us. I feel him scramble across the gravel toward his cottage, left unlocked because everyone in this town knows one another, and turn the brass doorknob before stalking forward into the dim foyer. Still my lips don't part from his.

We move down hallways I once knew, past framed photos of Niamh that I force myself not to see, into the bedroom at the end of the hall where we used to lie together and make lazy love all afternoon. Knowing what's coming makes me feel like I'm a teenager about to lose her virginity. We were barely what you'd call experienced when we made love before; just two twentysomethings fumbling in the dark. He's older, *we're* older, now. He's no longer the innocent boy who once explored my body like a foreign country.

He settles me onto the bed and stands before me. His glasses are removed and folded carefully before being placed on a nearby dresser. Then he reaches back between his shoulder blades and draws his sweater over his head in one fell swoop. From the slivers of sunlight filtering in between the gauzy curtains, I can see every contour of his muscled abdomen. I reach out to run my fingers through the dusting of blond chest hair, and he captures my hand, pressing it flat to his skin. Beneath my fingertips, his heartbeat thrums a wild rhythm, letting me know just how much of himself he is holding back in this moment.

He looks down at me, stroking a thumb over the back of my hand. The desire in his eyes is so visceral it steals my breath. "I told myself I'd take it slow."

His voice is a growl, a plea, a prayer for strength.

I let my hand fall from his grasp to trail down the center of his stomach before hooking a finger into his waistband. "Twelve years is pretty slow."

My words unravel his resolve, and he at last allows himself to be pulled down to me. His lips crash into mine, urgent and needy, teeth tugging at my bottom lip with such force I'm nearly certain he's going to draw blood. I don't care, I decide. Let me bleed. Let him rip me open and take whatever it is he needs to be whole again. To repair what I broke.

His forehead tilts to mine, gasping breaths buffeting my face as he whispers, "I remember you."

I cradle his jaw in my hands and look into his eyes, which seem endless in the shadows. "I never forgot."

"Leona," he moans, raking his hands over my chest and squeezing the swell of my breasts beneath the thin fabric of my sweater. Just as I'm arching into his touch, his hands travel farther south, finding my waistband and searching for the button that will release me from their entrapment.

"Don't call me that," I gasp, bucking my hips as his hand now slips inside my jeans, too urgent to be delayed by something as frivolous as removing my pants. He draws a fingertip along the wetness I'm sure is soaking through my panties before pressing into my clit, the glorious pressure snapping whatever tethers still linked me to sanity.

He props himself on an elbow, smirking down at me while his other hand still works its magic. "Oh?" His finger moves away from my clit and begins trailing the band of my panties, teasing me. "And what would you like me to call you instead?"

I cry out in desperation, tilting my hips toward those fingers that stay infuriatingly close but not close enough. "You know what I want."

One finger skirts along my lips, testing the wetness between them, but retreats before delving any deeper.

"I want you to say it." His eyes are glimmering with heat and mischief, like a sparkler on the Fourth of July. His finger sweeps into my slit, spreading me for him, but he hovers at my entrance, daring me to speak. "I want you to beg."

"Leo," I breathe, grinding into him on instinct alone. "I want you to call me Leo. And I *need* you to stop teasing me. *Now*."

"I knew you liked that name." He grins, teeth glinting in the buttery strands of sunlight. His finger finally drives into my core, curling and stroking in all the right places that only serve to stoke the flame higher until I'm certain I'm going to be burned.

My nails carve harsh lines down his shoulder blades. I'm convinced that if I don't anchor myself in his flesh, I'm going to float away on the ecstasy of his touch. His thumb rubs my clit in sync with his strokes, and I find the hope of extinguishing these flames in sight. I arch toward it, and he withdraws his hand.

An involuntary whimper escapes my lips. "Callum, please."

"So demanding, Leo." He draws his fingers into his mouth and sucks the taste of me off them. A hum of appreciation vibrates in his throat. "I like this version of you."

He steps back off the bed but leans forward to loop his hands around my waistband and pull, peeling my jeans away from my skin. I'm drunk on the feeling of his gaze roaming the length of my thighs. His fingers trace the phantom path. It's the same thing he did when we were younger. Where other men made me want to cover up the thickest parts of myself, he has always touched each inch with reverence. With desire.

His exploration stops at the seam of my underwear, and he quirks an eyebrow as he rests one foot and then the other on his shoulders, pressing a tickling kiss against the arch of each before he begins tugging black lace over the curve of my ass.

"You shouldn't have let me see these this morning." He draws them painstakingly slowly over my legs, ending at my ankles right in front of his face. "I can smell how much you want me, Leo, and it makes me so damn hard I can barely stand it. I've been thinking about these panties all morning."

With that, he removes them and lets my legs fall to each side. The bundle of black lace, however, is tucked into his back pocket while a wicked grin stretches across his face. "I'm keeping them."

I can't control the sound that rips out of my lungs then, caught somewhere between a moan and a sigh and a yelp, but it drives him wild. I'm spread before him, and I don't feel an ounce of shame. Instead I'm consumed by the heavy want coursing through my veins.

He grabs one leg and tosses it over my other, turning me onto my side. Before I can process what is happening, his teeth sink into the flesh of my ass, and I cry out in pleasure. He covers it with a gentle press of his lips, then smiles up at me. "My favorite part of you. I'm so glad you kept it."

The shamrock tattoo in question is little more than a dark blob on my ass cheek after twelve years, but he strokes it with a calloused thumb like it's a miracle. I got it late one night in Dublin after one too many Baby Guinness shots and a lot of enthusiasm from Callum.

The memory brings a warmth to my heart that only serves to make the moment that much more intense. He surges forward, balancing himself over me so I feel his weight but am not responsible for it. When he presses his lips to mine once more, I can taste the faint remnants of myself on his tongue, and the resulting throb between my legs has me desperately fumbling with his zipper.

His hand moves from my exposed hip to roam beneath my sweater until he finds my breast and squeezes it, his thumb roughly grazing my nipple through the scant lace of my bralette. I roll flat onto my back once more, opening my thighs for him to settle between them. He falls into place like he never left.

I'm frantically pushing his waistband down, and he chuckles. "Why are you in such a rush, love? I want to take my time with you." He leans back as he draws my sweater upward. "I've missed you so."

The emotion that fills my throat is enough to drown in, so I simply nod. The last thing I see before my shirt travels over my head and steals my vision is his lazy grin and the dim rays of light reflected in his eyes.

His teeth graze my nipple before I'm even free of the sweater. As he flicks his tongue against the lace, his hand works the other nipple, pinching and rolling it exactly the way I've always loved. He either remembers or is a damn good guesser. My money's on the former.

His mouth travels to my rib cage, kissing and nipping me

there, which causes goose bumps to break out over my sensitive flesh. His golden hair glows in the moonlight, and I run my fingers through it, admiring the way it shines. He moans like I've just stroked the perfect spot, so I repeat the motion, tugging slightly harder at the waves I've gathered in my fist this time. What can only be described as a purr rumbles in his throat.

My gaze falls on the muscles in his back as he travels farther down my body. They move with a predator's grace, scarred by angry red lines where my nails traveled their surface. I'm so distracted by the broad expanse of his shoulders that I almost forget about my stomach. About the silver bands of memory that strike through my core, now bared on display for him.

I could ignore them. Am trying to. But then he presses gentle, featherlight kisses to them on his southern-bound path, and my heart roars to the surface, forcing my brain to take note. To still. To bear witness.

He must sense the shift in my mood. He was always good at that, at knowing when he'd found a new place to lick and suck based on the fervent way my hips would strive toward him without any command on my part. Likewise he immediately knew not to touch the bend of my knee by the way I froze the only time he ever did it, skin crawling for no good reason other than it just felt *wrong* to be touched there, in that hollow place.

His gaze flickers up to meet mine, taking a reading on my reaction before glancing back down at the skin he's just tasted. A soft chuckle passes over his lips. "Oh, love, you don't think a few stretch marks are going to turn me off, do you?" He grins a wicked, Cheshire smile before sitting back on his heels and holding out an arm for me to examine. There, on the swell of his bicep, a band of silver marks the pattern of his growth. "We've all got them; nothing to be embarrassed about."

And I try, damn it, to accept the out he's offering me. To swallow the guilt and the sadness and all the other darker unnamed emotions that swirl within me, but I can't breathe. Because Poppy is here, in this room with us. Her presence in those marks on my skin is so palpable I'm convinced I could reach down in this moment and feel her kick, like no time has passed at all since they first appeared.

He studies me with a curious tilt of his head. "What's wrong?" A rough thumb scrapes over my abdomen before he thinks better of it and withdraws his hand. "We don't have to keep going. I'll understand if you've changed your mind."

His kindness, which was meant to envelop me like a warm blanket but instead falls like shrapnel on my nerves, is my undoing. A single tear, rebellious and desperate, slips from the corner of my eye. He tracks its path, brow furrowed, before glancing at the stretch marks once more. "I don't understand. Leo, you're beautiful; you shouldn't be ashamed of your body growi—"

The words stall on his parted lips. His calloused hand flattens over my stomach, a single finger tracing the path of the mark closest to it. A stack of wrinkles form on his forehead as realization, then confusion, then denial take turns flickering in his eyes. He shakes his head, gently at first and then fervently, like he's begging me to disagree with the truth his mind has landed on.

"Leona," he chokes out, that finger moving reluctantly now along the only physical reminder I have that our daughter existed. That I housed her in my body. That I stretched to make room for her, for what little time she was here. He hesitates there, seeing but not quite believing, before looking up at me with anguish drenching his features. "How did you know what to do about morning sickness?"

I cannot bring myself to speak, to answer, and that is an answer in and of itself.

"And why were you so upset at the market that day?" he adds. "You bought something from that woman, the one with the toys. And you were upset. Why?"

So he *did* see. He saw me give her the money, and he may not have heard the words that were spoken, but the pain must've been apparent on my face. "Callum, I've been trying to find a way to tell you. It just never felt like the right time, and—"

"Leona," he whispers, removing his hand from my skin like he's been burned. "Do you have a child?"

Chapter Twenty-Eight

Callum

Even in the low light of the room, I can see the color drain from her face. Suddenly she's the same shade of white as the bedsheets rumpled beneath her. As pale as she's gone, the lightning strikes surrounding her navel are even lighter. Almost silver.

At first her reaction made no sense. Stretch marks are nothing to be ashamed of, and hell, what human alive doesn't have one or two from weight gain or building muscle or just growing a few inches over the course of one pubescent summer? Besides, the Leo I knew and loved never cared about her body's imperfections. Not around me, at least.

But her stillness. That lonely tear streaking down her face. After a double take, and then a triple, recognition like a branding iron seared the nape of my neck. I'd know these marks anywhere. Just five years ago I watched with wonder while Catherine's belly stretched to accommodate Niamh's presence, praising her even though she detested the way her skin was marked by those changes.

The pieces slowly fall into place. The haunted look in her eyes at the market that day. The somber way she told that guest how to combat morning sickness. Her fear that she'd only let people down.

Hurt ripples through me, turning over my stomach until I'm certain I'll be sick. Every emotion I went through the day Catherine walked away, every tear I wiped off our daughter's face while she grieved an absence she didn't understand, returns to the forefront of my mind for the first time in years. I've worked so hard to push away the anger, the sadness, the impossibility of it all, and in a matter of seconds all that work is undone.

Because here Leo is, stripped bare beneath me, with all the evidence of the one thing I can never forgive sitting like a brick wall between us.

"How could you leave your child?" I choke. I wish I sounded stronger, but my voice sounds like it's passed through a cheese grater. Her mouth opens to speak, the defenses flashing in her eyes, and I cut her off. "Don't deny it, Leona. Please don't lie to me. Not again."

My words strike a chord. *Good.*

Suddenly she's scrambling to get out from under me. I don't fight her. I don't have it in me. She leaps from the bed and gathers her discarded clothes, forcing herself into them with her back to me. Like I can ever forget what I've seen on the other side of her body.

My hands burn where they've touched her. My throat is scalding. Rage boils in my veins, and it takes everything I have to contain it. To even come close to resembling the man Granda thought I could be.

She abandoned her child. The most horrific, narcissistic, *selfish* act…

The word is a fist constricting around my heart. Selfish. That's exactly who she told me she was, and I couldn't believe her. Didn't want to believe her. I'm crushed beneath the weight of the revelation, so quickly drowning in my spiraling thoughts that I might've missed her leaving the room had she not slammed the door in her wake.

It jolts me out of the trance I've fallen into. I chase after her, not even bothering to find my shirt and replace it. She's halfway down the hall when I grab her bicep, whirling her to face me. Her expression is gaunt, the exact opposite of how she looked mere moments ago, spread out before me and drenched in pleasure.

I'm going to be sick. I'm nearly sure of it.

Her chin juts out in defiance even as it trembles. "Take me home, Callum."

"Leo, why? Why would you do this?" My knees buckle, threatening to bring me down, but I catch myself with an outstretched hand slapping against the wall. The framed photos of my daughter shake. Leo winces. I step away, letting her go, checking myself even as I feel like the world has fallen out from beneath me. "You knew. I told you what Catherine did to Niamh and me. You've seen the hurt she caused. How could you sit with us day in and day out, knowing you had a child at home who suffered the same?"

The image of my mother asking her to hold Niamh the night of the storm flashes in my mind. The way she recoiled, just like she is now. There was guilt, even then, and I silently curse myself for refusing to see it.

"I didn't leave my child," she bites out, crossing her arms over her chest. Her amulet dangles between her collarbones, glinting in the dim light of the hall. "Don't yell at me over things you know nothing about."

"I'm not yelling!" Even as I say the words, their volume reverberates back to me. I draw in a deep breath, trying desperately to get ahold of myself. I don't know what to say to make her understand, so I settle for the bare and honest truth. "Right now my head is in the worst possible place, Leo, and I don't know how to breathe. I've just barely let my walls down, and it feels like everything is caving in again."

She sucks in a shaky breath, and I can see the tears blanketing her cheeks. With two small steps backward, she places space between us that feels suffocating. Every part of me is confused. In the same heartbeat I simultaneously long to hold her *and* haul her ass back to Dublin and put her on a plane. I want to be wrong. I'm terrified that I'm right.

"Speak to me, damn it," I groan, nearly dropping to my knees to beg.

Fire sparks in the depths of her gaze, and it's almost a relief compared to the stillness that predated it. Her shoulders square as her arms drop to her sides. She stalks forward until she jabs a finger into the center of my chest, and I can see how badly she wishes it could pierce me.

"She died, Callum. I had a child, and she died." Her voice is granite, impenetrable and mighty. "Now take. Me. Home."

With that, she pivots on her heel and marches down the hallway. My front door opens and then slams shut, and in the distance I hear my car door do the same. The walls in this cottage are so thin I swear her grief and anger are lashing out at me even from outside.

Good. I deserve it. I deserve to be lashed with something far worse than her anger. I should personally deliver her a whip and kneel before her to take my punishment.

Dead. She had a child, and that child, a *daughter*, died.

With shame weighing heavy on my shoulders, I dare lift my gaze to one of the photos of Niamh hung along the wall. She's sitting in a high chair, celebrating her first birthday, impossibly small and fragile. I remember the fear that gripped my heart each night back then as she slept, worrying she'd never draw her next breath. I'd lie awake next to her crib and watch her sleep to allay my darkest fears.

Leo lived through those fears, every parent's worst nightmare, and I just threw that back in her face.

I've never experienced a feeling quite like this one. Like I want to rip my skin from my bones and muscle and sinew. I'm strangling on my own remorse. The earth could yawn open beneath me and swallow me whole, and still it would not be a punishment suitable for what I've done.

I stumble down the hall, take the turn toward the front of the house, and grab a jacket from the coatrack in the foyer. Once I've zipped it over my exposed chest, the cottage spits me out into the night, and I'm nearly gutted all over again when I see Leo's silhouette in the car.

How can I ever repair what I've just broken?

The answer is, I don't deserve to.

When I open the driver's side door to climb in, she leans away from me, and it lumps a fresh scoop of hot coals onto my head.

"Leo, I—"

"Home."

She never even looks at me.

We drive in silence, but not the comfortable kind. The kind that suffocates. The air turns to molasses around us, filling my lungs with that instead of air. I search my brain for the right words to repair the irreparable, and I come up empty.

When at last I come to a stop in front of the bed-and-break-fast, its vine-covered facade lit only by a gas lantern hung by the entrance, Leo reaches for the door immediately. She's halfway turned toward the curb when I clamp a hand down on her knee, and she freezes in place.

Her face tilts in my direction, but she doesn't lift her eyes to meet mine. Instead her lashes lay against her cheeks in solemnity. The corner of her mouth quivers, and it takes everything in me not to trace it with my thumb, to try to quell her shaking.

"I'm so sorry, Leo." The words feel impossibly small for

something of this magnitude, but they're all I have. "You didn't deserve that at all. I had no right—"

"It's not your fault," she whispers. It's the last thing I expected her to say, and I have to force my jaw not to drop. Her gaze at last lifts to mine, and I swear I could drown in the sorrow that fills her eyes. "How could you have known? After all, I never told you."

With that, she leaves, skirting around an elderly couple stepping out of the inn before I can even get out of the car. They glance from her retreating back to me with morbid curiosity painted on their faces. I ignore them as I lurch toward the door. I'm nearly certain I'm going to be sick on the sidewalk, but I force one foot in front of another, desperate to reach her, to apologize again, to absolve her of the guilt she's falsely placed on herself.

When the hallway spreads out before me, she's already gone. Her footsteps thunder up the distant staircase, but I remain halted in my tracks. Mam leans a hip against the makeshift front desk, arms crossed over her chest as she studies me.

"Care to explain?" she asks, one eyebrow perked.

"I think I just ruined everything," I reply before stumbling into my mother's embrace.

If I told Darren that my uselessness at work this week could be attributed to the same girl who nearly got me fired from my unpaid internship all those years ago, he'd probably threaten to castrate me.

I've joined our virtual stand-ups late each morning with undeniable bedhead and ducked out early nearly every afternoon. The reports I'm responsible for showed up a day past their due in his inbox, and on top of that I've been dodging his calls. I'm a wreck, and I have no way of masking it, so I go the route of avoidance instead.

"What have you brought for Leona today?" Niamh chirps, gazing at the small gift bag dangling from my clenched fist.

The sun is high and bright, beating down on my shoulders while I hold open the door for her to enter the bed-and-breakfast. It's nearly lunchtime, and most of the guests are either long departed to their various excursions or checked out and moving on in their travels. I rolled out of bed too late to get Niamh here *and* attend stand-up, so I decided Mam didn't need an extra set of hands at breakfast that badly and let my daughter sleep in for once instead.

"A pretty magnet I saw at the store." I jiggle the bag at her for emphasis. "Think she'll like it?"

Niamh's nose scrunches up like she's caught a whiff of something vile. "A maggot? Why not a toy? Or flowers? Rapunzel likes flowers!"

"A *magnet*, you maggot." I ruffle her hair, which hangs in loose ringlets over her shoulders. No time for plaits today. "And what a coincidence; it happens to be a magnet that looks like a flower."

She shrugs her shoulders and then breaks into a sprint down the hall, her light footsteps echoing as she makes her way to Mam's room where her stash of stuffed animals awaits.

Mam is stoking the fire in the living room, sending showers of hissing embers onto the brick floor of the hearth. I join my hands at the base of my back, the small gift bag resting against my ass. Out of sight, out of further judgment by another Walsh woman.

"How's it going today, Mam?"

"You're awfully late," she responds, ignoring my question. She stores the fire poker in the wrought-iron stand to the right of the hearth and turns to examine me. I swear her eyes glint with amusement at her sad, lovesick puppy of a son before the corners of her mouth turn downward. "Another bad day, I'm afraid. She's still asleep last I checked."

A wave of sour shame coats my stomach.

Mam nods once, as if satisfied by my discomfort, before reclining in the chaise to the right side of the fireplace. "And what are you after bringing our girl today?"

Despite everything that happened between us, and the sheer unlikelihood of reconciliation, a small thrill runs down my spine when Mam refers to Leona as *our girl.* Like she's a part of the odd family Mam, Niamh, Padraig, and I have created. Like she belongs.

After all that she has lost, I wonder if she needs to hear that as much as I did. Possibly more.

I remove the small, metallic trinket from the bag, holding it up for Mam to see. She narrows her eyes like that might bring it into focus.

"It's a poppy flower," I explain, turning it over in my palm. "I saw it at the shop yesterday and thought she'd like it."

In all honesty, Niamh had gone looking for a snack and found the cupboards barren due to my terrible parenting, and I was forced to trek to the store to replenish our supplies. In the checkout lane a tower of kitschy tourist items lay in wait, and when the bright red petals of the magnet caught my eye, I immediately thought of Leo. Not the version of her I know now, but the twenty-year-old American girl who'd just seen a field of poppies bloom in the Irish countryside for the first time in her life. For a moment I could still feel the excitement crackling off her. I could taste her salty skin as I laid her out on a blanket and kissed her in the middle of that field.

"I don't know that she's ready yet, son." Mam gives a rueful smile. "She hasn't come out of her room except to use the bathroom. I don't think sausage rolls and little trinkets are quite enough to mend that type of grief."

I wince but nod. When said aloud like that, my little attempts at brightening Leo's days sound a lot more pathetic.

Out of the corner of my eye, my own movements reflected back at me draw my gaze to the antique mirror hung on the wall. I look haggard, with purplish bruises visible beneath the rim of my glasses and a week's worth of stubble accumulated on my chin. My scar has completely disappeared beneath the unruly overgrowth of facial hair.

The pendulum of my emotions is making me dizzy. How is it that in a little over a month I've managed to swing from hating Leo and wanting her gone to being eaten alive by guilt at having driven her away?

"What do I do, Mam?" I croak. "How do I fix this?"

She clicks her tongue at me, not in chastisement but in sadness. Her mouth forms a grim line. With a heavy breath drawn in through her nose, her chest inflates, and then it all flows out of her. She seems smaller afterward, somehow.

"When she's ready, the two of you will talk." Her gaze drifts down to her hands where they lie folded in her lap. "I'm not saying things will be perfect. A grief like that never goes away, and from what I've seen, she's carried it alone for a long, long time. But when she's ready to talk to you, remember how it felt to lash out at her without an ounce of grace for how she's suffered. Remember how it felt to judge her too harshly. To reach for anger rather than compassion. Don't repeat your mistake."

I stay planted in place for so long my feet consider growing roots. Mam never looks up or explains why she thinks Leo has suffered alone. After all, her daughter had to have come sometime after her marriage. After I blocked all knowledge and news of her out of my life. Surely her husband was there for her, at least in the beginning.

Anger lashes through me at the same time my thoughts whisper, *What if that bastard let her suffer alone?*

As if she senses this, Mam looks up, and the rest of her message lands like a cool balm on the burns of my rage. *Don't repeat your mistake.*

With a tight nod, I slip out of the room and up the stairwell, settling my pathetic peace offering in front of Leo's door. I pause to listen, but there is no sound coming from the room. After a long moment spent weighing my options, I walk away from the gift bag, knowing it's not enough but hoping nonetheless.

Chapter Twenty-Nine

Leona

My eyes burn from straining to see in the low light cast by the oil lantern on the bedside table. If I turn on the overhead lights, I'll certainly be able to see the baseboards I'm scrubbing a bit better, but then the light will filter under the closed door and nosy innkeepers might be tempted to see who's occupying what should be an empty room.

The lamp will have to suffice.

The nightmares are worse since my confrontation with Callum. Suddenly it's no longer me who can't get to the baby as the doctor takes her from the room. Instead, with strength that defies logic, I hold Callum's arms in a vise grip, stopping him from going after our daughter.

As the images press on my brain, I scrub harder, trying to make something, *anything* clean in the midst of this fucking mess.

I had my chance to tell him, and I chickened out. I convinced myself he was better off not knowing, and then the universe handed me my karma on a silver platter. It was certainly efficient, I must admit. Efficiently excruciating.

Lost in my thoughts, I miss the creaking of the door as it opens behind me. I'd probably have missed the bedsprings groaning beneath Siobhan's weight, too, if I hadn't turned to rinse my sponge in the bucket of warm, soapy water at my side.

"Siobhan, Christ," I gasp, dropping the sponge into the water and splashing myself in the process. "You scared me half to death."

"Only half?" she says, chuckling. "So still no ghost for the inn, I suppose. Better luck next time."

I grimace at her before looking away. I've managed to keep contact to a minimum this week while I figure out what the hell to do. Or at least, while I come to terms with what I *know* I have to do.

I have to tell Callum the truth, and then I need to leave this place. Staying so long has only increased the amount of pain that I will inevitably cause. I can't keep stretching out the days, spending time with Siobhan and the guests, when that will only make things worse in the end.

Siobhan sighs heavily as if I've said my thoughts aloud. I bring a soapy hand to my lips, checking to see if they've moved against my will.

"You know, Leona, my son can certainly be a stubborn arse, but he means well." She shifts on the bed, but I don't dare turn around. I can't face her. Not without spilling all my secrets. "He just loves so hard that it sometimes gets away from him and he ends up doing things he wouldn't otherwise be doing. Or saying. Do you understand?"

My teeth clamp down on the inside of my cheek. I know exactly what she means. I've been on the receiving end of that love. There was a time when I thought I was capable of giving it right back, but not anymore.

"Callum says you lost a child."

The bucket of water nearly topples over when I try to grip it for strength. Glancing over my shoulder at Siobhan, I'm met with an expression of somber understanding. Not undeserved pity, like

Callum wore, or tired sympathy like the nurses who delivered Poppy tried to offer. Her face is open and anguished in a way that feels familiar.

I nod, because it's all I can do, and she smiles gently in return.

"I suspected you and I were the same, though I've never wished to be wrong about anything more."

My face must betray my confusion, because her head tilts to the side and she pats the mattress beside her. I do as she asks, rising to my feet with a scream of pain shooting down my back before settling onto the uncomfortable springs next to her.

Her wrinkled hand comes to rest on my knee, and I cover it with my own.

"When you were here the first time, what seems like a lifetime ago, Callum would begrudgingly answer my calls once or twice a month in the few spare moments he wasn't with you." I start to interrupt, to apologize, but she squeezes my knee and I fall silent. "He was generally such a private child, but there was just something about you. He'd have shouted your name from the rooftops if there were a rooftop accessible to him.

"Once, I caught him just after the two of you had returned from a hiking trip in Wicklow. Callum told me all about how you took turns holding ten schoolchildren from a bus tour up on your shoulders to let them see the eggs in a bird's nest at the mouth of the trail." A huff of amusement passes over her parted lips. "He was so taken with you, you know that?"

I shake my head at the wallpaper rather than at her. It's different from the one in my attic. A dark, forest green with golden vines winding the length of it fills the room, making it feel smaller. Or maybe it's just because I'm feeling too big all of a sudden. Too seen.

"I don't understand. What does that have to do with anything?" I ask the wall.

Her hand on my knee grows firm like she's holding on to me for dear life.

"I had another baby, before Callum." Her voice is gravel. It's gargled water. It's a gasping breath.

I look at her, seeing clearly for the first time in days. Her skin is weathered and soft around her eyes, but her spirit is as evergreen as her irises. The memories sparking to life within her now are as real and as raw as if they'd happened yesterday.

For her, they must've. Just as mine did for me.

"He doesn't know about it, and I'd appreciate it if you'd keep things that way."

"I would never—"

"I know," she interjects. Her lips form a sad phantom of a smile. "I know you wouldn't, Leona." Her voice warbles, and I want to tell her that it's okay. That she doesn't have to tell me. But I know from experience how lonely it is to carry someone's whole life story within yourself. To have no one to share it with. So I stay silent.

"I miscarried. It was just around the twenty-week mark, by my count. Everything was fine. I was young, had no health problems, and didn't have a reason in the world to be worried. But then one day I started bleeding, and it didn't stop.

"The doctor said there was nothing he could do. I had to deliver that tiny, tiny baby. A girl, if you can believe it." She grins at the memory even as tears leak from the corners of her eyes. "I had a little girl. Then they took her away. In those days, the doctors didn't even let you see the baby, though I've no idea why. I didn't even get to say goodbye. I didn't even get to bury her."

Before I know it, my own tears are falling, and the only sound in the room is our respective sniffling. It feels as though we've run into an old friend that we failed to discover we both know before now. Grief, that long lost link, embraces us, and we embrace each other, completing the circle.

"Now look at me, blubbering like a baby," Siobhan scoffs, drawing back just enough to pat her eyes dry before offering her handkerchief to me. I shake my head, opting instead to wipe my eyes with my cotton sleeve.

"I had a daughter, too. She was stillborn at the beginning of my third trimester." I stare at our feet where they dangle off the edge of the bed. Siobhan waits, not rushing to fill the silence after my admission. I hesitate on the precipice of honesty. "How did you know? That we were the same?"

"After I lost the baby, it hurt too much to talk about. It's a pain a man could never understand. Even his father, the bastard, could only grieve her so much. But I felt her; I carried her. She was as real to me as Callum," she whispers. I wonder if she knows that her arms have wrapped around her middle like mine so often do, cradling someone who is no longer there. "That's why he left. When we finally had Callum, I obsessed over the boy. I didn't save any of myself for the marriage. Can't be blaming him for wanting more than a shell of a wife, you know."

I bite a chunk of skin off my lip, tasting metal. "But how could he leave Callum? After all that?"

She shakes her head. "It took years after the miscarriage before I could be in the room with another child. Or even see a pregnant woman without tearing up. I think, when Callum came along, it was like that for him, too. Maybe his grief manifested itself in that way." After a long pause, she lets out a harsh laugh while staring up at the ceiling. "Or maybe he was just a sorry bastard, and I'm giving him too much credit."

A laugh sputters out of me, and it does wonders to ease the tightness in my chest.

"I see that same thing in you, with the way you orbit Niamh." Her gaze falls to me, and I make myself meet it. "Nobody who lifts up ten children to see baby birds would keep that little ball of sunshine at arm's length the way you do. Not without a reason."

I feel suddenly exposed, and my skin catches flame. "I'm sorry, I never meant to—"

"Stop apologizing, Leona." She cups my cheek tenderly, forcing me not to break eye contact no matter how badly I want to. "I'm not accusing you or judging you, or any of it. I simply want you to know that I've been there, I've walked the path you are on, and I'm reaching back for you. You're going to make it, you hear me?"

A sob lodges in my throat, desperate to be let out. I can hardly breathe around it, but I nod.

She studies my face, stroking my cheek with her thumb in a calming metronome. "Was the baby Callum's?"

I can't hold it in any longer. I nod through the torrent of tears that flows over her hand. My trembling palm is pressed firmly against my chest, trying to suppress the ache that threatens to split me open. I wait for the admonishment. For the anger. For her to kick me out of this room for keeping this from her, but it never comes.

Instead she releases my face to wrap her arms around me and pull me into her. Her gray hair fills my vision, and the scent of jasmine invades my senses. It reminds me so acutely of my mother that I unravel even further.

"Callum's a lot of things. He's stubborn and a workaholic and not very sociable these days." Her lips move against my hair, tickling my scalp. I focus on the sensation as I try to steady my breaths. "He's grumpy as the Irish weather. But he's a damn good father to Niamh. He'd love to know he had another baby."

"He's going to hate me," I say, whimpering like a child.

"He's not going to hate you." She pulls back to look at me, smiling in that soft, knowing way that seasoned mothers do. "I don't think that boy could get an ounce of his body to hate you if he tried. You were barely more than a child yourself, Leona. He will be angry at first, like I imagine you were when you lost her.

Mad he got you into this in the first place. But it'll pass, and you'll both be better for it. You'll have each other to lean on."

I've spent so long feeling desperately alone in my grief, fearing the worst if I were to let anyone else in, that I can't hand myself completely over to relief all at once. But I see it there, on the table for me to pick up when I'm ready to believe it. When I'm ready to endure what must be endured to get to the other side.

When Poppy died, I saw my life laid out before me. For the first time it no longer felt too short for all the plans that I wanted to fit inside it. Instead the future felt impossibly long and complicated, like a labyrinth I had to pass through to get back to my daughter. Every day I survived was just one step closer to the day I'd hold her again. To the day I'd finally be whole.

But Siobhan's words have given birth to a glimmer of hope. Hope that my life doesn't have to be merely survived. Hope that I can love and be loved, with all my pain known and acknowledged. That I won't have to walk alone through any of it anymore.

Still, there is a quiet voice in the back of my head that remains unconvinced. That believes Siobhan's mistaken me for someone better, kinder than myself.

I lean away from her, studying the chipped polish on my left hand. "Is it selfish to tell him? Knowing it will only cause him pain?"

"No, love, it isn't selfish." She looses a sigh, filling the air between us with the scent of spearmint—an ingredient in her favorite nighttime tea. "There is pain in knowing the truth, but there is also a rare and precious joy. I'm sure you can agree that you'd rather grieve your daughter than to never have had her in the first place."

I nod, pressing my lips firmly together to hold another sob at bay. My tears have finally dried, and I'm not ready to reopen the floodgates just yet.

"Glad that's settled." She flops onto her back, the bed squeaking beneath her. Her arms fold behind her head, and she smiles up at the ceiling. "Now, would you tell me about my granddaughter?"

It spreads an earnest, cheek-aching smile across my face. To hear someone else refer to my daughter like that. Even my own mother, in her sworn secrecy, has never talked this openly about Poppy. It makes her feel as real as she was, as she continues to be, for me.

I join Siobhan, reclining beside her and staring up at the cream-colored ceiling. And for the first time outside my letters, I tell the story of my baby girl. Of her life and death, and what an honor it was to carry her for as long as she was here.

Chapter Thirty

Callum

"This can't be good."

I glance up at Padraig, then down at the collection of empty beer glasses littering the table in front of me. Across the dimly lit room, Dermot watches the exchange. He removes his flat cap and smooths what few strands of hair remain on his freckled scalp before putting it back in place.

"It's been a long week," I grumble. With a nod in Dermot's direction, two freshly poured pints head our way. He leaves the empty glasses on my table, probably to remind me to pace myself.

"Long week my ass." Padraig swings the wooden chair around backward before straddling it and leveling me with a hard stare. "Whatever it is, it can't have been that bad. After all, I haven't seen your one wandering the streets in the rain all week, as she's prone to do when you fuck things up."

I huff into my glass, and the liquid ripples away from me. "That's because she hasn't been leaving her room."

His jaw nearly hits the table. I reach over and slap it back into place. Lightly. For the most part.

"Sorry, lad." He rubs at his chin absent-mindedly. "What did you do? Last I heard, the two of you's were off to Kerry on one of your little adventures, or so you said."

The stone wall becomes a fascinating thing to look at. At least it remains unchanged and nonjudgmental. And it's capable of hiding how disappointed it is in my erroneous ways, unlike my friend.

"We went to Kerry. And things were good. Not completely back to the way they were, but better in a lot of ways, if I'm honest." I take a sip of red ale, my least favorite because I'm apparently a masochist tonight, and continue studying the different shades of brown and gray that form the cavernous room. "We, erm, got close when we got home. I made some pretty awful assumptions about something I saw, and it ended horribly."

I finally test a glance in Padraig's direction. His eyebrows are so screwed up they've nearly merged into one. "Cal, I appreciate that you're being protective of the lady's privacy, but I'm going to need a bit more clarity before I can offer any sound advice."

"As if you've ever," I scoff. He doesn't let up, though, and I find myself squirming in my seat. "She has stretch marks on her stomach that she reacted badly to me seeing. That, combined with some other things she's said and done, had me jumping to conclusions. I panicked and accused her of abandoning a child. But she didn't. She had a daughter, and that daughter died."

"*Oh my God.*" Padraig's voice is muffled by the hand clamped over his mouth. His halfway empty beer lies in wait on the table between us. I down the rest of mine.

"I know."

"Well, I suppose if you wanted to run her back to America, that was the most efficient way to do it." He scratches at his graying temple while studying a knot in the wood grain of the table. "My God, Callum. That poor girl. Can you imagine?"

I gulp. "I've been trying not to."

He nods like he understands completely. As if he, too, is

imagining a world without Niamh in it and can't stomach the idea. "Did she tell you what happened?"

"I didn't exactly feel like I had any right to ask, you know. Given I'd just accused her of something horrific, not to mention insensitive." The hand I run through my hair is trembling with anger. Anger at myself, at Leo's loss, at the incredible mess I've managed to make of things. "I've been trying to apologize every day, but she won't come out of her room."

"Is that why your mam canceled Sunday dinner last weekend?"

I give a curt nod, and he returns it.

Dermot shuffles across the room, greeting a few new patrons in passing on his way to us. The bar is less crowded at this hour than usual. It's part of the reason I asked Padraig to meet me earlier, after logging off at half past three and dodging two calls from Darren. I didn't want to drown my sorrows entirely; I simply wanted to teach them how to swim. And I didn't necessarily want a large audience when doing so.

"You two kids want another round?" Dermot asks, eyeing the collection of glasses pointedly.

My mouth opens, but Padraig cuts me off. "We're all right, Der. This one's had his fill."

"Glad we agree." The old man sighs and then starts gathering my discarded glasses with gnarled hands that are no less nimble after years of tending his bar. He manages five pint glasses in one hand. "I was running low on these thanks to you."

Following a long glare from Padraig, I call after Dermot, "I'll settle up when you're ready."

"I was ready the moment you walked in looking like you'd killed another one of Eoin's sheep."

Padraig snickers as I puff out my chest indignantly. "I didn't kill one of his sheep!"

Dermot doesn't bother looking over his shoulder. "That's not what your little girl told me at the shop a few weeks ago. Your mam backed her up."

"Women," I moan, digging my hand into my pocket to retrieve my wallet.

"Speaking of women," Padraig segues, "how are you going to fix things with Leona?"

For too long I remain silent, not because I don't want to answer but because I don't know how to. It's what I've contemplated all week long, and I'm no closer to a solution than I was on Monday when I got the brilliant idea to start dropping gifts in front of her closed door.

"Tell me you're going to fix things with her? Callum, she's the best thing to happen to you in all the time I've known you. You can't give up like this. Sure, you were a right arse, but—"

"I'm not giving up," I interject, cutting off whatever insult was about to exit his mouth. "I'm trying, okay? It takes a lot to pivot from keeping everyone as far away as possible to begging someone to come closer in a matter of a month. I'm out of practice. And I fucked up *badly*."

His lips flatline, and the crow's feet around his eyes deepen as he squints at me. "Maybe start with telling her that."

"That becomes difficult to do when she won't leave her room."

"Give her time," he says, unknowingly echoing my mother. "She'll be ready eventually. Just make sure you are, too."

I nod. Dermot catches my eye from behind the counter, waving the card machine in the air to let me know he's not making another trip over here. The legs of my chair scrape loudly against the floorboards as I push it back, standing and feeling every ounce of beer rush straight to my bladder.

Padraig is right, and so is my mam. I have to wait for Leo to be ready to talk. In the meantime I need to work on having the right words to say when she finally is. I'll learn how to apologize in every language if it will somehow balm the wound that I've ripped open.

And then I'll find a way to convince her she's not alone in her grief anymore. That I'm here, and I'm willing to shoulder it if only she'll let me. I don't know what happened with her ex to make her feel like the burden is hers and hers alone, but I'll do everything in my power to help.

The aroma of curry floats down the hall and slaps me in the nose the moment I open the turquoise door of the inn. It's not our usual Sunday dinner, and not one Mam's guests will be particularly fond of when the fumes linger long after we're done eating, but my stomach growls enthusiastically despite all that.

"We're having curry!" Niamh squeals, tugging at my shirt. "Do you think Granny got prawn crackers?"

"I'll bet you she did," I offer. "Why don't you go on and check."

Niamh scampers ahead, disappearing through the open kitchen door.

I try not to stare at the landing of the staircase. I do my best not to picture Leo padding down the steps, pausing when she sees me, and bracing herself on the banister. What I cannot prevent is the phantom feeling of her lips against my ear as she whispers that she's dreamed of me.

When I turn the corner into the kitchen, I leave the ghost in the hall.

Mam is poised over the stove, stirring the simmering liquid gently. "Come have a taste, son. Tell me if it's missing anything."

I do as I'm told, taking the spoon from her hand and blowing on the sauce before tasting it. "Mmm, that's perfect."

"Is it spicy enough?" she asks, eyebrows knit with worry.

I chuckle and step up to the counter where Niamh is sitting, munching on a bowl full of prawn crackers. "Any spicier and this one wouldn't be eating it." I remove the bowl from her lap, much to her dismay. "Leave room for dinner, Niamh."

She pouts so adorably I almost relent.

But then my eye catches over her shoulder, through the window, on the silhouette in the garden. She's reclining in a chair, curled up under a thick blanket to combat the chill in the air. With the sun low on the horizon, her hair glows more chocolate than midnight sky.

"I'll be right back," I tell my daughter, returning the bowl to her.

Mam's gaze tracks me to the back door; I can feel it burning between my shoulder blades. Just as I tug it open, she says, "Remember what I told you."

"I remember," I murmur, slipping out into the evening.

Leo hears my voice or my footsteps, one, because she turns to the side the moment my feet hit the grass. She doesn't address me though, and I can't say I'm surprised. Disappointed, maybe, but not surprised.

I make it all the way to her side before she finally looks up at me, locking her gaze with mine. In the depths of her eyes, which reflect the golden sunlight like the surface of the ocean, I see none of the agony that was present last I saw her. Instead I find acceptance, like she's stared down her fate and made peace with it.

The desire to get down on my knees and grovel is overwhelming.

I remain standing, just barely, but the words spill over my lips in a rush. "Leo, I can't tell you how sorry I am. The things I said…I'll understand if you can never forgive me for them. But I wanted you to know that—"

"Did you know," she interjects, tilting her head to the side, "that poppies are a symbol of remembrance?"

I'm confused for a moment, tipped off-center, until my gaze falls to her lap. There, in the palm of her hand, a small, metallic poppy flower winks up at me.

Chapter Thirty-One

Leona

Even though I know he's a mere foot away from me, I see Callum as if through a kaleidoscope. At once far away and incredibly close. Full of color and light. I can't help but cling to the image for another heartbeat, knowing what darkness is on the horizon.

I wonder if this is how the doctor felt the moment he had to break the news to me. Did he look down at the young woman with a thin paper sheet laid over her lap for modesty and see a person whose life he was about to ruin? Because right now, looking at Callum, that's all I can see.

I pat the chair to my right. "Would you sit?"

He doesn't sit. Instead he drops to his knees on the grass. It brings him closer. Closer than he'll want to be when this is all over.

The sharp edge of the metallic flower stem digs into my palm as I squeeze it shut. When I opened my door and saw yet another of Callum's gifts on the floor outside, I wanted to dig a giant hole and crawl into it. When I saw what was inside, I wanted that hole to take me straight to hell.

"When I found out the baby was…dying—" I choke on the

word. With a deep breath, I push past it. "I read a lot of blogs. Some said not to name her. That it would make things easier." My lower lip quivers. I have to take three measured breaths before I feel I can go on. "But I couldn't leave her nameless. When I pictured her, I never pictured her sick. In my mind she was beautiful and healthy and full of light." A soft smile pulls at the corners of my mouth. "I imagined her running through that field of poppies we found that summer. The meaning just solidified my choice, because I knew I'd remember her for my whole life."

Callum watches me with devastation mottling his features. He places a hand over mine, and I savor the warmth. I memorize the feeling of his rough calluses against my knuckles, the way his hand makes mine look tiny in comparison. There was a time when I thought I would've liked to know it was the last time he would touch me, all those years ago. Now that I do, now that I'm faced with saying goodbye and knowing its permanence, I realize how much better it was to remain in the dark.

"I'm so sorry you had to go through that, Leo." His thumb scrapes over my skin, back and forth. "I can't begin to fathom how it felt."

A piece of my heart falls away like land from a cliffside. I'm permanently altered by the breaking.

"Is that why you and your ex got divorced?" Heat flares in his eyes, burning off the fog of concern. I can see the battle for control rippling just under his skin. Anger—at Nick, perhaps, or the universe in its entirety—flushes his cheeks red. But he grapples with it. He overcomes. "Did he leave you to deal with this alone?"

He's kneeling next to me, and all around him is grass as green as his irises and the beautiful inn I've come to think of as home and beyond that, the sea. I think for a moment I can smell the brine in the air. I wonder if it can wash me clean.

I shake my head, answering both of us.

"Callum," I whimper. I want it to sound braver, but it just doesn't. Removing my hand from beneath his, I settle it over the milky white amulet that rests against my heartbeat. "I found out I was pregnant three months after I got home from Ireland."

It's the stuff of myths, the way he turns to stone. An otherworldly stillness settles over his body. The only thing giving away his humanity is the clenching and unclenching of his jaw.

Instead of waiting for him to speak or to scream or to walk away, I do what I came here to do. I give him the pieces of our daughter that I've clung to all these years. I plant her in his heart and hope she'll bloom.

"I was in shock. I was knee-deep in junior year, missing you terribly, and then I realized my period wasn't coming. I'd been blaming it on stress, but it had been months at that point. The test showed two lines right away. I made an appointment with our campus clinic immediately. When I left that day, it was with a referral to an OB-GYN and the suggestion that something wasn't right."

I tear my gaze away from him because I can't keep going when he looks at me that way. Like I'm some stranger sitting in front of him. The world is spinning around me so badly I have to focus on my knees to avoid getting sick.

"Then it was confirmed. Our daughter had something called Trisomy 18. Her heart, her body, her brain…none of it would develop as it should. She was terminal." Tears pool in my eyes, blurring my vision. Good. Good riddance. I'm so tired of seeing a world without her in it. "I don't have any excuses, Callum. I should've called you. I should've explained. You would've come; I know you would've. But all I could think about was saving my baby. *My* baby. So selfish, I know. There was no part of me that could fathom how the universe could give her to me just to take her away. There was no room for anything else in my world."

"Not even me."

His voice is paper thin, so fragile the evening breeze could slice it in two. I blink the tears away until he comes into focus. He's removed his glasses and folded them. They give his fist something to wrap around. With his face bare, for a moment he's twenty-two again. I imagine we've stepped back in time and we're crying over ultrasound pictures, together in our grief, rather than separated by everything I kept from him all these years.

I shake my head gently. "No, not even you."

His head bobs once and then he tucks his chin, staring down at the blades of grass between us. "When did she pass?"

"Sometime in the middle of the night the week I entered my third trimester." I gulp down the knot in my throat. I force myself to keep going. "Just like that. She was here and then she was gone, and I couldn't fathom why she didn't take me with her. I delivered her on the seventh of March."

His eyes go round despite himself. "The day before your birthday?"

"The day before my birthday." My lips press into a grim line, wet with the stickiness of tears. The memory of my mother sleeping on the couch beneath the hospital window as dawn came on my twenty-first birthday fills my mind. I laid in that bed and prayed for time to turn back. For the sun to sink below the horizon and the clock to rewind and my daughter to be with me again. It's the last birthday wish I ever made.

"She'd be, what, eleven now?" He studies his hands as he counts up the years. He peers up at me. "Niamh would have a big sister."

It's in that moment that he comes unraveled. His face crumples like fisted paper. Tears stream down his cheeks and fall to the grass below. He braces himself on me, not because he wants to touch me, but because he can barely remain upright. I hesitate with my hand outstretched over him, desperately wanting to comfort him while not feeling I have any right to witness him processing the cumulative grief I've been shouldering for years, all at once.

It's too much. It's all my fault.

"I'm so sorry, Callum," I whisper. It's the most my voice can do. "I understand if you hate me. I hate myself."

His fingers dig into my bicep. "Why?" he chokes. His gaze travels upward, landing on the place where he's grabbing me, and suddenly he lets go.

"I told you, I was selfish. I was angry." I suck in the biting winter air and let it burn my lungs. "I was consumed by grief."

He jolts to his feet, towering over me. His hand moves to rake through his hair, and the vein on his forehead pulses. The sudden movement makes me recoil, and in that moment the back door of the inn flies open and I'm reminded that we aren't alone in the world.

"Now, Callum," I hear Siobhan say. With a glance spared in her direction, I see she's bracing herself against the doorframe. Behind her, Padraig scoops Niamh up and disappears into the hall.

"Relax, Mam," he growls. He staggers away from me but never breaks eye contact. "I'm not asking why you didn't tell me," he says, lowering his voice so it can remain just between us.

I swallow thickly, wiping my face with the sleeve of my sweater. "What are you asking?"

"Why do you hate yourself, Leo?"

The world tilts on its axis and nearly spills me over its side. I imagine him not as he is but as a priest on the other side of a confessional. Only he can *see* me; he has always been able to see me. And he wants to know the truth.

The truth that I've buried away, out of sight even from myself. Because the fact is, I don't hate myself for being selfish or ignorant; I don't hate myself for making the wrong decisions at twenty years old. I don't even hate myself for never returning to Ireland or for marrying Nick or for breaking my own heart to fit into the life I received as a consolation when the one I wanted could no longer be had.

He stares down at me, unmoving. Unrelenting. There's no place to go, to hide. There's only the two of us. There's only ever been the two of us.

"My body failed our daughter," I say at last. "I can never forgive myself for that."

He winces like he's taken a blow. For a moment I don't think he'll respond at all. But he glances over at his mother, communicating silently, and then his gaze returns to mine and he nods. "Well, I don't hate you, Leo." His voice is gentle, solemn. Full of more grace than I've ever deserved. "I'm in shock. I'm devastated. But I don't hate you." He takes one step toward the door and then another, never once looking away from me. "I just… need some time. I need some time."

With that, he turns and brushes past his mother into the inn.

And every knot holding me together comes unraveled.

The sound of Siobhan's footfall on the grass barely makes it past the roaring in my ears. Soon I'm being yanked from my chair and her arms are encircling me, holding me up. She presses my face into the curve of her neck and she sways back and forth, as if she's rocking a baby. I cry until nothing comes out. I cry until my throat goes raw.

Even after the tears have subsided, she strokes my hair and shushes me softly. We continue our gentle sway, like a slow dance in the garden, until even the hiccups have stopped shaking my body.

"What do you want me to do?" she asks, using her soft, weathered hands to cup my cheeks and face me head-on. Her tone is unrelenting, but her gaze is kind. "How can I help?"

I bite down hard on my lower lip, nibbling away at the tender flesh. My gaze lifts to the darkening sky and the birds that fly overhead and this feeling that I haven't felt in years bubbles to the top of my heart.

"I want to talk to my mom."

Siobhan nods and gives a gentle grin. "Then let's go give your mam a call."

"She'll be busy with dinner," I mumble.

"It's earlier there," she says, guiding me toward the inn, past the simmering pot of curry and up the stairs to my room. She opens the door for me and walks me over to my bed, retrieves my phone from the bedside table, and settles it in my lap. "And besides, no matter the time, she'd want you to call her." She presses a kiss against my forehead. "That's what mothers are for."

"Thank you," I say, my voice wavering.

"Anytime." She pads over to the doorway but turns to look at me before disappearing into the hall. "Oh and Leona?"

"Yes?"

With a gentle smile and a sympathetic tilt of her head, she scans my face. "It takes time. But time is all it takes."

I nod because it's all I can do, and the door snicks closed behind her.

Chapter Thirty-Two

Callum

"Daddy, come have tea with me!"

I glance up at Niamh's little face peering out of the window of her tree house. She's clutching her raggedy bear to her chest and pleading with large, round eyes for me to scurry up the ladder and stuff myself through that impossibly small entrance Padraig mismeasured. Even if I were a contortionist, there'd be no getting through it without detaching my arms.

"Sorry, love, I can't fit up there," I call with a shrug. "Too broad."

Her eyebrows scrunch together. "What's broad?"

I cast my hands wide and puff out my cheeks before stomping around my back garden. "Big, like a giant troll!"

She giggles but then brings her bear's muzzle to her ear and tilts her head like she's listening. "Sleepy says he's a bear and he still fits."

"Rather small bear," I huff.

"Rude!" she shouts, and then she drops away from sight. The only hint of life coming from the plain wooden tree house is a trill of giggles floating on the breeze.

A half smile is all I can offer. For the past twenty-four hours I've been desperately trying to grasp this new reality. One where Leo and I had a child. One where that child is no longer in this world.

Suddenly the timeline of her cutting me off makes so much more sense. She'd grown distant around the time she would've discovered she was pregnant. Her responses went from instantaneous to sporadic to meager at best. Then I reached out to wish her a happy birthday, and I never heard from her again.

For years I've been feeling sorry for myself. In those weeks and months after, I would work long hours just to fill my time with something other than staring at the phone, waiting for her to call. Many nights were spent lying in bed with my eyes wide open and watering. *So this is my life*, I thought back then. *I've had the very best, and nothing else will ever compare.*

Now I look back and realize that on the other side of the ocean, Leo was probably lying awake as well. But it wasn't me she was missing desperately. It was never about me at all.

Maybe it was never about me with any of them.

I should've gone to her, I realize. I should've bought a ticket and showed up on her doorstep. Imagine how differently it would've all turned out if for once I hadn't let my fear of being left behind overpower the possibility of having something good in my life. Something—*someone*—I could keep.

"The garden looks so different without all the flowers."

I turn to find my mother standing with the garden gate thrown open beside her, both hands buried in her trouser pockets. Her hair is pulled back from her face and pinned behind her ears, making her appear younger. Even though her curls are silver. Even though the skin on her face falls in soft folds around her sympathetic eyes.

I nod while digging the tip of my shoe in the grass. "They'll be back come spring." Pausing, I glance at the enormous hydrangea bushes that have gone dormant for the winter. "Always are."

"Nothing if not dependable, those things." She makes her way to my side and loops an arm around my waist. "How are you holding up?"

The snort that rips out of me is entirely involuntary and far too harsh. There's nothing I can do but let it dissipate in the wind. I quickly glance up. Niamh goes on playing, random squeaks and babbles coming down from the tree house as she hosts a tea party with her closest stuffed friends. Satisfied that she's out of earshot, I smile grimly at my mother.

"I've certainly had better days."

She nods like this is the answer she was expecting. She, too, is studying the tree house. "Darren called."

"Did he now," I say, not asking really. The only shocking thing about it is that it took him this long to resort to phoning his sister.

"Oh yeah," she says, releasing me to fold her arms over her chest in an attempt to ward off the cold. "Says you were a useless sap last week and then you're after calling out today."

A heavy sigh passes over my lips as I rake my hand through my hair. "Sorry, mam, I'll give him a call tomorrow. I just—"

"No need, Callum. My brother may be a workaholic but he's not heartless. He was concerned about you, that's all. I told him you had some things come up that needed your attention and you'd be back to it when you could be. He understood."

For some reason, that weight being lifted off my shoulders is my undoing. I stagger backward, suddenly lightheaded, and drop into the uncomfortable iron bistro chair left behind by my long dead gran.

"You all right?" Mam asks, kneeling in front of me with concern darkening her eyes. She quickly scans my body, looking for anything amiss.

"I'm fine," I groan. A deep inhale calms the spinning in my head, but the air burns on its way down my throat. Or perhaps it's my tears, lodged there and waiting for an excuse to fall. "I'm grand." I stare past my mam, past the garden where my daughter is playing, and onward to the mountains in the distance. I will the lie to become the truth.

She clicks her tongue in disapproval. "You don't have to be fine, Callum."

I shake my head, because how do I explain to her the way it feels to be me right now? To be barely above water, treading in the sadness and grief and anger all at once, and still trying to do right by the little girl a few meters away in a tree house. To still work and put a roof over her head and cook her warm meals when all I want is to curl up in a ball and let the universe sort itself out, because clearly things have gotten tangled up.

She frowns as she takes me in, reading me in the way only our parents can. She braces a hand on each of my biceps and squeezes, then shakes me slightly, zeroing my focus in on her.

"Talk to me, son." Another little shake, a bit more desperate this time. "Let me be there for you."

Granda always talked about the importance of being Niamh's safe place to land. Suddenly I'm filled with regret that in all the time I spent learning to be that for her, I never thanked him for being mine. I never asked him who would take over when he was no longer here.

Mam is gazing at me earnestly, offering a life rope. If Granda were here, he'd tell me a real man knows when to accept help. I decide it's time to grab on with all I've got.

"Did you know?" My voice warbles, but it's clear enough. "About Leo? And the baby?"

She nods almost imperceptibly and then takes the other seat and drags it over to sit right in front of me. "I had my suspicions, but they were confirmed after the fight you two had."

My hands are trembling where they rest on my knees. "How could she have kept my daughter from me?"

"I don't think that was her intention, Callum. Even if that's what ended up happening." She frowns and the light fades from green eyes that are a mirror image of mine. It's the last thing I see before her gaze drops to her lap. "I never told you this, but your father and I had another baby before you. A little girl. I miscarried her halfway through the pregnancy, and it was a long time before I could look at myself in the mirror. An even longer time before I could forgive myself. I felt like I had failed her. Like it was my fault she died."

Shock reverberates through my system. "I never knew you went through all that."

"It's so difficult to talk about. Society doesn't want to hear it. Or if they do, there's a shelf life for how long they'll let you grieve before they think you should've moved on. But you don't move on. That's your *child,* for Christ's sake." She fiddles with a claddagh ring on her finger. A teardrop falls onto the back of her hand that she makes no move to wipe away. "Your granda gave me this ring when he found out I was pregnant with her. For a long time it sat in my jewelry box gathering dust. I'd pull it out late at night when I missed her more than I could bear. I've grieved her my entire life. I'll keep grieving her until I'm dead and gone and can be with her again."

I place my hand over hers and squeeze, settling her fidgeting and wiping off her tear in the same motion. "I'm so sorry, Mam."

She finally glances up at me, and it's the first time in my life I've sensed her seeing me as her equal. Not as her child but as her peer. A feeling of camaraderie passes between us, like we are soldiers in the same trenches, fighting shoulder to shoulder. Like she knows what my enemy looks like because she's been facing it since before I was born.

"All I wanted to say is, I know you are hurting. I know that what Leo did hurt you." She squeezes my hand. "I will leave it to her to tell you her story, but I'll say this: that girl has spent the last decade punishing herself. She doesn't need your help to do it. It is entirely up to you if you want to be a part of each other's lives, and I will support you no matter what, but just know that if your father had loved you as much as she loved that little girl of yours, I never would've let him go. I'd have followed him to the ends of the Earth."

She doesn't say it to wound me. My father's lack of interest in my life is not news. But it still stings nonetheless.

"I don't know where to go from here," I say weakly.

She shrugs. "Neither did she. Why do you think it took her so long?"

A tear spills out of the corner of my eye, and she swipes it away with her thumb, pinching my cheek on the retreat.

"Granny!" Niamh shrieks, leaping down from the ladder and landing with a firm thud. She runs across the garden, rosy-cheeked beneath layers of wool, with her teddy bear swinging from her grasp. Mam scoops her into a hug, grunting softly at the impact, and smiles the world's saddest smile over Niamh's shoulder at me.

Looking at my curly-haired, bright-eyed daughter, I force myself to imagine what I'd do if I lost her. From the moment Catherine got the positive test, I was Niamh's father. I felt it in my bones. The universe shifted into place, and I was where I was always meant to end up. If she'd been sick, I would've been devastated. If she'd died, my whole reason for living would've gone with her.

Suddenly the woman Leo has become, the more reserved one who holds herself back from the joys of life we used to take for ourselves unabashedly, makes perfect sense to me. She's a moon without a planet to pull her close. She's had to rebuild her world from scratch, alone.

"What can I do?" I ask. Niamh looks from me to Mam, trying to ascertain what exactly she's missed. Mam holds my gaze steadily, but the corners of her mouth turn down.

"I overheard her talking to her mother last night." She squeezes Niamh close, strategically covering her ears in the process. "There were talks of plane tickets."

My heart sinks all the way to my feet. "I can't lose her again."

Mam nods, her eyes sparking for the first time since she arrived. "Then don't."

"But how?" I plead. "If she wants to leave, I can't stop her."

She lets Niamh loose after planting a sloppy kiss on her cheek, which my daughter promptly wipes off. "Can we get take-away?" Niamh asks.

Mam smiles down at her. "Sure, love. Go hop in the car; I'll be there in a second."

"Yay!" Niamh cries, spinning around and making a beeline for the car.

"If she wants to leave," Mam says, drawing my attention back to her, "then you're right, you can't stop her." She steps forward and grasps each of my shoulders, our eyes nearly level with her standing while I'm still seated. "But you can give her a reason not to go."

I swallow thickly and nod because I don't trust myself to speak. Mam returns the gesture before following after Niamh, leaving me to figure out how to be something I've never quite mastered: someone worth staying for.

Chapter Thirty-Three

Leona

It's amazing how neatly a life can fit into a suitcase. All my clothes, toiletries, and miscellaneous items have stretched the bag to its limits, but it finally zips when I put my back into it. Glancing around the room, which I've stripped of its linens for washing, it's like the past month and a half never happened. I'll go and some weary traveler will take my place here, and the universe will slowly heal the laceration of my brief presence.

The thought of yet again crashing my parents' empty nest leaves my bones heavy. Maybe I'll get a job at a hotel nearby running their housekeeping services. I've been surprised to discover I like the manual labor and the logistics of timing it perfectly. I could rent my own place. Make a meager but mostly painless life for myself.

Just as I'm about to leave the converted attic space, my gaze catches on the floral cover of Poppy's journal. My heart lurches. How could I have almost forgotten it? I scoop it up and go to place it in one of the exterior pockets of my suitcase, only to find there's no room left.

I sit down on top of my suitcase and start thumbing through

the pages. The letters date back almost a decade, starting on the first anniversary of Poppy's passing. Buried under the grief and crawling toward graduation, I turned to writing to her as a way to off-load some of the pain. It helped. Infinitesimally at first, but more with each honest word I was able to lay out on paper.

The journal is nearly full. I hadn't noticed until now, but there are only a handful of blank pages left at the end of the book. It breaks me at the same time that it balms a hidden wound, like I'm running out of time to talk to her while also realizing I've done what I needed to do in telling her story. There's not much more that needs to be said.

I flip to the first entry and stare at the scrawled words of a shattered mother trying to come to terms with an unfathomable loss. The memory is as fresh to me today as it was the first time I wrote it down.

My Darling Poppy,

I've never imagined myself dying quietly, slipping into the night without a word edgewise. In my head I'll get a chance to put up a fight. I'll battle an illness to the brutal end, or I'll be caught in the crosshairs of a shooting and die shielding innocents with my body. I'll be sprawled out on the pavement after a car crash, tracing my goodbyes into the asphalt. It's not that I hope for it; it's just that it's all I've ever been able to imagine. Death wouldn't be this thing that happened to me. I'd be an active participant.

But you, my darling girl, had no such plans.

That night, you kept me up kicking just as hard as

any other night. Over the past year I've tried to convince myself that there was some detectable difference, some measurable withdrawal. But there wasn't any; I know it in my soul. You gave it your all, like you had your whole life, and then sometime between falling asleep at 1 a.m. and rolling down my waistband for the ultrasound tech that morning, you slipped away. Quietly. Unannounced. Our favorite tech just looked at me and I knew. I knew you were gone.

They prepared for the delivery right away. I called my mom. I don't know what she told Dad or what he thought was going on, but she came. And then she settled in beside me with that ironclad strength that only women have, and she helped her daughter do the hardest thing she'd ever have to do.

When you were born, the room, which had previously been a cacophony of machines whirring and nurses giving orders, fell completely silent. Even the monitors stopped beeping. We all refrained from breathing, to leave more oxygen for you. But you were already gone when they laid you on my chest, sweet girl. You were perfect, and perfectly still. And oh, how I loved you.

I clamp the journal shut. I can't read anymore. It's real enough for me in my own memories; I don't need the reminder to see the scene clear as day.

As my hand grazes over the floral cover, I realize that I'm not the one I've been writing this for all along. I know Poppy. I know every second of her existence down to the very heartbeat, because it is so intrinsically intertwined with mine. But Callum doesn't, because I didn't let him.

There are sad memories here, but there are happy ones, too. There are stories of the first time I felt her move, the first time she got the hiccups. There are fantasies about what we'd be doing now, as a family. Everything I could never bring myself to tell him is written here, and it's time for me to let it go. To show him all the parts of our daughter I love so that he can love her, too.

I tuck the journal under my arm and drag my suitcase toward the stairs, not chancing another look over my shoulder at the beautiful attic room that finally gave me back my life.

My phone buzzes in my pocket, and I remove it to see Padraig's reply come through.

LEONA

I need a lift.

PODGE

One ride, coming your way.

I chuckle despite myself and then shove the phone back into my pocket.

At the foot of the stairs, the sound of Niamh playing in Siobhan's room drifts to me. I'm halfway tempted to say goodbye to her, but I remind myself it's not my place. Maybe one day Callum will tell her about her older sister, but it will be his decision. And his decision if he wants to include me in that narrative at all. Soon

I'll be just another faceless guest in her memory, and it's for the best.

My footsteps echo down the hall, reaching Siobhan at the front desk long before I do. She turns to look, and an expression of acceptance rather than surprise passes over her face.

"That's it then? You're leaving us?" she asks, leaning her hip against the check-in counter.

I shrug at the same time my gaze hits the floor. It's the best I can do to avoid bursting into tears. "It's about time. I long overstayed my welcome."

"Nonsense," she scoffs, drawing my gaze to her. She's smiling, but it doesn't quite reach her eyes. "You're always welcome here, Leona."

My heart swells in my chest. Why does leaving feel so like I'm losing something that I can never get back?

"Thank you for everything. I owe you."

"Are you kidding? As clean as this place is, I'd say you were severely underpaid." She pinches my shoulder playfully. "Our reviews are going straight for the gutter without you here."

I laugh half-heartedly, and then silence falls over both of us. Her smile falters.

"Come here, you," she says and then she grabs me and pulls me in. I pinch the journal to my side so it doesn't fall as I'm swallowed up by her fierce embrace. Before I realize what's happening, her mouth finds my ear, and she whispers, "I want you to know that you are an incredibly strong person that was dealt a terrible hand. One that no one can ever be prepared for. You were so young, Leona. You can't keep punishing yourself." She pauses for a moment before adding, "You were the absolute best mother you could be to that little girl while you had her."

She releases me, and I stagger backward. I move the journal over my heart and draw in a jagged breath. "Thank you. I needed that more than you know."

She nods as if she does in fact know. "You're doing the best you can now. I can see it. Callum can see it. He just has this filter through which he sees the world, formed by his own bad experiences with his father and Catherine and…well, he'll get past it, is what I'm trying to say. You both will. Life has been incredibly unfair to you both, but it's all about to turn around. I promise you that."

Before I can say anything, the front door swings open behind me. We both turn to see Padraig standing in the doorway with his arms crossed over his chest and a solemn expression on his face as he examines my luggage.

"Don't suppose you're off to the shops, then?" he mumbles.

I shake my head with my lips pressed into a thin line. "I was wondering if you'd take me up to the train station in Killarney so I could skip the bus. I'll pay, of course."

He opens his mouth, but when he sees my face, he stops midprotest. Instead he turns to Siobhan. "And you're just okay with this?"

She shakes her head at him but forces a grim smile onto her face before squeezing me one last time. "Don't be a stranger, Leona."

"Thank you again, Siobhan. For everything."

Padraig looks from her to me in disbelief. "I just want it to be known that I in no way support what is happening here." He eyeballs my suitcase but then turns to walk away. "In fact, I won't be carrying your luggage to the car. I'm protesting."

With a sigh, I hoist the hefty bag over the threshold and follow him to his taxicab, not allowing myself one more word to Siobhan. I've been saving my tears for the hardest goodbye. I can't waste anymore here.

Once I've deposited my suitcase in the trunk, I take my seat on the passenger side. Padraig is staring straight ahead, making no noise aside from the *swish-swish* of his tracksuit as he shifts the car into gear.

"Before we head to Killarney," I say, drawing his attention briefly from the road before he remembers that he's mad at me, "I need to make one stop."

He sighs heavily like he's just realized his decision to give me the silent treatment isn't really going to fly. Nor is he exactly a pro at keeping quiet. "Where to?"

"Callum's, if you don't mind."

His gaze cuts to me briefly before he regains his composure. "Callum's it is."

As if the universe knows this is the last time I'll ever see this place, the overcast winter sky parts just as we crest the hill leading to the cottage. Dense gray gives way to buttery sunlight, warming the air by a few degrees. I still tuck my hands into my armpits while walking across the gravel to the front door in an attempt to warm them. I can feel Padraig's gaze burning a hole between my shoulder blades from where he waits in the car, but I fight the urge to turn around and plead for his help. This is something I have to do alone.

Callum opens the door before I've even knocked twice, like he's been waiting there for this exact moment. For me.

No matter how many times I see him, I'll never get tired of his face. Even as stressed as he clearly is, beneath the worried crease between his eyes and purple bags from sleeplessness, he is the most beautiful man I've ever seen. The loops and swirls of his blond hair are especially chaotic today, and longer than usual, like he's in desperate need of a cut. He's let his facial hair grow out. There's a pang of sadness in my heart that I won't get to see his scarred chin one last time. I have to swallow back the lump that rises in my throat.

"Leo," he says, and it's like the past six weeks never happened. It's the very first day, after a long time away. I have a chance to do it all over again. To tell him the truth from the beginning.

I uncross my arms, letting the journal fall away from my chest. His gaze drops to it, and the crease between his brows deepens. "What are yo—"

"I want you to have this," I say, thrusting it toward him. If he doesn't take it right now, my resolve will falter. When he hesitantly reaches for it, I let it go like it's on fire.

"Your diary?"

"It's not a diary. Not exactly, anyway." I shift my weight from one foot to another, staring at the journal rather than at him. "It's full of letters I've written to Poppy over the years, starting on the first anniversary of... I'm sorry." I draw in air, but it doesn't quite do what it's supposed to. My lungs are now full, but I still feel like I'm drowning.

Callum sees me struggling, and he quickly wraps an arm around my back and urges me toward the door. "Come inside for a second."

"I...can't. I'm sorry, it's just that—"

His gaze has traveled past me, to where Padraig is sitting in his cab, waiting. Realization dawns on his face. "Are you leaving?"

I bite down hard on my lower lip and nod, though it's more of a tremor.

Panic flashes in his emerald eyes. "No. You're not, Leo. You can't leave. You can't shut me out again."

Sobs begin to bubble in my chest, and it takes everything in me to breathe normally. Or as close to normal as I can get. "I've done enough damage here. It's time for me to go. I've got a ticket. Padraig's going to take me to catch the train, and then I'll be out of your hair for good."

"Except I don't want you out of my hair!" He sucks in an exasperated breath. "Don't run. *Please* don't run again. I'll cover your plane ticket, whatever the cost. I don't care. Just stay."

The tears fall in hot streaks down my face. "Why would you want me to stay? All I do is hurt you."

His mouth opens to speak before he reconsiders. He takes my hand and pulls me into the house, letting the door fall closed behind me so we are out of sight of his friend. When we've reached the living room, he sets the journal down carefully on the nearest side table and then turns to face me. "Look, Leo, I'm pretty sure all this time what we've really been doing is hurting ourselves."

A sickly laugh-cough spurts out of me. "What are you talking about?"

"I was afraid everyone I loved would leave me, and so I put myself into positions where that was the only possible outcome. You were afraid no one would ever forgive you for losing our daughter, and so you never forgave yourself. But I forgive you, Leo."

My knees give out beneath me, but he's right there to catch me, loop his arms around my waist and pull me to him. There is no space between us. There is only our lungs and our hearts thrumming in tandem against one another.

"You forgive me?" I say, hesitant in the face of mercy.

"I do. I forgive you for not telling me about her. But Leo, you have never needed forgiving for losing her, because it wasn't your fault. I don't need to read that journal to know how much you loved her. To know you would've given anything to save her. I know you would've because I know *you*." He scrapes a calloused thumb over my cheek, brushing away my tears. His lips are a breath away. "I know you, and I love you."

My heart stills in my chest when he releases my face. His hands trail along my body as he kneels in front of me, his touch traveling down my neck and across my shoulders, over my arms and steadying at my waist. When his knees hit the floor, he looks up at me with tears in his eyes, along with a question.

"I love you, too, Callum. It's one of the few things I've ever been sure of."

It's the answer he was looking for. Instead of responding, he tucks his thumbs under the hem of my sweater and lifts them up, exposing my abdomen.

"What are you doi—"

He interrupts my question with a kiss, placed against the angry red lightning strike that sits just below my navel. "Our girl was a fighter," he whispers, his lips brushing against another stretch mark. There are only a handful. I wasn't done growing when I lost her. "And so are you."

I can't hold myself up anymore. I drop to my knees in front of him and find his gaze. My fingers comb through the hair at his temples before locking together against the nape of his neck. "I'm so sorry."

"So am I." He smiles ruefully, cups my jaw, and tilts my lips toward his. "I should've gotten on a plane and come for you all those years ago."

I shake my head gently. "I wasn't ready for you then."

"But you are now?"

I let our mouths brush against each other once, twice. "I am."

"Does this mean you aren't leaving?" His eyebrows arch, gaze alight with hope.

"I'm here for as long as you'll have me."

I feel a flicker of a smile on his lips. "So forever then?"

"I suppose I could make that work."

As soon as the words leave my mouth, he covers it with his. He clings to me so tightly I'm not sure where one of us ends and the other begins. Our lips part to one another, and then his tongue traces along mine. The warmth heals something inside of me that had long been frozen over. I melt into his touch, savoring each pass of his strong hand over my waist, my spine, my hip. His other hand continues to cup my jaw, holding on to me for dear life.

Finally we have to come up for air. I suck in a breath as he groans, "Leo, I've waited twelve years to make love to you again. I'm not doing it on the floor."

Before I can respond, he stands, then scoops me into his arms and marches toward the hall. I'm thrown onto the bed with very little grace, and then his shirt flies over his head, fluttering to the ground somewhere behind him. He removes his glasses and tosses them in the same general direction. His belt and pants follow suit, and then his underwear. When he's finally naked, I stare at him with my mouth agape.

"It's like having my own personal viewing of David."

His eyebrow quirks. "Don't talk about other guys right now."

"It's a *statue!*" I squeal.

"I'll show you something that's rock-hard."

I groan, but it does something miraculous for my heart to joke again after all that has happened. "So you're no better at dirty talk than you were at twenty-two. Noted."

"Oh, Leo," he growls, stalking forward and planting a hand on either side of me. "You have no idea."

Chapter Thirty-Four

Callum

"Take your clothes off."

She balks, then quickly recovers, settling onto her back and grabbing the hem of her sweater to drag it over her head. She's wearing that same black lace bra from last time, and the realization goes straight to my dick.

"All of them," I add when she pauses like her job is done.

She smirks but begins working on her zipper. "What happened to not wanting to be rushed?"

"That was before." She slides her jeans down as best she can with me towering over her, and I take them the rest of the way off. Not waiting for her help, I grab her panties and scale the length of her legs with them, too. "Now I need you so badly I can barely breathe."

A sigh passes over her parted lips. "So you *have* gotten better at talking."

"Told you so." I hook my arm under her hips and move her up the bed so there is room for me to stretch out over her. Then my hand trails up her spine, and I undo the clasp of her bra. She takes over, tugging the straps from her shoulders and tossing the bra to the side. She's bare beneath me, and it's the most beautiful thing I've ever seen.

The last time I made love to Leo, we were barely more than teenagers. Neither of us had any meat on our bones, any stories to tell, any idea the rarity of our feelings for each other. But now she's a woman. Her hips are wider and her breasts fuller. Her nipples are dark and pebbled in the cool air. Those stretch marks from the child she carried for us nearly bring me to my fucking knees.

"I'm going to spend the rest of my life showing you just how beautiful I think you are." I capture her nipple between my teeth and suck.

Her back arches beneath me, pressing her even closer. I can feel every swell and curve of her body. I ache for her in a way I'd forgotten I could.

"Spread your legs for me, baby," I say, my breath causing goose bumps to rise on her breasts, and she does. I settle into the welcome embrace of her thighs, feeling the heat and wetness of her against the length of me. A groan rips through me. It's nearly the end of me before we've even begun. "This is going to be embarrassingly quick, and I'm so sorry but I cannot wait. I'll make it up to you afterward, okay?"

She nods, while at the same time digging her heels into my ass cheeks, urging me closer. "We've got the rest of our lives to take our time."

"That's the sexiest thing you could've said." I dip my head to take her other nipple into my mouth, capturing the other with my fingers and pinching it. She cries out and grinds into me, and my vision goes white at the edges.

I lick and suck my way up her breast to her collarbone and then to her neck, finally landing at her ear where I draw the lobe in between my teeth. My breath flows over her skin, causing her to shiver. At the same time my hand dips between us and I spread her lips before burying a finger and then two inside her.

"This feels a lot like taking it slow," she gasps, bucking her hips. I grind my palm into her clit in response, still stroking her with my fingers. "I need you, not your hand."

"Sorry, I got distracted." I pull out of her, and she whimpers. I nip her bottom lip and then reach for the bedside table, retrieving a condom from the top drawer and tearing it open with my teeth. I offer it to her with a lazy grin. "Would you do the honors?"

She giggles but takes the offered condom and unrolls it on my cock. Just the feeling of her doing so is nearly enough to end me.

I guide myself to her entrance, feeling her stretch around me as I push forward with painstaking slowness. Her head tilts back, and her mouth opens on a moan. I rock my hips steadily, taking more of her each time until I'm buried completely within her.

Her heat envelops me, and suddenly I'm starved and she's the first thing I've tasted in a decade. I thrust into her with everything I have, and she cries out in response. Her arms come around me and her nails anchor into my shoulder blades and it's a glorious pain coupled with the pleasure I'm feeling. Her eyelids flutter closed as she loses herself in the rhythm, and her hand moves between us to rub her clit in tandem with my thrusts.

"Fuck, I love it when you touch yourself." I flick my tongue over her nipple in the way I remember her liking, and feel her muscles convulse around me. "Leo, I need you to look at me while you get yourself off."

Her eyes open and she finds me in the dim light of the room. I lose myself in the feeling of her and the endless blue of her gaze and the swell of emotion in my chest. It crashes over me like a wave, and I let myself drown in it.

"I'm not ready for this to be over yet," I say.

She tilts her hips upward, which drives me deeper into her core. "It's just beginning, Callum," she whispers. Her fingers continue circling her clit while she uses her other hand to reach for a pillow, which she tucks beneath her elevated hips. The new range of motion fills me with ecstasy on every stroke, and the moan that rolls out of her tells me I'm not alone.

To see her so confident in herself, in what she wants, makes me fall even further in love with her. It makes me want to give her the world. My life. My *soul*.

She's always had it, I remind myself. To think otherwise all this time was simply idiocy on my part.

Her dark, wild hair is splayed over my sheets, and her skin is flushed as her back arches with pleasure. It's a beauty that's raw and unabashed. It's every wet dream I've had of her since the day she walked into my life.

Unable to hold myself back any longer, I thrust into her with everything I have. Steady rhythm gives way to desperation. I need to be as close to her as possible. She's the sun, and I'm ready to burn.

Her inner walls tighten around me, and her hand locks onto my bicep, anchoring herself as her own orgasm builds.

"I'm going to come," she cries.

"I'm right here with you."

Stars explode across my vision, but I watch her through it all. The pleasure between us swells into a beautiful crescendo, and then we come down together, the way we always should've been.

When the aftershocks have subsided, I roll off her and discard the condom. She turns to her side, leaving a place for me behind her, and sighs contentedly when I curve around the half-moon of her body.

"I've missed you so badly," I whisper against the slick skin of her neck. I follow it up by licking her, and she laughs.

"Stop, that tickles!" she shrieks, and then she rolls to face me. Her expression grows serious. She traces a hand along my cheek, around the shell of my ear, and down my jawline, following it with her gaze. "I've missed you, too. More than you know."

I smile down at her, basking in the glow of her happiness. It's the first time I truly recognize her, without the guards she's built up around herself all these years. She's got the beginnings of laugh lines around her lips, and it thrills me to see it. To know she's been laughing, even in her grief. To know that there is still joy to come.

Her hand moves from me to find the amulet that dangles between her breasts. The one she always has on. I cover her hand with mine and turn our palms over to take a better look at it. The milky white stone is unlike any I've ever seen, cut into an oval and set on a thin, gold chain. I tilt it in the low light, trying to figure out exactly what it is.

"It's made from some of Poppy's ashes," she says, answering my unspoken question.

Tears prick at my eyes, but I blink them away. This is a happy moment, her sharing our daughter with me. I don't want to cry now.

I bring the stone to my lips and kiss it before letting it fall back against her skin. She looks up at me with her mouth parted but doesn't say a word.

"Tell me about her."

She starts to roll toward the edge of the bed. "I brought the journal so you could read—"

I grab her hip and steady her in place. "I want to hear it from you."

She draws her bottom lip between her teeth.

"Hey," I murmur, pressing my lips to her forehead. "It doesn't have to be the sad things. Tell me the happy things."

"Like what?"

I press my lips together and squint at her as I consider the endless list of details I want to know. "Like what did you crave when you were pregnant with her?"

She laughs, and the sound is like music. "Takis and cherry Pepsi. Not at the same time."

"But you hate spicy food!"

Leona rolls onto her back so she can stare at the ceiling, unseeing, and picture that time. "I know, but pregnancy makes you do crazy things."

"What else?" I prop myself up with one arm, drinking in the vision of her naked body. "I want to know everything."

"She loved when I would sing to her," she muses, smiling softly. "Especially Christmas music. I wasn't showing yet when I went home for Christmas that semester. Aside from the morning sickness, I didn't even *feel* pregnant. But one night Momma and I were dancing together while 'Rocking Around the Christmas Tree' was playing, and that was the first time I felt her kick. Even after Christmas had come and gone, I kept singing carols to make her happy."

I can see it so clearly in my mind that for a moment I don't trust myself to speak for fear my voice will break.

She must notice the shift in my expression, because she turns to look at me. "Are you okay?"

I nod as my hand falls to brush her hair back from her forehead. "I just love you so much."

Her eyes soften. "I never thought you'd be able to feel that for me again after everything that's happened."

"I don't know how *not* to love you. It's as natural to me as breathing."

She stills beneath my touch. "I'm not the same person anymore, Callum. Losing the baby changed me. I had to grow up really, really quickly." A tear trickles over the precipice of her eye. "I could never—*will* never—be that person again. She died with our daughter that day."

I pull her to me and press my lips against her forehead. "I'd have you no differently."

After a long moment she draws back abruptly with her eyes wide. "What will Niamh think?"

"She'll think 'Thank God, someone who finally knows how to do plaits.'"

We both erupt into laughter, and it's the best kind of euphoria I've ever felt. Happiness after so much darkness. Pleasure after a decade of pain.

"Do you think your mom has already sold off my room?"

I glance at my imaginary watch, then drop my arm with a huff. "Doubt she's even looked at it. Before you, those rooms would sit as long as she could get away with before she could be bothered to clean them. Luggage would be piling up in the foyer."

She swats my chest. "Be nice to your mom. She only let my suitcase sit for half a day." She pauses for a moment, then shoots upright. "Fuck, my suitcase!" She clambers out of bed and starts grabbing for her clothes while heat travels straight to her ears. "Oh God, do you think Podge has been waiting this whole time?"

Before I can answer, she's jogging down the hallway toward the front door. I quickly step back into my pants and follow suit, finding her standing in the open doorway looking down at her luggage. No taxicab in sight.

Her hand finds her hips as she scans the horizon before turning to me. "How long do you think he waited?"

My phone buzzes from the back pocket where I left it. As soon as I unlock it and the message appears before me, I can't help but laugh. "I think he was gone the moment we shut the door."

"What?" Her eyebrows furrow as she turns to me. When she realizes I'm looking at my phone, she stretches onto her tiptoes to see what it is that I'm reading. I tilt the phone toward her so she can see.

PODGE

Did you get the shift?

"Jesus, Podge," she grumbles, eyes rolling. "What are we, teenagers?"

A snort rips out of me as I lock my phone. "Seems that way." I step around her and hoist the suitcase over the threshold before shutting the door once more. Then I take a step toward her and encircle her waist. "Now, I believe I said I'd make it up to you for my quick performance."

Her gaze cuts to me, eyes wide. "We just finished!"

"Still"—I cock my head—"I didn't get to taste you."

Desire swirls in the blue of her irises, and her lips part softly. "Callum Walsh, you *have* gotten better with your words."

"Among other things," I say, smirking, and then I toss her over my shoulder and head for the bedroom.

Chapter Thirty-Five

Leona

The shrill harmonica intro of "Dirty Old Town" by The Pogues scrapes against my eardrums when I step into the cool, dim light of Callum's favorite pub. Dermot winks at me from behind the bar as soon as he sees our joined hands dangling between us. He doesn't act the least bit surprised, no doubt thanks to Siobhan's propensity for gossip.

Still, it is a new feeling for me. Or a new-old feeling. I remember how it was to be Callum's before, but I'm a different person and so is he, and we are walking on soil that feels both fresh and hallowed. I let him lead me to where Padraig sits at their usual table, marveling at the sense of ease that flows through me.

"Listen, I'm happy for the two of you's, don't get me wrong," Padraig says, pointing to me and then Callum in turn. "But I refuse to let you become the type of man who brings his girl to lads' night."

Callum takes a seat opposite his friend and looks up at me with an eyebrow quirked. I rise to the unspoken challenge.

"What, you don't think I can hang with the best of them?" Laughing, I reach for Padraig's stout and take a sip while trying to hide my grimace as the bitter liquid slides down my throat. "*Gah!*

I'll never understand how you guys drink that stuff." I wipe my mouth and involuntarily shudder. "And relax, I'm not here to stay."

He slides his beer back across the table from where I've set it down, watching me curiously the entire time. Callum eyes both of us while trying to suppress a smile.

"First, I've yet to forget you drinking me under the table that night. So I know you can *hang.*" He takes a sip of his beer as he rolls his eyes. "Second, what can I help you with? Do you need a *ride?*"

"Watch it," Callum warns.

I smile at Callum and his hackles lower. Satisfied, my gaze flits to Padraig. "I just wanted to stop by and say thank you. You know. For everything."

The corner of Padraig's mouth twitches. "You mean for leaving your luggage so you'd have a fresh pair of undies to change into after your big make-up session?"

"All right, I'm leaving." I pivot on my heel but stop myself midturn and bend over to press a kiss against Callum's cheek. "That's the last time I try to be nice."

Callum catches my wrist on the retreat and pulls me back to him, not settling for a peck on the cheek. He pinches my chin between his thumb and forefinger and covers my mouth with his, dragging his teeth across my lower lip just enough to drive me mad.

When I draw back, I'm a little unsteady on my feet. Padraig clears his throat, and Callum's eyes sparkle with mischief. I swear even Dermot chuckles from his place behind the bar.

"Pay him no mind," Callum says. "He jokes, but he's secretly very proud of himself that all his meddling paid off."

"He and your mother both," I say.

Padraig finishes off his beer and flags Dermot for another. "I don't know what you two are talking about."

Callum nods at Dermot to request a beer for himself and shakes his head when Dermot points to me with a brow raised in question.

"Likely story." I try to smirk at Padraig, but the front falls away and my raw emotions come shining through against my better judgment. They live so close to the surface these days that it's become difficult to keep them hidden. "I mean it, though, Podge. Thanks for always listening. For picking me up in the rain."

He smiles and raises his fresh beer to me. Dermot scuttles away with the empty glass. "Anytime. I was just doing my job."

Callum raises his to clink against Padraig's. "Best taxi driver in Cahersiveen."

"*Only* taxi driver in Cahersiveen!" Dermot calls.

We all laugh, and it feels so good. To be here. To belong.

To not be afraid.

Callum's watching me over the rim of his glass. He sees where my mind travels. Maybe not the specific destination, but the route certainly. His hand encloses mine, and he brings my knuckles to his lips. "I'll see you tonight when I come to get Niamh?"

I smile softly down at him, and for a moment we're alone in this space despite being surrounded. After so long spent thinking this day would never come, I'm nearly tempted to pinch myself to make sure it's real.

Instead I squeeze his hand. "I'll see you tonight."

"*Blech.*"

"On that note," I say, glaring at Padraig, "I'm leaving. Don't party too hard, you two."

"Take celebratory shots, you say?" Padraig grins. "Consider it done!"

I head for the door, tossing a look Dermot's way that says, *Keep an eye on them.* To which he tips his cap.

The walk back to Bridge Street Bed-and-Breakfast is a quick one, and thank God for that. The wind bites at my cheeks the entire way. As November settles itself in, the blanket of early evening darkness makes the air seem colder than it is. I shove my hands into the pockets of my coat in an effort to preserve the warmth of Callum's lips against them.

Stepping into the foyer, warmth kisses my face. I can hear firewood crackling in the living room down the hall, and the smell of the burning fire is so familiar to me at this point, my body registers it as synonymous with home. I don't know how I got here from where I was when I first arrived, adrift and floundering simultaneously. The gap from there to this felt so impossibly broad at the time.

And yet, piece by piece, they have all helped me bridge it. Callum, Siobhan, Padraig, even Niamh. Without knowing it, they saved me from drowning in the life I'd created for myself. The one that was meant to keep me safe from ever enduring pain like losing Poppy again.

Maybe the best thing I can do with that pain is to feel it as honestly as possible, and to let those who want to shoulder the weight of it do so. Maybe that's the only way the pain gives way to love. To gratitude, for her life and my role in it, however brief.

"Oh, you're back!" Siobhan says, startling me from my reverie. She's got her jacket on and a wool scarf snaked around her neck. "Perfect timing. I thought I'd go pick up takeaway for the three of us. Have ourselves a girls' night."

"Takeaway sounds great!" I glance over her shoulder. "Where's Niamh?"

Siobhan follows my gaze. "Oh, she's playing in the living room. Could you watch her while I get dinner?"

An uneasiness sprouts in my belly and winds its way up my throat, blocking out the brittle euphoria from a moment ago.

"Or I could just go get dinner? Let the two of you hang out here where it's warm."

"Nonsense," she scoffs, patting my shoulder. "You've just gotten back, and I'm already bundled up and ready to go." Her gaze lifts to meet mine, and there's a flash of recognition in it as she takes in my expression. Head tilted to the side, she clicks her tongue softly. "You'll be grand, Leona. Niamh loves you. But if you aren't ready, just say the word and I'll stay."

Twenty minutes of babysitting. Insignificant to some, but I can feel the weight of responsibility in the shape of a still infant on my chest.

I look at Siobhan for one brief, stilted heartbeat. In that moment we share a grief that's so big it could swallow us both. We also share the determination not to let it.

I nod once. "I'll stay."

Her mouth stretches into a thin-lipped smile. "Atta girl."

She pats my shoulder once more and then steps out into the night. When the door closes behind her, the foyer seems suddenly too small, so I make my way down the hall.

I peek into the living room and see Niamh playing on the couch with two plastic horses. She makes them race and leap over the cracks between cushions before they argue over who was faster and have to do it all again. She's so focused on her game that she doesn't notice me taking a seat in the chaise across from her.

"What are the horses' names?" I ask.

She whips her head around, but pride won't let her admit she's startled. She simply brushes it off by squaring her shoulders and drawing in a dramatic breath. "This is Belle," she says, holding up the chestnut-colored horse first before lifting the white one. "And this is Ariel."

"Are those your favorite princesses?"

Her head bobs up and down in excitement. "Yes, because

Belle likes to read like me, and Daddy says I can learn to swim in the summer like Ariel. I'll be big enough then."

"That'll be so fun." I smile. "I love to read and swim, too."

Silence falls between us as she puzzles over how to respond. I know I'm being awkward, as if we haven't been around each other pretty much daily for the past two months, but the pressure of being alone with her, of being alone with *any* child for the first time in years, is getting to my head.

"Where is Daddy?" she finally asks while turning back to her horses.

"He's with Podge. You know they always hang out on Friday afternoons."

"Yeah," she says thoughtfully. "But I just thought he'd be with you."

I lean back in the chaise and cross one leg over the other. "Why's that?"

She shrugs her shoulders. "'Cause you like each other now."

The laugh that shakes out of me eases some of the nerves still bubbling in my gut. "We've always liked each other, Niamh."

Her unruly braid flies through the air as she whips her head around to look at me with more sass than should logically fit in her tiny body. "He did *not* like you in the beginning. At all."

Leave it to a kid to humble you with their honesty.

"Fair enough."

She considers me for a moment, studying my face and the space between us. Finally she circumnavigates the coffee table and is standing right in front of me, horses lying abandoned on the couch. She clasps her hands together behind her back and stares at the floral-patterned fabric of the chair rather than my face. "You do like him, right?"

Total honesty feels like the best course of action. "Yes, I do."

"Do you like me?"

I smile, and the rest of the nerves dissipate. "I do, Niamh. I think you're great."

The corner of her mouth twitches toward a smile, but she stops it. "Will you keep us, then?"

It's such a big question from such a small girl. One she doesn't understand all the implications of. One that it's too soon to answer. But still, I look at her and I can't help it. I catch a glimpse of the family I always wanted. I see the little girl my daughter never got to be, and then I see the almost-eleven-year-old she would be now. I imagine the two of them here, arguing over something senseless, while I wish for some peace and quiet.

Now I long for the chaos.

Suddenly I'm filled with the desire to grab hold of Niamh and squeeze her so tight. To never let her go.

"Would it be okay if I hugged you?" I ask quietly.

She nods and offers her open arms.

The moment she folds into my embrace, I half expect myself to splinter into a thousand pieces. I'm surprised to find those pieces mending instead. Every part of me that ached for eleven years to hold the baby I lost sighs in relief, because at last I have someone to cling to. Someone to cherish. Someone to protect and care for, in the ways I never got to with Poppy.

It reminds me of this type of Japanese pottery I saw once in a museum, where the shattered bits were glued back together with lacquer and then painted gold at the seams. *Kintsugi,* it was called, in which the places where it had once been broken were the most beautiful of all.

I squeeze her tightly for good measure and then pull back, taking her in. "I'll keep you if you'll keep me."

She smiles, showing off the gap between her front teeth. "Deal."

"I got everything ordered and was ready to pay when I discovered someone has removed my card from my wallet—*oh.*"

Siobhan pauses in the doorway. Her gaze locks on the place where my hands still brace on either side of Niamh's shoulders, and her face, flushed with color from the brisk wind, softens. "You two are having fun, I take it?"

I nod in unison with Niamh, who says, "Leona said she'll keep us!"

"Did she now?" Amusement sparks in Siobhan's eyes. "And what'd you promise her in exchange?"

Niamh glances at me as if for assurance and then replies, "That we'd keep her."

Siobhan nods and grins, like that is exactly the answer she was hoping for. "Sounds like a bargain to me. Now, would you happen to know where my card is?"

Niamh grimaces, causing her dimple to pop. "I was playing shop earlier. I'll go grab it!"

Siobhan steps out of the way to let her granddaughter fly past in a run that's made clumsy by her tangle of knobby elbows and knees. When I reach Siobhan's side, she surprises me by wrapping her arms around my shoulders. A young couple that checked in earlier avert their eyes as they pass by, like they've stumbled upon something private.

"I told you you'd be grand," she whispers fiercely into my ear.

I blink back the tears burning my eyes. "You were right."

"Always am."

She lets me go just as Niamh rounds the corner, credit card held triumphantly up in the air, and soon a moment that felt so incredibly important gives way to the normalcy of a Friday evening.

But it's there inside me, like a door that's finally been opened. I resign myself to step through it fully now that I'm finally ready to see the other side.

Chapter Thirty-Six

Callum

For about the tenth time in as many minutes, I sneeze.

The attic is dusty and disorganized, which is partially my fault. After Granda passed, when Niamh and I moved in, I simply tossed what few keepsakes we had into the darkness and didn't bother organizing what was left behind. Now that's coming back to bite me.

There are boxes full of photos and papers the subject matter of which I couldn't begin to guess. If someone told me the original copies of some biblical scrolls were up here, I'd be tempted to believe them. The air is frigid, causing my breath to come out in puffs that are just visible in the beam of my flashlight.

"*Shit.*" I trip over a warped floorboard, pitching forward into a stack of clothes that reek of mold, and sneeze again.

"Callum! Are you up there?"

Leo's voice drifts up from the garage below, sounding like music from this far away.

"Yeah," I groan, my toe still aching from the sudden impact. "You can join me if you like." *If you dare,* I'm tempted to add, but I refrain.

Heavy footsteps thud against the wooden ladder, and then the top of her head comes into view. The stubborn step that I've been meaning to fix squeaks under her weight when she hits it, and I can just barely see her eyes go wide in the dim light.

"Is this ladder safe?"

"Of course, why wouldn't it be?"

She hoists herself the rest of the way through the opening, sitting first and then drawing her legs upward. "I don't know, because this house and everything in it belongs in a museum?"

"Everything in it?" I say, hand over my heart. "I'm flattered that you think I'm museum-worthy."

That earns a flat look in return.

"I'd argue, but I did compare you to David, so not much of a leg to stand on there." She squints, finally realizing I'm not upright. "Speaking of which…"

"I tripped." Using a nearby trunk to maintain my balance, I rise. "Granda turned this space into an obstacle course."

Her eyes glint with amusement. "Or it's booby-trapped."

"Knowing that old man, I wouldn't be surprised," I say, chuckling. She joins in while finally trusting the floorboards enough to get to her feet. I turn the flashlight toward her and drink her in.

She's wearing a black long-sleeved shirt that's tucked into her jeans just in the front. The pants hang off her hips and arse in a way that's perfectly flattering and incredibly distracting. The light might be blinding her, but she smiles at me anyway, and it makes my knees weak. After so long spent denying how she makes me feel, allowing it all in is a bit overwhelming.

"Did you get a good enough look? Because the spotlight is a bit much," she jokes.

"Fine, fine." I drop the light, and she blinks against the sudden darkness. "I suppose you deserve to see, too."

"Lest I fall through the hole in the floor, yes." She steps toward me, eyeing the opening she just came through until she's clear of it. "What are you doing up here?"

I set down the light and reach for her, pulling her flush against me and brushing a kiss over her lips. "I could ask you the same thing."

"Podge gave me a lift," she says, jabbing her finger against my chest. "Your turn."

I step away from her and gesture broadly to the crowded, dusty attic. "Somewhere in this mess is a Christmas tree that a certain little girl downstairs would very much like me to put up."

"This early?" Her eyebrows rise nearly to her hairline. "You are a sucker."

I smile and roll my eyes. "A couple extra weeks of Christmas never hurt anybody."

"I suppose you're right." She scans the room, looking for anything treelike. "And besides, what the princess wants, the princess gets."

"Ah, so she's trained you as well?"

We laugh in unison before dissolving into a fit of sneezes.

After we've both regained our ability to breathe normally, she trudges into the thick of the boxes to my right, trailing a hand over each dusty surface she passes. I try to get back to searching, but I continue watching her out of the corner of my eye. Having her comb through these pieces of mine and my family's history feels oddly intimate, like she's walking through the caverns of my heart. She treads so lightly, and yet I can feel her there, filling up each space she enters.

"Killer lamp." She points at a hand-carved lamp base made to look like two mermaids entwined to hold up the bulb.

"What can I say, good taste runs in the family."

She finds a stack of photographs and holds one up. "Clearly."

I walk over to her, careful to avoid the floorboard that caught my toe before, and peer down at the stack while bracing my hands on her shoulders.

"Well, in fairness, I had no say in that outfit. I was a toddler."

"Uh-huh." She giggles, tucking the picture of me in a sailor's uniform into her back pocket. "Keeping that one for my own entertainment."

"More like ammunition, but all right."

She thumbs through a few more photos of my early years, including one where Granda is holding me in one of the wrought-iron bistro chairs in the garden. I pluck that one from the stack, revealing another, more faded image beneath it. In it, a young woman stands in front of our hydrangea bushes cradling her rounded belly while a proud smile shines on her face.

"Is this Siobhan?" Leo breathes.

"Mhm," I hum, flipping it over to read the handwritten date. "June, nineteen seventy-nine."

Our gazes meet as the realization dawns on both of us. The air grows noticeably thicker.

"Mam did say she was pregnant before me." I rub a thumb over the image, my heart thudding rapidly in my chest.

A gentle smile forms on Leo's face. Even in the low light, I can see the glistening moisture in her eyes. I don't suspect it's from the dust.

"We should bring it to the inn for her," Leo says, reaching for the polaroid. "I think she might like to have it. I know I would."

My gaze flickers instinctually to her stomach. "Are there any pictures?"

"There's a couple of me in the hospital that Momma took, in case I ever wanted them. They're in the memory box I have for Poppy with her sonograms and her urn."

She sets the picture of Mam on a nearby wooden table and

turns back to the array of boxes to resume her search, but the added weight doesn't leave her slumped shoulders. I move on instinct, wrapping my arms around her middle from behind and tucking her against me. My hands trail over her stomach as I nuzzle her neck, the citrus scent of her shampoo clearing even the memory of dust from my senses. I'm so full of love for her and my daughter, both my daughters, that I can barely breathe.

One of her trembling hands settles over mine and draws it upward, till my palm rests against her chest. No, not just her chest. The amulet that contains our daughter.

"I love that you still carry her with you."

"I'll carry her forever."

I press a kiss against her neck, her jaw, her temple. Everywhere I can reach without letting an inch of space come between us, even for the moment it would take to turn her around.

"People say grief gets easier as time passes. And maybe for them it does. But a mother isn't supposed to bury her child, and that's the kind of wound that never really heals."

I rest my chin against the crown of her head and squeeze her tighter.

There have been so many days where I'm tempted to pick up the phone and ring Granda for advice, only to realize all over again that he's gone. That I'll never hear his voice again. As painful as those moments are, and as much as I ache for the child I never knew, I realize that none of it can compare to what Leo feels. Suddenly the very marrow in my bones wishes to absolve her of it. And it's crushing to know that I can't.

"There was a song my mother sent to me, back when I lost her," Leo says, voice distant, "that talked about God taking the baby and showing her how time began. Holding her for the mother. But no one could care for my baby better than me. Not even God. It's horrible to say, but it's how I feel."

As the raw ache in her voice reaches my ears, the desire to fix it goes into overdrive. I want to do anything, *be* anything, that can make it better. I have to.

Granda's voice echoes in the back of my mind. *She doesn't need you to fix it. She just needs a soft place to land.*

I can be that, for both my girls.

"It's not horrible," I whisper. "It's okay to feel angry. I'd be shocked if you didn't. *I'm* angry, and I'm not even the one who carried her."

She turns in my arms and looks up at me, eyes wide and so honest it breaks my heart.

"Do you think that's where she is?" She swallows thickly, and so do I. "Heaven, I mean."

I move to cradle her face so she cannot look away. I want her to hear these words, every honest inch of them, and absorb them into her soul.

"Leo, you and I may not get a heaven, because I can be an ornery bastard and you keep secrets like the devil. But our girls? There's nothing but goodness and light for them, forever."

She lets out a laugh even as tears fill her eyes. I wipe them away.

"Thank you," she says, and it sounds a bit like a prayer. The kind you offer up when life hands you some unexpected sweetness in the midst of all the pain. Suddenly a flicker passes over her face. "You called them *our* girls."

My heart skips a beat. *I did, didn't I?*

I remove my glasses and drag a hand over my face. I don't know when I started to think of Niamh as ours instead of mine. Maybe I hadn't until this very moment. But it's there, laid out between us, and I can't take it back. I can only hope she feels the same.

"Do you not…do you not want me to think of Niamh as ours?"

Once the words are out, my lungs remain empty. Deflated. I

can't bring myself to draw another breath as I wait for her answer. After all, it's the only thing we wouldn't be able to get past. If she won't have my daughter, then I can't have her. Panic constricts my throat. Is it possible she doesn't want Niamh? After everything—

"Of course I do, Callum. I just—"

I don't let her finish her sentence. I swallow her words like they're a breath of fresh air.

Her lips move hesitantly against mine at first, and then they part and I reach out to taste her. It's a combination of strawberries and something intrinsically her, and I wish I could have it for every meal for the rest of my life, this taste. This relief. This euphoria.

"Callum," she says, coming up for air.

I open my eyes to see she's flushed with desire and probably a bit of leftover sadness. When I tuck a dark wave behind her ear, it's red, too.

"I'm sorry, that got away from me a bit. I just thought you were upset about Niamh, and she's my whole world. I couldn't bear it if..." I trail off, unable to say the words.

Leo smooths a hand over my cheek, anchoring my anxious thoughts to her and this moment we're in together.

"I love Niamh. You don't ever have to worry about that, okay?"

I nod, and she returns the gesture, satisfied.

Her head tilts to the side as she studies my face. "Do you know last night she asked if she could keep me?"

A huff of laughter passes over my lips, even as nervous energy continues bubbling in my stomach. "And how did that make you feel?"

"Honestly?" she asks, and I nod. "It was everything I've ever wanted. I'm not trying to replace Niamh's mom, nor could I ever, but I…I want to be in her life. I want to be something, *anything*, to her."

They're the exact words I needed to hear. The last piece that needed to fall into place in order for me to give myself over to her fully. After Catherine left, I thought I'd be alone forever because I'd never be able to trust a woman to love my daughter the way that I do. But I can see it there in Leo's wide blue eyes. Even in the dim light of the attic, her love for Niamh shines through. She's nervous, but not because she doesn't care for her enough. It's because she cares for her so much that the idea of not being a part of her life terrifies her.

"So does that mean we get to keep you?" I ask, grinning like a madman.

She draws her bottom lip in between her teeth. "That's what I need to talk to you about."

The joy that was my buoy moments ago sinks like a stone in my stomach. I step away from her to lean against an old wooden desk. She folds her arms around herself to replace the warmth I've taken with me.

"What is it?" I ask while bracing myself for the worst.

Her gaze is locked on my face, reading my every emotion. I suspect, not for the first time, that she can see down to the trenches of my soul.

"When I came here, I didn't really make any preparations. I didn't know how long I would stay. So I just bought a flight and came as a tourist." She pauses to let me process this before adding, "I don't have a visa like last time."

I shake my head. "What does that mean?"

Her chest rises and falls around a deep breath. A breath full of dust and all the memories this room contains. I'm surprised she gets it down without choking on it all.

"It means I can only stay in the country for three months.

Then I have to leave and apply for the appropriate visa in order to return."

I shift my weight in an attempt to steady myself. "Can't you do it from here?"

Her eyes tell me the answer before her mouth does.

"I'm so sorry, but no. I was up all night looking for ways around it, Callum. But I have to do it the right way. I can't risk getting in trouble and not being able to come back at all."

Her voice vibrates with panic at the idea of being apart from me, from Niamh, permanently. She looks at me, raw with fear that this will be the thing that ends us. The barrier we can't overcome. After all, wasn't I the one to tell her my greatest fear was being left behind?

But seeing her panic quells mine. Knowing she's as scared to lose us as I am to lose her makes my decision the easiest I've ever had to make.

This is the woman who fought her demons for me. She bared her soul over the most painful moment of her life, fearing the worst but knowing she had to do it for our daughter. For me. This, her leaving, is my demon to face, and it's my turn to fight for her.

I take her hands, unraveling them from her stomach, and cradle them between us. First one and then the other are pressed against my lips, and when I finish, tears spill from her eyes.

"The idea of you leaving terrifies me. I'm not going to sugar-coat it. But the idea of you never coming back is worse." I pull her to me and hold on for dear life. "So here's what we're going to do. We're going to enjoy these next few weeks as much as possible, and then I'll take you to that fucking airport for the very last time, and I'll be right there waiting when you come home to me. Because this *is* your home."

"*You're* my home," she corrects, and then she laces her fingers into the hair at the nape of my neck and pulls me down to her.

Every ounce of passion I poured into our kiss before, she

gives back to me now tenfold. Her teeth graze against my bottom lip; then her tongue sweeps over to dull the pain. She locks her arms around my neck, and I slide my hands down to cup her arse, lifting her so she's easier to reach.

Now I can take my time tasting her, enjoying every response my touch elicits. I trace her lips, which are swollen beneath mine, her ear, which draws a sigh from her lips, and her neck, which tightens her thighs around me. I grow hard in response, and I know she feels it. I cling to her as I stumble toward the desk, setting her down in the only clear space and then finding the button for her jeans in the dark.

"Daddy, did you find it?"

Leo's eyes pop open and lock with mine. We both go still as statues, and she covers her mouth with her hand.

"Not yet, hon, but I'm sure we will soon!" I yell, my voice coming out strained.

"'We'?"

I stick out my tongue at Leo, who has dissolved into a fit of silent laughter beneath me. "Leo's here!"

"Hi, Leona!" Niamh calls up, sounding terribly close.

"Hi, Niamh!" Leo replies, voice cracking on my daughter's name.

"I can come help!" Niamh offers, and then that telltale step on the ladder creaks.

"No!" we yell simultaneously before I add, "It's too danger-ous, love. We'll be down in just a bit."

Leo scrambles off the desk, landing beside me with a soft thud. We're both out of breath and flushed with embarrassment, but when her hand weaves itself into mine and she glances up at me, I've never felt more in love.

"Hurry up then, Daddy!" Niamh's voice sounds farther away, thank God. We both let out a sigh of relief followed by a bark of laughter from Leo.

"I'm glad you think this is funny," I say, shaking my head. "Welcome to life with a five-year-old."

"*Almost* five," she corrects. She smooths a hand over her hair, trying to hide the evidence of our tryst. "And I've never wanted anything more."

Her smile hits me right in the chest. How will I ever let this woman leave?

Chapter Thirty-Seven

Leona

For the first time in twelve years, time doesn't crawl. It absolutely flies.

One minute I have weeks to come to terms with the idea of leaving, and the next, the day has come. Anxious energy reverberates through me as I shower, towel off, and don the thick wool sweater Siobhan got me as a parting gift. *To take a bit of Ireland with you,* she said. Like I'm not leaving my whole heart here when I go.

I sit at the edge of the mattress and face the mirror that leans against the wall. My cheeks are fuller than when I arrived, my eyes brighter. I look like me again. The girl I knew before I became the woman I am.

Perhaps pieces of both can coexist.

The lightest knock draws my gaze. "Come in!" I call, and then two wide, teary green eyes peek around the opening door.

"Oh Niamh." I stretch my arms wide. "Come here."

She runs across the room and throws herself against my chest, squeezing the breath out of me. "Do you have to go?"

Her loose curls tickle my chin, and the scent of her strawberry kids' shampoo wafts up to my nose. I don't have the words to comfort her, because right now with her cradled against me, I'm not sure how I'll be able to say goodbye either.

Callum steps into the room and leans against the floral wall, arms crossed and head bowed. I know this hurts him as much as it hurts me, but he's trying to be strong for Niamh. He doesn't want to pass on his fear of goodbyes to his daughter. He wants to write a new story for her, one where people come back. Where they keep their promises.

Two nights ago, when we lay tucked into one another in the lazy evening light of this room, he whispered it all to me. His hopes and fears for her, and for himself. The ways he feels he doesn't measure up. All the steps he's taking to be the father he never had, despite it all.

It's a version of him that's new to me in the midst of everything I already thought I knew. This man, stoic and seemingly carved from granite in his stillness as he watches me with his daughter, is both the person I've always loved and someone new that I get to fall in love with for the very first time.

And I am. Because every fear is the flipside of a coin, and the other side is a man who loves his daughter so much he wants to be everything she needs. A man who can't see that he already is.

I smile at him and lay my cheek against the crown of our girl's head, blinking away tears. In those quiet conversations, I promised to be the one to tell him every day how good he's doing. I promised to help him write that new story for Niamh by coming home.

He clears his throat, but his voice still comes out thick with emotion. "She has to go, love. But she'll be back before we know it."

"Before I'm five?" Niamh mutters against my chest.

"No, not before you're five." I sit back, bracing a hand on

each of her shoulders, and meet her gaze. "And I'm so sorry to miss it. But when I come back, we'll have a big party to cover everything I've missed. It'll be Christmas and your birthday and anything else all wrapped into one!"

A cheeky grin stretches across her face, revealing her dimple. "Will there be presents?"

I wink at her. "More than you can handle."

"I can handle a lot!"

"That she can," Callum muses. The corner of his mouth finally lifts as he strides across the room to squat next to us. "This one was hoping someone would plait her hair one last time." He glances up at me, the green in his eyes sparkling with unshed tears. "I never could master the double plait."

I laugh, spin Niamh around in my lap, and study the two of us in the mirror. Despite a complete lack of shared genes, the ring of gold in our eyes makes us look somehow related, and it warms a piece of my heart. Like she was always meant to be mine, and I hers. I run my fingers through the fine strands of her blonde hair, separating it into equal parts. "Did you bring hair ties?"

"Daddy?" Niamh asks, peeking up at him.

He chuckles and shoves a hand into his back pocket, drawing out two small rubber ties. I retrieve them and loop them over my fingers so they're available when I'm ready.

"Ready for your first official lesson in braiding?" I tease.

Callum rolls his eyes. "You think you can teach me something the Internet hasn't tried to already?"

Niamh meets my gaze in the mirror and I wink. "I know I can."

The drive to Dublin consists of four hours of rolling green hills, windmills in the distance, and music filling the somber silence that hangs in the air between us. We've said all the words we have for one another over the past few weeks, preparing ourselves for this pain. All that's left to do is endure it.

We make it to our hotel just as the world grows dark around us. My flight leaves early tomorrow morning, so we'll stay in the city for the night and then say our goodbyes before the sun has even risen. It is all so familiar that the sense of déjà vu is debilitating.

I stretch out on the bed and stare up at the ceiling, with its smooth white surface and lack of wooden beams, and ache for the inn that has been my home for three months. Despite knowing this is what has to be done, every part of me wishes I could turn tail and run all the way back to Cahersiveen, bidding the Irish government good luck in kicking me out.

Callum's bare feet thud softly against the floor as he crosses the room, climbs into bed, and settles on top of me, careful to balance his own weight. There is pressure but no heaviness. There is no pain, but there is no pleasure, either.

He traces a thumb across my cheek, along my jawline, into the softness of my bottom lip. "Have I mentioned how much I will miss you?"

"You have," I whisper, and it aches—the yearning. "But tell me again."

"I will miss you when I drop Niamh off in the mornings and you are not there with a dollop of fresh cream smattered on your nose." He kisses the phantom mess, and I watch him as he does. "I will miss you when Saturday morning comes and I have to eat both sausage rolls myself."

I snort softly. "Don't blame me if you gain weight."

"I will blame you, and there's nothing you can do to stop me."

He nips at my bottom lip. "I will miss you at Sunday dinner, making bedroom eyes at me across the table."

"I'm sure Padraig and Siobhan won't be missing that."

He pauses, locking eyes with me. Without his glasses, I can see every shade of green, and it's beautiful.

"What?" I ask, breathless.

He shakes his head with a half smile splayed on his lips. "Nothing, you just said that the way an Irish person would. 'Won't be missing.'" His lips brush against my nose. "We're rubbing off on you."

Warmth spreads across my chest, and my heart yawns up into my throat. Pride and sadness and love exist simultaneously, filling every available inch of space.

"What else will you miss?" I whisper.

"This," he says, and then he covers my mouth with his. My lips part, and he slides his tongue against mine, tasting me. Memorizing me.

I trace my fingertips along the length of his spine, coming to rest at the hem of his shirt, and tug it upward. His lips stall against mine, and he pulls back despite my whimper at his retreat.

"Make love to me." I don't even care that I'm begging. I need him, and I need him to know it.

The low light cast by the bedside lamp dances in the shades of his hair. He smiles crookedly at me and shakes his head. "I will, but we have somewhere to be first."

I raise an eyebrow at him, and he smooths it over with his thumb. "You'll see."

My stomach growls, reminding me of the long drive and lack of food during. "Is there food involved? Tell me there's food involved."

"You'll see," he repeats, and then he's up and I'm empty, longing for his weight again.

We retrieve his car from the valet and drive in the opposite direction I'd hoped. Away from the thick of the city, where restaurants exist in abundance, and out toward the more residential areas. Streets packed with rows of brick apartment buildings give way to tall, tightly situated single family homes, and then we're climbing, and there are only a few houses amid stretches of thick woods.

A sense of recognition starts at the base of my neck and trickles down my spine. I blink against the yellow light cast by the occasional streetlamp as I step back through time. When we reach a familiar winding gravel road, I'm twenty again, and we're in the kind of love that only happens once in a lifetime.

But it happened for us twice, and I'll never be able to thank the universe enough for that.

We stop in front of that same gate, now even more rusted with the ravages of time, and I don't hesitate. I hop out of the car and yank it open, allowing Callum to pass through. It creaks in protest when I close it behind us. I return to my seat, quiet with anticipation.

There is only one other car parked at the viewpoint, off to the left with the windows fogged over. We could blame it on the heater building condensation on the glass where it meets the cool night air, but that would make us naive. I look away from the silhouettes to give them privacy.

Below us, the city is alight. Windows form a thousand glittering embers. Headlights zipping along the winding streets dance like fireflies. From so high up, it's easy to forget that for every light there is a person, and for every person, a life. When I was younger, I looked at them all and just admired their beauty. Now I wonder if they're happy. I hope that they are.

"Thank you," I say, unshed tears coating my throat.

Callum's hand finds mine in the dark of the cabin, and then he climbs over the center console and pulls me along. He's broader than he was at twenty-two. His shoulders strain against the seams of a blue sweater, and I run my hands along them, over the swells of his biceps, across his corded forearms, until our hands can at last intertwine. There is trepidation in our touch, and tenderness, too.

"I'll miss you when I sit down to read and you're not there to distract me by asking what the book is about," I say; then I press my lips against that scar in his chin. He releases my hands and finds the edge of my sweater, then draws it over my head.

"I'll miss you when I have to go fill out paperwork at a government office, and you're not there to buy me a magnet to mark it as a special occasion."

I strip his sweater from his body, and then my bra from mine, so that our skin is bare and hot and soft against the other's.

"I'll miss you every time it rains, because I'll imagine we're together by the inn's fireplace, with Niamh cuddled up between us."

We separate long enough to remove our pants and underwear. It's clumsy yet romantic in its honesty. I straddle him once more, this time with nothing left to separate us.

"I will miss you every second," he breathes.

"So will I," I say, and I cannot even bring myself to cry because I'm so grateful that I get to love someone this much.

A smile quirks his lips. "Should we skip the condom again? Take our chances?"

I throw my head back and laugh so hard it hurts. So hard that the sadness gives way to joy.

When at last I'm able to catch my breath, I grin at him and shake my head. "No, not this time. If you're going to get me pregnant again, let's do it when I get to stay right here with you."

The words tumble out of me without a thought, but then his eyes soften and my heartbeat trips over itself.

"I'd like that," he whispers.

"I would, too," I say, and realize that I mean it.

He retrieves a condom from his pants pocket, the confident bastard, and rolls it onto himself. Then he's inside me and all around me, and I move against him in a slow rhythm meant to build rather than break. His lips find my ear and then my neck, and then he draws my head backward with a fistful of my hair and flicks his tongue over my nipple. The resulting moan passes over my lips and echoes from his.

I roll my hips, feeling my clit rub against him, and that arcs my pleasure higher. His rough hands fall to my waist, keeping my rhythm steady while he licks and sucks and nibbles at my breasts. It is all-encompassing, the feeling of him inside me and touching me and loving me. I give myself over to him, and he does so in return.

He groans, low at first, and then louder when he reaches that peak. His fingertips dig into the soft flesh of my hips as he thrusts up into me, losing himself in the pleasure he finds. I capture the sound of his orgasm with my lips, swallowing his air the moment he breathes it.

He shudders beneath me, and his eyelids flutter open. "What do you need?"

I shake my head. There's too much emotion in me to think about finishing. "Just this."

He nods as if he can hear what I haven't said, and then lets his forehead rest against mine. "Is it crazy to think we were meant for each other."

"It'd be crazy to believe we weren't."

A sigh escapes his lips, tickling mine. "Promise you'll come back to me."

My throat constricts at the familiar words. In my head I see us as we were. I see the positive test lying on my college apartment's bathroom counter. I see the sonograms and my rounded belly, and I see our daughter, still against my chest.

But I also see the house at the end of the gravel road, with hydrangeas growing in the backyard. I see Niamh running to greet me with her arms open wide, and I see Callum leaning against the doorframe with a smile as bright as the sun spread across his face.

"I promise," I say, and I mean it.

Chapter Thirty-Eight

Callum

The best day of my life doesn't start the way I thought it would. For the past eight months, when I pictured the day Leo would return to Ireland, it involved a silver-screen level of romanticism. I'd be standing just outside airport security, dressed to the nines with a large bouquet of roses in my hands, ready to welcome her the moment she stepped over the threshold.

Instead my fingers are tangled in Niamh's curls, trying to turn them into some semblance of a plait. But I can never do it the way Leo does it, according to my daughter. Now that she's tasted perfection, she'll settle for nothing less.

"Would you prefer to go to school with your hair down?" I ask, peering down at her uniform to check for any specks of powdered sugar. I made crepes to celebrate the occasion, not realizing the potential mess I was signing up for when I did.

She contemplates the question, her blonde eyebrows scrunching into one long line of indecisiveness. "Can Leona call to remind you how?"

I snort. "It's three in the morning her time."

What Niamh doesn't know, because we've decided to surprise

her, is that the real reason Leo can't video chat is because she's currently landing in Dublin airport, over three-hundred kilometers away. Padraig's there in the receiving line, taking my rightful place sans roses. It irks me, but I couldn't bear to miss my daughter's first day of school, nor would Leo ask me to.

Niamh sighs dramatically before hoisting herself off the chair and skipping over to the antique mirror hung in the hall. She looks over her wild curls, turning her head this way and that, before squaring her shoulders and turning to me.

"I'll wear it down."

"Will you now?"

She gives a curt nod.

Surprised sadness ripples through me when I realize how quickly she's grown up before my very eyes. Not just because of her choice to go without the plait, but because she's somehow old enough to go off to school without me. After a lifetime spent with myself or my mam, it feels impossible that she could be so independent. Yet here she is, without a shred of fear on her face.

She didn't get that from her dad.

"Right then, are you ready?"

She giggles. We've been practicing this.

"I was *born* ready."

"That's my girl." I grab her backpack from the kitchen counter and follow her lead to the door. A quick glance at my phone tells me Leo will have made her way to customs by now. The last stop before she's clear to enter the country, and Padraig can bring her home at last.

The drive to Niamh's primary school takes no time at all, and then she's eagerly jumping from the car to race to the door. She's bolder than I've ever been, and twice as smart. She'll have no trouble today, while I'll be an emotional mess.

"Are you not going to say goodbye to your dad?" I call to her, and she whips around with a broad smile on her face.

"Sorry, I forgot!" She runs into my waiting arms.

"Forgot me already. I'm wounded!" I place a kiss on the crown of her head and then step back to take her in. My whole heart outside my body. I'll never get used to it.

"I could never forget you," she says sweetly. She glances over her shoulder, eager to be off, and I decide to stop making this about me. If she's fine, I should be, too.

"Okay, love"—I crouch so we're face level—"you have the best day ever, and there will be a surprise waiting for you when you get home. Sound good?"

She nods eagerly, the gap in her two front teeth showing in her cheeky grin.

"All right. I love you," I say, but she's already turned and I'm speaking to the back of her head.

"Love you, too, Daddy," she calls over her shoulder, and then she disappears into her classroom. Just like that, everything changes in an instant. For the first time in a while, though, I know it's only getting better.

Leona

I thought the moment I made it through customs, with my hard-won paperwork approved, that I'd feel settled. After all, that would be the moment everything was official. Every email, online application, and detailed letter trying to prove my eligibility would finally be worth it. All the long hours working as a house-keeping manager at a local hotel these last eight months would pay off. Something I'd done so I had job experience to show the Irish government that I really was capable of taking the role

Siobhan was offering me, therefore earning my more permanent work visa. Turns out I couldn't quote my time at the Bridge Street Bed-and-Breakfast for qualification purposes since I did it under the table.

But even after my luggage was loaded into Padraig's taxi and we'd hit the road toward Cahersiveen, anxiety still rippled through my muscles, making me jumpy. Now, as we round the last bend in the road that leads to the main street through town, it ramps up higher. I'm nearly tempted to throw open the door and run all the way past downtown, through the fields of sheep, to that cottage where Callum is waiting for me.

"If you don't stop shaking your leg, *I'm* going to have an anxiety attack," Padraig warns.

I glare in his direction, but do my best to tamp down the jitters to a minimum.

"Thank you." He eyes Bridge Street as it comes into view, hovering his hand over the turn signal. "Want to drop off your suitcases first?"

I can't be held responsible for how loudly I yell, "No!"

He smirks but removes his hand. "Straight to Cal's then. Noted." His gaze flickers over the dashboard. "Though I might need to stop for petrol…"

"Podge, if you so much as stop for one of Eoin's sheep, I might have to murder you."

He snickers. "You know I'm only teasing."

Relaxing back into my seat as best I can, I force myself to gaze out the window. The town is alive in the late summer heat. Fishermen have come in from their morning trips, stopping in at the chipper on the corner. We pass Dermot's pub, and if I squint I can see his silhouette through the window. The large cathedral at the edge of town is surrounded by blooming flowers, and mourners fill the cemetery to tend the gardens for their loved ones.

When we turn onto the road where Padraig picked me up in the rain nearly a year ago, my heart leaps right into my throat. Bright purple foxgloves sway in the breeze, framing our path. I roll down the window and let the scent of fresh rain and blooming flowers and the hint of brine from the nearby sea flow in on the breeze.

Just up ahead, I can see the road that will take me home, yet it feels like we're crawling toward it. I try my best to be patient, to wait for Padraig to reach it, but blood begins to rush through my veins and my lungs tighten and I know that he's there and all I have to do is get to him.

"I'm sorry, Podge," I gasp, and then I open the door and stumble out, barely catching myself before I fall face-first into the gravel. But my feet are as desperate to reach him as my heart, so they fall into pace quickly. I'm sprinting down the road, heat flooding my cheeks, and soon I can see it. The cottage, with a ray of light shining on it like the sun knows exactly what's happening, appears on the horizon. The windows are cracked, letting the light breeze dance through the gauzy curtains. The door swings open, and I can see nothing else.

Him. He's here, and he's real. He's every thought I've had, every dream I've remembered since the day I left this place. His blond, disheveled hair and his beautiful green eyes and those arms, spread wide to catch me when I throw myself into them.

"You're here," he sighs against my neck.

"I'm here," I breathe.

His arms tighten around my waist so he can lift me and spin us around in circles. I laugh and laugh and then I'm crying because this is real. Because after everything we've been through, after all the anger and beauty and grief and joy, we are together. Despite all our brokenness, we are whole.

He steps away just enough to bring his hands up between us

and cradle my face. "Niamh will be home this afternoon. She has no idea you're coming."

"I can't wait to see her. To hear all about her first day of school." I shake my head. "I wish I could've been here to see her off."

He chuckles. "She wished that, too. Apparently my hair-styling skills are no longer needed."

He smiles, and it takes over his entire face. His glasses have fallen down the bridge of his nose, and the scar in his chin shines white in the sunshine. His skin is smattered with freckles from a summer spent playing in the backyard with Niamh. Her tree house received an upgrade, and I followed along through video calls and pictures. Even from the other side of an ocean, I got to be here with them in spirit until I could be for real.

"You are so beautiful," he says, brushing a tear away from my cheek. "I've missed you every day."

My face crumples, but he holds me steady. Every moment of anxiety and hope, of anticipation and impatience is coming out of me in the form of tears I can't stop. He doesn't complain, though. He simply captures each one with his lips until at last they dissipate.

When I finally trust myself to speak, I draw in a deep breath and shrug out of my backpack, letting it slip off my shoulders and into my arms between us. "There's something I need to show you."

His eyebrows furrow as I unzip the pack. When I feel smooth brass beneath my fingertips, I close my hand around the impossibly small object and remove it, letting the bag fall to the ground.

I cradle the heart-shaped urn between us, engraved simply with Poppy's name and the date I lost her. It seems impossible that my entire reason for living could be held by something so delicate. I have to remind myself that she isn't in there, not really. She's a part of me and of Callum. She lives on in her sister, too.

Her memory, and the love born of it, will be her legacy long after we're gone.

She won't be forgotten, and that's all a mother could ask.

When I look up at Callum at last, there are tears filling his eyes and a smile on his face. "You brought our daughter home," he says, and he covers my hands with his. "Both my girls are home."

Then he kisses me, with our daughter cradled between us. On the front porch of the cottage, with the scent of hydrangeas flooding my senses and a light rain starting to fall.

It's the closest to heaven that I'll ever get.

Epilogue

Leona

My Darling Poppy,

It's the middle of June, and my feet are so swollen I can barely walk. The third trimester has been a doozy, and what would normally be mild summer heat feels like an inferno to me. I barely wear anything other than sports bras and stretchy shorts these days because I'm hot and my belly is too big. Your daddy doesn't mind though; he thinks it's cute. Guess he's into whales.

Your father loves you dearly, I hope you know. Watching him be so filled with excitement and love through this pregnancy has made me ache for that time he didn't get with you. He would've been so good. He would've read to you and even sung to you. Okay, you might've hated that because he's a terrible singer. But he would've laughed with you and tickled you where you kicked. He would've told you deadpan jokes that he thought were funny. We are the luckiest girls, you and I and Niamh, to be loved by him. And your brother, the littlest of the family, will be lucky, too.

He'll be born in just a few weeks, and then Mom and Dad will fly over for a month to meet their new granddaughter and help with the arrival of their grandson. We wanted to wait for this day until he was here, until they could be too, but the poppy fields are full of fresh blooms. Miles and miles of that beautiful orange-y red as far as the eye can see. It felt too perfect not to do it today. Like you were telling us it was time. Like you were welcoming him in.

So this afternoon, your father, sister, and I will drive out to the poppy fields, loaded down with a picnic basket full of sausage rolls and a rock shandy for each of us. We'll eat our lunch and talk about your life and what you mean to us, and then we'll spread your ashes amongst the flowers. You'll be in every poppy that grows, every blade of grass. You'll be in the rain and the trees and every breath your momma takes until we're together again.

This isn't goodbye, of course. This is just another way for you to be. A place I can go and visit you and feel your presence. A field your siblings can play in, and their children, and their children's children. When I go, I'll join you there, and so will Daddy. It'll be our place, and it'll be perfect.

Promise me this, though, love. That you'll watch out for your brother and sister. Maybe you already do. That you'll watch out for me. I want to be a good mother to each of you, and a good partner to Callum. Somewhere in all of that, I also want to be good to myself. It's something I'm working on, but of course, I could always use your help. You were my first; you'll always know me best.

I've got to go now. Your daddy has the car loaded up, and it takes me at least ten minutes to put on my shoes. I just wanted to take a moment to thank you for choosing me to be your momma. It is the greatest title I'll ever wear. And I'll shout it from the rooftops until my dying breath, "This is Poppy, and I was lucky enough to love her."

I'll be seeing you, my sweet girl. And until then, I'll carry you with me for my whole life, just as I did for yours.

Love you forever,
Momma

Acknowledgments

Every book I write has a special place in my heart, but this one takes up the most real estate.

I owe a lot of gratitude to my fiancé, Andrew, for rooting for me while I pursue my dreams. Thank you for listening to me drone on about comma placement and plot lines and promo materials, even when all you want to do is watch the movie that's playing. Your patience and steadfast love are my inspiration.

Thank you to my incredible team of beta and sensitivity readers—Sam, Michelle, Jennalee, Stephanie, Margaret, Katie, and Paige. Your loving critique and unhinged commentary made these characters what they are. I'm so grateful that you ladies have loved and championed my stories, even when I'm down with a bad case of imposter syndrome. You mean a great deal to me. I'm so lucky to have you all in my corner.

I'd be lost without Sarah Estep's constant flow of memes and commiseration. Thank you for believing in me even when I don't. You're incredible. Jackie Egan, our voice note frenzies give me life when I desperately need it. Thank you for waiting in giddy anticipation for each new plot I send your way. You're the reason I'll write all of them, I'm sure.

To my editor and big sister, Lea Ann—you are brave, strong, and feisty. You're also incredibly tender when needed. I'm blessed to know each facet of you. Thank you for lending your expertise to this story, and for flagging every single period that wasn't italicized when it should've been. I don't think anyone but us would've noticed, but it's that type of neurosis that confirms we're definitely related.

Thank you to Jenni for believing in this book so much that you shout about it from the rooftops. Jessica Joyce, thank you for taking the time to read and blurb this book. It is such an honor. Kristen, thank you for driving all the way to Canada to hang out with me (and thank you for formatting this book)!

Patrice, thank you for looking the other way when I make sex jokes on the Internet but liking every other post I make. You're the best mother-in-love I ever could've asked for. Danniele, you and Lea Ann blazed this trail. It's a privilege to be your baby sister, and to follow in your footsteps.

To the K Club crew of 2017, thank you for giving me the best summer ever. From the gaff parties to Dicey's to the late-night McDonald's sessions, I am forever indebted to you all. I truly had the time of my life, and I'll never shut up about it. Sorry to everyone else. To Aoife, who has remained my friend even after all these years and the ocean that separates us, I love you dearly. Thank you for reading this book to make sure I didn't misrepresent your entire country. I'll repay you with a lifetime supply of Sour Patch Kids. And to Ciaran, thank you for giving me Cahersiveen.

To my mother, who endured something no mother should ever have to. Thank you for sharing your story with me. For speaking about Brandy throughout my life, so that she is always near to me. I think of her when December rolls around and when people ask about my older siblings, and I smile when *You're a Fine Girl* comes on. It feels like I'm dancing with my sister. Your love for us kids is a badge of honor you've always worn on your sleeve, Momma, and I'm so grateful for you. You are stronger than you've ever believed. Us girls got it from our momma.

Finally, as always, dear reader. I write these stories, but you all are the ones who give them life. You've made my dreams come true, and I'll never be able to thank you enough for that.

About Hannah Bird

Hannah's accolades include a second-grade teacher who said her story about bats had "very good potential" and enough accelerated reading medals to sink a body at sea. Her goals in life are to write novels that will make you cry, and to check everything off the bucket list she wrote at seventeen.

Hannah resides among the rolling hills of Tennessee with her other half and their clingy golden retrievers. When she is not writing, she is trying to outrun her sweet tooth in the gym.

You can travel along with Hannah on her writing journey at her website, hannahbirdauthor.com, and at all the bookish destinations below:

facebook.com/hannahbirdauthor

instagram.com/hannahbirdauthor

amazon.com/author/hannahbird

goodreads.com/hannahbird

tiktok.com/hannahbirdauthor